D1315193

A TASTE OF THINGS TO COME

Nick lifted his head, spotted my car. He started toward me.

My heart fluttered. I nearly panicked and drove away, not wanting him to ask me what I thought I was doing. It felt like an hour watching him walk to my car. He went around to the passenger door, opened it, and got in.

I went warm inside. Having him near, feeling the heat of his skin inches away, was an instant aphrodisiac.

He held up the present I'd left for him. The plastic wrapping gleamed in the moonlight. "Edible underwear?" he asked.

Other books by Jennifer Ashley:

THE CARE & FEEDING OF PIRATES
THE PIRATE HUNTER
THE PIRATE NEXT DOOR
PERILS OF THE HEART

CONFESSIONS
of a
LINGERIE
ADDICT

JENNIFER ASHLEY

LOVE SPELL NEW YORK CITY

LOVE SPELL®

June 2005

Published by

Dorchester Publishing Co., Inc.
200 Madison Avenue
New York, NY 10016

ISBN 0-505-52636-0

The name "Love Spell" and its logo are trademarks of Dorchester Publishing Co., Inc.

Printed in the United States of America.

Visit us on the web at www.dorchesterpub.com.

ACKNOWLEDGMENTS

Special thanks to Jeff and Maya Bohnhoff for letting me borrow the title of their hilarious music CD, *Aliens Ate My Homework* (Mystic Fig Records). You guys are brilliant. As always, thanks go to author Glenda Garland for her beyond-the-call-of-duty critiquing, terrific advice, and editing skills. Also, thanks to my editor Kate Seaver, for her patience, solid advice, and being such a delight to work with. And, of course, to Forrest, for his unconditional support and for teaching me how to laugh.

CONFESSIONS
of a
LINGERIE ADDICT

1

New Year's

On New Year's morning, I woke up with a man I didn't know.

I sat up. He sat up. We stared at each other.

He had blond hair sticking out every which way, bloodshot blue eyes, and a chin stubbled with red-gold bristles. He also had a very nice chest and muscular shoulders, which were bronzed and tanned.

We were in my bed in my apartment, and the New Year's party that had raged all night in the living room was finally quiet. We were both stark naked.

I had no clue who he was.

He said, "Unh."

I said, "Oh, God."

He scrambled out of bed, holding part of the sheet over him. I got a wonderful view of his chest and arms and lower abdomen, that slice between the belly button and what a nice girl shouldn't want to see.

He grabbed his clothes. He held them over himself and dropped the sheet. Then he ran.

He had the nicest butt I'd ever seen in my life.

I sat there, bewildered and in pain. I, Brenda Scott, mousy, quiet, never-rocks-the-boat Brenda, had just slept with a beautiful-bodied blond man whose name I didn't know.

And I didn't remember anything about it.

On December 31, my boss, Tony Beale, the owner of KCLP FM, had decided that the best way for him to get a ratings bounce was to see how high he could make the DJs bounce.

He drove all of us to the Coronado Bridge to set up a re-mote broadcast in the freezing wind from San Diego Bay.

"This will work, Brenda," he said, rubbing his hands. His eyes lit with that fanatic glow they got when he was excited about one of his crazy ideas. "This is going to be great."

"Sure, Tony," I said, my teeth chattering.

Tony was always trying to make KCLP one of the top five stations in the city, and he had idea after stupid idea to help us claw our way up. None of them ever worked, of course.

Today, he'd decided to hook up the DJs with wire-less mikes, strap them to bungee cords, and throw them over the side of the Coronado Bridge. He didn't throw me over because I wasn't one of the stars. All I had to do was stand at the top, shivering, and describe the scene.

So I told San Diego which DJ was going over; then I turned off the mike and cried, because that morning, my boyfriend, Mr. Perfect, had called me and said, "This isn't going to work, Brenda."

He meant that he wanted to break up with me but couldn't think of a good excuse why. The truth was that he, Larry Bryant, one of the richest men in southern California, had gotten tired of mousy, nobody, little Brenda Scott.

I'd seen the breakup coming. Larry Bryant, a perfect man with a perfect career, a perfect life, a perfect house, and perfect looks had expected his girlfriend to be perfect, too.

I'm not perfect. I'm five foot four and have red hair that mostly sticks out. My eyes are blue—a washed-out blue, not deep, dark, and soulful. I have a good nose, but it's freckled. I wear a size eight, and that's all I'm going to say about that.

I suppose Larry wanted me to get tucked and sucked and lifted until I was five nine with a great figure and glowing blond hair. I wouldn't, I couldn't, and so he didn't want me around any more.

Tony, when he'd found out about the breakup, had been livid. "For God's sake, Brenda, get him back! He's our best advertiser."

Larry was one of the few businessmen that bothered to advertise with KCLP, probably because our rates were so cheap, and Tony gave him extra spots for free. That's how I'd met Larry; he had come to the station to talk to Tony about landing the choicest times for his spots. Larry's family owned a successful local chain of sporting goods stores, and he was ready to open branches in Los Angeles. Yes, *that* Larry Bryant.

"I know you're upset," Mr. Perfect had said that morning in his I-know-what's-best-for-you voice. "You tell Tony you need a little time to pull yourself together, then you'll be all right."

I'd hung up on him.

Tony had decided that the breakup had been my fault and refused to give me any sympathy.

Out on the bridge, the morning show host, Tim, refused to jump. Tony finally got him shoved into place, turned on Tim's microphone, and told him to jump. Tim wouldn't do it, so Tony pushed him over.

The people of San Diego got to hear scream after terrified scream as Tim went down, down, down, and then— nothing. They got to hear me standing up top bleating, "There goes Tim. Sounds like he's having fun." And then, "Oh, God."

And then silence. Dead air is one of the scariest things for radio stations. According to the engineers back in the studio and the FCC, I treated greater San Diego to one minute and twelve seconds of dead air before I finally said shakily, "He's still breathing, isn't he?"

Tim was still breathing when they pulled him back up to the bridge. His cord hadn't been too long, he hadn't hit his head or banged into the side of the bridge, or any of those things I'd feared. He'd passed out from terror.

He woke up as they pulled him back over the side, snarling every foul word he knew at Tony Beale. His mike was still on. The engineers were laughing so hard that no one thought to cut him off the air.

More FCC fines for KCLP.

The day dragged on, the sun went down, the weather grew colder, and still I stood on the bridge while the DJs joked and laughed and pushed each other over the side.

I missed lunch; then I missed dinner. Someone brought sub sandwiches, but the jumpers ate them all while I kept up the on-air chatter.

My stomach growled, the hours went by, and I thought of the New Year's party my roommate would be throwing. I had planned to spend New Year's Eve at an expensive restaurant with Mr. Perfect. Instead I'd be spending it at home with my weird roommate and her even weirder friends.

Finally the day was over. Marty, the producer, wrapped

up the mike cords, and I hurried to my car, hoping the heater would work.

Tony caught up to me as I unlocked my car. Tony, at fifty, had round eyes, a good paunch, and barely any hair on his head. "Talk to Larry, Brenda," he said. "That's a good girl. You tell him you're sorry for whatever you did and that you won't do it again."

"Mind your own business, Tony," I growled.

"It is my business. I want his money."

I got into my car. "Happy New Year," I said.

He leaned down and called through the window. "I'll expect good news on Monday, Brenda."

I started the car and gunned it. Tony jumped out of the way, and I peeled out and slid into traffic, heading back toward San Diego.

By the time I got home, it was dark and Clarissa's crowded, ear-splitting party was in full swing. My living room was crammed with people I didn't know, many looking as though they could try out for parts in a bondage flick. As I dragged myself in, a dominatrix-looking woman handed me a martini.

I downed it. It burned all the way to my stomach—almost straight vodka. I headed for the food, which was mostly gone except for a few tortilla chips and the remnants of salsa that smelled like stale onions.

Before I could eat even that, someone put another martini into my hand. I drank it while I yelled over the music to Clarissa, making up some excuse why I'd decided to come to the party instead of going out with Larry. She looked at me with her eyeliner-black eyes and smiled. I have no idea if she even heard me.

I could have lived with the dominatrixes and the music and the lack of food. I could have just shut myself in my bedroom with my martini to have a private cry. But the next time I looked up, I saw Larry walk in.

I jumped. What was he doing here? Sure, Clarissa had invited him, but why would he come when we'd broken up? Had he not had enough of humiliating me that he had to come and give me some more in person?

He scanned the crowd, looking for me, probably. I grabbed martini number three and hid myself behind two guys with very white faces who were wearing black leather and chains.

As Larry made his way through the teeming crowd, the third martini went down the hatch, and then all the pain went away.

And so did I. At least the conscious part of me. As far as I know, I went over like a tree in a high wind.

The next thing I remember is waking up next to my tight-butted blond man, who took one look at me and fled into the dawn.

I grabbed my clothes and jerked them on, leaving off half my underwear. I stumbled out of the room—and straight into Mr. Perfect.

To this day, I have no clue what he was doing there, why he'd come back. Clarissa shouldn't have let him in. He was shaved and dressed and looked like he was ready to go to work—on New Year's Day when the rest of the world was still climbing out of its fuzzy cocoon and mumbling, "Huh?"

I knew by his expression that he'd seen my mystery man run out of the room. He gazed down at me, baffled, his perfect brows arched.

"Brenda?"

I stood there, my mouth open, my panties in my hand, while Larry stared at me in a mixture of horror and fascination. "Brenda? What do you think you're doing?"

I don't know where it came from. Brenda Scott had always been quiet, shy, and mousy. I did what I was told, showed up to work on time, laughed at everyone's jokes. I had been the obedient and obliging girlfriend, going to parties I didn't want to go to and talking to people I didn't want to talk to, to make my boyfriend look good.

But standing there with my shirt half-buttoned, while Mr. Perfect gave me the what-has-my-stupid-girlfriend-gotten-herself-into-now look, a new Brenda Scott woke up.

This Brenda Scott threw back martinis and slept with men she didn't know. This Brenda Scott was wild, sexy, and daring—this Brenda was a woman who could do anything.

I looked Mr. Perfect right in the eye.

"Hey, Larry," I said. "Hand me my bra, will you?"

The next day, I waltzed into the San Diego branch of Lili Duoma, an exclusive lingerie clothier from Beverly Hills. I don't know why I decided to go in there, but while I was driving by, a parking space opened up right in front of the store.

I took that as a sign. Parking spaces in downtown San Diego don't just appear for no reason. I would have been thumbing my nose at Fate if I hadn't taken it.

Ten minutes later, I stood in front of a mannequin modeling a camisole and thong that were mostly sheer, mostly black, and covered mostly nothing.

Under my dress today, I wore white (boring) high-waisted briefs and a large bra that could have doubled as a slingshot. I bought my underwear at discount stores, one pair for every day of the week, with one left over for laundry day. I'd never in a million years wear panties that were skimpy and sexy and not machine washable.

But this was the new Brenda. The wild Brenda who gulped martinis and seduced men under her ex-boyfriend's nose.

Before I knew what happened, my hand reached out of its own accord and picked up a sheer silk thong.

I looked at the slinky thing in my hands, felt the silk

caress my skin, and heard the black-haired saleswoman whose name was either Zoe or Chloe say, "Ah, yes, zo excellent a choice for you."

I bought it. I took home said thong and a catalog that Zoe (or Chloe) pushed on me, and entered a new world.

No one but me knew I wore that skimpy, silky thong the next day at work under my skirt and sweater. I felt just a little wicked, walking around looking frumpy on top and sexy underneath.

Right then and there I knew—no more pale high-waisted boring briefs for Brenda Scott.

I thumbed through that Italian catalog until it was dog-eared, called stores in New York and L.A., ordered whisper-soft camisoles, silken tanks, sheer slips, body stockings, lace hosiery, and sweet little teddies. I made pilgrimages to Beverly Hills and La Jolla and shopped and shopped.

I shopped, I bought, I brought it home. Then I bought a lingerie chest to keep it all in.

Me. The girl who got through college in the wimpiest cotton briefs and thought even colored panty hose were way too sexy.

Some people smoke, some people get drunk, I buy lingerie.

It doesn't matter. It's only me who ever sees it.

Now about my family.

About two months after my New Year's adventure, my brother David moved back to San Diego.

David had gone off to Chicago seven years before to get rich, and he had. He'd found a yuppie job, made lots of yuppie money, and married a yuppie wife. Alicia had sleek blond hair and a stick-thin figure, came from the right family, and knew all the right people. Mr. Perfect would have loved her.

In March, David returned to San Diego without her. He carried a red duffel bag that held all his worldly goods. It turned out that he'd lost his yuppie job and all his stocks and all his money, and in the end, his yuppie wife had thrown his yuppie butt out.

He moved back in with my mom in the house we'd grown up in, a rambling suburban place that sat up on a hill overlooking Mission Bay.

My mother had lived in that house for more than thirty years. After my dad passed away, she'd stayed up there alone. She liked it there, she said. She didn't change anything in the house, but I noticed that after my dad died, she started buying fresh flowers, drinking wine coolers, and eating organic vegetables.

My father had kept a sailboat down in Mission Bay, and my mom still had it, although she never used it. Whenever my dad had sailed out, my mother had sat up on the patio with her binoculars and watched him.

Mom rarely went out in the boat because she said she got too seasick. I just think she didn't want to listen to my father yell. He liked to do that when he got on the boat. Captain Bligh had nothing on my dad.

After my father died, my mom still sat on her patio every afternoon and watched the boats going in and out of Mission Bay.

David had been my father's pride and joy. David had gone through college with honors, then landed a job as an engineer at a company that made incredibly sophisticated computer terminals for airlines.

What happened to him wasn't his fault. David explained that the airlines had started getting crunched, and many decided to go with an alternate company that offered the same service as David's, but for less. David's company got fewer and fewer orders and finally folded altogether.

Poor David. Mom welcomed him with open arms. David ran straight into them and gave her all his laundry.

David didn't come home alone. He brought a friend with him called Jerry Murphy. Mom invited Jerry to stay up at the house with David for a while. I finally met Jerry when we all sat down to have a welcome home dinner at the house for David.

David introduced Jerry to the new, improved Brenda. Jerry was in his thirties. Jerry was good looking. Jerry had dark hair and gorgeous brown eyes. Jerry wasn't married, and he was thinking about moving to San Diego permanently. I liked Jerry.

I sat across from him wearing a leather skirt, not too short, and a satin blouse. Underneath I wore black lace thigh-highs, a lace camisole, and black silk bikinis. I stared at Jerry and daydreamed about him taking them off me.

I need to give up on daydreams.

I had to admit that Mom looked better since David's return. She'd got her hair cut short, and it looked good. Tonight she had on jeans and a turtleneck and had put on makeup. I was glad. She'd had been hanging out on the patio in her robe for too long.

"Jerry had a boat repair business in Chicago," Mom announced as she handed around the chicken.

Jerry smiled and thanked her as he took the platter. Polite to parents, I noted. Another plus for Jerry.

"He thinks he'll do better starting one out here," David added. "It's warmer here anyway."

"Brenda works for a radio station," Mom said. "Maybe she can get you advertising on the radio."

"Does Jerry talk?" I asked, sending Jerry a coy smile. He gave me a dark-eyed wink.

A good beginning, I thought.

I was so wrong.

Jerry came down to KCLP the next day. He had a smooth way about him and made friends easily with everyone. Even Tony Beale liked him. Tony shook his hand. Told him it was a pleasure doing business with him. Told me to take him out to lunch.

"Keep him happy, Brenda," Tony said warningly. He was still annoyed with me for breaking up with Mr. Perfect. I kept reminding him that Mr. Perfect had broken up with *me,* but he insisted that if I'd been more of an obliging female, Larry would have stayed around.

I obliged and took Jerry to lunch. I would do my best to keep him happy. No problem, Tony.

I took Jerry to Saba's, a gourmet sandwich place. I was wearing black satin panties, a matching lace bustier, and pinstripe tights under a denim skirt and black cashmere sweater. Jerry wore a sweatshirt that stretched across his muscles. I enjoyed myself looking at his muscles.

"My dad had a boat," I said as we ate.

"I know. Sarah was telling me."

It took me two heartbeats to figure out that Sarah was my mother.

"We still have it," I said around my arugula and raspberry salad. "It probably needs your expert repairing."

I daydreamed about me showing Jerry the boat, the cabin, the bunks. Just me and him and the water and the sunshine.

"I know," he said. "I've seen it. We're going to take it out Saturday."

"Oh." My dream died. "Who's we?"

"Your mom said she'd let me sail it. Why don't you come along?"

I sat silently. I didn't want a family trip. But I supposed it was better than nothing. Mom could be nostalgic, David could show off everything he knew about sailing, and I could smile at Jerry and his muscles.

11

Jennifer Ashley

"Sure," I said. I tried to sound bright. "Saturday. Can't wait."

On Saturday afternoon, David called me. "Hey, Brenda." He sounded tired and annoyed. "Can you pick me up?"

"Where are you?" I asked. "I thought we were going out to Dad's boat."

David said, "Huh?"

"Aren't you calling from Dad's boat?" I asked.

"No, I had a job interview. I don't have enough money to take the bus back to Mom's house. Can you give me a ride?"

I held onto the phone, trying to stem my disappointment. "Sure. Where are you?"

"Garnet Street," he said and gave me the directions.

I growled something and hung up the phone. I had resigned myself to going out on the water as a family party, but maybe Mom and David had changed their minds about going at all.

Then I perked up. I'd take David home and convince Jerry to go out to the boat with me. I could show it to him alone, as I'd originally planned. We could take it out, have wine on the deck while we watched the sun set. . . .

Happy in my fantasy, I drove to Garnet Street, picked up David, and drove him up the hill to Mom's house.

We got there. We parked the car. We got out. David unlocked the door. Everything was quiet.

Maybe Jerry was sunbathing on the patio, I thought. In a skimpy bathing suit. I started to go look.

Just then, Jerry Murphy walked out of my mom's bedroom. In his underwear. Bright red bikini briefs that looked great on him.

Mom walked out behind him. In her robe.

David and I froze to the living room carpet.

12

After a long, tense moment, Mom said, "You two really should have called first."

David turned as red as Jerry's underwear. He shouted, "What the *hell?*"

2

The Mystery Man

David wanted to move in with me. An hour after we'd found out what Mom was doing up at her house with Jerry Murphy, David stood in the doorway of my apartment with his duffel bag slung across his back.

"You can't stay here," I told him.

"Well, I'm not staying up there with Mom and *him*."

"He's your friend. You brought him."

"I brought him for you, Brenda. You were supposed to show him around. Why didn't you?"

"Mom beat me to it."

David's face got red. "I told Jerry how nice you were. He said he wanted to get to know you." David looked me up and down, from my striped silk blouse to the fishnet stockings under my cutoff shorts. "What happened to you, anyway? You look weird."

I started to close the door. "You can't live with me, David."

He put his shoulder against it. "Just until I can find a place of my own."

"I already have a roommate. You won't have anywhere to sleep."

"I'll sleep on the couch. I don't care. You can't throw me out. I'm your brother. I don't have anywhere else to go."

Good old familial guilt. Who was it that said that the definition of family is that, when you go to them, they have to take you in? I think I'm misquoting. Anyway, I knew David really didn't have any place to go. Damn him. I opened the door.

"I'm not doing your laundry," I said darkly.

He looked disappointed as he slung his duffel bag to the floor. "You used to."

"I've changed."

"Obviously."

The apartment I shared with Clarissa had two master suites, each with a bedroom and attached bathroom, one suite on either side of the living room and kitchen.

I warned David that I'd have to talk to Clarissa about him staying—whenever she woke up—and he said, "Whatever." He dragged his duffel bag into my room.

Clarissa had no job and spent most of her time sleeping in her room or messing up the kitchen or having parties. But she paid her half of the rent on time without fail and always seemed to have plenty of money. I'd had roommates in the past who'd eaten all my food, then stuck me with the rent, so I decided to put up with her eccentricities. Clarissa bought her own food, mostly candy bars and beer. She stayed impossibly thin on this diet.

David had obviously decided that though he'd sleep on the couch, the rest of his stuff could share my room. He started combining the contents of two of my dresser drawers into one.

I leaned against the doorframe, watching him. "So Jerry's staying?"

"Yes," David said tightly. He grabbed my T-shirts and stuffed them into the drawer with my camisoles and tanks. "They're in love. I would have stayed on Dad's boat, but guess who's teaching her to sail it?"

I looked at him in surprise. "Mom always said she hated sailing."

"I guess she doesn't any more." He came out of my drawer with his hands full of panties. "Good God, Brenda, how much underwear do you need?"

"Will you leave my stuff alone?"

I grabbed the satin panties and thongs from him and crammed them into my lingerie chest. They didn't fit, which was why I'd moved them to the dresser.

He shrugged. He unzipped his duffel bag and up-ended it into the drawer. A rain of wrinkled underwear, shirts, pants, and black socks fell out. He mashed it all down, then slammed the drawer shut.

"Geez, David," I said. "No wonder Alicia kicked you out."

He turned around. He dropped the duffel bag. His face was white, his eyes dilated. He looked like someone had just kicked him.

"I don't want to talk about it," he said. He stalked into my bathroom, slammed the door, locked it, and wouldn't come out.

I left him in the bathroom, changed my clothes, and drove downtown to an Italian restaurant called Tonio's, which just happened to be across the street from Lili Duoma. I'd come to the restaurant because I wanted to think and also so that I could use their bathroom.

Tonio's had decorated the bathroom floor to ceiling with black-and-white posters of Italian male models. I found them restful. I could gaze at those hunky men with their muscles and their dark smiles and their tight leather pants, and they didn't talk back or go out with my mother. The life-sized one admiring me in the stall was particularly handsome.

I dried my hands, said a silent good-bye to Stefano flexing his biceps above the towel holder, and went back to my table and my arriving pasta.

I ate. The waitress, who'd wearily said her name was Terri and she'd be serving me today, wasn't interested in a table for one, especially not a female one. The busboy tried to flirt with me, but I wasn't in the mood for banter.

My stomach full, my bladder empty, I started across the street to Lili Duoma. I'd feel better if I bought some new stockings, I told myself, and maybe a camisole to go with them.

I stepped blindly into the narrow street, never seeing the red convertible driving serenely toward me. Good thing the driver saw me.

Tires screeched. People shouted. I turned and saw the red car sliding toward me. I should have dived behind a parked car. Instead, I stood there, eyes wide, picturing myself flying up over the hood of the convertible car and being plastered against the windshield like a bug in spike-heeled boots.

At the last second, the car stopped. It rocked back and forth, the bumper two inches from my shins.

The driver threw off his seat belt and hiked himself high over the windshield. "Hey, are you OK?"

I stood there, slowly realizing I hadn't actually been squashed on the windshield.

As my breath came back, I worked out how utterly stupid I was. People were staring. They already knew how stupid I was.

"You OK?" the concerned motorist repeated.

"Angh," I said.

The driver had blond hair, slightly frizzy. The last time

I'd seen it had been New Year's, two months before, when I'd opened my eyes as a new woman.

We stared at each other for a few agonizing moments. I told myself he'd never remember me. I started to slink away.

Another car flew around the corner and whizzed past us, narrowly missing me. I jumped back in front of my mystery man's car, heart in my throat.

I heard him get out. I scuttled across the now-empty street. I heard him tramping determinedly after me, so I ducked inside the lingerie store. He was a guy. He'd never follow me in.

He did.

"Hey," he said.

I dodged behind a rack of sky-blue teddies, then took a deep breath and turned and faced him. Be brave, Brenda.

There he was in the flesh, my mystery man from New Year's. A casual T-shirt stretched across broad shoulders and chest muscles that had been honed to precision. He was taller than I was, looking down from a handsome face and blue eyes that were no longer bloodshot. He had a swipe of blond stubble on his jaw, probably where he'd missed with the razor.

I suddenly knew how Tim had felt when Tony had pushed him off the Coronado Bridge. I felt like I was falling a long, long way into nothing. But I never wanted to stop.

Zoe, or Chloe, watched with interest from across the store. We'd gotten to know each other well since January, me and Zoe. Or Chloe.

His hair was not as frizzy as I remembered it from New Year's morning. It was curly but it looked silken. He'd tried to brush it flat on his head, but it stuck out here and there. I liked it.

I couldn't think of anything to say. I could only stand

there with my heart hammering and study his good-looking face and hair that wasn't quite perfect. His nose was crooked as well. I liked that. I was tired of perfect men.

"Hi," he said.

"Hi." The word creaked from my mouth.

He faced me over the teddies, his eyes the same blue as the satin fabric. "I guess there was a reason I decided to turn down this street today," he said.

"Kismet," I said faintly.

"How have you been?"

"Oh, you know. OK."

We could have been casual friends meeting up after going our separate ways.

"Good."

He kept looking at me hard with those blue eyes. I flushed. I wondered just how wild I'd been on New Year's Eve.

"So, would you—uh—like to talk about it?" he asked.

"We are talking about it," I said. I hoped I sounded smooth and glib, like I did this all the time.

My mystery man suddenly looked at the rack that separated me from him. I watched it dawn on him what was hanging from it and what kind of a store he'd followed me into. His face reddened and he took a step back.

Some women might be turned off by a man's embarrassment over women's underwear. But not me. I'd just come off of a year of Mr.-Take-Charge-And-We-Do-Everything-I-Want. Mr. Perfect was charm personified, and he walked over everyone.

I warmed to my blond, slightly imperfect man.

Suddenly he smiled. His mouth turned up on one side, his blue eyes crinkled, and my heartbeat went right off the scale.

In college, I'd read a ton of historical romances in which strong, beautiful heroines fell head over heels in love with stoic and sexy men. When the heroes in those paperbacks smiled, the heroines melted.

I'd always thought that simply a convention of the stories. But looking at him, I suddenly understood what all those long-skirted, petal-skinned heroines had felt when their heroes had gazed at them with devastating blue eyes and smiled the way my mystery man was smiling at me now.

He said, "I mean I want to talk for real. Want to go for coffee?"

Yes, yes, yes!

"Right now?" I gasped. I had to purchase lingerie right now. If I was going to have coffee with him, I had to buy something to wear.

"Why not? How about Swesto's on India Street? Meet you there? Say in an hour?"

I couldn't think of a reason to refuse, and the way my legs were shaking, I knew I didn't want to refuse. "Um, sure."

"Terrific," he said. His smile could melt butter.

"See you then," I answered.

He gazed at me for another long and heart-melting moment, then turned away.

Beyond the window display of French corsets, I saw a police cart stop next to his car. A young woman in black began scribbling gleefully in her ticket book. His smile died. He said, "Crap," and tore out of the store.

A gust of cool spring air wafted over me as the door glided closed. I hadn't realized how hot I'd been.

Zoe, or Chloe, walked over to me with a midnight-blue silk camisole in her hands.

"He is beautiful, zat young man," she said. "Perhaps zis would be good for you?" She thrust the camisole at me. The price tag read one hundred dollars.

What can I say? I bought it.

* * *

So there I was at Swesto's.

The sun was just going down, bathing San Diego in golden, liquid light. Far out west a cloud bank hovered in the blue dark, but the sky above was clear, clear.

I'd put on the camisole in the dressing room before I left Lili Duoma's. It was incredibly soft, and the silk rubbed along my breasts better than Mr. Perfect ever had.

My blond man wasn't there yet. I ordered an espresso from the coffee bar, carried it to an empty table in the corner, sat down, and idly studied the markings on the table that were supposed to make it look like a coffee crate.

The best thing about a coffeehouse is that no one cares if you show up alone. If you agree to meet someone and they stand you up, you can just pretend you came in to catch up on a novel or extra work from the office. You stay for a believable amount of time, then you go, no one the wiser. It's painless, unhumiliating, easy.

I kept telling myself that as minutes ticked by. I picked up the home and garden section of the newspaper and read all about how a sunroom could brighten up my house and increase its value.

When I looked up from the details of laying Saltillo tile, he was standing there.

My breathing constricted. For two months I'd been mourning getting dumped by Mr. Perfect. But looking up at this man's blue eyes and his brawny arms stretching his T-shirt, Mr. Perfect was rapidly fading from my thoughts.

Instead I started thinking about this guy in the shower. With me soaping him down.

"Hi again," he said.

"Hi," I answered.

We were off to a Hepburn-and-Grant start.

"I'll get some coffee," he said. "Do you want any?"

I'd already finished my espresso. I thought about asking him to order me another one. I thought about how jittery I'd be after I drank it. The first time we'd met, I'd been falling-down drunk on martinis; this time I could be bouncing up and down on caffeine.

"No, thanks," I said.

He moved off and ordered his coffee. He leaned against the high counter, offering me a good view of the back of his jeans. Those jeans smoothed over his nice, tight butt, the one I'd seen on New Year's. I wanted to slide my hand into his back pocket and keep it there a while.

I had actually made love with this guy. He'd touched me with his tanned hands, kissed me with his lips.

I wished I could remember it.

My heart beat hard and fast as he shifted his weight to take his wallet out. I could pass out just looking at him. I'd be spread out on the floor with a smile on my face.

He was almost done. I sat up straight and tried to smooth my hair. I crossed my legs, letting the lace tops of my stockings peep from under my skirt. I uncrossed my legs, crossed them the other way. I uncrossed them totally and tucked them under my chair.

I didn't like the chair. I stood up to move—and bumped right into my mystery man.

He jumped. So did the coffee, but fortunately it landed back in the cup.

I plopped down into my chair again. "Sorry."

He carefully set down the coffee and took the chair across from me. Smart man. He'd put the entire table between myself and him.

"Brenda," he said.

He knew my name. I searched my memories of the New Year's party. Couldn't remember a thing. Was it John? Sean? Don? Brawn?

"Brenda," he said patiently, "I'm apologizing."

I blinked and realized he'd been talking. "Sorry. Go on."

"I'm trying to explain why I left so fast New Year's morning. When you rolled over and saw me, you looked horrified. I realized I couldn't be a great sight to wake up to, so I decided it was best for both of us if I got out of there."

Sure, I thought.

He went on, "Then when I was halfway home, I realized how stupid that was. I went back to the apartment, but everyone was gone. Including you. I knew your name was Brenda, and that was it. I'd gone to that party with a friend of your roommate's, and I was tempted to ask him for your number, but then I imagined the look on your face when I called you. I imagined you hanging up on me. I thought I'd give my ego a break and let it go."

"I would have talked to you," I said.

Or would I have? I wondered. Would I, mortified, have pretended he had the wrong number and hung up?

"I had to leave town the next day," he said. "I spent the past two months in San Antonio with my brother, helping him move his business. I only got back a few days ago. I figured you'd have forgotten all about me by now."

"No," I croaked. "I didn't forget."

He smiled at me. I started thinking about him in the shower again.

"Why don't we start all over?" he asked. He held out his hand. "I'm Nick."

Nick.

Nope, still didn't ring a bell.

I took his hand. His fingers were strong. "Brenda."

He looked at me across the table with his blue, blue eyes, and said, "This is kind of lame."

I blinked. What was lame? This coffeehouse? Seeing me again? My outfit? Me wanting him in the shower?

"I have to go to an office party next weekend," he said.

"You know, one of those employee picnics? I wondered if you would go with me."

He looked nonchalant. Larry had always sounded smooth when he asked me out, and kind of condescending, like he was doing me a favor.

Nick watched my face. He laughed softly. "I was right, it's lame. Do you like basketball? I can get tickets. Or concert tickets—for whatever you'd like to see. Or movies—there's a new sci-fi coming up that's supposed to be huge."

I could get tickets, too, working at a radio station. At radio stations, free tickets are rained on you to promote shows and concerts and whatever. Except at our radio station, we didn't get Ozzy; we got pig pickins out in the farmlands.

"I don't care," I said.

"I'm trying to be so cool here." He spoke lightly, but his blue eyes watched me. "Cool Nick asking out sexy Brenda."

Sexy? Me?

Me.

Sexy.

I stirred dregs of coffee with my little straw, tried to look coy. "You could sound a little more enthusiastic."

He leaned forward, his arms resting a few inches from mine. He didn't have the brutally fair, freckled skin that some blond men have; his forearms were dark with tan, the hairs golden. "Last time we met, you didn't exactly look happy to see me."

"Last time we met, you almost hit me with your car."

He grinned. "I meant before that."

I leaned down to the coffee so he wouldn't see me blush. "You didn't look happy to see me then, either."

"I was embarrassed."

Wow. A guy admitting he was embarrassed. Mr. Per-

24

fect would never have admitted that in a million years. I started to really, really like Nick.

I looked up. He watched me, and he was so heart-breakingly cute. Shy Brenda was about to blush and stammer and screw this whole thing up.

So I let the new, brazen Brenda reach out and put her hand on his tanned and muscled arm.

"Maybe we could try again," I heard myself say.

He looked surprised. And hopeful? Did he look hope-ful? I hoped he looked hopeful.

"Get to know each other all over again," Brazen Brenda went on. "In all ways."

I couldn't believe those words had come out of my mouth. But the new Brenda is wild, she's adventurous, she wears sexy lingerie.

He closed his warm hand over mine.

The romance heroine inside woke up and started to swoon. And drool. And pant.

Wordlessly, I trailed my fingers across Nick's forearm. The old Brenda would never have done that. Even the new Brenda shook at her daring, but I kept my finger on his skin.

His arm was hard with muscle, wiry strength under bronzed skin. I thought again about waking up next to him. His body had been warm and strong, his muscled chest looking good only half-covered with my sheet.

"You want to get to know me again?" he asked.

I shrugged like I didn't care. "Sure. Why not?"

The look he gave me put Stefano to shame. "All right. When?" He was pretending he didn't care either. Or maybe he really didn't.

"You doing anything tonight?" I asked.

A swallow moved from his jaw all the way down his throat. "Just talking to you."

I leaned closer. He smelled good, and not like aftershave. Some men think that if they drench themselves in cologne, women will come running. Some men believe anything they see on TV.

I'd never asked a guy to have sex with me before. I wasn't quite sure how I was supposed to ask a guy to have sex with me.

I couldn't suggest we go back to my apartment, not with David there, not with Clarissa and her strange, black-eyed stare. Besides, Clarissa was having another party. I cringed from suggesting a hotel room. That would be really, really cheesy.

He didn't offer to take me to his apartment, either. Maybe he had an embarrassing roommate, too.

Then I thought of my dad's boat. Mom and Jerry hadn't gone out there. Neither had David. It was sufficiently private.

My heart beating hard, I mentioned the boat to Nick.

"Sounds good," he said softly.

I stammered out directions to the marina on Mission Bay. Nick nodded like he knew the place. We agreed to meet there at seven that evening.

He stood up. I looked across the table at his flat abs and the button on jeans. Wild Brenda wanted to reach over and run her finger right down the zipper.

He abruptly leaned down and brushed a brief kiss to my lips.

Something electric sparkled through me and I got all hot and bothered, not to mention damp in some places. It was only a little kiss, for God's sake, I told myself, but my body felt suddenly warm and pliant and happy.

He looked at me for a long moment, his blue eyes darkening. Then he smiled and walked away. The door buzzer rang as he exited the coffeehouse.

I had to sit there for ten minutes waiting for my legs to stop shaking before I could get up and leave, too.

The only other person in the coffeehouse now was the

barista, a college-aged guy who leaned against the counter reading *Madame Bovary.* He looked up and gave me a big smile.

Ok, so maybe people at coffeehouses didn't completely mind their own business. I put five dollars in his tip jar and walked out.

3

The Trouble with Boats and Older Brothers

When I got into my car again, who should call me but Mr. Perfect.

I looked at his number on the readout on my cell and debated whether to answer. Two months ago, I would have panted to hear Larry's voice again. Today I had just spent half an hour with blue-eyed, warm-smiling Nick. Larry had officially become second banana.

I decided I might as well answer. I settled back in my seat and thumbed the button. "Hello," I said, sounding neither happy nor annoyed.

"Brenda." Larry's voice was friendly. "How are you?"

When Larry sounded friendly, that meant he was up to something. "Oh, fine," I answered. "You?"

"I miss you," he said.

Two months ago, I would have danced for joy at those

words. But time apart from him had made me wary. "Miss you too, Larry," I said neutrally.

"I mean, I really miss you." He sounded sincere. "I'd like to see you. How about tonight?"

"I'm busy tonight." I clenched my fist and made a *yesss!* gesture. *Thank you, Nick.* "Tomorrow?"

He paused. "Oh, hmm."

Messed up your schedule, did I? Ha! He'd cleared a window for me, and I hadn't jumped through it.

After a long pause, he said, "Can you talk right now?"

I leaned my elbow on the window. A driver who'd wanted my parking space gave me a pissed-off look and roared past. "What do you want to talk about?"

"You." His voice got more pleasing. Larry really knew how to turn it on. "I think I know where we went wrong."

Yes, I said I'd go out with you in the first place.

He said, "I think we never got to know each other. We kept going without really taking time, you know?"

"Maybe," I said.

"For instance, I never realized, well, how hot you were. I mean, I knew you were hot, of course I did, but I took it for granted."

Hot? Me? Larry had never thought of me as anything but lukewarm.

Not that he'd been all that great himself. He was Mr. Perfect everywhere but in bed. Larry had certainly never read the *Kama Sutra* or even *How to Make Your Girlfriend Even Remotely Orgasmic.*

I smiled into the phone. "So what are you going to do about it?"

He chuckled. "Get to know you better. I'll tell you what. Next weekend, my parents are spending time at the house in Dana Point. Why don't we go up there and join them?"

I removed the phone from my ear and shook it. I put it back to my ear. "Did you say we should join your parents at their house in Dana Point?"

He'd never once, in the year I'd gone out with him, suggested bringing me home to Mother. I'd never known whether he'd been ashamed of me, or of them, or both.

"Yes, they want to meet you," he said.

"Why?" I asked, more suspicious than ever.

I mean, why did a guy take you to meet his parents? Not to get into your pants. If he wanted that, he'd try to get you drunk. He didn't suggest dinner at the house with Mom and Dad. What was he up to?

"I've told them so much about you," Larry continued. "They think it's time we all got together. So, next Saturday, OK?"

I thought about Nick and his blue eyes and the way his arm had felt under my fingertips. I held onto that and said, "Um, I don't know, Larry."

Larry became solicitous. "I don't want to rush you. Why don't you let me know tomorrow, and I'll tell my mom and dad whether we're coming?"

He was pushy. He'd always been pushy.

Suddenly I smiled. He was handing me the chance to do something I'd always wanted to do to Mr. Perfect. Every day that I'd gone out with him he'd made my decisions for me. I'd never been able to put him off and tell him what I really thought. If I took time to think, he simply did things his way and dragged me along. And then, if I'd asked him to do anything for *me*, he gave me the *I'm really busy, honey, I'll get back to you, OK?* excuse.

Now, he wanted something from me, but he no longer had a hold over me. The power wasn't his any more. It was mine.

I studied my fingernails and sat back in my seat. "You

know what, Larry?" I said. "I'm really busy right now. I'll get back to you, OK?"

I heard him spluttering as I clicked the phone off.

I tossed the phone on the seat beside me, shook my hands through my hair, and screamed, "Woo hoo!" It felt so good. I threw back my head and laughed.

The phone rang again. Larry's number showed up on the readout. I turned on the radio and cranked it up. A snappy song by Jet drowned out the ringing. I started to sing along.

A guy was blocking traffic a little way behind my car, his blinker on. He was going to get my parking space, come hell or high water. I peeled out and let him have the space, waving at him as I left. Sometimes stupid persistence should be rewarded.

OK, when you read about romantic assignations in novels, the hero and heroine never have to worry about logistics. They are already conveniently someplace private, like in a rose-covered gazebo in the middle of the night, where they just start kissing and shedding their clothes.

No one mentions the heroine weaving through weekend traffic, hunting for a parking space, hiking through a marina while seagulls strafe her, and worrying the whole time that the hero won't even show up.

As I drove, hunted, hiked, and ducked seagulls, I worried that Nick would go to the wrong marina, that he'd never find the right slip, that he'd change his mind halfway there and leave me waiting on the dock like a fool.

He didn't. My heart pounded hard when I saw his red convertible T-bird pulling into the marina behind me.

He parked his car and met me at the gate that led down to the boats. We didn't say anything, but he smiled at me. My tongue cleaved to the bottom of my mouth. I couldn't have said anything even if I could have thought of anything to say.

I unlocked the gate and took him through. We walked down the dock, our footsteps on the boards too loud for comfort.

When we reached my father's boat, the woman who owned the neighboring boat came out on her deck and waved at us. "Brenda," she said cheerfully. "How's your mom?"

Mom had called me after I'd gone home that afternoon, trying to talk to me about the recent blow-up. She'd told me, somewhat defiantly, that she was taking Jerry to a fancy restaurant in La Jolla tonight. I'd said, "Fine, whatever," and hung up.

"She's great," I answered lamely. *She's just up in La Jolla sharing foie gras with a man half her age, that's all.*

"I'm so glad to see her coming out here again, and her nephew, too. It's nice of him to spend time with her."

Nephew? Had my mom told her that, or had she just assumed? "Uh, yeah, he's great."

The neighbor glanced at Nick, then winked and smiled. "Have a good night."

"Right. You too."

I climbed up to the deck and nearly dragged Nick on board.

My dad's boat was a forty-five-foot sloop with a painfully white deck and lots of polished wood in the cabin. My dad had loved it, called it his home away from home—probably because he'd spent most of his off-work time here instead of in his real house up on the hill.

I could tell that my mom had been out here recently, because a trash bag hanging from a cabinet handle held an empty wine cooler box. My father would have died before he'd have drunk a wine cooler. I imagined handsome Jerry and my mom drinking them out here, and I quickly turned my back.

I turned on the lights and closed the shades. Two bunks reposed opposite each other, doubling as seats during the day. "So," I said, tossing my purse on one. "What do you think?"

Nick touched a beam. "Nice." He had that gleam in his eye that men get when they behold vehicles of any kind. "Your dad's, you said?"

"My mom's now. My dad died a few years ago."

"I'm sorry." He looked sorry. His blue eyes held compassion. One up on Mr. Perfect.

I arrested my thought. I didn't want Larry intruding right now. Right now, I wanted to be with Nick, my mystery man.

I wanted to be spontaneous. I wanted to be uninhibited. I wanted to be less scared than I was.

While he stood with his hand resting on the beam, I started unbuttoning my blouse. My fingers were shaking. He just watched me, his gaze intense.

I realized when I was halfway down the shirt that this would be the first time anyone would see what I'd taken to wearing under my clothes. Yes, the camisole was tasteful and chic (and expensive). But I'd never revealed that part of myself. Not even to Clarissa, who shared my home.

I froze, my fingers on the buttons. I wondered if I looked panicked.

He watched me a while longer, and then he said, "Brenda," in a soft voice and came over to me.

He took my hands, lowering them from the shirt, then leaned down and kissed me.

He kissed me like he meant it. His lips were smooth and dry and his fingers caressed my wrists. I loosened my hands from his and wrapped my arms around him.

He had a nice strong back. I ran my hands up and down it, feeling his muscles, enjoying the firmness of them. Any minute now, memories of the night we spent together would come back to me. Any minute.

Meanwhile, he brought his hands up to the unopened buttons and started undoing them himself. I flattened myself against the corner between the bunk and the wall as he slid the cloth-covered buttons through the holes. He kissed my throat.

His hair smelled nice. He'd just washed it. I'd never liked blond men before. I liked them dark-haired, like Jerry Murphy. Jerry Murphy who was now eating fancy French food with my mom up in La Jolla.

Nick's eyes were so blue. Under the harsh glare of the bulb over us, they were deep blue. Forget Stefano and his smoldering brown eyes. Stefano was stuck on a bathroom wall.

At last Nick opened my blouse. The camisole beneath was blue, kind of like his eyes.

"I don't remember this," he murmured.

"I bought it today. At the lingerie store."

He looked at me like he was searching for something. "What for?"

"Because I was meeting you."

He smiled. He slid his hand under one of the straps. His fingers were warm. I got a big lump in my throat.

He kissed better than any man I'd ever kissed before. Nice eyes, great kisser—why, why, why didn't I remember him? I kept waiting for those post-drunken memories to come back—something should have triggered it, right? But I got nothing.

I decided it didn't really matter. I reached behind me and snapped off the light.

Now it was black and I could focus on Nick's lips and his hands on me, how good his hair felt under my fingers. He skimmed his tongue into my mouth, warm and spicy.

I was enjoying myself. I was really, really enjoying myself. My encounters with Mr. Perfect were planned by him, orchestrated by him, dictated by him. I'd simply shown up and followed along.

Nick was different. He didn't start off with a checklist of what we were going to do. He just kissed me like he liked kissing me and didn't really care what we would end up doing.

This was adventure. This was excitement. I wanted this.

We sat down on the edge of the bunk and kissed, then decided we liked it better lying down.

My heart beat extra fast. He was turning me on just kissing me. My legs shook and my thighs were hot and bothered.

He nuzzled my neck. I laced my fingers through his warm hair and hooked my foot around his leg. He pulled down the straps of my camisole. Cool air touched my breasts.

It was dark, but he found me with his mouth.

"Nick," I whispered.

"Mmm?"

"I'm glad you almost ran over me today."

He laughed, low and sexy.

"I was having a really, really bad day," I said. "It's better now."

"Brenda." He scooted up until his face hung over mine. I could just see it in the moonlight.

"What?"

"Shh." He kissed me again. I shut up and surrendered.

His hand roved my body, moving under the camisole. He knew how to touch me. His finger moved in a circle around my areola, and it tightened and lifted.

He kissed his way down my throat, brushed his tongue over the hard tip of my breast. I felt the firm, blunt length of his penis pressing his zipper.

"Brenda," he whispered.

"Hmm?"

"I hate to tell you this."

A slight worry pricked me. "Tell me what?" *I'm gay?* No, he felt randy and ready to go. *I'm married?*

Oh, God, please don't let him say *I'm gay and married.*

"I didn't bring a condom," he finished.

"Oh," I said. My worry dissolved. "I brought one."

He lifted his head. His sexy smile returned. "You did?"

"Yes."

He looked at me a long time; then his smiled widened. I wondered if he was happy, or if he was laughing at me. "I've never met a girl like you, Brenda."

"No?" I said.

"No. You're wild and fun and a little bit crazy." His voice softened. "I like that. I need that."

"You do?"

"So if you don't mind," he said, leaning to kiss my breast again with his warm mouth, "I'm going to celebrate."

I wasn't thinking of stopping him. I ran my fingers across the hard muscle of his shoulder blades, seeking the concave curve of his spine.

He inched his way up my body again. His lips were smooth and soft like warm satin when he kissed me. He dipped his tongue into my mouth, swirling heat and the sharp spice of him.

He cupped my shoulder, rubbing his thumb across the hollow of my throat. I was warm, warm, warm, and excited and ready for him. I'd never felt like this before.

Something thumped on the deck above us. I gasped and jumped. Nick rose, his hand under one of my straps. "What's the matter?"

"I thought I heard something."

We listened. Water licked the hull below us, and a

breeze jingled wind chimes on the boat next door. "I don't hear anything," he whispered.

I exhaled, trying to relax. "Never mind." I turned his face to me. "Kiss me some more."

He obliged. Our mouths met in a frenzy.

He smelled good. He felt good. He tasted good. I buried myself in his goodness.

The cabin door slammed open. Feet sounded on the ladder; then something thumped to the floor.

"Oh, God." I sat up and shoved Nick away. His hand caught in my camisole and it tore, a tiny, heartbreaking sound.

The light snapped on. The blazing glare fell on the unmistakable red canvas of my brother's duffel bag and David standing behind it.

David looked at Nick, who scowled back at him. He looked at me lying there with my shirt open and my camisole ripped.

"Brenda!" he bellowed. He threw up his hands, turned around, and stomped up to the deck, leaving his duffel bag behind.

"Jesus," we heard him say. "What is wrong with the women in this family?"

4

Drive Time at KCLP

"I'll go," Nick said.

I swung out of the bunk and started buttoning my shirt over the ripped camisole. "No, don't. I'll get rid of him."

Unlike me, Nick hadn't undressed. He didn't need to button or zip or snap anything.

"Who is that, anyway?" he asked.

"My brother. He's supposed to be staying at my apartment. I don't know what he's doing here."

His face softened. "It looks like he needs the boat more than we do," he said. "I'll go."

He was being nice. My brother had interrupted him getting free, no-strings-attached sex, and he was being *nice*.

I opened my mouth to beg him to stay. He stepped close to me and cupped my face in his hand, and I forgot how to talk. "You're great, Brenda," he said. "Will you call me?"

Great? Me? "Sure," I babbled. "Yes. I'll call. Often."

He gave me another smile that melted my heart, then turned around and climbed up to the deck.

I kept hastily buttoning my blouse. When I reached the top, I realized I'd missed a button and the whole shirt was crooked. Who cared? I ran out onto the deck. David was sitting on the bench by the wheel. He didn't say one word to me as I scrambled off the boat after Nick.

Nick was walking away fast. I slipped and stumbled after him in my stupid high heels. "Hey, Nick."

He stopped when he reached the gate, watched me catch up to him. I wanted to say *good night* and *thanks* and other meaningless stuff. Instead, I raised on tiptoe and kissed him.

He put his thumb on the corner of my mouth and returned the kiss softly. "Thank you, Brenda," he murmured.

Thank you for what? I wanted to ask. For nothing?

He looked down at me for a moment, then, without a word, he opened the gate and strode silently through it.

Not until he'd crossed the parking lot, started his car and driven away did I realize that I didn't know his last name, or his phone number, or where he lived, or anything else about him. He'd probably given me all that information on New Year's and figured I'd remember. I should at least know his last name. He remembered my name, right? I hadn't bothered asking him for his phone number again.

That's because I am too stupid to live.

When I got back to the boat, David had gone inside. I found him sitting on the bunk opposite the one Nick and I had kissed in. He looked morose.

I sat down and regarded him glumly.

"I guess I messed up your date." David kicked his duffel bag. "You could have warned me."

"It's OK." I couldn't bring myself to explain it wasn't a date; we'd just decided to have sex. Or, wait, maybe that was a date. "What are you doing out here, anyway?"

"I came to get some sleep. Your roommate is having a party."

Clarissa liked to throw parties, like the one on New Year's. She had a lot of friends from all walks of life, and once in a while she'd invite them over to drink and eat and hang loose in my living room.

"You'll hate staying at my apartment," I told David. "You should get one of those weekly hotel rooms until you find something."

"With what? I'm cleaned out."

"Put it on a credit card. I'll even pay the bill. Or send it to Mom. She should pay for it."

He sat, unblinking, his eyes pure anguish. "I don't have any credit cards. I lost everything, Brenda. Every last thing. They took away my credit cards and my house and my whole effing life."

We sat in silence. Outside the wind died. It got so quiet we could hear the faint *swish, swish* of water against the hull.

"I'm really sorry, David," I said softly. "I didn't know."

He looked past me, his anguish palpable. "What did Alicia *want?* I gave her a house and a car and everything she asked for. I moved up so fast, made so much money. I was going to join a country club. Me, your dweeb brother. And then the shit hit the wall, and I had to file for bankruptcy. You know, I think Alicia would have stayed even with everything else, except for the bankruptcy. She was embarrassed. *Embarrassed*, do you believe it? She got a big lawyer and is suing me for everything I haven't got."

He sat folded in on himself, like he was hiding from the world.

I watched him, my heart burning. I'd been so wrapped up in my own problems that I hadn't had time for his.

Poor David. He'd run back home like a frightened child, thinking his mom would pat his head, say, "There, there," and fix him spaghetti and meatballs. Instead, the friend he'd brought with him had started dating his mother, and the kitchen was closed.

I swung my foot a little, my heart heavy. "Mom will help you," I said. "You know she will."

"I don't want her to."

I knew he didn't. He was angry and hurt. "We'll think of something," I said. My words echoed in the stuffy little room, like they didn't mean anything. "Come on, let's get some dinner. I'll buy."

"I don't want dinner."

He glowered. He didn't want help; he wanted to pout. I could have scolded him, but I didn't have the heart, because I didn't blame him. I wanted to pout, too.

"Sleep here on the boat, then," I said. "I'm used to Clarissa's parties."

He nodded once, then he looked around the cabin, made a face, and stood up. "I'm not staying here. You were screwing. Mom was probably screwing, too. I'll have nightmares."

"Thanks a lot. And we weren't screwing." *We never got the chance.*

"You can do what you want, Brenda, I just don't want to know about it." David lifted his duffel bag, his face dark with sorrow. "Man, everyone's screwing but me."

I convinced him to have dinner with me anyway at a pancake house. David had always loved sourdough pancakes, but tonight he ordered a plain old short stack and squished butter and syrup all over them until he made a mess. He didn't eat very much.

While I watched him and felt sorry for him, I wondered if I'd ever see Nick again. I still tasted his kisses on my tongue and felt his hands on my body. I thought of his face in the moonlight, hovering so close to mine, and how his eyes got warm and blue when he smiled. I remembered the feeling of his body under my hands, firm muscles smooth beneath my palms.

I swore to myself I'd find him again. If I had to call every Nick in the San Diego phone book or walk up and down the streets jumping in front of every red T-bird, I would do it.

David and I finished with the pancakes and went home. Clarissa's party had wound down, and only one reveler was left. She used our arrival to kick him out, then she went to bed, leaving all the ashtrays piled with cigarettes and candy wrappers.

The next day was Sunday. We all slept late, and then I took everyone out for lunch. It was a mournful meal, and David embarrassed me by telling Clarissa all the gory details of finding me with Nick the night before. She just ate her salad and acted like she wasn't listening.

I woke up Monday relieved that I had to go back to work. It's bad when your weekend sucks so much that you look forward to Monday.

I didn't go on the air until two, but Tony liked me there most of the day so I could record spots and help the other DJs and get on the phones and sell advertising. I'd told him the very first day that no way was I making coffee for everyone all the time. He'd just smiled and stuck me with all the other crap jobs instead.

I tuned the radio to KCLP as I headed down the interstate. Tim, the morning guy, was broadcasting from inside the shark tank at Sea World. He had some sort of hookup where he could stay underwater and talk through a mike. His voice wavered. His board op was obviously watching him from outside the tank.

"Look out, Tim!" the board op shouted. "You aren't nervous, are you? Sharks only attack when you're nervous."

Tim's voice came back. He was trying to laugh and pretend he didn't care that a couple hundred sharks were swimming around him.

"You gotta stay in there ten more hours, Tim," his board op said. "Anyone who wants to win an hour in the shark tank with Tim, give us a call right here at—"

My right hand snaked down, punched a button, and Tim's shaking voice disappeared.

I hit KBZ, our rival. KBZ hugged the number five slot and had kept KCLP out for years. They drove me crazy. It was hard trying to sell advertising to tightwad businessmen who pointed out that they could run an ad for the same money on KBZ and be on the fifth highest rated station in the city.

I'd always have to promise to throw in free time slots on the overnights and tickets to the county fair or the plus-size women's mud-wrestling tournament. A few clients implied that if I threw in a private strip tease, they'd give me as much business as I wanted. I usually rolled my eyes and left, although Tony, without a doubt, would encourage me to grant their wishes if he'd known about them.

The KBZ DJ came on the air. "Hi, San Diego, this is Nick Jordan."

I almost slammed into the trunk of a bright yellow Honda before I jammed on my brakes. Tires squealed. Horns honked. I stared at the radio in frozen shock.

Nick.

I saw again his blond hair and blue eyes, his sexy body, felt his kisses. Hot, wild kisses that threatened to boil my blood away.

Nick—my Nick—was a DJ on KBZ.

My car swerved. Someone screamed an obscenity. Nick started talking again.

"I'm your new voice on KBZ mornings from five to nine, driving you to work."

I started shaking. Commuters whizzed around and in front of me, in and out, on and off the freeway. My eyes were wide, fixed in place as Nick kept talking.

"I had a hot date this weekend," he said. "You know, one of those nights you'll never forget." The sound effect of applause came on. "Her name was Brenda, and she was beautiful. But you know what? I don't have her phone number." The sound of a group groan came on. "So I tell you what. I'm going to play her a song, and she can call me here. This one's for you, Brenda." His voice went away and the strains of "Crazy" by the Dave Matthews Band came over the airwaves. A sweet love song.

My heart pounding, I dove off the nearest exit, even though I was five exits away from the one I needed. Somehow I got into a parking lot of a grocery store. I stopped the car. The radio wailed that Nick thought I was a lovely lady.

Perfect. My life was just perfect.

I laid my head on the steering wheel and groaned.

I staggered into KCLP sick to my stomach. I didn't get the chance to rush to the bathroom because Tony Beale cornered me. He held onto a rolled-up newspaper, which he shook at me like I was a bad dog.

"You have to do the afternoon drive time today, Brenda."

"What?"

"Afternoon drive time is yours. I fired Hans."

Any other day of my life, I would have grabbed at the chance to entertain San Diego while they were stuck in five o'clock traffic.

Today my nerves were raw, my emotions fragile. How

could I be bright and chirpy at four in the afternoon when my world whirled around me like I'd just stepped off a roller coaster?

Tony tapped my arm with the newspaper. "You awake, Brenda? Drive time. This afternoon. Play music. Answer phones. Talk to people. You do remember how to be a DJ, right?"

Crap. "Right."

So why hadn't Nick told me he worked in radio? Maybe he had told me, along with all the other stuff he'd poured out to me on New Year's.

Geez, what had I told him? I didn't remember telling him anything about my life, my job, or even my last name.

We'd both wanted a brief encounter. Excitement, fun, no commitment.

Ha. Now he was broadcasting far and wide that he'd had a date and wanted to see her—me—again.

I turned on the radio, ignored Tim's pleas to get that hammerhead away from him, and switched to KBZ.

A girl was on the phone with Nick. "Hey, Nick, you don't find her, you call me, OK?"

Nick laughed, warm and sweet. "Sure thing." He hung up. "The phones are lighting up all over the place. I promise I'll get to you as fast as I can." He went to commercial, one of the clients I'd tried to book and couldn't.

I snapped off the radio.

Tony stormed past me down the hall to the studio. No one was in there but Marty the producer, making sure the remote went OK.

I followed Tony, figuring I should do something other than bang my head against the wall.

Tony entered the studio just when Tim's team went to commercial. He grabbed the phone. "Tim!" he bellowed.

Tim couldn't answer, being with the sharks, but his

board op—the guy who was running the soundmixer—must have. Tony kept yelling. "Why aren't we getting any calls? Listeners should be all over this shark thing."

I stopped myself groaning. We weren't getting any calls because everyone was calling KBZ about Nick's mystery date.

"What?" Tony shouted. He glared over the phone at Marty, who was unwrapping a candy bar. "Turn on KBZ."

Marty took a bite of chocolate-covered nougat, then turned one of the dials in front of him.

Nick's voice filled the studio. "I have a pair of tickets to Incubus for whoever can find my mystery date. I'll throw in a dinner for two at Tonio's. The lady's name is Brenda," Nick said.

I shot Tony Beale a frozen look, waiting for him to turn around, waiting for him to scream at me, waiting for him to tell me I was fired. He'd assume I was conspiring with a rival radio station.

Marty bit his candy bar. Had he heard and understood and was waiting to watch the fireworks?

Tony stared at the radio; then he turned to me, his expression puzzled. "Why is that so interesting? Sharks are more interesting. Aren't sharks more interesting?" he asked Marty.

"Yeah, sharks," Marty replied. "Interesting."

Tony looked right through me. The idea that Nick's mystery Brenda was the Brenda who worked for him never occurred to him.

Insulting prick.

All morning I listened to Nick's show. It was like a car accident. I didn't want to look, but I couldn't turn away.

Nick signed off his show at nine, but the phones kept ringing. The next DJ, annoyed that he was taking Nick's calls but probably having his manager breathing down his neck, answered like a good sport.

"Hi. Nick's not here. . . ."

A frantic female voice. "Tell him I'm his mystery date. Tell him I want to meet him."

"This is KBZ, I'm not Nick. . . ."

"Hey, I'll change my name to Brenda if he wants me to!"

"KBZ, I bet you want me to talk to Nick. . . ."

"Any woman who wouldn't call Nick back is a stupid *beep*ing *beep!*" a lady with a grating voice shouted. "I love you, Nick!"

"Turn that off!" Tony bellowed.

My hand moved without my brain telling it to and snapped the radio off.

"They have enough ratings without us listening, too. What are we going to do about it?"

He was frothing at the mouth. Really. Bubbly spit dribbled down the side of his lip.

I looked at him for a stunned moment, waiting for him to fire me on the spot, and then something happened.

Just like when Larry had caught me stumbling out of my bedroom on New Year's, the fed-up Brenda inside me woke up. Nick was broadcasting our failed date and taking the listeners from my station and Tony, who'd finally figured out that I was Nick's Brenda, was blaming me.

I could go home and sulk in my room, or I could let the lingerie addict in me stand up and take over.

I raised my head. The light in my eyes must have been scary, because Tony Beale took a hesitant step back.

"Put me on the air," I said.

Tony blinked at me. "What?"

"Put me on the air. Right now."

"But we're in the shark tank today—"

I stood up. I wasn't very tall, but then, neither was Tony.

47

Too many meals spooned into him by his Italian mama had spread Tony's girth so that it nearly touched me.

"I'm getting on the air and stealing our audience back," I said.

Tony looked at me a little longer. "What are you going to do, Brenda? Flirt with him on the air? Get all cooey with him? You should have told me what he was going to do; I would have had a bit all set up. But did you tell Tony what was going on? Nooooo."

"I didn't know," I said. "But I'll fix it now. Just put me on."

His little eyes narrowed. "Nick is looking for a sexy, hot woman. Not you. The listeners will never buy it. And then your butt's fired."

I drew myself up. I thought about the lingerie under my clothes, slinky and sexy, and how Nick's eyes had darkened when he'd unbuttoned my blouse. "I'm more than meets the eye, Tony. You put me on, and I swear to you, the listeners will flock over here. The shark tank is sunk."

The canny salesman that lurked inside him watched me speculatively. "OK. You can try. But if it doesn't work, you're back to running the boards on overnight *and* getting the DJs coffee."

"Fine," I said, shaking in my heels.

"Fine," he said. His eyes were razor-sharp. He didn't think I could do it.

We barged into the studio, interrupting Marty, who was eating another candy bar.

"Yank the sharks," Tony snarled.

Marty stopped midbite and stared at him.

I slid into the pilot seat, put on the headphones, and adjusted the volume on my mike. On the other side of the glass, Marty tossed down his candy wrapper and segued into a commercial.

While I half-listened to an annoying male voice

scream about Uncle Lewee's no-credit used cars, I tore through our CD collection until I found what I wanted, readied my mike, and watched Marty blandly switch the broadcasting from the shark tank and back to the studio.

I made my mind go blank. If I thought about it, I wouldn't be able to do it.

I listened to the station identification—read by some babe with a sexy voice because Tony thought the voice would better attract the male listeners sixteen to nineteen.

Marty cued me with a limp finger. I said, "Hey, we're back in the studio. This is Brenda Scott taking over for the sharks."

Tony Beale watched me, face white. I drew a long, deep breath, made my voice oh-so-funny and fun. "I heard that a guy at a rival station has to beg for girls to call him. He's looking for Brenda. So I'm Brenda. What do you think, should I call him? I'm waiting for your answer. Should we give him his Brenda? This is for you, Nick."

I clicked in my CD and the wailing tones of "Stand by Your Man" filled the air.

I killed the mike because I knew Tony was going to yell.

"That's not on the playlist!" he shouted. "It's not even from this century. We play urban contemporary, Brenda. Rap and dance. Hip stuff for the kids today."

The last time Tony Beale had been hip was in 1973. I'd seen a picture of him with waist-length hair and an even longer beard and a scruffy T-shirt with a ZZ Top logo on it. He must have been twenty years old, but even then he'd had a receding hairline and a slight paunch.

"Sharks and a playlist aren't going to win the listeners," I said. "Nick set it up, now I'm reeling it in."

Tony stared at me in surprise. Was this the Brenda who did what she was told and came in early and tried (and failed) to get phone interviews with rappers at the crack of dawn?

Meet the new Brenda, Tony. She lures men to bed and wears a sexual superhero's outfit under her clothes.

Tony looked at me for a long time. But he hadn't survived in this business for thirty years for nothing.

"Good girl," Tony said. He patted my shoulder. "Bring them home to daddy."

Before I could tell him how so non-PC that was, Patsy Cline ended her tune.

"Look," I said. The computer screen was filled with a huge list of calls. Tony stared at it in awe. Marty scrambled to answer the lines. He looked pissed. I don't think he'd ever had to answer more than one call per show before.

"This is Brenda," said the new Brenda in a bright voice. "Talk to me."

A man's voice came on. For a heart-stopping moment, I thought it was Nick himself, but then realized the voice was wrong. "Forget this Nick guy," he said. "He's got half the women in the city calling him. You don't need him."

The next was a guy with the same attitude. "You don't need a show-off. You need a reeeal man." Like himself, presumably.

"I bet you're real, all right," I said. "But I'll wait to hear from Nick. If he's up to the challenge."

"Be my babe, Brenda!" the third man shouted. "Screw Nick!"

I'd love to screw Nick, I thought, then said, "You're sweet, but I'll give Nick a chance. Just one, though."

I had girls calling me, too. Some told me I was a bitch for being mean to Nick. Others said, "You go, girl!" "Guys shouldn't have everything their way." "You make him fight for you."

The point was, they all called me, not KBZ.

"What's with that Nick?" another man asked me. "Begging a girl to call him back over the air? What a smooth guy."

My hand went to a CD and dropped in Santana and Rob Thomas. "Yeah," I said. "Real smooth." I started the CD. OK, so that was lame, but I was desperate.

Tony stood there with his mouth open as the Latin sound filled the room. "We were alternative last year, Brenda. This year we're hip-hop."

"And we were country-western the year before that," I reminded him, which was why I could find Patsy Cline at an urban contemporary station. Tony liked to change formats. He did it all the time—he could, since he was one of the few independent station owners these days. He was always trying something new to grab more listeners, and ergo, more sponsors.

Tony kept standing there, his manager genes fighting his salesman's ambition.

The phones kept ringing. Marty was sweating, his half-eaten candy bar forgotten.

For the next two hours, San Diego called me and told me not to call Nick. I played whatever music came to mind, from U2 to the Proclaimers all the way back to Barry White.

Format and clock went out the window. Tony watched me, white-faced.

"Just play the spots, Brenda," Tony said, his voice weak. "At least play the spots. Uncle Lewee's bought almost the whole midday."

I looked at him. I was shaking badly, and I knew whenever I got out of here, I'd fall over, right on my face. "Hey, Tony, after this, you can get any account you want," I said. "Uncle Lewee's can bite us."

Tony stared at me again. He looked like a fish. Then his eyes took on a kind of glow.

Before the next song finished, I heard him out yelling at the sales guys, telling them to get out there and land more advertising, *right now.*

The new, sexy Brenda with her black lace teddy and satin tights told the city that Nick should call *her* if he wanted her so bad.

The old Brenda would have gone into the bathroom to throw up. The new Brenda hung on and kept talking.

Because I was mad. I had been so excited to go on that date with Nick, so thrilled to try out my lingerie persona on a guy who didn't know the old Brenda. But it wasn't just that. When he kissed me, my heart went pitter-pat.

Ok, thud, thud, thud, drool, swoon.

I thought maybe, just maybe, he liked me too. Now, he was using our date to get publicity for KBZ, like they needed it.

That's what he was doing, using that charming voice and his sweet songs to get himself more listeners.

Ha. Let him see a publicity stunt. I could play the game. He probably had expected me to quietly call him, and then he'd tease me on the air while his audience laughed. *Nothing doing, gorgeous man.*

Geez, why did he have to be so gorgeous?

By the time the afternoon DJ came in, I was wound up, hot, shaking, and exhausted.

Tony himself helped me from the chair and led me out of the studio.

"You're drive time tomorrow morning, Brenda," he said, handing me the choicest slot like it was nothing. "Be here at five."

Five. I barely knew my own name at five. "What about Tim?" I managed.

"Tim, ah." Tony flushed. "Tim went to the hospital."

I raised my brows. "Really?"

"Yeah. Shark bit him."

I wondered how long it would be before Tim sued

KCLP. Right now, I didn't care. Tony walked me out to my car and said, "See you tomorrow, sweetie. Early. Get some sleep."

And that was how Brenda Scott landed herself morning drive time in a top ten market.

5

Mom, Ten—Brenda, Zero

"Is Clarissa a lesbian?" David asked me when I got home.

"What?" I was still shaky. I wanted a shower and a drink, not in that order. Maybe I could have my drink in the shower.

"Is Clarissa a lesbian?" he repeated. "She never talks to me."

"She never talks to anyone."

David clicked off the TV and slumped in the chair. "I figure either my ability to attract women is totally gone, or she's a lesbian."

"She's not a lesbian. She just doesn't talk to anyone."

I went past him, through the bedroom, and into the bathroom. David's stuff was everywhere. He'd gotten shaving cream on the mirror.

I shoved everything aside, closed the door, stripped off my clothes. While the shower warmed up, I stood looking at myself, stark naked, in the mirror.

My skin was bloodless white, the kind of skin red-heads have. Forget tanning. Buy lots of sunscreen. Against my skin, my nipples stood out brownish pink. My eyes were wide and dark, my spread pupils drowning the blue.

What did Nick see in me, a freckle-faced, pale-skinned redhead?

I knew what I saw in him. Wide shoulders, blue eyes, lips that could kiss. Oh, baby, did he know how to kiss. I remembered his lips on mine, his tongue stroking my mouth. He'd tasted fantastic.

I wasn't sure what to make of him putting our date on the air. Cheap publicity for his show? That didn't go with what he seemed like at the coffeehouse or out at my dad's boat.

He'd seemed warm, friendly, funny. Or maybe I was a rotten judge of character. Look at my track record.

Did he truly want to find me? Was he being romantic? *You're great, Brenda,* he'd said before he'd left me. And *thank you.*

What would he do if I did call him? Broadcast the call on the air? Without telling me? That would be just perfect.

I imagined my voice going out over the airwaves. *So, Nick, I really liked rolling around on the bunk with you, can we do it again?* Tony Beale would have a stroke.

Or would Nick turn off the mike and talk to me for real?

What kind of guy asks a girl to call him on the radio? And rips a hundred-dollar camisole and doesn't say he's sorry?

I sighed. My taste in men was just priceless.

I got tired of staring into the mirror and wondering why guys thought breasts were attractive. I stepped into the shower.

The water felt good. Geez, I was tired.

55

Someone banged on the door. I got shampoo in my eyes. "What?"

The door opened. Steam swirled. "Your phone's ringing," David announced. He held up my cell phone in his big hand.

Great. "Who is it?"

"It's Mom."

I waited. He waited. The phone kept jingling.

I said, "Are you going to answer it?"

"No. Are you?"

"No."

"OK." David put the phone on the counter. It stopped ringing.

He left the room and slammed the door. Steam swirled some more.

I finished shampooing and rinsed my hair. Over the water, I heard the phone beep. Mom had left a voice mail.

More swirling steam as the door opened again. "Brenda," Clarissa's sleepy voice floated to me. "Can I borrow your shoes?"

Clarissa wore two sizes smaller than me, but she was always borrowing my shoes. She also often contemplated getting plastic surgery on her feet, the kind that shortened the toes so a woman could cram her feet into tiny, spike-heeled shoes.

"Sure," I said.

The door stayed open for a minute. "I'm going to take your brother out tonight, OK?"

Borrow your shoes, borrow your brother. At least she never asked me for money.

"Where are you going?" I asked, trying not to sound like the bossy sister.

"A party. Friend of mine."

More waiting. The sound of falling water filled the silence.

"OK," I said. "Have a good time."

She still didn't leave. "I heard you on the air."

For some reason, I was flattered. She'd never showed any interest in my job before. Smart enough not to be impressed, I'd always thought.

"Yeah?" I prompted.

"Is Nick the guy you went out with Saturday? On your dad's boat?"

"Yep, that's him."

"Oh." She stood there, her black hair stark against the white steam. "You should call him. He sounds cute."

I didn't answer.

"There's a message on your phone," she said. Then she drifted out and closed the door again, sending a cold draft into the shower.

I stayed under the water a good long time. I still couldn't believe that, A, I'd boldly gone on the air and done what I'd done; B, I hadn't dropped dead in the middle of it; and, C, Tony Beale had given me the morning drive time slot. I guess the saying, "No guts, no glory," is true.

By the time I got out, my fingers were shriveled and I'd stopped shaking. But I still wanted a drink.

I listened to the voice mail while I dried my hair. "Brenda, it's me," my mother said. "Will you still go shopping with me this weekend?" Since my father's death, my mom and I had had a standing shopping date one Saturday a month. We'd go to malls, get a manicure, have lunch or tea—you know, girly stuff. I'd always looked forward to it.

"Call me, Brenda," she said. "We need to talk."

Boy, did we.

I erased the message.

Mom tried to call me two more times that day. I didn't answer and erased those messages, too. David and Clarissa left for their party. Knowing I'd have to pry myself out of bed the next morning at four, I tried to go to sleep.

But when you know you have to sleep, you can't. Besides I was too keyed up. I was wound from this morning and wound from anticipating tomorrow.

My cell rang again. I didn't recognize the number, and it didn't have a name. A telemarketer? Or—

My heart beat faster—Nick?

I answered. "Hello?"

"Brenda? This is Jerry. We need to talk."

"No, we don't," I said and hung up.

I turned off the cell phone and stuck it in the drawer of my nightstand.

I knew I was acting like a baby. I knew, in an adult, rational way, that my mother was a grown-up and didn't have to answer to me and that she could sleep with whomever she wanted.

But I'd seen a gorgeous hunk of a man who put Tonio's bathroom models to shame coming out of my mother's bedroom, stark naked. Or almost naked. And my mother coming out after him looking as though she had just been thoroughly and pleasantly sexed. My mother was sleeping with a guy nearly twenty years younger than she was, a guy I had been thinking about trying to sleep with myself.

Was I supposed to say? *Woo-hoo, way to go, Mom*?

Maybe someday I would be able to say it. Maybe someday the adult, rational part of me would tell the spoiled kid in me to shut up, and I would rejoice in her success.

But right then, I just wasn't ready.

The next morning, I made it to the station with three minutes to spare.

Tony Beale looked at me in agony. "Come on, Brenda, you're on!"

He looked fresh and clean and bright-eyed. He made

me sick. I hadn't slept at all, and I felt like I'd been run over by a truck.

I threw my stuff on the floor and sat down in my chair. I rubbed sleep out of my eyes and tried to adjust the microphone levels. "How's Tim?" I asked.

"Who? Oh, Tim. He's uh, fine."

Tony hadn't even checked up on him. Tony, such a fine, caring, upstanding human being.

Poor Tim. Upstaged by a shark and a lingerie addict.

On one of the speakers, I pulled up KBZ. Nick was just going on the air. "Good morning, San Diego," he said.

At the sound of his voice, my whole world stopped. I wanted to melt on top of the speaker and croon, "Good morning, Nick."

"Brenda never called me," he went on. "Maybe she'll call me today."

The commercial on our station cut out. "Hey, San Diego," I said. From somewhere in the depths of my gut, I found the perky, bold woman who wore hundred-dollar lingerie and spike-heeled shoes and wasn't afraid of anything.

"This is Brenda Scott, filling in for Tim Turner who got a little too friendly with a great white yesterday. So have you all heard Nick today? He's still looking for Brenda."

Nick started playing Bill Withers's "Lean on Me" from the ancient past. I countered with the Eurythmics belting out "Sisters Are Doing It for Themselves."

Tony came screaming in before the song was done. "What are we now, the best of the eighties?"

"Just let me do this, Tony." I was not in the mood to be badgered by Tony after two hours of sleep. Just as I'd drifted off early that morning, Clarissa and David had come in. They'd sat up talking until four. At least, David talked. And talked. I don't know what Clarissa did. Fell asleep, probably.

Nick was on the air again. "I hear Brenda's awake," he said. "Why don't you call me, Brenda? We'll talk about old times."

Old times? Did he mean our one-night stand and our near one-night stand?

How can you have two one-night stands with the same guy? What is that, a two-night stand?

His calls started pouring in thick and fast. Some people thought Nick's challenge was romantic. Others thought it was tacky, and that we were publicity hounds.

I wasn't sure what I was doing. I just knew that I had to keep up my end of this thing. If I didn't, I'd be drooling all over him, publicity stunt or not.

Some women were already drooling over Nick. "Why do you want her?" a girl asked plaintively.

"Brenda's gorgeous," Nick said. "She's got red hair and big blue eyes. She's beautiful."

"She's not worth it, Nick!" the girl wailed and hung up.

Men called him, too. "Hey, if Brenda doesn't want to call you, maybe she'll call me."

In your dreams, I thought.

I said to my audience, "So why doesn't Nick call Brenda? That's the way it's supposed to work."

I played The Calling, to keep the music in this decade. Tony still wasn't happy. "Hip-hop, Brenda. We are supposed to be playing hip-hop and rap."

"Have you heard anyone complaining?" I indicated the phones, which were lit up with people wanting to talk about Nick and Brenda.

"Well, no, but—"

"How much advertising did you sell yesterday, Tony?" I asked him.

His eyes took on a dreamy, faraway look. "Lots."

"Then shut up."

He looked at me, and grinned. Somewhere in there, I saw the cool DJ from the seventies who schmoozed with

Alice Cooper and Steve Tyler. "I love you, Brenda," he said.

"Go call Tim," I told him. "He got nibbled on for you."

Tony still looked dreamy. "Right, right."

I started answering the phones. I got indecent proposals. I got people making fun of Nick. I got people making fun of me. Tony stood behind me, rubbing his hands, looking like he wanted to smoke an after-sex cigarette.

Nick retaliated. He didn't sound pissed; he sounded like he hadn't had such a good time in years. "Hey, Brenda. This is for you. Thanks for Saturday night." He played "Rock the Boat," another seventies classic.

I countered with music from Nickelback, and he stayed in the '70s. I imagined his program manager jumping up and down, telling him to stick to alternative rock. The calls flooded in to my station and his.

The last hour of my shift, I was standing up, taunting Nick, and he was laughing back at me. His callers challenged me to call him, mine told me to tell him to screw himself. To keep Tony happy, I played all the spots he'd sold the day before.

Another call came through. Marty the producer, who was finally getting into it after looking mad all morning because he actually had to answer phones and push buttons, sent the call through. "Here's another one, Bren."

"This is Brenda," said the new, fired-up Brenda who could do anything. "Talk to me."

"Hi, Brenda. This is your mother."

Everything screeched to a halt. In the background, the Gin Blossoms played on. Behind the glass, Marty grinned.

Tony ran in, his eyes wide, his face red. "Dead air, Brenda. Talk, for crying out loud."

I didn't want to. My mom had called into the radio station before when I was on the air (probably because no one else would). The listeners loved it. I'd heard of a radio show out in Arizona in which the DJ's mom called him all the time. The bit was very popular.

"Mom," I said. It was the only word my mouth could form. "Um, did you want to say whether I should call Nick?"

"Well, I'm kind of old-fashioned," Mom said. "I think the boy should call the girl."

Old-fashioned? Did she just say *old-fashioned*?

"Are you still there?" she asked. "Actually, I called to find out if we were on for Saturday."

I just stood there staring at the sound-absorbing padding on the walls. The crosshatch pattern made me dizzy.

"We're on for shopping, right, Brenda?" Mom chirped again.

She was putting it on as much as I was.

What was I going to say in front of millions of listeners? OK, thousands of listeners. OK, maybe a couple hundred. *Forget it, Mom, I don't want to see you until you kick out your thirty-five-year-old boyfriend*?

"Sure, that sounds great," I said.

"Come to the house at two. And you can tell me all about Nick."

I groaned inwardly. I'd hoped that the world would think this back and forth with me and Nick a joke, a publicity stunt.

But no. They took it way too seriously. And so did my mother.

"Sure thing, Mom," I said. "See you then."

"Don't be late," she said happily.

She hung up and Marty cut the line.

"Why did you put that through?" I yelled at him.

He looked at me like I was crazy. "What, I was going to hang up on your mom? I like your mom."

I gave up. Mom always knew how to get to me. She'd had more than two decades of practice.

6

Brenda Makes a Date

By Friday morning, Tony Beale couldn't take it any more.

"Brenda, you've got to call this guy at KBZ."

I stared at him. Behind the window, Marty opened his fourth candy bar of the morning, the crackling of the wrapper loud in my headphones.

I pulled off the headphones, scowled up at Tony Beale.

All that week, Nick and I had done our on-air tease. We'd played music from all over the map, up and down the decades, and had tons of calls. Tony had landed advertising from clients he'd only dreamed of. Tony was there every morning when I showed up, eyes gleaming, drooling for more.

I hadn't slept in four days. I was wired about doing drive time, about Nick, about my mother's on-air ambush, about Tony wanting more and more calls, and more and more ads. I'd go to bed and stare at the ceiling for hours. Then, when I finally started to drop off, David and Clarissa would come home.

I didn't know what was up with them. Clarissa kept taking David out—to parties, to bars, to restaurants. She paid for everything.

David wasn't divorced yet. He was still in the process. I knew from watching other people go through it that things could take a year, sometimes more, depending on the circumstances. David's wife seemed to be ready for a long, brutal fight, and if she suspected he had a new girlfriend, she could make his life even more hellish.

But I didn't think that David and Clarissa were having sex. Whenever they returned from their outings, they'd sit in the living room and talk.

At least, David talked. I heard him going on and on and on as I tried to shut him out and go to sleep. He talked mostly about his wife and all the things he did in Chicago, but sometimes about his life before that, like hanging out with his friends and where he'd liked to go.

Part of me wondered why Clarissa listened to him. I went out once to get a drink of water and saw her sitting with her thin legs in glued-on jeans curled up to her chest, listening without looking bored.

Part of me was slightly envious, because David never wanted to talk to me about anything. He shut me out every time I tried. I only knew what had gone wrong in his life because I overheard what he said to Clarissa.

David talked about the clubs his wife had dragged him to in Chicago, expecting him to schmooze guys who could boost him up another rung of the corporate ladder. He'd hated the false friendships, hated smiling at people he despised, hated pretending he liked the teams they liked and the food they liked and the people they liked.

"But I did it," I heard him say one night. "Because I knew if I didn't, she'd never let me into her pants again."

"That is so uncool," Clarissa had replied.

"I was stupid about her. You know, she was so beautiful and so smart and so rich, and she wanted *me*."

It sounded like David had suffered from the same disease as I had.

Now I stared at Tony with sleep-deprived eyes and said, "What are you talking about? This is a good bit."

"They're getting bored, Brenda." He handed me a newspaper, a morning edition of the *San Diego Chronicle*.

Yesterday, the local news section had showed a photo of me in my headphones grimacing into the mike, and one of Nick in his phones, smiling like he knew a good secret.

I had cut out the picture of Nick in his T-shirt, his muscles pressing the thin fabric, his blond hair glinting under the photographer's lights. I'd taken it home and stuck it into the drawer next to my bed where I could pull it out whenever I wanted to and gaze adoringly at it. OK, so I'm a sorry case.

The article had said, "Will She or Won't She? San Diego's Morning DJs Play Dating Game."

The article was stupid, full of innuendo and dumb jokes. Tony had said, "Hey, it's publicity."

They did man-on-the-street interviews—or at least women at malls and men skating on Pacific Beach. "I think she should go out with him," one woman said. "He's cute and he has a job."

A man said, "I think Brenda is too good for Nick. She's smart and funny. If she wants to go out with me, my number is . . ."

More than one woman was quoted screaming: "We love you, Nick!"

However, in a total flip-flop, today's newspaper read, "Enough Already: San Diego's Morning DJs Go On and On."

The article oozed sarcasm about how we were pounding this thing into the ground. "In an effort to gain publicity, stations KBZ and KCLP try to get a one-up on reality TV. Reality radio? Puh-leeze! The DJs keep up a dialog straight out of hack romance novels and play music from long-departed and best-forgotten eras. Give us a break. Bring back Tim and the sharks already. At least the sharks don't talk."

The article was written by a guy who lived to tear down radio and TV stations and local celebrities.

Tony breathed on my neck as he read over my shoulder. "Call Nick," he said. "Keep this thing moving. We'll set up a date and let Tim interview you when you're on it. We can do a remote. Nick and Brenda's date."

"What?" I cried.

"Come on, Brenda. You don't have to sleep with the guy. Although a hint that that's coming next would work. You could do a morning-after show. And if it works out between you two, we could broadcast the wedding—"

"Tony!"

"Just call the guy, Brenda. We racked up more sponsors this week than we did all year. I want to keep them happy, 'cause I want to keep my job. Is that too much to ask?"

Yes, I wanted to scream at him.

It was one thing to tease Nick over the radio, another to talk to him directly. What if he was doing this just for publicity? What if he never wanted to see me again? What if he'd rather sit for five days in a shark tank than go out with me? He and Tim could play underwater cards or something.

"You want to keep your job, too, right, Brenda?" Tony asked. He smiled like a shark.

All of a sudden, bungee jumping off Coronado Bridge didn't seem so bad.

* * *

Ten minutes later, I had the phone in my hand. Tony had punched the number for KBZ and shoved the receiver into my damp fingers.

My mouth was dry, and I wanted to pee. I took a gulp from the bottle of water next to me. It tasted like dirt.

I was choking it down when Nick's beautiful voice said, "KBZ, this is Nick. You're on the air, talk to me."

A huge cough came out. Then my voice, weak and scratchy. "Hi, Nick. It's Brenda."

Dead silence.

He knew it was me, the real Brenda, not some hysterical woman calling from her car claiming to be the Brenda he wanted.

He knew it was me because I sounded more like an idiot than any of those other women had.

I heard him take a breath. I imagined all of San Diego waiting for his next words. Would he welcome me warmly, or would he laugh and say, *What a sucker! You fell for my big joke.*

"Hi, Brenda," he said. I heard the smile in his voice. "What took you so long?"

"Uh," I said.

Tony Beale leaned over, his mouth inches from the receiver. "Tell him you want to go out with him."

I angrily waved him back. "I've been busy," I said.

"I heard."

"So, um, how've you been?"

Tony rolled his eyes. I was shaking all over, my hand sweating so much that the phone almost slid out of my grasp.

"I've been great," Nick said, totally in command. "I've been thinking about you."

"Yeah, so I heard."

"How's your brother?"

I imagined everyone on his side snickering. I wondered how much of the story he'd told them.

"Oh, he's fine."

"Great. Well, Brenda, I want to see you again, if you didn't pick up on that yet. How about Saturday? Tonio's restaurant has offered to sponsor our second date."

Tonio's. My Italian restaurant with the hunks on the bathroom walls. My voice started shaking. "Uh, sure, Saturday sounds fine."

"I'll make a reservation for two o'clock." He laughed. "You won't stand me up, will you?"

"No. I'll be there."

"I'm glad. See you then."

He hung up the phone. I sat there with the receiver in my hand, unable to move. Tony pried it from me and pushed the "off" button.

He smiled with glee. "This is terrific. We'll have Marty there and do a remote. All you have to do is eat pasta and smile at Nick."

I stood up. I wanted to puke. "Tony, you are not broadcasting my date."

"Oh, yes, I am. Saturday ratings always suck. We'll pull some in. Offer to let the listeners come down and watch. We'll give away prizes, tickets, whatever."

"Oh, God," I said.

I had to get out of that room. It was hot, and Tony's aftershave filled it with a cloying reek. I swung around, ready to flee, and almost ran right in to Mr. Perfect.

Larry stood in the doorway, his Armani suit perfectly pressed, his perfect shoes, custom fitted, hugging his perfect feet. He held a newspaper and had a stunned look on his face.

Great, just what I needed to make my day better.

"What the hell are you doing here?" I demanded.

Tony's eyes widened. "Don't insult the sponsors, Brenda."

Larry was staring at me like I was a strangely formed cockroach. "Nick Jordan's Brenda is *you?*"

"Yes, of course," I said crossly. "Where've you been?"

I tried to charge past him. Mr. Perfect closed his hand around my upper arm, manicured fingers clenching tight. "Brenda?

"What?"

"You're going out with Nick Jordan of KBZ?"

"Yes. Haven't you been listening?"

His blue eyes flashed like a neon sign. "You made a date for Saturday. You're supposed to come with me to Dana Point. To meet my parents."

I twisted myself from his grasp. "No, I'm going out with Nick on Saturday. At Tonio's. You can come along and watch. Apparently everyone else in San Diego will be there."

Larry's face was white, his lips pinched at the corners. "Brenda, if you go out with him, I'll pull all my advertising from this station."

Behind me, Tony made a squeaking sound.

I drew myself up to my five-foot-four height. New Brenda tilted her head back, looked Mr. Perfect right in the eye. "A week ago, that would have scared us, Larry. But we've landed so many accounts this week that yours will be pushed out of the prime slots anyway."

Larry actually spluttered. He got spittle on his perfect chin. "You can't do that, and you know it."

Tony made more strangled noises as though a shark had just gotten him.

I said, "If you paid us what those prime slots were worth, Larry, we'd give them back to you. But you're too cheap. So the top payers get them." I put my hands on my hips. "Go ahead and pull your ads. Lose business. See if I care."

I knew that when Larry thought he'd lose a dollar for

any reason, he had to have a drink and lie down to recover.

Larry's face went a strange shade of green. "I have a contract!" He switched his glare to Tony, who stood rooted in the middle of the studio floor. Marty was grinning through the glass.

"Well," I said sweetly, "you won't if you pull your spots. Now get out of my way. I have to go to the bathroom."

Mr. Perfect remained planted. Mr. Perfect always wanted to have the last word. "How do you even know Nick Jordan, Brenda? When did you meet him?"

I smiled. "On New Year's. You remember."

He drew breath to deny it, and then he realized what I meant.

His jaw dropped as he remembered me stumbling from my bedroom, half-dressed, the bedroom in which Nick and I had been doing—whatever it was we'd been doing. I still couldn't remember.

Larry's face went red. A vein pulsed in his perfect forehead. He started to say, "F—"

I shoved him aside and marched to the bathroom.

I didn't throw up, much as I wanted to. I sat in the stall and cried. I wasn't upset; it was just release. Men swear and hit walls; women cry.

I washed my hands, washed my face, brushed my hair, reapplied my makeup, and rubbed lotion on all my exposed skin. After I'd done everything femininely possible to make myself feel better, I ventured outside the bathroom.

Mr. Perfect was gone. Thank God.

Tony Beale was still in the studio. He'd thrown on some tunes (rap from this year) in my absence.

"Brenda, Brenda, Brenda," he said. "Don't *do* that. You gave me a heart attack."

"What did he say?" I asked, resuming my seat. I was incredibly calm.

"He said he might buy some more time," Tony said; then he grinned.

I smiled like I wasn't quivering inside. "Hey, I know Larry. All you have to do is imply that someone else will make more money than he will, and he falls all over himself trying to one-up them. He loves money and nothing else."

I'd finally realized that this was true. Larry had a perfectly compartmentalized world. You mattered to him on the scale of how much money he'd make or lose because of you.

He'd broken up with me because I was too far in the red. He'd called me again because for some reason I'd moved back into the black. I wondered where he'd put me on the chart after our encounter today.

The song finished. I stuck on another one because I did not want to talk to San Diego right now. Tony acted like he'd hover over me ready to criticize every word I said, but, thank God, one of the sales guys needed to talk to him. The sales guy looked excited. That made Tony excited. Tony hurried out into the hall saying, "What? What?"

"Hey Brennnn-da," Marty said to me over my headphones. "You got a phone call."

"I don't want to talk right now," I said. Ms. Perky DJ had run out of things to say.

"It's Nick."

I swung around in the chair and stared at him. He grinned back. Marty was skinny and had lank black hair and friendly blue eyes. Now those blue eyes twinkled as he grinned at me. "He said not to put it on the air. What do you want me to do?"

I sat there for a stunned minute. I could broadcast the call, let San Diego have more laughs. Or I could talk to Nick and hope he wasn't broadcasting or recording it on his side.

I turned on the speaker from KBZ. A song was playing. I nodded at Marty. "Put it through."

I took a deep breath, picked up the phone. "Hi," I said brightly.

"Brenda." Nick's smooth, deep voice came to me. "I wanted to talk to you off the air about this whole thing."

"Why?" I asked. "To break it off?"

He laughed. Geez, he had a good laugh. "No. I need to warn you that my program manager wants to do a remote from Tonio's."

"So does mine," I said glumly.

"I'll understand if you don't want to go. I'll eat it."

"No." I clung to the phone as the word burst from me. If we called it off, would I ever see him again? I strove to make my voice nonchalant. "Let's do it. What the heck?"

"I really do want to see you again, Brenda. It's not just this radio thing."

I started to feel warm. "So why didn't you call me the normal way? You could have said, 'Hey, Brenda, I had fun, even with your stupid brother screwing everything up. I'd like to go out again. How about Saturday?'"

He laughed again. "I didn't know your phone number. You're unlisted, did you know that? I didn't know you were Brenda at KCLP until you got on the air on Monday. Really."

"Sure, I believe you." I wasn't sure at all, but I made it sound like a joke.

"And then it got out of hand."

"Yeah, it got out of hand here, too."

"You know why I picked Tonio's?"

I leaned back in my chair, stretched out my toes in my strappy red shoes. "Because you like their fettuccine gorgonzola?"

He chuckled. I imagined his smile, his warm blue eyes, the thick blond lashes that framed them. "No, because it's across the street from that lingerie shop. You know, the spot where you jumped out in front of my car."

"Where you almost ran me over, you mean." I kept my tone light.

He laughed again. His lips would be curved into his sweet smile. "That's the place. After the remote is over and everyone's bored with us, I want to take you shopping. I tore your slip, so I'll buy you a new one."

I remembered his hand on my shoulder, the heartbreak of the ripped hundred-dollar silk.

"Camisole," I said.

"What?"

"It was a camisole. Not a slip."

"Whatever. I'll buy you a new one. An even better one."

"You'd help me pick it out? I'd have to try a few things on." I had a sudden vision of myself coming out of the dressing room to model lingerie for him—all the other customers and Zoe/Chloe would conveniently disappear, of course.

My throat got dry. I shouldn't think about things like that.

He just laughed. "Sure. And then you'll wear it when we go out Saturday night. Just the two of us."

Alone. No Tony, no Marty, no audience, no remote, no brother.

Alone with Nick. Nick who kissed like hot lava. Nick whose body was solid and sexy.

I licked my lips. "I guess."

"Good. See you at Tonio's."

My song was coming to an end. So was his. "Hey, Nick," I said.

"Yeah, Brenda?"

"You aren't taping this, are you? When I hang up, I'm not going to hear it coming out of your station, right?"

"I'm a gentleman, Brenda. I'd never do that."

Well, I'd gone out with gentlemen before. "Sure, I believe you. See you, Nick."

"See you, Brenda."

I hung up. My heart beat fast and hard. Marty still grinned.

I kept KBZ on the speaker and listened to it with one ear the rest of my shift. Nick never played our conversation. That didn't mean he wouldn't save it up to shoot me down with some other time.

People called me to congratulate me on landing the date, or to castigate me. "Aw, Brenda, you caved!" one guy said.

"I felt sorry for him," I assured him.

Another guy called. "So is that this Saturday you're going out?"

"Yeah," I said. "Come and join us at Tonio's. We'll be giving away some great stuff." Whatever it was. Tony would tell me at the last possible minute.

"But isn't Saturday when you're supposed to meet your mom? I was listening the other day, and you promised to go shopping with her."

I had totally spaced that. Probably because I'd wanted to.

I slid off the headphones and laid my face on the console. I hated when other people knew my life better than I did.

7

Jerry Ruins a Date

My mom had heard the broadcast. I called her. She sounded so understanding—you know, the way mothers do when they make you want to feel two inches tall.

I tried to cancel with her, but she suggested, her tone reasonable and sunny, that we move it back a few hours. I'd arrive at the house at ten; then we'd go out shopping and to lunch.

I pointed out that I was supposed to eat at Tonio's with Nick at two and I didn't want to eat two lunches. She told me I could make do with a salad.

I knew I wasn't going to win.

David didn't want me to go. He told me on Saturday morning to stand her up.

"I can't stand up my own mother," I retorted. I'd put on jeans and a sheer black blouse over a tight lace undershirt and silk bikinis. "It's the bargain, David. She had the labor pains, we show up when she asks us to."

"I'll show up when she throws out my so-called friend."

Clarissa yawned and stretched. It was like watching a cat. I looked with envy at her very long, very slender limbs as she arched her back, curled her toes, and lifted her hands above her head.

"What's wrong with your mom dating this guy?" she asked.

David glared at her, though I noticed he let his gaze glide over her legs as she folded them on the sofa.

"Because it's frigging embarrassing, that's why," he growled. "The guy's only a few years older than I am. When Mom was having her labor pains with me, he was five years old!"

"Well, he's not five years old now," Clarissa said. "It's different when you're older. I'd go out with a guy who was fifty."

"That's totally different."

"No, it's not."

"So," David said, his voice challenging, "you'd go out with a guy fifteen years younger than you?"

Clarissa laughed, languid and low. "No. A guy fifteen years younger than me would be thirteen. But if I was forty, I'd go out with a guy who was twenty-five. Why not?"

"What is it with women? You're all crazy."

"Thanks a lot, David," I said.

"Well, you are." He transferred his glare to me. I grabbed my purse and headed out the door.

David was pissed because he'd gotten a call that morning from his wife's lawyer. I'd watched him take the call, watched the veins on his neck stand out and his face get redder and redder.

He'd thrown the phone across the room after the lawyer had hung up. I'd retrieved it and was thankful he hadn't broken it.

"How can she want more money?" he'd screamed. "I'm bankrupt. Doesn't he know what that means? What does he care anyway? That lawyer makes more money than I ever did. Stupid bastard."

I knew David needed help. If he didn't get himself a good lawyer, he'd get screwed over bad. But what lawyer wanted to take his case when he'd just lost all his money?

The thing was, if I'd stayed with Mr. Perfect, Larry could have found a lawyer for him. He'd have found a friend who owed him a favor, and the friend would have helped David out pro bono.

But I'd told Larry to kiss off. I wasn't about to go crawling back to him, even if I could help my brother. Any help Larry gave us would carry a high price, anyway. He held grudges forever.

Tony Beale must know lawyers, I thought. He couldn't work thirty years in radio without needing them. But I hesitated to trust any lawyer Tony recommended. Case in point, the one we occasionally consulted with at the station was a total shyster.

I left David and Clarissa to argue and made it up to the house on the hill at five past ten. I parked in the circular drive in front and knocked on the door.

I felt funny knocking. Any other day, I'd just walk in, or unlock the door with my key if Mom was gone. Now here I was, knocking at the door of the house in which I'd grown up. But I certainly didn't want to walk in while my mother and Jerry were rolling around on the sofa, or on the patio, or in her bed. I never wanted to see that as long as I lived.

Jerry Murphy opened the door.

I took a step back and nearly tripped over the welcome mat. Jerry wore jeans and a red T-shirt that went well with his tanned skin and dark brown hair. I didn't like the fact that I still appreciated how good looking he was.

"Where's Mom?" I asked in a hard voice.

"Come in," he suggested.

He opened the door wider, backed out of the way. I stalked in past him and threw my purse on the antique Mexican high-backed chair in the foyer.

This house had been built in the 1970s, when it was still affordable to live well in San Diego. It was a California ranch-style house, which meant that it was long and rambling with lots of connecting rooms, and had a huge master suite separated by the length of the house from the kids' bedrooms.

The sunken living room had a fireplace and a bank of windows that looked out to the patio and the fabulous view of Mission Bay and the ocean. My parents' bedroom had glass doors that went out to the same patio. Mom and Jerry probably had breakfast together out there on nice mornings.

My mom and dad had refurbished the house a couple of times, throwing out linoleum for Mexican tile and ripping out the wall-to-wall carpet in favor of hardwood. They'd been home improvement geeks before it was trendy to be home improvement geeks.

I plopped myself down on an overstuffed leather couch and folded my arms. "Where's Mom?" I repeated.

Jerry sat on the raised brick hearth near the couch. "She went out for a few minutes."

"What for? She knew I was coming."

"She needed to get a few things from the store."

"So I'm alone here with you?"

He nodded. "It'll give us time to talk."

I stood up. "I'll wait in my car."

He stood up too, moved in front of me. "Brenda."

I was getting tired of men standing where I wanted to walk. "Move," I snapped.

He looked at me with his soulful brown eyes. "Stay here and talk to me. Please. We need to talk."

"About what? You and my mother? I really don't want to talk about that."

"Brenda, you need to get past this."

"Get past it?" I spluttered. "How am I supposed to get past it? She set me up, luring me here, pretending she wants to go shopping."

"She does. This was my idea."

"Ah. Should have known."

"I know you're mad at us," he said. "But I want to explain things to you. I want to explain that Sarah is the best thing that ever happened to me. I'm in love with her."

"Really?"

"Yes. She is," he said firmly. "I want you to tell David that. I wasn't trying to take advantage of his hospitality. That was never my intent."

He looked bothered by the fact that he'd upset David. Listening in on David and Clarissa's conversations, I'd learned that Jerry had been a very good friend to David in Chicago. Had been one of the few people who'd stood by David when he'd lost everything. He'd even helped David buy his plane ticket home.

Part of me wanted to like the guy; part of me wanted to cry out in anger. He said he hadn't intended to hurt David, but that hadn't stopped him from doing it.

I folded my arms. "Tell me something, how would you feel if David started going out with *your* mother?"

"I'd question her taste," he began with a smile, then the smile died. "I'm sorry. I know you're not joking. I don't know. I probably would not like it. But I'd try to see it from her point of view."

"Huh," I said. I sat back down. I didn't want to play dodge with him to try to get out the door. I was mad and I was tired.

"I would," he insisted. "Look at it from your mom's point of view. She's up here all alone. From what I

79

gather, she and your dad weren't all that happy the last couple years of their marriage."

"Don't drag my dad into this."

But I knew he was right. Mom and Dad hadn't been happy for a good long time. They had stayed together, I knew, mostly out of habit, and because they both felt too old to want to start over again. Plus they didn't want to upset David and me.

"She wanted someone to talk to," Jerry said. "And I let her talk to me."

"Oh, is that what you call it?"

"Brenda, stop it. Can't you even try to see Sarah's side?"

I made a face. "OK, I know she was lonely. I was hoping she'd meet someone. But you weren't really who I had in mind."

Jerry said, "I like her and she likes me. I've never known someone so easy to talk to in my life. We like a lot of the same things. We finish each other's sentences. It's like we've known each other forever, even though it's only been a few weeks."

"Touching," I said.

"If you're trying to make me mad so I'll dump her, it won't work. I won't do anything to hurt her. But you're hurting her by turning your back. That's why I'm asking you to get over it. You can hate me all you like, but don't hurt Sarah."

I sat in silence for a moment. Outside, a jeweled hummingbird dove at an open red flower and enjoyed itself sucking nectar.

"I don't hate you," I said reluctantly. "But you should have told us. If the two of you had sat us down and said, 'You know, we like each other and we want to go out,' it wouldn't have been so bad. It would still be weird, but not such a shock. But to see you coming out of her bedroom—my parents' bedroom, mostly naked—that's just wrong."

"I know." He flushed. "I felt really bad about that."

"But you did it anyway. By the way, nice underwear."

He reddened. "I'm still sorry it happened that way. But it happened. We like each other, and we aren't planning to change that."

He sat back down on the hearth, leaning forward with his elbows on his knees. He was telling me, *You don't get to rule here. Your mom is shutting a door, and you don't get to go in.*

I realized, watching him, what was the matter with me. Jerry had gained something, an intimacy—and I don't mean sex—with my mother that I'd never had. That I never would have.

My mom had always been a good mother—took care of us when we were little, rushed us to the emergency room when we broke bones, gave us tea with honey when we were sick. She took us to school and band practice and football practice and all our other practices.

She cooked dinner and cleaned the house and did all the things that a woman did when she was born in the fifties and married in the seventies right before women's lib really took hold.

She made my dad lunch, put up with him flirting with his secretaries, and had sex with him when he wanted it. She let him have his boat and listened to him boss her around, and she did it all with cool detachment. Because that's how she grew up, that's what middle-class women were supposed to do. It was her job.

And now Jerry Murphy had come along saying he wanted to be her friend, wanted to be her lover. A gorgeous guy with a great body who wore red bikini briefs and was probably great in bed.

Mom was saying, *Whether you like it or not Brenda, I want this.*

And I was jealous. Of Jerry.

"It's weird," I said. "It's just weird."

"OK, I admit that I never thought the woman of my dreams would be fifty," Jerry said with a grin. "But she is. I'm fine with it."

I frowned. "Did you ever think that maybe she's going out with you only because you're hot? Like a guy going through a midlife crisis who picks up a babe twenty years younger than him?"

Jerry looked at me, confused, and then started to laugh. "I don't think so."

"Why not?"

"Your mom and I fell in love because we talked and got to know each other. Besides, I don't think I'm that hot."

"Oh, please. You're gorgeous. And you have a great ass."

I must have been over-the-top upset. I would never have told a man he had a great ass if I was in my right mind. Brenda Scott never said that.

"You're flattering."

I folded my arms. "One reason I think it's weird you're dating my mom is because I wanted to go out with you myself. I was working up the courage to ask you out when— Geez, what would have happened if David and I had come in ten minutes earlier?"

He lost his smile. "Maybe if you and your brother respected your mother's privacy, it wouldn't have happened at all. This is her house. You wouldn't like her walking right into your house when you had a date."

He was telling me that what went on in the house where I grew up was no longer my business. That I had to move on and never come back. I had moved out, he was moving in, and he got to close the door behind me.

I sprang up. "This is my *life*," I said, looking around at the Mexican tile and the fresh, bright nautical paintings.

"It's hers, too," Jerry said. He paused. "You really

82

were going to ask me out? I never caught that. Why didn't you?"

"Mom beat me to it. She worked fast."

He smiled faintly. "No, I worked fast. I met her and I liked her. I wanted her to like me. Besides, aren't you going out with that Nick guy from the radio?"

I shrugged. "That's just—a thing."

What kind of thing, I didn't know. Maybe I'd find out today. Unless I got down to Tonio's and found out it was all a big joke, on me.

I heard the garage door open, then the hum of a car.

"Sarah's back," Jerry said, in case I didn't understand what the sounds meant. "Sit down. I can get you something to drink if you want it."

"I know where the kitchen is," I said. "I grew up here."

He frowned. "Be nice to her, Brenda. Go out on your shopping date, have lunch, talk to her. She told me she looks forward to your shopping trips. Don't take that away from her."

"Stop trying to be a family counselor," I snapped. I walked around the sofa and toward the back bedrooms. "I'm going to the bathroom. I won't jump out the window and run. OK?"

He just looked at me with the handsome eyes and handsome face that my mother had fallen for. I'd almost fallen for them, too.

I stalked away. Whenever I was upset, I had to pee. It must be a biological thing.

I went to the bathroom. I'd grown up in this bathroom. When I was five, I had a stepstool I could stand on so I could reach the sink. I pictured myself twenty years ago, in my nightgown, my red hair all over the place, climbing up on the stool and leaning way over to grab my toothbrush from the holder on the wall.

My mom had rewallpapered and painted when I was twelve. At the time, I was learning to put on makeup and having my first period. My brother David would stand outside and thump on the door and say, "Brenda, would you hurry up?"

I'd open the door and say quietly and viciously that if he didn't leave me alone, I'd tell Mom about how he locked himself in here with his *Playboy* magazines. He'd snarl at me, but we'd kept each other's secrets.

Since David and I had moved out, the bathroom had gone through another renovation. Gone was the old vanity; in came a pedestal sink and a pretty white cabinet, a claw-foot bathtub to replace the built-in, and wallpaper that was cute and old-fashioned.

The way Mom wanted it.

I finished, washed my hands in the sink I'd never used as a kid, patted my hair down even though I knew it would stick straight up again in five minutes, and left my childhood haven.

In the kitchen, Mom was standing with her arms around Jerry's waist. He framed her face in his hands, his thumbs skimming her cheekbones. Before I could say anything, he bent and kissed her, a long lover's kiss.

"Excuse me," I said.

Mom jumped away from him. Then she gave me a defiant look and took hold of Jerry's hand. "Brenda."

I raised my hands. "I'm sorry. I can't stay and deal with this right now. I have to deal on my own. OK?"

I turned around and walked away, regret churning in my stomach.

My mom said, "Brenda," pathetically.

Jerry said, "Let her go."

I ground my teeth as I marched from the house and slammed the door.

Let her go. Like Mom didn't need me any more. Like she only needed him.

8

Why Cell Phones Are Devices from Hell

I drove north. Traffic was terrible. I didn't care. I just wanted to go somewhere that was not my Mom's house with her kissing Jerry Murphy.

I drove my car to Torrey Pines Beach and parked in the lot that was surprisingly empty. This was always my favorite beach, where you could walk for a long time on the sandy strip between ocean and vertical cliffs.

People were snorkeling in the waves, mostly in wetsuits because the water in March was still cold. A few brave tourists, probably from North Dakota and thinking it was warm, were paddling in their bathing suits and lying out to tan.

Still, the beach was relatively empty. I stripped off my heels and lace stockings, rolled up my jeans, and strolled along the crumbling golden sand. Seagulls swooped past me, then lifted to the cliffs to rain droppings on the unwary on the nature trails far above.

I don't know why I was so upset. Jerry was right: Mom's life was her business.

Reason told me that. The dry voice in the back of my head, the one that told me I was stupid and childish, agreed that Mom could sleep with whomever she wanted to. Even if she'd wanted to go out with a nineteen-year-old circus clown, she was allowed. She was a grown-up.

But the part of me that would always be a child felt betrayed. Like David felt betrayed. He'd brought home a friend, and that friend had wormed his way past us to usurp what we'd taken for granted as ours.

I'd never been close to my dad. He'd been more interested in David and hadn't had much time for a daughter. He hadn't given extraordinary time to David, either, preferring his job and his boat to his family.

I remembered a friend I'd had in high school named Lola. She had five brothers and sisters. I'd go over to her house, and it would be chaos. They didn't have much money, so their house was small, and the eight of them overflowed all the rooms and out into the yard and into homes of their neighbors. Lola's father would come home and start shouting that he couldn't hear himself think in all the noise. But he'd say it with a smile on his face. He loved it and loved his huge, unruly family.

I'd always liked visiting them, even with the whole pack of Lola's family screaming at the tops of their lungs. At my house, things were always quiet—even the normal American household appliances were muffled.

My dad had been proud of David when he'd finished college with an engineering degree—just like the old man—and landed his good job in Chicago. I'd scraped along with my degree in communications and started working for minimum wage at radio stations, because I wanted to be in radio.

My dad hadn't been disappointed in me. I don't think he ever noticed what I did. When my dad died, David was still at the top of his game. So he died more or less happy.

Since then, my mom and I had been working on a closeness we'd never had when my father was around. She'd lived entirely for him. Now that we were alone, without Dad, without David, the two of us had finally started getting to know each other, like with our once-a-month Saturday shopping.

Jerry Murphy threatened this new closeness.

So here I was on a beach on a cloudy day, stepping through the sand getting my feet dirty and giving seagulls the eye.

I walked for a long time, until the curve of cliff cut me off from going farther. At low tide, it was possible to scoot along the cliff and keep walking on the far beach, but I'd come at the wrong time, of course.

I picked a dry spot in the sand and sat down. I watched joggers running along the water's edge and the occasional intrepid hiker picking his or her way down a precarious cliff path to the beach. One child busied herself building the mother of all sand castles.

I watched sailboats move slowly up the coast and other sailboats move back down. I felt sorry for myself for a while, then just watched the waves move in and out, in and out.

I would have sat there all morning and all afternoon if I hadn't been saved by my cell phone.

I wasn't going to answer it, but I saw that it was Tony Beale and the rest of my life came rushing back at me.

"Brenda, are you there?"

I could barely hear him over the swish of the ocean and the cliffs between me and downtown San Diego.

"Yes!" I shouted.

"What?"

I climbed to my feet, trying to hold onto the phone at the same time.

"Where are you?"

"Torrey Pines. I don't have to show up until two."

"It's two-thirty!"

"What?"

I dug my watch out of my pocket where I'd shoved it to keep it dry and sand-free. Sure enough the little hand was on the two and the big hand was on the six.

"Get your butt down here, Brenda. Nick's ready to leave."

Crap, crap, crap.

"Tell him to wait for me. Tell him I'm in La Jolla, but I'm on my way."

"What?"

"Just tell him to wait!" I screamed.

"I can't hear you, Brenda. I'm going to convince him to wait another fifteen minutes. His manager is pissed. He's ready to roll."

"Not fifteen minutes. Give me half an hour!"

"What? I can't hear you. . . ."

The connection died. "Tony! Dammit." I started punching buttons. I reached Tony's cell again, but it went straight to his voice mail, then cut off before I could leave a message.

I screamed and kicked sand. A pelican who'd waddled in front of me looked offended.

I'd never make it off this beach, over to the freeway and down to Tonio's, not to mention parked, in fifteen minutes. I tried to hurry. The sand pulled at my feet, threatening to turn the half-mile stroll into a labored hike.

An aging hippie caught up to me, jogging. He had

long gray hair gathered in a ponytail and a lined, weathered face. "You know, those things take over your life," he said, gesturing to my cell phone. "They're devices of oppression, man. Free yourself. Throw it away."

I glared at him. He wore a faded tie-dyed Grateful Dead T-shirt. He'd probably moved here in the sixties and had been jogging on this beach ever since.

I threw my cell phone down. It sank a few inches into the sand.

"That's good," he said. "Let it go."

The phone rang. I picked it up. Sand trickled into my ear.

It was Tony. "Bring some flowers or something, Brenda. Make it like you were late because you were buying him a present."

"Tony, I don't have time!"

"Fifteen minutes," Tony said, then hung up.

"Your old man getting you down?" the hippie said.

"My boss."

"Aw. That's what happens when you subject yourself to social oppression. Those in power try to tell us how to live, you know?"

"If I don't get downtown in fifteen minutes, my butt is fired."

I hurried on toward the parking lot. The hippie jogged with me, keeping up a steady monologue. He told me he'd come out here with his old lady, started making wall hangings out of hemp and now had a huge store in Del Mar and another in Ocean Beach.

I couldn't shake him. His name was Billy and he loved jogging on this beach. He was determined to tell me what I could do if I just gave up all my material possessions and settled down in a little shack to weave. I asked him about his old lady, in case he was trying to pick me up.

He gave me a nostalgic smile. "Thirty-five years we've been married. Thirty-five. Can you believe it? I met her at a memorial party for Hendrix. Everyone said it wouldn't last."

I congratulated him on his connubial bliss and kept scurrying.

I made it to the stairway to the parking lot. I tried to balance myself on the railing and scrape the sand off my feet. I slid my stockings back on, grimacing as sand leaked out the lace holes. I jammed on my shoes and hurried up the steps to my car.

I'd shaken the hippie. No, there he was, wiping his face on a towel that he'd taken from a motorcycle.

I unlocked the door of my car, hopped in, and threw my sandy cell phone on the seat.

I turned my key in the ignition. The engine wheezed then clunked a few times and stopped.

"Oh, I don't believe this!" I yelled. "Come on."

I cranked the engine. It wheezed. It clunked. It died.

I stopped. I let myself fall forward until my head banged into the steering wheel.

"Car won't start?"

It was Billy, peering down at me through the window.

I made a noise somewhere between a snort and a scream.

"You need a lift? I have to go to my Ocean Beach store anyway."

I looked at him, looked at his bike, tried to start my car again, and considered my options.

"All right," I sighed.

I got out of my car and locked it up. He had put on a leather jacket, and he handed me a helmet. It was yellow with flowers on it. Probably belonged to his old lady.

He let me get on the bike first. It took me three tries to get my leg over. He pushed my ankle the last time.

I held the helmet in one hand and my phone in the

other while I called Tony back. "Tony!" I shouted. "Don't hang up. I'll be there in twenty minutes. Ok?"

"What? I can't hear you. Who is this?"

Billy kicked his leg over the front of the bike, then jumped on the starter. The bike roared to life.

I jammed on my helmet. Before I could grab hold of the bar behind me, Billy took off.

My legs flew out. The helmet slipped in front of my face. I grabbed it with one hand and Billy's jacket with the other.

My cell phone went flying. I yanked the helmet around in time to see the slim silver phone skitter into the lane of oncoming traffic. A bright green SUV's front tire crunched it into a million tiny pieces.

By the time Billy and I roared up in front of Tonio's, everyone was gone.

I yanked off the yellow helmet, shoved it down on the bike, and ran inside. I saw my hair in the reflection of the glass door. It was sticking straight up from my forehead.

I made it inside in time to see the waiters straightening out the tables for their regular customers.

Marty stood in one corner winding cords around his arm.

"Marty!"

"Hey, Brenda," he said, his usual grin gone. "Where you been?"

"Trying to get here. Why did Nick leave? What did he say?"

"He was pretty mad that you stood him up," Marty announced with unnecessary relish. "Tony is pissed, too."

"I told him to wait," I panted. "I told him."

Marty shrugged. "He didn't say you told him anything. You should have called."

I kicked a chair. Then I grabbed my foot and jumped up and down in pain.

Billy had come in behind me. He looked around, taking in Marty and the board he was packing up.

"Hey, are you the Brenda from the radio?"

"Yeah, that's me," I said. "That was me," I corrected darkly. Tony would probably fire me the minute he saw me again.

"You were supposed to meet that guy today," Billy said, awed. "Why did you go to the beach instead?"

I ignored him. "Marty, can you give me a ride? I lost my cell, my car wouldn't start—"

"I'm going to the studio. You want to go there?"

"No!"

I figured I'd better avoid Tony until he had time to calm down. I could probably avoid the station for a few years without a problem.

"I listened to you this week," Billy prattled. "You were cool. The music your station plays is a drag, though. You should play more Dirt Band."

I squeezed my eyes shut. "Can I use your phone, Marty?"

He let me. I dialed home. Neither Clarissa nor David answered. Instead I got my own radio voice saying, "This is Brenda. Clarissa and I can't answer right now, so leave a message."

I hung up. I dialed a couple of friends, but they weren't home either. I could always go to the station with Marty, but I really didn't want to do that.

Billy was still looking at me as though he'd just met Janis Joplin or something.

"Billy, can you give me a ride to an auto shop?" I asked him. "I need to get a tow, or at the very least, a jump start." If I couldn't save my job or my love life, maybe I could at least save my car.

"Sure. Tell you what, I'll take you to my store. My old lady would love to meet you. I've got a friend who's a mechanic. He can check out your car for you."

"All right," I sighed.

I got the helmet firmly on this time before Billy took off. I grabbed him around the waist and held on while San Diego went by at breakneck speed.

9

How Hippies Invented Sex

Billy's store in Ocean Beach was large, packed with arty trinkets, and filled with tourists.

"Oh, I *love* this," said a woman with a New Jersey accent, picking up a tiny lighthouse made of woven hemp. "It's so California."

I'd left the yellow flowered helmet on the bike, and I tried desperately to pat my hair down. It sprang from my hands, flying every which way.

"Katie," Billy bellowed. He strode through the store with the lanky walk of a jogger and parted a bead curtain. "I brought a guest. That Brenda from the radio."

Katie stood up. She had long braids of silver hair and a tiny body. She smiled at me, her blue eyes still as dreamy as they must have been when she'd put flowers in her hair and wept because Jimi had died.

"Oh, we listen to you all the time," she said. "Only I wish you'd play more Dirt Band."

Billy chortled. "That's what I said, too."

"Or Creedence."

"Yeah, we love them. You know that John Fogerty almost came to our wedding?"

"Really?" I asked politely.

"He was on his way, but he got the directions mixed up. Katie, Brenda needs a tow."

"Oh," Katie said brightly. "Call John."

Not John Fogerty, I assumed.

"Hey, that's what I said," Billy hooted.

No wonder they'd been together thirty-five years.

I sat in the back with Katie, and she gave me coffee while Billy made a loud and long call to his friend John.

"Did Billy tell you how we met?" Katie asked.

I nodded. "At a memorial service for Jimi Hendrix."

"Oh, yes. That was a sad day. We'd heard the news, so some friends and me put together a memorial party and invited everyone in town. I was standing by the window while they were playing 'Little Wing,' and crying hard, when Billy came up to me. He was nice, so understanding. He put his arms around me and let me cry on his shoulder, and then we went out to his van and made love."

She waited for my reaction. I gulped coffee. "That sounds, ah, romantic."

"It was so beautiful. He said he was driving to every state in the United States and asked me to go with him. So I did. We drove all over America, saw New England, and the South, and the Great Lakes, and the Rockies. We slept by the side of the road and made love every night."

She looked dreamy, her thoughts far away.

"It sounds nice."

I wasn't joking. I imagined myself sticking daisies in my stiff red hair and driving around in a beat up VW van with Nick. Going where we wanted, stopping where we wanted, making love all night. It sounded restful. Something Mr. Perfect would never dream of doing. Mr. Perfect would die before he got in a van or—horrors—camped.

Not that Nick would ever talk to me again. I felt tears coming on. I held them back. Once I started, I wouldn't stop.

Katie snapped back to the present and gave me a half smile. "Of course, that was before HIV and safe sex and all that. It's too bad. Kids today don't make love for love. They either want the high of sex and end up with six babies before they're twenty, or they're so uptight that they won't have sex at all. Sometimes I think we were the lucky generation. Our parents were uptight, our kids are uptight. We were the only ones who knew what making love really meant, you know?"

My mom was about the same age as this woman. If Mom had come from a different kind of family, maybe I'd have been conceived in the back of a van on the side of the road, too. Maybe her and Dad would have had a better life together.

Billy came breezing in. "OK, Brenda, you're all fixed up. John will take you back to Torrey Pines, then either give your car a jump or take it to his shop."

"That's really nice," I said. I was starting to unwind, and if I didn't clench my teeth, they'd chatter.

"He loves cars. He can feel what's wrong with them. He's in tune, you know?"

Katie handed me a thermos and a lump in plastic wrap. "Take this for the road. You look hungry."

I was. I'd missed lunch with Mom and my meal with Nick. "What is it?"

"Brownies. I baked them this morning."

I looked at her in alarm. She started laughing. So did Billy.

"Don't worry," Katie said, grinning. "There's nothing in them but chocolate, I swear."

I wiped the stupid expression off my face and thanked her. They really were nice people.

O.K, I know I could have come off my high horse and called my mom. She would happily have driven down the hill and picked me up and helped me out. But I couldn't. Not yet. I needed time to adjust to my mother being a real person before I went back to thinking she was my mother.

A pickup truck screeched to a halt in front of the door. Horns started going off behind it because the driver was blocking the lane in a narrow street.

The guy didn't get out of the truck. Billy opened the door for me, and Katie came to stand in the doorway and see me off.

The man inside had a gray-and-white beard and gray hair and wore a red bandana. The pick-up was fairly old, but the engine purred in a contented way that gave me hope that this guy could fix my car.

Billy boosted me inside, made sure I was settled with my thermos and brownies. He slammed the door. He waved. Katie waved. John put his foot on the gas and we were off.

John wove through Ocean Beach traffic toward the freeway to take me back to Torrey Pines. Billy must have told him all about me, because he started talking about radio back in the sixties.

"They didn't have playlists back then or automated stations like now. The DJs played what they wanted to, what was hip, what they liked. You know that the Doobie Brothers got famous because someone played the B side of a forty-five? No one would ever do that today. They don't even have forty-fives or turntables any more. Just CDs and computers."

"That's true," I said, because I couldn't deny it. No DJ had spun a forty-five in twenty years.

John swerved around three little Japanese cars, one

hand on the wheel. "I was in a band back in '69," he said. "We had a single on the charts. Made it to number seventy-five."

"Really?" I said to be polite.

He laughed. "Yeah, it was 'Black Mothers'. It was a 'Nam protest song. We were called Bohemian Love Child. Don't worry, no one's ever heard of us. We were sort of famous for about ten minutes. Then we broke up. One of the guys was sent to 'Nam right after that. Kind of ironic. But he was lucky. He made it back OK."

"Good," I said. I swallowed as we zipped around an eighteen-wheeler.

"Some Saturday nights we get together at a roadside coffeehouse in Imperial Beach. We get a good crowd down there. You should come."

I nodded. "Sure."

I might as well drive down to Imperial Beach and listen to hippie tunes, I thought. I'd never have another real date as long as I lived.

He turned into the parking lot at the beach and screeched to a halt beside my little car. Two kids perched on top of it. They watched us to see if they'd have to bother getting down.

I gave John my keys, and he climbed into my car and cranked the engine. "Nothing but your battery," he said cheerfully. He got out and waved his arms at the kids like he was driving away birds. They hopped off the hood and sauntered down the beach, music screaming in their headphones.

John rummaged in the back of his truck, dragged out jumper cables, then proceeded to hook my battery to the one under his red hood. The cables snaked from car to truck like IV lines.

He started my car again, and it roared to life.

"Follow me back to my shop," he said, throwing his

jumper cables into his truck. "I'll put another battery in for you."

"No, that's OK," I said tiredly. "I'll just take it in."

He waved his arms again. He liked doing that. "Naw. I'll give you one for free. Any friend of Billy and Katie."

"I just met them today," I said.

"So? Tell you what. You play some Golden Earring at your station, and I'll do it."

Since Tony had probably fired me, I had nothing to lose. I said, "Sure."

"Great." His face split in a grin. "Come on."

He charged off. I got in my car, followed him out.

I had to keep my foot hard on the accelerator so as not to lose him. We swerved through semis and weekend drivers and tourists at top speed. For hippies enjoying a laid-back lifestyle, Billy and John certainly drove damn fast.

He drove downtown to a mechanic's shop not far from Tonio's. It was closed today, but he unlocked the doors and waved my car into a bay.

He pressed power on the CD player, dropped in Cream and Eric Clapton, turned up the volume, and proceeded to change my battery.

"There you go." He slammed the hood of my car. "Brand new. Should last you three years. It goes bad, you just come back."

He wiped his hands on a red rag. "Thanks," I said, truly grateful, or I would have been if I hadn't been tired, depressed, and probably fired. "You guys have been really nice."

"Hey, we're all in this together. Come to the joint in Imperial Beach tonight. Tell them you're with the band." He winked.

That's all I needed. To be the groupie of a band who hadn't made a record since 1969.

"Thanks," I said. "I might."

He waved good-bye. "Peace and love, Brenda." He smiled. "It's not just for hippies anymore."

I said something feeble, then drove away.

I managed to get back to my apartment without any more problems. I parked the car and dragged myself up the stairs to my front door.

I found a note from David on the kitchen counter. He and Clarissa were taking the trolley down to the border and walking across to Tijuana to go shopping.

Great, I thought. His wife's lawyer is after him, so he leaves the country.

I went into my bedroom, closed and locked the door. I stripped off my black blouse and jeans stained with sand and lay down on the bed in my lace undershirt and bikinis.

Somewhere in the complex, kids were playing. They laughed and yelled at each other, having a great time. Downstairs someone was listening to Sarah MacLachlan.

I lay there and tried not to think about Nick sitting at a table in Tonio's surrounded by wires and mikes and his producer and manager. I tried not to think about Tony Beale pacing the floor, roaring at Marty, and attempting to grin weakly at Nick and say I'd be there any minute.

If this were just between Nick and me, I could call him up, explain, and we'd have a good laugh. But the entire city—heck, San Diego County and beyond—knew that I'd missed the date. That I'd humiliated Nick and KBZ and KCLP. That I was a total idiot.

Nick would never speak to me again. He probably regretted speaking to me in the first place. He must especially regret our rendezvous on New Year's.

If this had been only a publicity stunt, I wouldn't have cared. Sure, I'd lose my job, but that wasn't what made me cringe inside.

It was Nick and what he'd think of me. I liked Nick. I liked him a lot. I liked his blond hair that wasn't perfect and his blue eyes and the way he smiled. I liked remembering his lips and his hands in the dark. I liked his voice and his tanned muscles and the hollow of his throat.

I liked the way he had a little pucker between his brows when he frowned. I liked the way his mouth drooped a little in one corner when he smiled. I liked the way his cute backside filled out his jeans. And I liked the way he said my name.

The phone beside my bed rang, the land line. Without looking at it, I lifted it to my lips and mumbled, "Hello?"

"Hi, Brenda," Mr. Perfect purred. "I heard you dumped that DJ from KBZ. Good. I'm proud of you."

I squeezed my eyes shut. Just what I needed. Mr. Perfect calling and saying he approved of my being a total idiot.

"What do you want, Larry?" I sighed.

"To congratulate you. You did the right thing."

"No, I did a stupid thing. I didn't miss the date on purpose."

"Brenda." He had the patient, kind tone I especially hated. "You don't need that DJ. He's a jerk for broadcasting that he went out with you. He made up the whole thing to get his station publicity at your expense. Why did you fall for that?"

"You really wouldn't understand," I murmured.

"Did Tony fire you?"

"I don't know. I haven't talked to him." I never wanted to talk to Tony Beale again as long as I lived.

"It doesn't matter. You don't need to go out with the DJ. You don't need Tony Beale or your job. When you marry me, you won't need any of them. You'll have everything, I promise."

My eyes popped open. The whole world went very still. I couldn't hear the kids or the music downstairs.

"Did you just say—when I married you?"

He laughed, his manipulative, silken laugh. "When you marry me, yes. We should get married, Brenda. We're great together."

I knocked the receiver against the bed a few times, then put it back to my ear. "Am I hearing you OK? Since when were we great together?"

"We always were." He sounded hurt.

I closed my eyes again. "Larry, explain to me, in words of one syllable, why you and I are great together and should get married."

His patient tone returned. "Because I have money. Because you need money. Because you're nice to people, and they like you. Because my parents like you, and I like your mom."

"I've never met your parents," I pointed out.

"I know, but I've told them all about you. They're upset that KCLP made you make a fool of yourself on the air this week. They think I should pull all my ads."

Larry was always threatening to pull his ads. I wondered if this time Tony Beale would tell him where to stick it.

"They want to meet you," he continued. "And your mom."

I sat up. My strength was returning. No one but no one could make me mad like Larry Bryant could make me mad. Only before, when we'd been dating, I'd been too wimpy to do anything about it.

"My mother is dating a thirty-five-year-old man," I said.

Larry stopped. Dead silence reigned for almost a minute. "What was that?" he asked as though he hoped we had a bad connection and he'd heard wrong.

"I said, my mom is dating a thirty-five-year-old man," I told him loudly. "His name is Jerry. He is a friend of my brother's."

I imagined Larry taking a firm grip on the phone, his eyes going wide with horror. "You're kidding, right?"

"No, I'm not kidding. I was at my mom's house this morning. Talking to both of them."

I didn't tell him about my temper tantrum that screwed up the rest of the day. Some things Larry didn't need to know.

"Why is she dating a thirty-five-year-old man?" Larry demanded. "God, that's creepy. I'm thirty-four."

I boiled over. It was one thing for me to be upset about my mom's choice of lovers, but Larry had no business saying that my mother was creepy. "I don't know, Larry, maybe she likes him. Maybe he treats her better than my dad ever did."

"Stop yelling. You're not making sense."

"I'm making perfect sense. She can date whoever she wants. It's her business."

"She's probably going through a phase. Feeling lonely after losing your dad. It's natural she'd want to feel attractive to the younger generation. Old people get like that. She'll snap out of it."

I thought about the way my mother had kissed Jerry in the kitchen. I thought about how his eyes had softened when he'd said he was in love with her.

Tears welled up in my own eyes. "She's only fifty-three, and stop criticizing my mother."

"Don't get all upset. You always do this. Blow everything out of proportion. I still want you to come up to Dana Point for dinner. Tonight."

I stood up on the bed. The phone crackled. "Maybe I have plans tonight."

"No, you don't. You stood up this Nick guy, so you aren't going out with him. And your mother is embarrassing you, so you're not having dinner at her house. You don't have anything else to do, Brenda, so I want you up here tonight. Everything will work out."

Sure, Larry. The way you want it to. As always.

"I do have something to do," I said. "I'm going to a coffeehouse in Imperial Beach."

There was a moment of silence. "You're what?"

"Going to a coffeehouse in Imperial Beach. To listen to a band from the sixties. If you want to see me, come there."

He snorted. "Good God, what for? I'd never go down there. And you're not going either."

"Yes, I am. I was invited by one of the band."

"What are you, a groupie?"

"So what if I am?"

"Brenda." He finally got mad. He finally dropped his I'm-reasonable-and-so-much-smarter-than-you tone. "The only reason you're doing this is to punish me. You know that. You want to hurt me because I broke up with you, so you've started sleeping with any man who comes along. Well, you're only hurting yourself. I'm offering to take you back, even though you're acting like a slut. Stop being stupid."

I bounced up and down on the bed. "Well, maybe I slept with Nick because I liked him better than I like you. And maybe I'm this guy's groupie because he's a brilliant musician as well as good in the sack."

I crossed my fingers as I said that, because I had no intention of getting that friendly with John the mechanic, former member of Bohemian Love Child.

"I called you to help you, Brenda. I'm warning you, this is your last chance."

"Everything's about you, isn't it, Larry?"

"What are you talking about? I swear, if you don't start acting sensible, I'm going to hang up this phone and you'll never hear from me again."

"Promise?" I said.

"Don't tempt me, Brenda."

"You know what, Larry?" I held the receiver up against my mouth and shouted, "Bite me!"

I slammed down the phone.

The sound of plastic hitting plastic and the absence of his voice was exhilarating. I jumped up and down on the bed. I laughed loudly and jumped some more.

I kicked my legs out from under me and landed on my back, still bouncing. The lace shirt slithered against my skin. I loved it.

Larry could take his offer of marriage and his house in Dana Point and his dinner with his parents and his ads and insert them where the sun don't shine.

I wanted Nick back. I would get Nick back. I was Brenda Scott, drive time DJ, lingerie addict, bold, brash, wild woman. I was a groupie. I was free.

I screamed and kicked my legs, reveling in my freedom.

Then I grabbed the telephone book from underneath my nightstand and flipped pages until I found the ads for a couple of stores that shy Brenda Scott would never set foot in.

I was going to buy Nick a present.

10

Nothing Says Love Like Edible Underwear

I called Marty at the station. I told him to not let on it was me, and I bribed him with free food to find Nick's address for me. Nick Jordan wasn't listed in the phone book, but I knew Marty had friends all over the radio world, and he'd know someone at KBZ who would surreptitiously give him Nick's address.

While Marty did his research, I showered and dressed in my sexiest camisole and thong with a garter belt and pinstriped thigh-highs. Over this I put on a black sleeveless dress and a tight red jacket.

Marty called me back by the time I was done with my makeup. I wrote down the address and went out to do my shopping.

An hour and a half later, drawing on eight o'clock, I stopped in front of a house in a lovely neighborhood between Ocean Beach and Point Loma.

Nick lived in a two-story house that was very Old California, which meant stucco, arches, tiled roof, paved courtyard, fountain, and climbing vines and flowers over everything. The scene was quiet. A crooked brick-paved walk led to a gate to the courtyard. Inside the courtyard, a fountain trickled soothingly into a ceramic bowl.

I knew Nick was home. I'd dialed the phone number Marty had given me, a land line, not a cell number, and Nick had answered.

I'd hung up. I'd used a pay phone, so he couldn't caller ID me.

Brenda the lingerie addict, Brenda the groupie, was now Brenda the stalker.

I walked quietly to his front door and slid a thin package into the mailbox that hung next to it, making sure a corner of the package stuck out. Then I rang the doorbell and ran away as fast as my heels would let me.

Out of breath, I hunkered in the front seat of my car, panting and waiting. After what seemed like a long, long time, the front hall light went on, and Nick opened the door.

He peered through the screen into the darkness. I gripped the steering wheel, my heart thumping, but I didn't think he saw me. He stood there, looking, for a long time. Then he went back into the house. Without even glancing at the mailbox.

I growled.

I waited for ten agonizing minutes, giving him time to settle himself back in front of the TV or whatever he was doing.

I got out of the car and tiptoed up the walk and back through the little courtyard to the door. I took the envelope out of the mailbox and wedged it into the crack between the screen door and the frame. I rang the doorbell again and scuttled away.

Nick yanked the door open within seconds. He must have been watching out of the window. "Brenda?"

I'd just stepped through the gate into concealing darkness. I hurried to the car, dove in, and ducked down, trying to catch my breath. I rose slowly so that I could see out the driver-side window.

Nick hadn't opened the screen door. He was looking through it at the walk, trying to tell if he'd really spotted me. The corner of the package was sticking straight out at him, but he never noticed it.

After a long time, he quietly closed the door.

I screamed between my teeth. It's very hard to stalk someone who won't cooperate.

I waited another ten minutes, then another five. If I went back too soon, he'd catch me, and that would ruin the surprise.

At last, I got out of the car. My feet hurt from running in three-inch heels, but I couldn't take them off because I'd rip my stockings to shreds.

I reached the door. I tugged at the little package. It stuck.

I wiggled it, trying to loosen it. It wedged harder. I yanked. It came free. My elbow banged the doorbell, which went off.

Nick slammed the door open before I could move. "Brenda?"

I opened the screen door. I thrust the package against his chest. "Would you open it? Geez, Nick."

I turned away. I wanted to stay and admire how adorable he looked in his shirt and jeans with his hair messed up. But that wasn't the plan.

I clomped back down the walk and got into my car.

I watched him stare after me for a while. Then he looked at the package. He carefully unsealed the end of it then reached inside and drew out the cellophane packet.

Nick looked at it for a long time. I bit my lip. Would he

throw it down on the pretty tiles and storm inside? Or would he come and find me to thank me for my thoughtful gift?

He lifted his head, spotted my car. He started down the walk.

My heart fluttered. I nearly panicked and drove away, not wanting him to ask me what I thought I was doing. Mr. Perfect would have lectured me. I guess that's why I stopped giving him gifts. I never gave him the right ones.

It felt like an hour watching Nick walk to my car. He went around to the passenger door, opened it, and got in.

I went warm inside. Having him near, feeling the heat of his skin inches away, watching his lips turn upward in his smile, made all the stupidity I'd gone through that day worth it.

He held up the package. The plastic wrapping gleamed in the moonlight. "Edible underwear?" he asked.

I shrugged. "You offered to buy me lingerie. So I bought you some."

He started laughing. He leaned to me, put his arm around me. "Brenda," he said, his voice velvet-soft. "You drive me crazy."

He kissed me.

He kissed like sunshine, or like hot chocolate on a cold night. I twined my arms around his neck and held on.

I couldn't believe I was actually kissing him again. I couldn't believe he hadn't told me and my edible undies to go to hell and here, I'll drive you.

He tasted so good. He threaded his fingers through my hair. His body was hard and warm against mine.

I slid my hands under his T-shirt. His muscles were nice, sculpted by whatever weight machine he used. I let my fingers wander to his belt and beyond to his taut blue-denimed backside.

"Brenda." He raised his head.

He wanted to talk. I didn't want to talk. If I talked, I'd

say something stupid. I wanted to kiss, to give my mouth something to do so it didn't make a fool of me.

"Brenda."

I pressed him down to me again. "Kiss me some more."

"Mrs. Pankhurst is watching us. She's about to come over and ask me who you are."

My head popped up. "Who's Mrs. Pankhurst?"

"She lives across the street. She's known me since I was five."

"Oh." I peered over his shoulder. Sure enough, a woman stood on the front walk of the house across the street, trying to see what was going on in the car.

"I know why you didn't come to Tonio's today," Nick said.

"You do?" I wondered how the story of my adventures had reached him. Maybe Billy and his wife had called his station and told the story while they asked Nick to play more Dirt Band.

The lines around his eyes smoothed out as he lost his smile. "I don't blame you."

"You don't?"

"I mean, what kind of setup was that? You and me having our second date on the air? It was lame. I'm glad you stopped the fiasco."

"You are?"

"Do you think I wanted all those people around and microphones on the table while I tried to get to know you better? I mean what could we really talk about?

"Then why did you set it up?"

"Because I wanted to see you again." He cupped my cheek. "But I didn't think you wanted to see me."

"You didn't think I wanted to see *you*?"

"You weren't exactly happy on the boat."

I sat up. "That was because of David. I was mad at him. But I couldn't leave him alone. He's going through some stuff—"

"It's OK." He smoothed the hair from my forehead. "It doesn't matter now."

"No." His touch mesmerized me. I could sit here forever and let him touch me softly, even with Mrs. Pankhurst watching from across the street.

"So, you doing anything tonight?" he asked, smiling slightly.

"Going to a coffeehouse in Imperial Beach."

He looked puzzled. "You're what?"

Mr. Perfect had asked the same question. But Mr. Perfect's voice had held outrage. Nick only wanted to know.

I kissed him lightly, then turned in the seat and put the key into the ignition. "Want to come with me?"

He sat silently for a moment then he shrugged and said, "Why not?"

Under Mrs. Pankhurst's avid gaze, I started the car and pulled away from Nick's house.

In silence, I drove out of Ocean Beach, around the airport, and down the freeway south toward Coronado and Imperial Beach.

Nick didn't talk either. I was painfully aware of his nearness, and it made me nervous.

I wove the car through streets that tourists didn't see unless they were heading to Tijuana on the back roads.

I found the coffeehouse without much trouble. The small building was set well back from the street and had a dirt parking lot and weeds growing around the foundation. The Imperial Roadhouse wasn't really a coffeehouse or even a bar; it was more of an amateur musicians' hall, with a stage and rows of chairs and helpful people making coffee.

Nick held the door for me. When I walked in, John the mechanic was just strapping on a guitar on stage. Two other men in their fifties, one with a guitar and the other with a hand drum, were seating themselves behind him.

"Hey, Brenda!" John sang out, waving. I waved back.

He pointed to the front row. "Saved you a seat."

There weren't many people in the room, so we easily made our way to the front. John grinned down at me. "This your boyfriend?"

"This is Nick," I said.

Billy and Katie were in the front row, too. "Brenda!" They greeted me like a long-lost friend. I introduced Nick again.

"From the other radio station," Billy said. He grinned and shook Nick's hand. "I don't listen to you. I like Brenda."

Nick slid his arm around my shoulders. "So do I."

My heart went bump, bump, bump. I suddenly wanted to kiss and kiss him, and I was afraid I'd start doing it right there in front of everyone.

Someone yelled that it was time to start, so we sat down. The lights dimmed, and John and his band—"The remnants of Bohemian Love Child," John said—played.

They were good. They played their one hit single, which I'd never heard, but everyone else in the house obviously had. Including Nick. He looked at me in surprise when I claimed ignorance.

"Really?" he said "It was popular on a retro station I worked at in San Antonio."

I said, "Oh," and shrugged. He laughed.

I had a surprisingly good time. The band knew other tunes, some familiar, some not. Bohemian Love Child could play, they could sing, and they did it because they loved it. Their warmth filled the room, and in the end I was cheering and clapping and singing along with everyone else. So was Nick.

Mr. Perfect would have raised his groomed brows in disdain and said, "Let's go, Brenda," after the first song.

Billy and Katie invited us to a party at their place along with the band and pretty much everyone else in the room. Nick and I followed the convoy to their house in Coronado.

"My pad," Billy grinned when we walked in.

As I entered the spacious and well-decorated house, I decided that Billy's stores must do well. He'd come a long way from weaving hemp in a shack on the beach.

Katie served us beer and wine and food, and the band did some impromptu singing. Then we all sat on the floor in the living room and told stories about some significant thing that had happened in our lives, an event that had changed everything for us. A tambourine was passed from person to person; the one who held it had to tell the story, kind of like the talking stick in those male bonding rituals.

Katie handed the tambourine to me.

"Oh," I said, looking at it.

"Come on, Brenda," she said, smiling.

"Uh."

I cast around for some profound story about my life. I couldn't think of any. The stories told up to this point had been about the storyteller finding himself on a remote Pacific island, or losing her virginity among the ruins in Rome, or traveling to Bangladesh to help poor families learn to farm. I'd never done anything more deep than drive up the coast to find a lingerie store even more exclusive than Lili Duoma.

"It's there inside you," Katie said, trying to be helpful. "Look deep."

"Tell us how you decided to go into radio," Billy suggested.

Nick shot a sideways glance and a little smile at me. I wondered how he had gotten into radio. Most people do it in weird ways that were never planned.

But I suddenly remembered an event that had changed my outlook on life forever.

113

"My brother's wedding day," I began.

Collected heads nodded, and eyes turned to me, including Nick's.

"I was in college when my brother got married," I said, remembering with a bitter pang. "I was twenty. I was in the wedding party along with his wife Alicia's friends. The dress they gave me was beautiful. I decided to go in style, so I spent all that morning at the hairdresser's. Then I came home and spent an hour making myself up.

"I spent most of my money at that chic salon and the rest on the makeup. My mom and dad drove us all to the church. I thought I looked wonderful. My mom and dad were so elated and agitated about David getting married that I don't think they noticed me much, but that was fine. It was David's day."

I looked down at the tambourine, its shining silver disks slightly dusty. "Everything was fine until David was safely married, and we went outside for the pictures. Then the other bridesmaids took me aside and told me that Alicia had said she didn't want me in any of the photos.

"When I asked why not, they looked at each other, kind of smiling. One of them—Mary-Ann Ruben, I'll never forget her name—she was blond and slender and beautiful—told me in the friendliest way that my hair looked like a scouring pad and my face looked like someone had hit me. She advised me that when I started hunting for a job after college, I should choose some profession where looks didn't matter."

I heard murmurs of sympathy. I looked up. The circle of hippies, most with braids and beads and beards, gazed at me in indignation. "What a bitch," Katie muttered. "I bet she was prom queen."

I shrugged as though the hurt was too far away to feel any more. "Well, of course I locked myself in the bathroom and cried for the rest of the day. I don't know if what Mary-Ann said was actually true, because to this day, I can't find any pictures of myself at that wedding. But it made me wonder what kind of professions were out there where no one would care what I looked like. That's when it struck me that in radio, no one sees you. They hear your voice, and they make up their own version of you in their head. So I switched my major to communications, worked the summers at radio stations in town, and got hired at one when I graduated. And I've been in radio ever since."

Which meant that I had Mary-Ann Ruben to thank for the fact that Tony Beale was going to fire me when I showed up Monday. One more reason to find a picture of her and make a dartboard.

"I hope she's eating dirt," John said, "now that you're famous."

"I think she married a plastic surgeon," I said. She probably lived up in Rancho Santa Fe, drove a Mercedes, and spent her afternoons taking tennis lessons from a tanned hunk named Raoul.

Nick was looking at me, his eyes soft. I wondered if he felt sorry for poor young Brenda, or if he was thinking that my hair really did look like a scouring pad.

I handed him the tambourine. He dragged his gaze from my hair and looked at the instrument with a bemused expression.

I was willing to bet that Nick had lived a much more interesting life than I had, the girl who'd more or less never left home.

"I hiked across Europe when I was in college," he said, confirming my thoughts. "But I don't think that was the experience that made me. Looking back, it was pretty self-indulgent, pretending to be a free spirit on my parents' credit cards."

The circle laughed.

Nick ran blunt fingers over the tambourine. "No, I think the event that pushed me to where I am now happened at the end of the year I lived in San Antonio. I had been given a great contract at a station there—drive time, lots of money, lots of prestige. My parents had just passed away, and my younger brother had invited me to live with him out there. It seemed right that I should leave San Diego and start a new life."

He fixed his audience with his frank blue gaze. "At first I thought everything was perfect. I liked the town, the weather was great, and it was good to be with my brother again. I met a girl, and we hit it off."

I wanted to look away so that I wouldn't have to watch him talk about some woman he'd fallen in love with in Texas. But I didn't want to appear insecure, so I studied the line of his chiseled cheekbones, his hard jaw, the way his eyelashes flicked as he spoke.

"Her family was prominent in town," he went on, "and she introduced me to a lot of people. In Texas, if you're not from Texas, people don't always take to you all the way. But through her and her family, I was invited to high-society parties, and I got written about in the papers—the cool DJ from San Diego engaged to the socialite. I became very popular—it was easy to get a table at restaurants." He smiled self-deprecatingly. "I thought I had everything going for me."

I imagined Nick, despite what he said about needing help to get an "in," devastating the town with his warm smile and good looks. He'd probably had women drooling at his feet.

"Why did you come back?" I asked softly.

He met my gaze, his blue eyes never wavering. "I almost didn't. My fiancée's father told me that if I quit radio, I could join him in his business and work my way up pretty fast. He was talking about more money than I'd ever seen in my life. It was tempting."

My heart beat faster. A glamorous woman, an executive job, a truckload of money—and he'd turned it down to come back here and duel with me on the radio. Most people would think he was crazy. I thought he was crazy.

"Why did you turn it down?" I leaned closer to him. I sensed the circle listening, but it seemed as if Nick and I were having this conversation by ourselves. "Weren't you in love with her?"

"I thought I was," he said.

My heart burned with jealousy, and I tried to hide it. *Down, Brenda. Remember, he's on a date with you tonight, not a beautiful, rich woman in Texas.*

So I'd taken him to a hippie joint and brought him to a party where we sat on the floor and ate tortilla chips and spilled our guts. Could that compete with a glamorous gig with a beautiful woman?

I suddenly felt twenty years old again.

Nick went on with his story. "I thought I was in love, but I was just dazzled. Dazzled by money, by my popularity, by seeing myself in the newspaper all the time."

"Yeah, real stupid of you," I said sympathetically. "What undazzled you?"

His hand found mine. His strong fingers closed around mine absently, as though he wasn't even aware that he'd reached for me. "One night, we went to a big charity ball, one of those five-hundred-dollar-a-plate dinners. I went with my fiancée, her friends, her sister, and her sister's husband. When we walked out of the hotel, I saw a homeless guy sitting on the sidewalk in front. He was muttering to himself and probably drunk, but it was December and it was cold, and he was shivering. So I gave him my coat. I figured he was cold, I was going home in my warm car, and I could always buy another coat. I handed it to him and he cried and said thank you, and I walked away and caught up with the others. That was it; I probably didn't change his life or anything. I never saw him again."

Billy spoke up, "Did the socialites give you a hard time? I lived on the streets a while in San Francisco. I was always grateful when someone even gave me a quarter. But other people would get mad and say, 'Don't waste money on a bum.'" He grinned. "They should see me now."

His friends laughed.

Nick smiled wryly. "No, they didn't get mad. They never even noticed." He took a drink of his beer, still holding my hand.

"They didn't notice?" I asked, wondering what he meant.

"Oh, they noticed I didn't have my coat," Nick said, "My girlfriend asked me what happened to it. I told them I gave it to the homeless guy we'd passed, and they all said, 'What guy?' And that's when it hit me. They'd never even seen him. Never noticed that a man was sitting on the sidewalk shivering in the cold. They didn't view him with disgust—they never saw him at all. They *couldn't* see him. So I knew then that I could never be one of them, join their exclusive club. Because pretty soon I wouldn't be able to see him either. And I didn't want to be a person that couldn't see someone who wasn't as lucky as me."

"Oh, wow," Katie said. The others murmured their agreement.

"So," Nick said, handing the tambourine to the next person, "I decided to come back to San Diego. I missed the ocean and the mountains anyway. I realized I'd been trying to run away from myself and be someone I wasn't. I asked my fiancée to come back to San Diego with me, and she looked at me like I was crazy. So I came back alone." He slanted me a half smile. "I'm glad I did."

Everyone clapped.

I looked at him, my heart in my throat. I slid my arm around his waist and rested my head on his shoulder as the tambourine went on around the circle.

"I'm glad you came back, too," I whispered.

11

Really Good Sex Doesn't Hurt, Either

I drove the car back to Nick's house and parked in front of it. He'd kept his hand on my knee the whole trip.

"Come inside," he said.

I pretended to peer nervously across the street. "What about Mrs. Pankhurst?"

"She goes to bed at ten. Every night. On the dot."

It was well into the wee hours of the morning. "But she'll get up soon. I bet she's an early riser. And she'll see my car. What will she think?"

He laughed. "She'll think I got lucky. Come on. I want to show you the house."

"I like it already," I said as we got out and started up the walk.

"It belonged to my parents. My brother and I probably could sell it, but, I don't know, we don't want to." He unlocked the door and ushered me inside. "After they passed away, I brought in my own furniture and lived here. My brother and I decided that we'd save it for our kids."

"You have kids?" I asked, slightly panicked.

He smiled. "Not yet."

The house was as nice on the inside as it was outside. The decor was Old-World Spanish, with splashes of brightly colored tile, arched doorways, and carved wooden paneling. A staircase spiraled upward through a stucco tower.

"That goes to the bedrooms," Nick said, stopping behind me as I gazed up the staircase.

"Bedrooms?" I tried to sound coy. "Hmm, interesting."

He smiled. He took my hand and led me up the stairs.

Nick's bedroom was large and airy and overlooked the back of the house. The yard below was dark, and the lights of nearby houses dropped away sharply from it. I guessed that during the day, this window gave a fine view of the ocean.

I turned to find Nick watching me. He leaned against the doorframe, his arms folded, showing off his muscles. Backlit from the light in the hall, his torso was firm and lean.

I surveyed him from head to foot, pretending I was bold and sexy and sized up guys all the time. "I bet you've never been on a date quite like tonight," I said.

"No, I have to say it was original."

"Not as good as a five-hundred-dollar-a-plate dinner, probably."

He laughed and started walking toward me. My throat went dry.

"I like your friends," he said.

"I only met them today," I told him faintly.

"Really?"

He looked impressed. Why, I don't know. "Really," I said.

He slid his hands to the back of my neck and played with the fine hairs at my nape. "That's what I like about you, Brenda. You're spontaneous, not afraid to do what you want. You're everything I'm not. You're just what I need."

"I am?" I squeaked. I loved his fingers on the sensitive skin of my neck. "For what?"

"To take the stick out of my butt."

I smiled slyly and moved my hands to his beautiful backside. "Funny, I don't feel anything there."

"Trust me." He kissed my temple, smiling into my skin. "I love your hair."

I giggled, God help me.

"What's so funny?"

"It looks like a scouring pad."

"No, it doesn't." He kissed my hairline. "It's beautiful." More kisses. "Soft. Smells so good."

"So do you," I whispered.

He kissed me. A real kiss. He meant business. He parted my lips and pressed his tongue into my mouth. He tasted like cinnamon, spicy, not sweet.

I couldn't stop the moan. He felt so good. Lust crawled through my loins. I dug my fingers into his backside and pulled him hard against me.

"I want you so much," he murmured, his eyes half closed.

"OK," I said.

He peeled my coat down my arms, kissed my bared shoulders. "Did I tell you how much I like your dress?"

"No."

"I really like it."

He slid the coat all the way off and tossed it away. I put my arms around his waist again. He found the top of my zipper in the back, started easing it down my spine.

"Hey, wait a minute," I said.

He stopped. "What?"

"Why am I the only one getting undressed here?" Without waiting for his reaction, I grabbed the hem of his shirt and dragged it up over his head. He chuckled, slid his arms from the sleeves, and threw the shirt across the room.

I stepped back in admiration. Mr. Perfect had always seemed attractive to me, or at least he'd always kept himself groomed and in shape as part of his perfection. But this was different.

Nick was raw, male flesh. Where Mr. Perfect looked studied, like a magazine model, Nick had easy, natural virility. He didn't have to strike a pose or stand in the right light. Whichever way he moved, he looked good. Those sinews rippled in all the right places.

Of course Nick looked good standing still, too. I imagined unbuttoning his tight jeans, unzipping the zipper, pulling the fly open to reveal his taut abdomen and the top of his hips. I wet my lips, shivering in excitement.

I couldn't decide whether to keep looking at him or to jump on him and devour him.

Devouring won. I growled and launched myself at him.

Laughing, he caught me, then finished unzipping my dress. He slid the dress from my body, his hands smoothing the slippery fabric of my camisole beneath.

"You bought another one," he said.

I shrugged, burying my face in his neck. "I have hundreds." OK, maybe not hundreds. But dozens. No, what's that one that means twenty? A score. "I have scores," I said.

He lifted my chin. "What?"

"Nothing. Just kiss me. And take off your pants."

He kissed me. He held me with one hand and with the other unbuttoned and unzipped his jeans.

I helped him slide them down. He wore bikini briefs underneath, the cloth stretched tight over his buns, a nice playground for my fingers.

He kissed me again. "Get on the bed," he whispered.

"I can't with you holding onto me."

He turned me around, gave me a gentle push in the direction of his bed. The bed was king-sized, with blankets and lots of pillows. But it was tidy, every pillow lined up and the bedspread smooth. He hadn't known I was coming tonight, which meant his bed always looked like this. A sexy guy who made his bed. He couldn't be real.

I climbed aboard. I flopped onto my back, crossed my ankles and leaned back on my elbows. "Well?" I said.

"God, you're gorgeous, Brenda."

That's what I wanted to say about him. He stood at the foot of the bed in his underwear and looked me over. I returned the scrutiny with pleasure.

He had nice arms. That's the first thing I notice in a guy: the biceps, the forearms. Tight arms make me drool. Backsides are good, too. So are broad shoulders and hard pecs. Lucky me; Nick excelled in all these areas.

He leaned down and pulled off his bikinis.

Wow. He excelled in that area, too.

Unembarrassed, he let me look.

How did I not remember *that* from New Year's? I wished and wished that the fog would clear from New Year's Eve and let me remember me putting my hands all over this guy.

I wanted him inside me. Just looking at him made me want him inside me. I wanted to scream, "Come to Brenda, you beautiful hunk of man!" but all that came out of my mouth was, "Urk."

He tortured me a while longer by standing there.

I was crawling all over with wanting. I'd never felt

this way before, definitely not with Mr. Perfect. The very first time Larry had made love to me, I'd been excited with anticipation, but the longer we'd gone out, the more taking off my clothes for him hadn't seemed worth the effort.

I'd rip off every stitch for this guy. Anywhere. Any time.

Maybe I really was a slut, like Larry had called me today. I wanted to do it with Nick, now, and I wanted to do it with him in every position I could think of and many I didn't know.

I held back saying that. No use scaring him away.

He let out his breath as though he'd been holding it a while. "Brenda, you are so beautiful."

I wondered what Brenda he was talking to. "Well," I said, to hide my confusion. "Are you just going to stand there?"

He grinned. He took a step and then suddenly jumped on the bed and landed on top of me.

I squealed like a teenager. He backed up and looked at me in alarm. "Did I hurt you?"

"No. Come here."

I hauled him down and kissed him on the mouth. He was all bare and sliding on my silk underwear. My arms went around his naked back, and he nibbled his way down my neck. He nuzzled my breasts through the fabric and playfully bit one nipple that was ready to jab through the cloth.

"Nick," I whispered.

"Yes?" he asked, nipping at me.

I caressed his arms, loving his hard biceps. "I want to have mad, passionate sex with you."

I'd never in my life said that. I never said it to Mr. Perfect, because I always hoped he'd suddenly remember he had something else to do when we got to bed.

"That's the idea," Nick said.

"I want to have sex with you all night."

"Pretty much what I had in mind."

"I want you to strip me naked and lick me all over."

He grinned. "I'll make a list."

I raked my nails up his back, lightly, not to hurt. He pushed up the camisole, and I lifted my arms so he could tug it off me.

I lay there, my fists clenched, rocking back and forth as he licked my throat and shoulders and breasts. His tongue was hot and wet. I was almost screaming.

He trailed kisses down my torso, licked my belly button. I squeaked. He tickled me. I wrestled with him. It was fun.

My garter belt baffled him. "How does this work?" he asked, plucking at a lacy strap.

I reached down and unhooked the garters from my stockings, squirming to reach the back ones. Women don't wear garters any more, no matter what movies depict. They wear pantyhose, which are practical and cheap and unsexy and boring, but they're here to stay. Actresses in movies—and me—are the only females in America who regularly wear garter belts. Even finding garters isn't easy these days. Only snooty lingerie places like Lili Duoma or kinky places sell them.

I wondered if I was kinky or snooty? Both?

Nick stripped off the stockings and garter belt and my panties. I heard the tearing of a foil wrapper, which meant he'd thoughtfully brought out a condom. And then he was on me, body to body, nothing between.

He tried to be gentle with me, tried to work me up to taking him. I was wet and aching already. I seized his shaft, all warm and hard, and guided him to the ache. He slid inside and everything stopped.

He lay on me, his ribs moving in and out with his

breath. My legs were spread, his hips fitting between mine, his heart thudding against my chest. His pulse matched it on his temple, and his eyes were dark, watching me.

"Brenda," he said, his voice soft. "I think I've been trying to find you all my life."

I touched his cheek. I didn't tell him that he made me want to start crying.

He was stretching me wide, and it felt so good. I lifted my hips for more.

He slid out and back in again. He'd stopped laughing, his expression turning intense. He lifted his body, bracing himself on his hard arms.

I gripped his buttocks and let him ride me. I loved it. I couldn't believe I didn't remember this from New Year's. I must have been passed-out drunk. This time I was going to remember every glorious minute of it.

He was a fine man and knew how to make love. He touched me, he kissed me, he murmured my name. His shoulders bunched as he braced to keep his weight from crushing me.

He moved his hips rhythmically, driving deeper and faster into me. I urged him on.

And then it happened. I had the best orgasm of my life right there under him.

I'd had orgasms before, even with Mr. Perfect, in spite of his best efforts to make going to bed all about his needs. But never like this.

I couldn't see, I couldn't hear, I could only feel this wonderful feeling starting where Nick was inside me and ending, I don't know, on the other side of the universe. I moaned. I writhed. I babbled things; I don't know what.

Women who think they don't like sex have never had an orgasm like this. They should try it.

127

Next thing I knew, I was lying on the bed again, panting, my skin all wet. I held Nick close and laughed and laughed.

Now it was his turn for orgasm. His hips moved faster and faster. He closed his eyes. His face took on a beatific expression, and then he collapsed onto me, burying his face in my shoulder.

"Brenda," he whispered. "God, that was so good."

Then he fell asleep.

Some women make a big deal about guys who fall asleep right after sex. I didn't mind. At least, not with Nick.

I pulled him close and snuggled my cheek against his hair. I felt warm and heavy and free. No one knew where I was. No one could call me on my smashed cell phone. Not my mother, or Larry, or my brother, or Tony Beale.

I lay there enjoying the warmth of a man I wanted to be with and enjoying my freedom.

I liked watching him sleep. His blond lashes lay against his cheek, and his limbs were loose and relaxed. So he snored a little. I didn't care.

Around sunrise, I drifted to sleep, too. So this is falling in love, was my last coherent thought.

When I opened my eyes again, Nick was smiling at me from his pillow. Sunlight flooded the room. Kids were playing outside. A dog barked, and someone laughed.

"Hi," Nick said. "You're beautiful."

I knew I looked as good in the morning as an aging movie queen with too many facelifts. I wanted to jump up and run far and fast, just like I had on New Year's morning.

"Urgh," I said.

"A smooth-talking woman. I like it." He touched my cheek.

I pulled away, scooting to the far side of the bed. I put my hand to my hair. "I look like Little Orphan Annie."

"No, you don't." He shoved aside the sheets. We were still bare, because people really don't get up and put on their pajamas after sex like they do on TV.

That was fine, because I wanted to look at him. His body was delicious, sculpted perfection. His penis was stiff. Maybe waking up next to Little Orphan Annie turned him on.

"I am so horny," he said, giving me that warm smile. "I've been lying here imagining us doing all kinds of things."

"Like what?" I asked, coy Brenda.

He showed me. He pulled me on top of him, and we had more beautiful sex in the full light of the sun.

The clock beside the bed said it was twelve noon. At one-thirty we staggered to the shower and washed each other all over. Guess what? That led to more sex.

By three o'clock, we finally made it downstairs, and Nick cooked breakfast. Or lunch. Or whatever it is you eat at three o'clock in the afternoon when you've been having sex all morning and are famished.

Nick cooked real breakfast. French toast. I set the table while he broke open eggs and got out thick slices of bread and whisked together milk and sugar and cinnamon.

Nick obviously knew how to cook. I mean, he had whisks. No man has whisks unless he knows how to use them.

He cooked the slices of French toast on the griddle, then he brought them to me sprinkled with powdered sugar and drizzled with syrup. He was great in bed, and he could cook. How did this happen to Brenda?

He returned to the griddle and started frying his portion.

"Why aren't you married?" I asked him, licking the syrup from the back of my fork.

He fixed his gaze on his toast. "Why do you ask?"

I touched each of my fingers as I listed his attributes.

"You make breakfast, you like your family home, you make your bed, you're good in the sack. Why hasn't some woman snapped you up?"

He slid the spatula under the toast and tipped it onto a plate.

"I was about to get married," he said, bringing the plate to the table and sitting down next to me. He reached for the syrup. "Remember the story I told last night? The wedding was supposed to be this June." He plopped butter on his French toast and drizzled syrup on top of it.

"I can't believe she let you go without a fight," I said. "What did she say when you told her you were coming back here?"

It was none of my business. But I wanted to know.

He didn't meet my gaze. "We argued. She couldn't understand why I was giving up her father's help and his money." He poured on some more syrup. "She was mad, not hurt. That told me a lot."

I chewed the French toast. It was perfect; crispy outside, soft inside, sweet and buttery. "She was stupid. I'd have grabbed you and held on."

He smiled, his eyes warm. "You're sweet."

"I'm not sweet. I'm truthful."

He leaned to me and kissed a dab of syrup from the corner of my mouth. "No, you are sweet."

I gave him a sly look. "Syrup. Now that sounds fun."

He shook his head, returned to his food. "Why aren't *you* married?"

I hid my embarrassment by shrugging and looking wise. "Can't get enough of my carefree life."

The real reason was—no one had ever asked me. That is, unless I counted Mr. Perfect's proposal yesterday. If you could say that his "you should marry me, Brenda, it's for your own good" was a proposal. He'd forgotten the flowers and moonlight and, oh, yeah, being madly in love with me.

"I bet you have guys lining up to go out with you," he said.

I looked at him in surprise. If guys were lining up to go out with me, they were hiding it well. "No," I said.

"You're gorgeous. You make friends easily. You're fun. What's not to like?"

I must be dreaming. I must be asleep in my apartment, not sitting here eating French toast and listening to the gorgeous, sexy man who cooked it tell me that I was beautiful and fun. I'd wake up any minute. I held onto the table to make sure I was still there.

"No, really I—" I began, then I stopped myself.

What are you going to say, Brenda? That you're really a total loser? That you only had one serious boyfriend, and he turned out to be a jerk?

I smiled. "It doesn't matter," I said. "I'm with you now."

He grinned and turned his attention to his food.

I finished my French toast. I offered to help clean up. He said, no, not to worry about it. I stood up and took the dishes to the sink anyway.

Helping with the dishes let me stay there longer. Plus I got to learn my way around his kitchen. You know a guy well when you know where he keeps things in his kitchen.

After we'd loaded the dishwasher and put everything away and wiped down the counter and the stove and the tables, I couldn't put it off any longer. He hadn't invited me back upstairs, so I finally said the words.

"I should go."

He closed his hands around my arms. The warmth was like a magnet. I couldn't move, didn't want to break that pull.

"Do you have to?" he asked.

His voice conjured visions of last night, and this morning, and the shower, and promises of more to come.

My heart beat fast and hard. "Yes."

He nodded, but he looked disappointed. I glanced at him from under my lashes. "You're supposed to ask me why I have to go."

He took a step back, like he didn't care. "OK. Why do you have to go?"

"Because you didn't ask me to stay."

His smile came back. He cupped my shoulders, leaned down and kissed me. "Stay," he whispered.

"All right," I said, as though I'd been debating it. "But I'll need a toothbrush."

12

Another Reason Movies Aren't Like Real Life

OK, here comes the montage.

You know how in movies when the hero and heroine get together in the middle of the story, you get a montage of them walking in the park and riding roller coasters and having candlelit dinners and running through meadows?

The montage is short, probably a minute of screen time. It condenses the joy of the couple into bite-sized pieces so the audience doesn't get bored.

The movie condenses it, because what is so interesting to the couple—the way his hair shines in the sun, how warm his hand is when you walk along the beach, how he laughs when you share an ice cream cone and you smear ice cream all over your face—is only so interesting to the people who paid money for the movie ticket. Those people came to see the conflict, the argument, the

133

bitchy ex-wife who pops up in the middle of everything
and ruins the couple's happiness.

In real life, the montage is the longest part. All the
conflict leading up to the couple getting together is over,
and the montage is the reward.

Nick and I spent Sunday in our very own montage.
We walked hand in hand along the beach, dancing away
from the water when it snaked too close. We had drinks
in a beach bar, smiling at each other because the music
was too loud to talk over. We went to a tourist shop and
bought bright oversized T-shirts that said "San Diego"
on them over pictures of surfers and whales. Mine was
hot pink and clashed with my hair. I put it on over my
dress and wore it while we strolled back down the
beach. We stopped to kiss every once in a while.

Most montages lead to more sex. Ours did, too.

We made hot, wild love in his bedroom while it got
dark outside. Mrs. Pankhurst must have been having a
great time watching us come and go, and seeing that my
car was there all night both Saturday and Sunday.

We got in the shower and cleaned the sand off each
other's bodies. I slid my arms around him and laid my
cheek on his warm, water-covered torso. He held me
with strong arms and kissed me.

This was crazy. I wanted the montage to go on forever.
I actually wanted to run through tall grass with my
arms open, although where we'd find a convenient
meadow in the city I didn't know. I wanted to sing stupid, sappy songs. I wanted to laugh and cry and kiss
him some more.

I knew, however, that reality rushed back at us at
breakneck speed. The weekend would end, and we'd be
back to work as usual. We couldn't stop it. I decided to
have a damn good try, though.

In the shower, I closed my hand around his nice, slippery penis. He held onto me while I did that, and then all of a sudden, he lifted me and pressed me against the wall. The sex that followed was even crazier than before.

When we got hungry, we went downstairs for a late supper. Nick cooked again, making a snapper with wine sauce from ingredients he just happened to have on hand.

After that, we lay on the living room carpet and talked and touched each other before we, yes, had more sex.

By this time I'd told him all about David and his marriage and his troubles, and all about my dad; and about some of my own past, leaving out Mr. Perfect, because I didn't want to talk about him.

Nick told me about his brother and about his parents, who'd waited to have kids until their forties. They'd been a close, happy family. His father had been a chef and had owned several gourmet restaurants. Nick had worked for a time in a couple of them, which explained how he had learned to cook.

Then one day, he and his dad had done a radio interview for one of their restaurants, and Nick had fallen in love with radio. He'd quit the kitchen, bummed a board op job at a tiny station out in the middle of nowhere, and worked his way up from there.

We talked about the weirdness of radio and Tony Beale; then we fell asleep on the floor.

We woke up when Nick's alarm upstairs went off at four, reminding us that we were morning drive time DJs who had no business staying up all night.

I didn't have any clothes with me but the dress I'd worn for two days and my souvenir T-shirt. I put the T-shirt over the dress, trying to make it look like a cute two-piece skirt outfit. No one at the station ever paid attention to what I wore anyway.

We parted in the courtyard. Nick kissed me.

"I want to see you again," he said, resting his face against mine. "Tonight?"

"Twelve hours from now? Sure." I hesitated. "I should go home first after work. Change my clothes, you know? Then I could come back, if you want."

"I do want. Pack a bag." He winked at me.

I gulped, then kissed him. "See you later," I said, and hurried to my car.

Mrs. Pankhurst, up at four thirty in the morning for some reason, watched me drive away. She didn't wave.

At five sharp, time for drive time, I walked into the station, my head high.

Tony was there, of course. He stared at me. His domed forehead turned chartreuse. "What are you doing here? You'd better go back home and get some sleep, Brenda, because you're back on overnights."

I walked past him. "I don't think so."

Tim was in the studio, headphones on. Tim was about thirty, had black hair and nice brown eyes, and a shaky smile. His arm was wrapped in a large bandage, and he wore a sling.

Tim Turner had been in radio since he was eighteen. Nothing scared him anymore except Tony Beale. And maybe sharks.

"Hi, Tim," I said kindly. "How are you?"

"OK." Tim smiled and drew a breath. "I'm OK."

Tony had followed me. "Did you hear me, Brenda? After that debacle Saturday, I'm ready to fire you. I decided to give you a break and put you back on overnights."

My heart squeezed, but I wasn't about to let Tony know I was intimidated. "I didn't know you knew a word like 'debacle,' Tony."

"I'm not kidding, Brenda! Oh, and you have to take a pay cut, too."

"No," I said. I was shaking inside, but I sat down next to Tim and reached for a pair of headphones.

"If you go on the air you're fired," Tony said.

Tim looked up nervously. "Both of us?"

"No, Tim," I said. "Everything will be fine. Besides, Tony, you need me. Tim's minus an arm today, so how it he going to work the computer?"

"Marty will do it," Tony said. He glared at me. "Don't you dare sign on, Brenda."

I turned on my mike. "Hi, this is Brenda Scott, back from a fine weekend with KBZ's ultragorgeous DJ Nick Jordan. Wonder what's going on with Nick today?"

I turned up the speaker that had KBZ. Nick was just saying hello.

I knew right then that I was in love. I'd spent two nights and a day with Nick doing everything sexual we could possibly think of. We must have run through an entire box of condoms. I don't think I spent a minute without him.

And yet, when his voice floated through the airwaves, my heart turned over and I couldn't wait for this afternoon when I could run into his arms again. I wanted another montage, and I wanted it now.

"We ditched you," Nick said gleefully. "Me and Brenda. You all left at the wrong time. We had a wild weekend all right. Without anyone watching."

He spun a tune.

Tony stared at me. I stared back, daring him to say something. We were still on the air, no music playing or anyone talking. Just Tony and me staring at each other.

Tim, the pro, picked up the cue. "Wow, Brenda, sounds like you had a hot time." He started laughing, getting into the teasing DJ persona. "So you ditched the entire city of San Diego and went on a binge with KBZ's morning host. You ho."

"Hey," I said, sounding outraged. "Watch who you're calling a ho. You had a fling with a shark. What does that make you?"

"He bit me," Tim said, sounded offended.

"You should have checked that it was a female shark before you made your move," I joked.

"It might have been a girl shark," Tim said. "How was I supposed to know? How do you tell the sex of a shark?"

I knew we'd be getting calls from every geek in the city telling us how. The computer phone list was growing already.

"When it bites you, you know you got the wrong one," I went on, not even paying attention to what I was saying.

Tony grabbed the mike and clicked the switch off. "Why are you still talking, Brenda? You're fired."

I took the mike back. "No, I'm not."

He grabbed it back. "Oh, yes, you are."

I grabbed it. He held on. We had a tug of war. "No, I'm not," I gasped. I flipped the switch on again. "Tony's trying to fire me," I told my listeners. "Everyone call and boo him."

The calls started flooding in. Marty struggled to answer. He put every one on the air.

From every corner of the city, from every kind of voice, young, old, male, female, weak, strong, came long, drawn-out *booooooo*s. Tim clicked keys, recording them one-handed, and played them back one after another.

Tony relinquished the mike. He sank into a chair and looked worried for a while. At last, he sighed. "You have balls, Brenda."

I glanced down at myself in mock panic. "I hope not."

He gave me a narrow look. "Why did you think I wouldn't fire you?"

"I didn't. But you know, I'm going out with a guy at KBZ. He could probably get me a job if I asked."

Tony stood up. He seized my arm. "No, you don't. You're mine, Brenda. Mine, all mine."

"Go make sales, Tony," I said.

He smiled like a man in love. "OK." He drifted away.

Tim watched me with raised brows. "You charmed the snake."

I shrugged. I waited, timing the end of the spot, ready to take the mike again.

"Next time," Tim said, turning back to the computer, "*you're* going in with the sharks."

I went home after work. As soon as I walked in, I realized that no one had been in the apartment since I'd left it for Nick's house on Saturday evening.

The dishes in the kitchen lay in the same places with the same food drying on them. The note from David and Clarissa saying they'd gone to Tijuana still lay on the counter.

I checked the voice mail on our land line. Nothing from David or Clarissa. One call was for Clarissa from a guy I didn't know. One call for David from his wife's lawyer. Two were from Mr. Perfect asking where I was. I erased those.

I hung up and started washing the dishes, a little worried. Would David and Clarissa have stayed down in Tijuana, and what for? I had to admit that even though I'd lived with Clarissa for about a year, I didn't really know her. She paid her half of the rent and utilities and stayed out of my business, except for borrowing my shoes, but I didn't really *know* her.

Clarissa didn't work, but she had money. She had weird friends, some of them bordering on creepy, but I never said anything. She didn't let them stay in the apartment, and besides she paid her rent.

But now, for some reason, I was imagining Clarissa

taking my brother to Mexico and introducing him to drug-runners. Maybe Clarissa had decided that drug-running would solve David's financial problems. Maybe the FBI had followed them and were even now interrogating my clueless brother under hot lights.

I finished the dishes and straightened up the apartment, wondering what to do. I had no way to reach David to make sure he was OK. Clarissa, like my new hippie friends, didn't believe in cell phones, and David couldn't afford one.

So, they were in Mexico, cut off from home, being interrogated by the FBI.

Nick might know what to do. I almost called him, then I stopped. What would I say? *Hey, Nick, my brother is smuggling drugs from Mexico; do you know how I can find him?*

I sighed. Nick had a vision of me that I didn't want to shatter. I wanted him to think I was smart and funny and not related to a very strange family.

Maybe I would have to break down and call my mother, tell her I was worried about David, and what should we do?

I cringed from that. I didn't want Jerry gloating that Mom's stuck-up kids couldn't even take care of themselves.

Or maybe, I thought, I could mind my own business. Maybe Clarissa and David had hit it off and had decided to go to Acapulco and rent a condo on the beach. Clarissa had money. Maybe she'd suggested it, and David hadn't been able to resist her long legs and throaty voice.

So David had gone to Acapulco with Clarissa while his wife was trying to sue him for divorce. Oh, great, David.

I started worrying all over again.

I was supposed to go back to Nick's. Pack a bag. I could do that.

I stripped off my clothes and put the bright pink T-shirt in its own laundry pile so that it wouldn't ruin all my pristine undergarments. I took a shower and re-dressed from the skin out. Thinking of Nick, I put on a pink lace teddy and a sleeveless dress, one I could wear with sandals. I saw no reason to load up with clothes.

I swear, I'd had more sex in the past two days than in my whole relationship with Larry. It had been much better sex as well. I actually had rug burns. Was I a wild woman, or what?

I was tired, but I felt good. Stretched and warm and happy. At least, as long as I didn't find out my brother was a fugitive, I'd be happy.

I thought about my upcoming montage with Nick. What would it be tonight? Would he cook me another fine dinner, would we watch the sun set over the water, would we walk through a park, holding hands, smiling at the children?

The phone rang. Larry's number appeared in my phone's readout. The romantic movie squawked to a halt.

I let it ring. The last person on the planet I wanted to talk to was Larry. I would even have answered for my mother, because I was starting to feel really bad about how I'd been treating her.

The voice mail picked up the call. I closed my eyes. *I should turn around, take my bag, walk out of the house, and drive back to Nick's.*

But something made me wait. When my message light lit, I lifted the phone to see what Mr. Perfect had to say.

"Brenda? It's Larry. You need to call me. This is important. It's about your brother."

Click. *End of messages. To erase this message—*

I frantically slammed my finger to the "off" button, then pushed a key to call Larry back. He was still on my speed dial. I'd have to fix that.

Jennifer Ashley

"Larry Bryant," he answered his personal line cautiously.

"It's Brenda. What about my brother?"

"You were home when I called, weren't you?" Mr. Perfect asked in an annoyed voice. "You were letting the phone ring, knowing it was me."

"Larry," I said, panting. "What about my brother?"

"He's been arrested," Larry said, way too calmly. "In Mexico."

142

13

Mexican Radio

"Oh, God." I clutched the phone, panic rising. *For drug running?*

Larry went on. "One of the employees in my front office likes to listen to the radio from Tijuana. She asked if your brother's name was David Scott. When I asked why, she said that a David Scott had been arrested in Tijuana and was being held in jail there. I wondered if you even knew about it."

I clenched my fist and silently cursed. Why did an employee in Larry's office have to know about my personal life? And why did Mr. Perfect assume I didn't have my personal life under control and didn't know about David?

OK, so I didn't, but that was beside the point.

"Oh, God," I said again.

"Where have you been?" Larry demanded. "I've been trying to reach you on your cell."

My cell phone was a pile of plastic parts on Torrey Pines Road. "None of your business."

"Who have you been sleeping with this time?" he asked, sarcastic. "No, don't tell me, I don't want to know. I made some phone calls. I think I can get your brother let go, but I'll have to go down and make sure. I'll pick you up."

"Oh, no," I bleated. "No, no, no. I can drive to Mexico myself."

"No you can't. I've already got Mexican insurance on my car, so we can go right away. Besides, I'm not letting you go to a Mexican jail by yourself. You'd say something stupid and get yourself locked up for the rest of your life."

I hated him. At that moment, I hated him more than I'd ever hated him, even when we were dating and he had undercut my self-esteem one little comment at a time.

I hated him, because I needed him. He had the friends to get David free, and it was probably too late today for me to go to an agency and buy the special car insurance that you have to have before you can drive in Mexico, and I'd have to wait until tomorrow, and who knows, by then, David might be dead. Ok, I was panicking, but I wanted to go get David *now*, before they thought of some weird charge to make against him and we never saw him again.

Plus, I didn't want to call my mom. We'd caused her enough grief already. I'd go with Larry this one last time, I'd bring David home, and we'd explain to Mom after that. And then I'd kill David.

When I thought of Nick, I almost cried. I wanted my montage. I wanted to kiss him again. I wanted him to smile at me and tell me I was beautiful.

I could imagine me calling Nick and saying, *My brother's a fugitive, and me and my ex are driving to Mexico to spring him from the joint.*

He'd listen politely, hang up the phone, and never speak to me again.

I'd lose that beautiful, beautiful man, just when he was about to make me believe I might not be a loser after all. So went my life.

"Wait a minute," I asked Larry, "what about Clarrisa?"

"Clarissa? What about her?"

"She was with David. He went with her to Mexico."

"I don't know, Brenda. No one said anything about Clarissa."

I ground my teeth. If she'd run off and left David holding the bag, or whatever it was that drug-runners held, I'd have something to say to her. That is, if she ever came back. Maybe she'd gone to Acapulco with the leader of the gang.

"Just come and get me," I said.

"I'll be right there," Larry answered. He was gloating.

I slammed down the phone. I tossed my bag into the corner and screamed through my teeth. Damn David, damn Mr. Perfect, and damn Mexican radio.

Well before Larry arrived, I gathered my courage and called Nick.

"Hello," he said cheerfully.

My heart stuck in my throat. "Hey, Nick."

The other end of the line went silent. I tried to think of all kinds of things to say, and I did think of them, but my mouth wouldn't form words.

He finally said, "You aren't coming, are you?"

"No." I swallowed a sob. In a rush, I blurted, "I have to go to Mexico and pick up my brother."

Another pause. "Want company?"

The last thing I wanted was Nick in the car with Mr. Perfect. Or coming with me to a jail. Or listening to David explaining how he'd fallen in with drug-runners.

145

"No," I said quickly. "This is something I have to do alone. I'll—I'll tell you all about it later."

"Sure," he said. He meant, *I don't believe you, but I'll pretend I do.*

"I'll call you when I get back."

"Sure," he said again.

He hung up. I sat there staring at the receiver, my eyes stinging with tears.

Just when you think you have your life together—

I went outside to wait for Larry. I carried a jacket in case it got cold, but the cool air felt good on my arms.

I tried not to think about Nick in the shower, how good his skin looked all wet and slick, and how much fun it was to slide my own body over his.

I tried not to think about the tone of his voice on the phone just now when he'd said, "Sure."

I ground my teeth. I'd been rejoicing that at Nick's house no one could call me. All that time, David had been in trouble. Mr. Perfect had had to make sure I knew about my own family problems.

But then, David could have tried to call me at home, left a message that I would have at least gotten this morning. Or he could have tried to call the station.

Why hadn't he called? This was very weird.

I noticed a seedy-looking car parked near the entrance to the apartment complex, a squared-off Toyota from about fifteen years ago. The white paint had long ago turned a dull gray, and the chrome was dented and cloudy. A man sat in the car, staring up at the apartments. I had the feeling he was keeping an eye on my front door.

Just what I needed. A stalker.

Some DJs got them. People with not much to do and a slight kink in their brains decided that following around their favorite DJ was a good idea. So far I'd never been popular enough to worry about it.

Bravely, I walked past the car and to the entrance to wait for Larry.

The guy in the car was young, with crisp black hair and a clean-shaven face. He glanced at me, then away, uninterested, and resumed staring at the building.

OK, so the stalker was not stalking me. Or he could just be waiting for a friend. My imagination was on overdrive.

Larry pulled up, and I forgot about the guy in the dirty white Toyota.

Mr. Perfect drove a Lexus, of course. It was a gentle gray and the seats inside were leather. Every car gadget known to man was built into this car—a weather monitor, an internal temperature control, a satellite guidance system (I don't know what for, as Larry prided himself on knowing how to find any place, any time), a programmed, computerized music system, and the most comfortable car seats ever devised.

I disliked that car. It intimidated you. It said, "I am so much better than you, me and my form-adjusting leather seats."

When a car thought it was better than you, that was bad. Larry thought he was better than his car, and that was ten times worse.

Larry got out and came around to open the door for me. I opened it before he could reach me, not wanting to be his little woman any more. His expression cool, he ushered me into the car and closed the door behind me.

While I settled on the annoying perfect seats, he got back in. "Your preferences are still programmed," he said. He leaned over and flipped the switch that moved the seat to the height and width and firmness I'd liked before.

It was like the chair was trying to put me back the way I was, trying to mold me into the Brenda who'd been Larry's girlfriend. The girl who did whatever he said because she lacked the confidence to believe he was wrong.

I squirmed, trying to fight the chair with my butt. I flipped the switch again, and the chair moved back to the way it had been.

Larry glanced at me sideways, but said nothing. He pulled out onto the road and we headed south.

The seat was uncomfortable, too high and too far back, but it never paid to be too comfortable with Larry.

"I tried to call this weekend," he said. "Several times. Not just about this."

He rested his hand on the top of the steering wheel. His skin was pale, a man who didn't like the sun. Black hairs stood out on his fingers, but even they were flat and well-groomed. A tasteful silver ring encircled his third finger. When we'd first started going out, I'd bought him another ring, knowing he liked them. He'd never worn it.

"My cell phone broke," I explained. "I need to get another one."

The steering wheel twitched. "I told you not to buy cheap junk. I could have gotten you a state-of-the-art phone that would last forever. What happened to yours? I know a man who might be able to fix it."

"An SUV ran over it," I said, watching the scenery. "Does he have really good glue?"

I sensed him staring at me, even though I didn't look at him. I know what the stare would show—mild surprise and disapproval.

I didn't care. Only months ago, I would have felt like a fool telling him about the fate of my cell phone. I would let an accident be my fault, because it could have been prevented if I'd only listened to him.

Now I just wanted to laugh at him. What a jerk, worried about how much I spent or didn't spend on a cell phone. Like it was his business.

"I called your apartment, too," he said. "Were you not answering?"

I thought of the messages I'd erased. "I wasn't home, Larry."

"Where were you? With your mom? And her—uh—" He cleared his throat uncomfortably.

"No, Larry," I said. "I was with a man."

The steering wheel jerked again. We were going sixty miles an hour, so it was a little unnerving.

"Don't lie to make me jealous, Brenda."

"Are you jealous?" I asked, interested.

"No."

I believed him. Larry didn't get jealous. He got angry, in a selfish way. He didn't want me, but he didn't want anyone else to have me, either.

"I spent the weekend with Nick," I said. "He has a house near Point Loma. I was there all weekend." I emphasized it with a smile.

Larry's face got red. I half expected him to lean over, throw open the door, and push me out. He probably had a button by his steering wheel, the unwanted-passenger-ejector button. The car would open the door, extend the seat, dump out the unwanted person, and close everything back up again.

I'd have to walk to Mexico to get my brother. But I didn't care. The look on Larry's face was worth it.

"I thought you stood Nick up," he said.

"I changed my mind. He has a nice house. You'd like it."

Actually, he wouldn't. Nick's house was cozy. The furniture didn't match. The chandelier in the living room wasn't designer. The tile floors were worn by decades of people walking on them. It was a real house, lived in by real families.

Larry clenched his jaw. His skin was perfectly shaved. Barely a hint of whisker showed. "You're doing this to get back at me. That was a bad idea, Brenda."

"It didn't have anything to do with you," I said. "I went out with Nick because I like him."

"You know that's not true."

I burst out laughing. "It is true. Get it through your head, Larry. You broke up with me. I moved on. Why don't you?"

"Because I want you to marry me!" A vein pulsed in his perfect neck.

"Why?" I genuinely wanted to know.

He glanced at me, raked his gaze down my bare arms and sheath dress, looked back at the road. "I don't want you like this. Not this wild woman you're trying to be. I want you back the way you were."

"When I hung on every word you said?" I asked. "And thought you were right about everything? When I couldn't say a word for myself? I don't know, Larry, I like the new me better."

"Well, I don't."

I gave him a faint smile. "Too bad."

My heart was heavy because I knew Nick might never speak to me again, and I was nervous because I worried about David, but a little tiny part of me was having fun pissing Larry off.

I expected him to growl that he was turning the car around and my brother could just rot in the Tijuana jail, but to my surprise, he didn't.

We pulled up in the line at the border crossing. Larry had everything in order, of course. I had no doubt that he'd greased so many palms from Los Angeles to Puerto Vallarta that he never had problems going anywhere he wanted.

Larry drove on after they let us through, heading for downtown Tijuana in his beautiful, cushy Lexus.

I'd never been to the Tijuana jail before, but it was about what I'd expected. We pulled up in front of a grim and age-worn building with squared corners, a building that said you did not want to be there.

Larry parked, came around to help me out (of course),

and locked his car nonchalantly, as though he believed no one would dream of trying to steal his lovely, expensive car in the heart of a Mexican border town.

The first person I saw when we went inside was Clarissa. There was no place to sit, so she was standing next to the wall, her legs miles-long in her tight, hip-hugging jeans. She waved when we came in, and sauntered over to us like we were picking her up at a mall.

"Where's David?" I demanded, as soon as I could speak. *You drug-running whore.*

"They're getting him. Oh, there he is."

My brother walked out of a door in the back, looking dead-eyed and angry. His stride was quick, but he limped.

"David," I cried, flinging myself at him. I never knew until then how much I loved my annoying older brother.

He said, "No, Brenda, wait," but I'd already thrown my arms around his neck.

He stank like a latrine. I gagged and back-pedaled. I ran into two police officers who were dragging a smelly and very drunk man between them.

David grabbed my arm before I could fall over. "Let's just get out of here, OK?"

We walked. Fast. At the door, the guards gave us a hard-eyed stare, and I suddenly pictured us all being grabbed and thrown back into a cell, including Larry in his dapper suit.

But Larry seemed to have everything taped up. The guard held the door for us. Said, "Hasta luego." Politely.

When we approached the Lexus, Clarissa exclaimed— well, as much as she ever exclaimed—"Nice car, Larry. Have I seen this one?"

Larry didn't answer. He touched buttons on the combination lock, clicked his remote, and let us in.

Clarissa and David immediately climbed in the back. I had wanted to sit with David, but I resigned myself to the inevitable, getting in again beside Mr. Perfect.

Larry's fastidious nose wrinkled as he started the car. He gave the two in the back a fish-eyed stare in his mirror.

"What happened to you?" I asked, glaring around the seat at Clarissa.

She lifted her shoulders in a languid shrug. "They said we were shoplifting and arrested us. We weren't."

I looked to David for confirmation. He nodded. He was angry but not upset.

"So why didn't you call me?" I asked.

"They wouldn't let us use a phone for two days," David said. "They put me in a cell with like fourteen other guys. There wasn't room to sit down. They didn't even have toilet paper."

Larry's eyes widened. I could see the thought in his head: *And he's sitting on my leather seats.*

Clarissa scratched her arm. "Ick. I think one of the prostitutes gave me fleas."

Larry turned a strange shade of green. He slammed on the brake at an intersection, then took off north, as though he could outrun the smell and the fleas if he drove fast enough.

We had a much longer wait crossing back into the U.S. than we had going into Mexico. David fell asleep in the back and started to snore. Clarissa rested her head against his arm, her eyes closed. She probably didn't notice the stink, since she stank just as badly herself.

They let us pass pretty quickly once we made it to the front of the line. Larry said polite things to the border patrol, readily popped his trunk so that he could show he wasn't smuggling immigrants or bombs or drugs into the United States. They glanced in, waved us through. The magic of Mr. Perfect.

The sun had set, and twilight spread from the edge of the Pacific to the tall mountains east of the city. Stars pricked the clear sky. A beautiful evening.

Without asking permission, I rolled down my window and let the cold evening breeze flow over me. I got exhaust from other cars on the I-5, but that was better than smelling David.

Both jailbirds were sleeping hard by the time we pulled into our apartment complex. The stalker in the white Toyota had gone.

Larry got out of the car, tight-lipped. He followed the three of us upstairs, although I knew he must have been dying to take his car to be fumigated.

"Thanks, Larry," I said at the door. I was sincere. He had helped us when he hadn't needed to. He could have heard about David and shrugged it off.

No, wait, what was I talking about? Take-charge, I'm-always-right Larry? No way could he have left this alone.

"Go inside, Brenda," he said.

Typical. He followed me in and closed the door.

14

Clarissa Explains It All

I told David, "Go take a shower, and burn your clothes."

"I'm starving." He headed for the kitchen.

I yelped, ran after him, and headed him off. "Don't you go anywhere near my refrigerator. I'll make you a sandwich. Just go take a shower."

"I can't," David grumbled. "Larry's in there."

Sure enough, the first thing Larry had done was run into my bathroom. I heard the water in the sink running and running and running. He was probably using up all my expensive soap.

Clarissa had already disappeared into her bedroom to start her own shower.

"Don't sit down!" I yelled at David. I dragged out bread and lunch meat and mustard and quickly slapped together a sandwich.

Someone knocked on the door. David, the doofus, answered it.

A familiar voice floated to me, and my heart zoomed.

"I stopped by to see if you were all OK," Nick said. He broke off and coughed. "I hate to tell you this, David, but you really stink."

"Yeah," David said, opening the door wider so Nick could walk in. "I was in jail down in Mexico."

Nick closed the door. "In jail?"

He looked so good. He was casual in jeans and a pullover shirt and sneakers, a complete contrast to the Armani suit and tie of Mr. Perfect. Nick's hair was a little messy from the wind. I loved it that way.

I gazed at him like a high school girl gazes at her first sweetheart. Dreamily, I took a bite of David's sandwich.

"Why were you in jail in Mexico?" Nick asked David.

"A slight misunderstanding with the Mexican police. No big deal, though."

"Harsh," Nick said, sympathetic. He looked at me, his blue eyes amused. "Is that what you didn't want to tell me on the phone?"

I nodded, still incoherent. I'd put too much mustard on the sandwich.

"You ever been to a Mexican jail?" David went on. "This drunk guy was brought in, and while he was passed out, three other guys stripped him down to his underwear. When he woke up, they sold his clothes back to him. They laughed the whole time. Even the drunk guy laughed. It was surreal. Is that my sandwich?"

Wordlessly, I put the sandwich back on the plate and started to hand it to him. Then I jerked it back. "Wash your hands first."

"I will if Larry ever gets out of there. What's he doing, taking a sponge bath? Your boyfriends are weird, Brenda." He cocked an eye at Nick. "Oh, sorry, Fred, no offense."

"His name's Nick!" I yelled.

"Oh, sorry," David shrugged.

I almost threw his sandwich at him. He grabbed the

plate, trundled back into the kitchen, and snapped on the water in the sink.

Nick started to say something, and then Larry came out of my bedroom.

"Why did you pack, Brenda?" Larry asked, holding out my little overnight bag. "Where are you going?" He noticed Nick, and his expression turned sour. "Or is it somewhere you've been?"

I grabbed for the bag. Larry held onto it. "None of your business, Larry," I gasped. "Good-bye, Larry."

Larry eyed Nick behind me. "Aren't you going to introduce us?"

What did he think, we'd all be friends and have a party? "Go away, Larry."

I felt Nick next to me, his hard chest near my shoulder. "I think you should introduce us," he said. His voice was low, but he directed menace toward Larry.

Larry drew himself up. "I'm Larry Bryant." He waited for the name to sink in, then said, "I am Brenda's—"

"You are not Brenda's anything," I interrupted him. "And I want you to go away."

"I'm not going anywhere," the damned man said. "Not until we talk about some things."

"We've talked. On the phone, in the car. There's nothing else to talk about."

"There is plenty to talk about. Like why you are picking up men right and left. You're on the rebound, and you're going to get yourself into trouble."

"I am not on the rebound." I ground my teeth. "I am over you. And spending one weekend with Nick isn't picking up men right and left."

Larry's brows climbed. "One thing we need to talk about, Brenda, is your morals."

"*Larry!*"

"I think that's enough," Nick said quietly.

His tone cut through the heated words that Larry and I were throwing at each other.

Larry, looking startled, actually closed his mouth. David leaned against the kitchen counter, watching with enjoyment while he chewed his sandwich.

"I don't really know what's going on here," Nick said. "But I do know that I don't like you talking to Brenda like that."

I shot Larry a triumphant look.

Nick's strong hand closed on my shoulder. "Brenda, why don't we talk outside?"

"If you walk out that door, Brenda," Larry said, "the engagement's off."

Nick's lips whitened. I could have cheerfully strangled Larry Bryant right then. I wondered why I hadn't done that a long time ago. It would have saved me so much trouble.

"There is no engagement," I told Larry. "No engagement," I emphasized to Nick.

Nick walked out. He said nothing; he simply turned and walked out the door. I glared at Larry. I snatched my bag from him, did a one-eighty, and ran out after Nick.

I caught up to Nick at the bottom of the stairs. He said absolutely nothing until we got to his car. He opened the door, but didn't get in. He draped one arm over the open door, resting the other on the convertible's top.

"Nick," I blurted. "I'm sorry."

Nick didn't answer. He seemed calm, uncaring, even, but his eyes held quiet anger.

Small wonder, when he'd come to my apartment, seen Larry coming out of my bedroom, and realized that I'd lied about my trip to Mexico, or at least, I hadn't told the whole truth.

"I was never engaged to him," I said. "I swear it. I was

157

going out with him, yes, but we broke up. On New Year's. Before you and I met."

His eyes flickered, and my voice dragged to a halt.

How stupid was I? On New Year's Eve, after Larry had broken up with me, I'd gotten drunk and jumped into bed with a handsome guy called Nick Jordan.

I bet I'd just made Nick feel really, really special.

Nick bent his head and looked away, but not before I saw the flash in his blue eyes. He knew exactly what I'd done. Anything I could say, any denial that I'd not gone to him on New Year's to make myself feel better would sound like a lie.

I'd gotten drunk that night, because Larry had dumped me. I'd likely went along with Nick's suggestion that we go to bed, because Larry had dumped me. Nick hadn't known that, but he knew it, now.

To my surprise, Nick didn't jump into his car and race away, leaving me in the dust.

"It doesn't matter," he said quietly.

"Yes, it does. Please believe that I am not, not, not seeing him any more. He asked me to marry him just this Saturday. I told him what he could do with his proposal."

Nick's expression didn't change. I bit my lip. Maybe it hadn't been such a good idea to tell him that I'd run out and bought him edible underwear and took him to bed after getting mad at Larry. He might see a false pattern in my behavior.

"Saturday," he repeated. "When you missed our on-air date?"

"No! Later. I missed the date because I got stuck on the beach."

He didn't look amused. He straightened up.

"I'm going to go, Brenda," he said. "Before you say anything else. This weekend was fun. We'll do it again. Let's leave it at that."

He was pissed, and I really didn't blame him. But I

panicked. Leave it at that? Maybe never see him again? Never have another montage?

I clung to his car door. "Nick, wait. I did this all wrong. I should have told you the truth, but I wanted you to like me. I was too embarrassed to tell you what was really going on. I'll throw Larry out. I just needed him to get David out of jail."

He gazed at me steadily. "OK."

"No, not OK. Larry is an interfering, nosy pain in the ass, but he has connections, lots of connections. I knew that if anyone could get David free, it would be Larry, much as I hate him."

"OK," he said again, still way too calm. "You asked him to help you out. He did. You don't have to explain."

"Yes, I do. I didn't sleep with him, if that's what is worrying you."

His mouth tightened. "I never said that."

My heart started racing again as I realized I was digging the pit deeper and deeper. "I'm finished with him, Nick. He's my ex with a capital X. I loathe him. I despise him. He is excrement." I ground my heel into the pavement like I was crushing a bug.

"I didn't think you'd gone back to him," he said mildly.

"I mean, I've—" I stopped, looked at him. "You didn't?"

"No."

"Oh." My heart warmed. "Why not?"

"I'm hoping you have much better taste."

"I do," I said fervently. "I do, Nick. Much better taste than to go running back to him."

"Besides, you're not very good at being sneaky."

"No." I broke off, affronted. "What do you mean, I'm not very good at it?"

The ghost of a smile touched his lips. "When you don't want a guy to catch you leaving him underwear, you should drive away, not ring the doorbell three times."

"Well, if you would have looked in the mailbox." I stopped and blew out my breath. "Never mind. Does this mean you're not mad at me?"

"I didn't say that, either."

"So you are mad."

"Yes, but I plan to get over it."

My hope held on. I already liked him much better than I'd ever liked Larry. When Larry got angry, he shouted and raged and blamed me. Nick was trying to remain reasonable. He was having a hard time with it, because I was truly an idiot, but he was trying.

I said softly, "I'll never go back to him, Nick. Never. I'm not that stupid. And I really, really want to be with you." I hefted my bag. "See? I packed."

Nick looked at the bag and looked at me.

Suddenly he seized my shoulders and pulled me close. His breath was hot on my face, and the bag was squished between us.

"I want you bad, Brenda," he said hoarsely. "But I want you all to myself. No brother, no ex-boyfriend. You take some time to figure out what you want to do, then you call me, OK? When you're ready."

He kissed me. His lips bruised mine. I loved it.

He let me go. I gently probed my scraped lip with my tongue. My heart beat fast, and my insides performed lustful cartwheels.

"Nick," I started. "I—"

He put his fingers over my lips. Just the heat of his hand made me melt. "No. Don't say another word. You decide what you want. I won't decide for you."

I stared at him, dazed. I nodded.

He brushed his lips across mine one more time; then he got into his car. He closed the door. He started the engine.

Through the open window he said, "I'll be waiting by the phone."

I nodded, hugging my bag to my chest.

Sure, I'd take time to find myself or whatever. In the meantime, I'd imagine him kissing me like that again and touching me all over, turning the lustful cartwheels to full-out flips.

I'd be calling him in ten minutes.

I watched him back out and drive away. The red convertible flashed as he pulled into traffic, and was gone.

By the time I got back up to my apartment, Clarissa had finished her shower. She was sitting on the couch with a big towel wrapped around her slender frame and another towel turbaned over her hair. She was filing her nails and seemed oblivious to the fact that Larry was still there.

"Will you get out?" I demanded of him. I dumped my bag in the corner.

"Not until I talk to you. Will you sit still and listen?"

"No!" I plopped down on the couch, but only because I didn't want to stand next to him. "I'm tired of you, I'm tired of your lectures, I'm tired of hearing your voice. You chose to walk out of my life, so why don't you stay out? You only came back because whatever chick you dated after me got wise and dumped you."

"You're wrong about that," Larry said angrily. "I broke up with her."

Ha. That had been a stab in the dark, but I felt pleased that I'd guessed right. "Really? Then you only came back to me because—OK, I have no idea. But I don't want you back. Get that through your head."

Clarissa's thin murmur broke in. "Your mom owns prime property."

Her voice was so soft that both Larry and I turned to stare at her.

"What?" I screwed up my face, trying to figure out why she was dropping in that particular non sequitur.

"Your mom's house is worth a lot of money," Clarissa said patiently, as though explaining to children. "David told me that Larry thinks your mom should move into a smaller place, maybe a condo, and sell the house to Larry. Because she's a bereaved widow who doesn't want to live with the memories, right, Larry?" She gave Larry a little smile.

Larry huffed. "So what? I'm only trying to help out. Brenda's mom could realize a good profit."

Clarissa concentrated on her nails again. "Except that the amount you told David you'd pay is like five times less than what the house is worth. I have a friend who's a realtor. She says that Brenda's mom's house is worth a couple million now. You'd buy it from Brenda's mom for a song, telling her that she'd have to do too many repairs to get a higher price. Then you'd get some contractor friends to renovate it cheap and turn around and sell it for two million. Reaping yourself about a million or so in the process."

My mouth went dry. My mother's house was worth two million dollars? Well, it was up on that hill overlooking the Pacific, a neighborhood that had grown from nothing to being coveted by millionaires and movie stars.

I wondered what the millionaires and movie stars thought about my mom's new boyfriend.

I folded my arms. "Yeah, that sounds like Larry. Did you think my brother would be too stupid to check you out, Larry? Or did you think you'd make me fall in love with you again so I'd convince my mom to hand it over?"

Larry didn't look ashamed or even mad that he'd been found out. "You don't know everything," he said to Clarissa, who went on buffing her nails. "It doesn't matter if I'd make money on the deal. I still want to help

Brenda's mom out. She can't be happy living there, and she'd at least get a good half million for it."

"My mother seems like she's having a great time," I informed him.

"Oh, yeah, with a guy half her age, you told me. A guy who's probably after her money. At least I didn't try to sleep with her for it."

"Maybe he just likes her," I said hotly.

"Sure, Brenda. What guy my age goes out with a woman your mom's age? It's disgusting."

I sprang up. "My mother is not disgusting!"

"Don't be stupid, I didn't say that."

I marched to the door, opened it. "Get out, Larry. Now."

I wondered how I ever thought him good looking. His face was twisted with rage and superiority, and his eyes were cold. I must have mistaken good grooming for good looks.

"Brenda," he began.

"Yeah, get out, Larry," Clarissa said languidly. "We don't want you here."

"She lives here, too," I told him. "So she has a say in who stays or goes."

"Don't give me that. I got her out of jail, you know."

Clarissa shook her head. "No, you didn't. My friends did."

I said, "What?"

She inspected the cuticle of one pristine nail. "When they finally let me near a phone, I called a friend. He's a judge, and he's friends with a judge in Tijuana. The Tijuana judge got the case dropped."

I gaped in surprise, then swung on Larry. "Ha!"

Larry turned purple. He probably *had* called half his contacts in Tijuana, but I bet that by the time Larry's friends had contacted the police, David and Clarissa had already been free.

"Ha!" I screamed again, though I know I sounded stupid. "Nyah nyah nyah nyah nyah."

He glared at me. "Don't be so childish."

But he finally left. He stomped out the door, and I slammed it good and hard.

"What's going on?"

David sauntered out of the bathroom, also wearing nothing but a towel. I started to feel overdressed.

"We just threw Larry out," Clarissa said. She smiled at him.

David smiled back. "Good. He's such a jerk."

They were so happy together, the jailbirds in their towels.

I left them alone and ran to take my own shower. I scrubbed off the smells of David and the jail, as well as the smarmy feeling I'd gotten from riding in Larry's car. I had to scrub long and hard before I felt clean again.

I dragged myself through that week. I wanted to call Nick at least fifty times, but I was afraid of pushing him too hard and too soon. Or I'd say something *really* stupid, and Nick would hang up and never talk to me again.

I wanted to go very, very carefully here and not screw up what I had before it even got started. My budding relationship with Nick was new and fragile and so easily broken.

I directed my fury at Larry. I was furious with him for trying to use my family to make himself more money. He'd played David, who was feeling low after the fiasco with his wife. Actually, I was proud of David for resisting Larry. David needed money badly and Larry had probably offered him a cut.

I was furious with Larry for trying to play me, too. *Poor, lonely Brenda*, he must have thought. *I'll offer to marry her, and she'll be so dazzled, she'll let me do anything.*

But Larry didn't know that Brenda had changed.

Brenda was now spontaneous, fun, and crazy. Wasn't she? Nick liked her.

To reinforce that Brenda, I went to Lili Duoma and bought three new camisoles, a half dozen pair of sexy stockings, and a new garter belt.

I was also furious at Larry for implying that my mother was old and used up. She was only fifty-three, for crying out loud, and she was very pretty. She had a charming and sweet personality. I loved her.

I started crying when I thought about that. Tony Beale came up behind me in the studio.

"What are you crying for, Brenda?"

I reached for a tissue. "I love my mother."

"Aw," Tony said. "Ain't that sweet?" He glared at me. "That has nothing to do with the show!"

I sniffled. "Shut up, Tony."

He rolled his eyes. "Whatever."

He was already mad at me because I didn't want to do Nick and Brenda. "You have to do Nick and Brenda!" he had screamed when I came in Tuesday morning. "The accounts all want Nick and Brenda. You have to do Nick and Brenda."

"No," I said firmly. "Not this week. People are sick of it anyway, you said. Put me in the shark tank with Tim. I'll do that."

A few hours swimming with sharks wouldn't be half so bad as my pain over Nick. Not even if one of them bit me.

Tim, next to me, had gone pale. "Oh, no. No more sharks."

"Sheesh," said Tony. "I don't know why I don't fire you two losers."

"Because you love us," I said, making a mock kissing noise. Tony rolled his eyes and stormed off.

All week, Tim and I played songs and took phone calls and talked about what was going on in the city. We didn't talk about Nick and Brenda, and we lost one or two advertisers as the week progressed. Now it was Tony's turn to cry.

By Thursday, I was missing Nick bad.

I wanted to do things with him I'd never wanted to do with Larry. And I don't mean the fabulous sex—although that didn't hurt. I wanted to be able to call him for no reason and have him think it was great that I called. I wanted to buy him presents and let him cook for me. I wanted to go away for weekends with him and find those flower-strewn meadows.

I'd backed off long enough. Hadn't I?

Thursday afternoon, I went home, shut myself in my bedroom, and called Nick.

As I listened to the phone ring, my heart bumped and thumped. What if he didn't answer? Should I leave a message? What kind of message? Or should I just hang up? I'd probably not hang up fast enough, and I'd treat him to a few seconds of panicked, heavy breathing. He'd think he had a stalker.

Speaking of stalkers, the guy in the dirty white Toyota showed up again. But he still didn't seem very interested in me. I didn't get it. If he was a stalker, he wasn't doing it right. Or maybe he was following Clarissa. She was just weird enough to have one of her strange friends following her around. Well, I'd warn her and keep my eye on him.

Nick answered the phone. I froze.

"Hello?" he said again.

I knew that in another second, he'd hang up. "Nick?" I croaked.

"Brenda," he said. It was not a question.

"Don't hang up."

"Ok." He sounded surprised that I'd assumed he would.

I held onto the phone in both hands. "Um, while I'm

taking time and figuring out what I really want, can we maybe have dinner? Tonight?" I paused. "Don't say no."

He chuckled. I lay down on the bed and let the warmth of his laughter flow over me. I love men's voices. So deep, so rich. Yum.

"If you already decided what you want me to say, why are you asking me?" he said.

"I mean, don't say no right away. Give it some thought."

"Yes."

"I mean—" I gulped. "What?"

"I said, yes, I'll have dinner with you."

"Oh."

"Why do you sound so disappointed?"

I wiggled on the bed, happy to listen to his voice and wishing he were lying next to me. "I thought I'd have to talk you into it. I had all these arguments ready."

"Like what?" I could hear the smile in his question.

I'd planned to describe the lingerie I would dazzle him with, or things we could do in bed. I really wanted to see him. I'd given up being proud.

"Never mind," I said quickly. "You've already said yes."

"Tonio's?" He suggested, naming the scene of our misbegotten date and the hunks on the bathroom wall.

"OK," I said hesitantly.

"Pick you up?" he offered.

"No," I said. "I'll pick you up."

He waited another minute. I closed my eyes, willing him not to change his mind.

"All right," he said at last.

I told him seven and didn't ask if that was OK. I didn't want to give him any more chances to say no.

I hung up, then spent the next three hours deciding what to wear.

15

Why Flashing at a Restaurant Is Not Always a Bad Thing

It's not easy to decide what to wear on a date with a man who isn't sure he wants to see you any more. It's a delicate decision-making process. I stripped down to my underwear (La Perla slip and cami over silk bikinis) and tried on dress after dress.

Some were too frumpy, some too trashy, some too girly, some not girly enough. After an hour and a half, all my clothes lay limp on the bed, the silhouettes of fashions that didn't make the cut.

Finally I stripped off my underwear as well and tried on lingerie, deciding that what I wore underneath would determine what I'd wear on top.

I pulled on a sheer black body stocking, one that covered me from neck to toes, but was very sexy, if I did say so myself. Over that went a one-piece dress with slits up the sides, cut low to show off generous amounts of the body stocking.

I did a 360 in front of the mirror and sauntered confidently out to my car. In the parking lot I did a 180, ran back to my apartment, slammed the door to my bedroom shut behind me, and ripped everything off.

I scooped up a bustier I'd discarded earlier. It was rust-colored with lacing that pushed my breasts high, making me look like I actually had cleavage.

Over this I slipped on a black dress that zipped up the front. I tugged on thigh-high stockings that had elastic to keep them up and ran out into the living room with black high-heels in hand.

"Are you going out, Brenda?" Clarissa said in her sleepy voice. She was in the kitchen dishing up her meal of a candy bar. "With Nick?"

"Yes," I said. I hopped on one foot, trying to stick a shoe on the other. "Don't wait up."

"I won't." She took a bite of chocolate and coconut. "I'll take David out for a cheeseburger."

I glanced around the quiet apartment. "Where is David?"

"Job hunting," she said. "He won't find one."

I scowled. "Why do you say that? He's smart, he graduated with honors, he's worked his way up the ranks in a big company—"

"I know, but he's too upset. He needs to chill for a while, figure out what he really wants."

I snorted. "What's he supposed to live on while he's figuring out what he really wants?"

Clarissa shrugged. "He sleeps on our couch, and I take him out for cheeseburgers."

She had a point. I said, "Don't get thrown in jail this time, all right?"

"OK," she answered, her face straight.

169

I shut the door.

When I pulled up in front of Nick's house, my heart was pounding, and I was panting and puffing. Ok, Brenda, I told myself. Stay calm. It's only a date.

Mrs. Pankhurst across the street was sweeping her front walk. I waved to her. She leaned on her broom handle and stared back at me.

I wondered if she was thinking, *Oh, look, there's that tart that spent the weekend with Nick. He'd better watch out for her.*

I knocked on the door. Nick answered right away, which meant he'd been watching for me. He looked me up and down, his expression neutral.

I cringed. I knew I shouldn't have changed out of the body stocking. A body stocking said *sexy and quietly alluring*. The bustier pushed my breasts to my chin and screamed *slut*.

Nick didn't say anything. We walked out to the car together. Nick waved to Mrs. Pankhurst. She immediately waved back.

On the way downtown, we listened to the radio—by silent consent, neither of the stations we worked for. The passionate strains of "Rescue Me" accompanied us through the crush of traffic on Harbor Boulevard and into the cavern of downtown.

Tonio's was fairly empty. It was Thursday night, and the tourists wouldn't crowd us out until summer. I over-tipped a guy who turned out to be a busboy to get us a secluded table in the back.

Instead of a tired waitress, we got a smooth-talking waiter, who told us the specials like he was reciting a Shakespearean sonnet. I ordered the walnut and gorgonzola salad, and Nick had some kind of exotic chicken dish.

We didn't have much to say to each other. I felt awkward, but consoled myself by looking at him. His shoulders and chest stretched out his button-up shirt in an enticing way. His collar had folded in on one edge, and I wished I could be the woman privileged enough to straighten it for him.

We ate in silence except for comments on how good the food was. After I finished my salad, I headed to the bathroom, because I'd drunk way too many glasses of water trying to fill the quiet between us.

I eyed Stefano over the towel holder. His oiled Italian biceps bulged, but he no longer looked as good to me. I'd seen Nick's biceps. They were every bit as good as Stefano's, and the bonus was, Nick was real. I could run my hands over his skin and feel his warmth and feel him touching me back.

When I returned to the table, the waiter asked us if we wanted dessert. I turned him down, but Nick ordered the tiramisu and offered me half.

I scooped up the lady fingers and mascarpone cheese laden with rum and sucked it off my fork. I loved tiramisu, but hadn't wanted to look like a pig. Maybe Nick liked women who ate like birds.

Then again, have you ever watched birds eat? I used to have a feeder on my balcony. One sparrow would gobble every bit of the seed, chasing away all other birds but his girlfriend. And look at pigeons. I'm surprised they can still fly.

With this interesting debate raging in my head, I missed that Nick had said something to me.

"Huh?" So elegant, was Brenda.

"I asked if your brother was OK. After having spent two days in jail."

"He's fine." I cleaned my fork with my tongue. "Actually, he seems better than usual. I thought he'd be depressed, but he seems reenergized. He's back out there looking for a job."

"Good." He sounded glad, as if he actually cared. "Would he be interested in doing anything in radio?"

I laughed. "David says that people in radio are nerds who never grew up and don't know how to." I looked at his face. "Oh, sorry."

"I think David's right," Nick said.

"You do?"

"Sure," he answered. "I pretend to be responsible and adult, but inside, I still want to be a kid."

"You think that about me, too?"

"Yes."

I huffed. He smiled. God, I loved his smile. His mouth creased in the corner, almost a dimple. "That's why I like you," he said. Something tingled inside me.

I was glad he was sympathetic with David, but I was a little irritated that he said I still wanted to be a kid. I'd hated being a kid. Awkward, redheaded Brenda had been picked on and laughed at—that is, when she wasn't being overlooked.

"I know why you like me," I said, wild Brenda taking over.

His smile deepened. "Why?"

I put my finger on the zipper of my dress and drew it gently downward.

OK, so my back was to the rest of the restaurant, we were in a dark corner, and no one sat at the tables around us. The waiter and busboy were nowhere in sight.

Nick's eyes widened. "What are you doing?"

"Reminding you why you like me." The zipper went down, slowly, slowly. My bustier, lacy and pretty, came into view.

Nick was a man. He proved it by being unable to wrench his gaze from the bustier and my breasts curving over it.

"Brenda," he said, his voice strangled.

I smiled. I slowly worked the zipper up again.

"Would madam care for more water?"

I jumped half out of my seat. The waiter hovered at my elbow, a dripping pitcher in his hand.

I gulped. I turned beet red. "Sure."

He poured. Before he pivoted and glided away, he winked at me.

I turned to Nick in frozen horror. I expected him to glare at me, to tell me I was too embarrassing to be around. He'd jump up and stalk off, sticking me with the bill.

Nick had his napkin pressed to his face, and he was shaking all over.

I glared at him. He put his elbows on the table and snorted. I said scathingly, "You could have warned me he was coming."

"Didn't have a chance." He gasped for breath, reaching for his own water. "I bet we get great service the rest of the night. God, you're beautiful."

I squirmed a little under his attention. His eyes were hot and blue, his smile like bright sunshine.

Nick was right: the waiter was very attentive. He even brought us chocolate-covered strawberries on the house and took a little off the bill. On the way out, he patted Nick on the arm as if to say, "Way to go, boy!"

I blushed hard as we walked out and made our way to my car.

As I pulled away from the curb, I noticed a dirty white Toyota not far away. It was empty, and I couldn't tell as I drove past whether it was the same car I'd seen before. My incompetent stalker again? Or just another white Toyota that needed a wash?

We still didn't have much to say to each other, Nick and I, as we drove back around the bay to Point Loma. A few clouds obscured the moon, but the night was pleasant enough.

Mrs. Pankhurst had finished sweeping her walk by the time we got back. Now she was sitting in an Adirondack chair on her lawn. Looking at the stars, was she?

Nick took my hand and started pulling me across the street. "Come on," he said.

I dug my heels in. "What for?"

"Let's get it over with."

I let him persuade me. We climbed the curb to Mrs. Pankhurst's front walk. Nick lifted his hand in greeting. "Hi, Mrs. Pankhurst."

She got up. She glanced sharply at me, but when she looked back at Nick, her expression softened. "Nicky," she said. "How are you?"

"I'm fine, Mrs. Pankhurst. This is Brenda Scott, my girlfriend. Maybe you've heard her on the radio."

"No," Mrs. Pankhurst said. She held out her hand for me to shake anyway, then pulled it back almost as soon as we'd touched.

She was a smallish woman in her sixties, still retaining the plumpness of her younger years. Her house was genteel crumbling pink stucco with bougainvillea and roses growing all over it.

She looked genteel and slightly crumbling herself, an elegant woman slowly fading, but down-to-earth. She swept her walk and sat in the front yard because she wanted to, not because she had nothing else to do.

Keeping an eye on Nick must have been entertaining, as well.

"She's on KCLP," Nick went on, blithely ignoring the curious stare the woman gave me. "She's very popular."

"Is that so?"

Nick grinned as though she'd paid me a compliment. "That's so. Good night, Mrs. Pankhurst."

"Good night, Nicky." She looked back at me, forced out some manners. "Good night, Miss Scott." She emphasized *Miss*.

No one had ever called me "Miss Scott" before. No one said "Miss" any more, did they?

Nick and I walked back across the street hand in hand. A breeze wafted up the hill below his house, bringing scented, slightly humid air from the ocean.

"She doesn't like me," I said as Nick led me through the courtyard and unlocked the door.

Nick glanced back through the gate to Mrs. Pankhurst's front yard. She had resumed her seat in the Adirondack chair. "Her bark's worse than her bite," he said. "I've known her forever."

"She knows what we do in here," I said darkly.

Nick opened the door and ushered me in. "We're grown-ups, Brenda. What do you think she's going to do?"

I wasn't sure. She'd probably tell her friends up and down the street and at her bridge club. Somehow this network would work around the coast and up the hill to my mom.

My mom, who was sleeping with a thirty-five-year-old man in red bikini briefs. The world was upside down from where it was supposed to be.

The house was dark. I wandered into the living room and looked out the windows. Clouds no longer blocked the moon which reflected on the distant sea, stretching a path of white light to the horizon. The tiny sparks of fishing boats and naval vessels floated in the darkness.

Nick put his arms around me from behind and rested his cheek against mine.

"It's beautiful here," I murmured.

And so peaceful. No Clarissa and her weird friends, no David complaining about his life, no Tony Beale and his crazy schemes, no Larry calling to accuse me of being a slut. Just me and Nick and the pretty night.

OK, and Mrs. Pankhurst in her yard across the street. I wondered if she'd gotten out her binoculars so she could peer through Nick's windows.

But I still felt the peace of the place, the contentment.

Nick had been happy here. I could feel it. The whole house had been saturated in happiness.

"I should resist you, Brenda," he whispered, his breath hot on my skin. "I really should."

"No, you shouldn't," I said, smiling in the dark.

"I should," he repeated. "But I can't."

He slid down the zipper that I'd so brazenly lowered at Tonio's and slipped his hand inside my dress.

His touch was warm through the bustier. He cupped my breast in his hand and kissed my neck, his hair silken against my skin.

I knew right then that I was truly in love. This had nothing to do with comparing Nick to Mr. Perfect. I wanted Nick, and Nick was all I wanted. The photo in my mind of perfect Larry Bryant crumpled and burned, reducing itself to ash.

I wanted to kiss Nick, and kiss him and kiss him. I turned around in his arms, pulled his head down to mine.

Our mouths met and met again. Heroines in romance novels had nothing on me. They were too busy fighting off pirates. I got to stand in Nick's living room and kiss him.

He smelled like garlic and tiramisu, and I tasted rum and chocolate on his tongue. He kissed me slowly, leisurely, as if we had all night.

I suppose we did. But I was impatient. Something in me feared that if I didn't get him into bed in the next ten minutes, he'd shove me out the door. There I'd be on his doorstep, hot and horny with my heart ripping in two, while Mrs. Pankhurst watched me through her binoculars.

I grabbed the waistband of his pants and started frantically unbuttoning and unzipping. He started to say something, but before he could, I yanked down his pants and his underwear. There he was, all bare and warm.

I sank my fingers into his tight buns and kissed him again. His legs, strong with muscle, pressed into mine.

"Brenda," he said, laughter in his voice. "Slow down."

"Can't," I said.

"You going somewhere?"

"No."

I slid my hand between his legs. His balls were warm and taut against my palm. He made a raw sound.

I moved to his shaft and drew my fingers along it. I found the tip and lightly circled the flange. His eyes half closed, he studied me with a gleam of heat.

"I don't think we'll make it upstairs," he murmured.

"That's fine," I said.

He slid my dress from my arms, then unlaced the bustier with clumsy fingers, pushing it down to free my breasts. I was holding onto his hips as though we'd fall if I let go. He gently pried my hands away and lowered himself to his knees as he pulled the bustier all the way down.

His tongue flicked my navel, brushed across my abdomen. I laced my fingers in his hair and stifled a groan.

He slid the bustier from my body, then took off my panties. I stood there in nothing but my thigh-high stockings and shoes while his tongue played between my legs.

I was a bad, bad girl. But nothing had ever felt so heavenly as Nick's tongue dipping into me. I felt hot and sexy and excited.

I was going to come right there. I didn't want to. I wanted to save it for when he was inside me. My body, on the other hand, didn't really care what I wanted. I screamed out loud, closing my fingers on his sleek hair.

He kept licking me. It was pure torture. I screamed

again and told him how much I wanted him, how I wanted him inside me. The words *I love you* might have come out of my mouth, but if they did, he didn't seem to notice.

By the time he laid me down on the floor, I was sobbing in joy. "Shh," he said, stroking my hair.

"I hate you," I whispered. "Why do you make me feel like this?"

He smiled and kissed my face. He lay full-length on top of me, his warm, damp skin on mine. He fumbled with a condom, which he produced from somewhere, probably when I was busy screaming. Then, with one hand, he parted my legs and pushed himself inside me.

I arched and bumped against the floor, trying to get as much of him into me as I could. He kissed me. I lifted my legs and wrapped my ankles, my feet still in heels, around his back.

I'd never had sex like this before. This was crazy; this was new; feelings swept over me until I was drowning.

Nick pumped inside me, his face tight with concentration. When he came, his back got slick with sweat and so did his face. Sweat beaded under his eyes, around his lips, on his eyelashes. He kissed me, probing every inch of my mouth with his tongue.

I unwound my legs, pretty sure he'd have marks embedded in his back. He kept kissing me, still inside me, and I lay there and enjoyed it.

He buried his face in my neck and held onto me. I amused myself by tracing his firm biceps around to his triceps and up the backs of his arms to his shoulders. His body was beautiful. My fingers moved down his shoulder blades and the tight muscles of his spine to the slight indentations above his hips.

He raised up on his elbows, and I thought he was going to say something, but he just looked at me. His gaze roved my face.

"What?" I whispered.

He kept searching me with his gaze, as though he was studying every inch of me that he could see. His eyes were warm. "We should go upstairs," he murmured. "It's getting cold."

The cool night air must have been chilly against his sweat. I was perfectly warm and happy with him on top of me. The carpet was prickly, but I didn't care.

"OK," I said. I wrapped my arms around his neck and kissed him.

He gave a little laugh when he broke the kiss. He got off me and stood up, then reached down and pulled me to my feet. He held me for a little bit, then he bent over and gathered up our clothes, while I admired the view.

Naked and unembarrassed, he carried the clothes and led me up the stairs to his bedroom, where we made love again on his bed. After that, he wrapped me in sheets and snuggled down beside me.

16

Format Change at KCLP

This is what happiness feels like, I thought. Lying here in the cool dark with Nick's warmth next to me, his arm heavy across my waist. The night was quiet, and I had nowhere else I wanted to be.

"What are we going to do with you, Brenda?" Nick murmured.

"Mmm." I kissed his ear. "Why do we need to do anything about me?"

"You make me crazy," he said. "I never know what's really up with you."

"Is that bad?"

"I should tell you to go and never see you again."

I held him tighter. "Let me stay. I brought a change of clothes this time. And a toothbrush."

He chuckled. "I have no intention of letting you go. That's what I mean. I can't trust myself around you."

I wondered, when he went to work tomorrow and wasn't around me, what he'd decide. Would he take the not trusting himself thing seriously, and convince himself not to see me again?

I held him a little tighter. "I don't know. You seem calm, levelheaded, sensible."

"Not about you."

I turned my head to look at him nose to nose. I was limp and exhausted by lovemaking and my own feelings. "I'm just a girl who likes you. Nothing wrong at all."

"I'm calm, levelheaded, and sensible until I'm with you." He touched the tip of my nose. "And then everything gets crazy. I've always been good—you know, I'm the nice boy who remembers his mother's birthday, doesn't drink too much, and drives the speed limit."

I laughed. "Then how did you end up a DJ?"

"By working hard and not screwing up. I always show up to work on time, I never say anything controversial, I don't mess up. I'm so anal."

I raised up on my elbow. The sheet covered him to the middle of his abdomen, and I covertly studied the planes of his pectorals and shoulders. "What are you talking about, never say anything controversial? You wooed me on the air!"

"That wasn't controversial. I played the ads exactly on time and brought good publicity to the station."

My heart burned. "Is that the only reason you did it?"

"It was one reason."

"Oh. Thanks."

"Not the only reason," he said, but the little hurt in my heart didn't go away. "But I never would have dreamed of talking about my personal life on the air before I met you. Before you dragged me out to your father's boat and started undressing in front of me."

I swallowed. "I was afraid that if we just talked that night, you wouldn't like me."

"You're kidding, right? And then you bought me edible underwear."

"Which is still out in my car," I said, realizing. "Probably stuck under a seat."

"Never mind," he said with his half smile. "It's the thought that counts."

I settled back down, but I was a tad uneasy. "If I make you so insane, why did you agree to go out with me tonight?"

"Mmm. I can't resist you."

"Good. I thought you were really mad at me."

"I was."

I bit my lip. His eyes were still and dark. "Are you still mad at me?" I asked in a small voice.

He stroked my hair. "I told you I'd get over it. But yeah, I was crazy jealous when I saw your ex-boyfriend come out of your bedroom. And more when you told me you'd let him help you. That day when you called me, I knew something was wrong, and I was mad that you didn't tell me the truth."

I rubbed my arms. "I didn't want to hit you with my dysfunctional family too soon. At all, actually."

"You didn't think I could help you," he said. "Or that I'd even want to. That kind of burned."

"Really?" I asked nervously. "You seemed calm."

The point between Nick's brows creased in a cute way. "I wasn't calm. I was ready to beat Larry up right there."

"Oh, good." I smiled. "I mean, would you really?"

"Sure. See? You turn me into a crazy man."

I lay my head on his warm, broad shoulder. "That's nice."

"I haven't wanted to beat up a guy since I was fifteen."

I drew my fingers along the inside of his arm. "How did you woo girls when you were fifteen? Beat up their boyfriends?"

"No." He laughed a little. "I carried book bags and opened doors."

"Did it work?" I asked.

"Like a charm."

I bet he was charming then, even as a gangly and awkward teenager. He was certainly charming now. Not to mention *not* gangly and awkward. He had a body that could get a girl wet in two seconds.

"Well, you don't have to beat Larry up," I said. "Unless you really want to. He's out of my life."

He ran his hand through my tangled hair. "You're getting my hopes up."

"Hopes of what?" I asked.

"That you're all mine."

He stroked my hair again, languidly, then his touch gradually stilled.

"I am," I whispered.

I waited a while to gather my courage. "In fact," I went on softly, "I love you."

Nick said nothing. I lay quietly, wondering if I'd said the wrong thing. Would he tell me to leave, or would he gather me up and kiss me and say, "I love you too, Brenda?"

Silence filled the room. At last I lifted my head and looked at him.

Nick's eyes were closed. He lay with his head pillowed on his bent arm. His face was relaxed, his eyelashes resting against his cheek. A soft snore drifted from his mouth.

I gazed at him for a long time. Then I lay back down and snuggled against him, smiling a little.

Nick's alarm clock reminded us again that we were morning drive DJs, so we showered, threw on our clothes, and drove our separate ways to work.

Nick cooked breakfast before we left. He'd thrown together a waffle batter the night before while he waited for me to pick him up. In the morning, while I showered, he grilled the waffles. So I walked into KCLP stuffed with Belgian waffles and whipped cream and strawberries. Going out with Nick was going to make me fat.

Tony sat in the control booth. He looked haggard, circles bagging his already baggy eyes.

"About time you showed up," he said.

I was five minutes early. "Why are you playing The Doors?" I asked. Synthesizer music leaked through the speakers. "I think I can safely say they never did any hip-hop."

Tony stared at me like I'd asked him why we had a roof on the building. "The format changed, Brenda. I told you last week we were doing it today. The babyboomers have the money, and they want the Doors. We were dark all night. Weren't you listening?"

I tossed down my bag. "If we were off the air all night, how could I listen? And no, I was out." OK, he might have mentioned the format change to me last week. Or not. With my mind full of Nick, I never heard him.

Tony got up. Behind the glass, Marty peeled open another candy bar. He and Clarissa should have compared notes.

"So we're classic rock now," Tony said. "Zeppelin, ZZ, Dire Straits."

I patted his arm. "You're in heaven, aren't you, Tony?"

A grin split his face. "Yeah. Back to music I understand, for a change. All these rappers and alternative groups—here today, gone tomorrow. I can't keep track."

"Top Forty radio is stressful, Tony," I said, pretending sympathy. "Do we have any Dirt Band?"

I slid into my seat, picked up the phones. One thing you learn in radio is that change happens, and it happens fast. A flexible DJ is an employed DJ.

"I brought out a whole library," Tony said. He hauled a CD tower over to me. "Go for it."

"What about Bohemian Love Child?" I asked, flipping through the disks.

"Who?"

"They had one hit. Thirty-six years ago. You know, here today, gone tomorrow."

Tony shrugged as if he didn't understand what I was talking about. "Doesn't ring a bell," he said.

The disks were filed alphabetically by band. I skimmed the Bs. Badfinger, Black Sabbath, Blue Öyster Cult, Boston. No Bohemian Love Child. Poor John.

"So where's Tim?" I asked. "Interviewing aging rock stars?"

"I fired Tim."

I glanced up in surprise. "You fired him? Why?"

Tony looked slightly guilty. "Tim's too jumpy. It seemed like every time I walked in the room, he'd either leap out of his chair or scream."

I snatched up a Dirt Band CD. "Well, let's see, you pushed him off a bridge, then you threw him into a tank full of sharks. I'd be jumpy, too."

Tony took on an innocent expression. "He'll be OK, Brenda. He's got a good on-air personality and has lots of experience. He'll find another job."

"You have a lot of heart, Tony." I slid the CD into the slot and turned on my mike. "Hi, San Diego, this is Brenda on the new classic KCLP. If you're awake, Katie and Billy, this one's for you."

I played the track. Tony looked happy. Marty, who was about twenty, looked confused.

The phones started going. Marty put a call through to me. "Hi, KCLP, this is Brenda." The Dirt Band's harmonica wailed in the background.

Nick said, "Hey, Brenda. What are you guys doing over there?"

"Changing format. It happens."

My mouth talked, but my mind whirled with the memory of waking up next to him that morning, his arm wrapped around me, trapping me in the bed while he slept. The sun had just touched the horizon, showing me his bronzed body against the white sheets. Nick was gorgeous when he was asleep.

He wasn't bad awake, either.

"I want to see you again tonight," he said.

I stared at the wall. I could have sworn that he'd just said he wanted to see me again tonight.

"It's Friday," he said. "Neither of us have to get up early tomorrow."

"You're a wild man, Nick. Staying out late on a Friday night."

"I know, what can I say? There's a restaurant I want to take you to. My dad used to own it, and the food is fantastic." He paused. "I'll pick you up this time."

"You're sweeping me off my feet, Nick." He really was; I had to sit down.

"Don't sound so excited. You'll like it." He fixed a pickup time of eight and hung up.

I remained staring at the wall. Tony plucked the phone from my hand and put it down. The song ended, and Tony had to click to the next single. "Brenda."

I jumped. "What?"

"You look all googley-eyed. Like you're twelve years old with your first crush."

I frowned, started flipping through CDs again. "It's not a crush."

"No, you're in looovvvve," he chirped. "When's the wedding?"

"No wedding, Tony."

"Come on, we need a wedding. We'll do the engagement announcement on the air and have a big party. The guests can win free stays in a honeymoon suite or something."

"We've already talked about this," I said angrily. "No way are you turning my relationship with Nick into a radio show from a honeymoon suite."

"Oh, come on, Brenda, it's just an idea. Besides, you owe me. Larry Bryant pulled all his advertising this morning because of you."

I stopped. "Really? How do you know it's because of me?"

"He said, 'I'm pulling all my ads because of Brenda.'"

I spilled half a dozen CDs onto the floor. I leaned over to snatch them up. "I'm really sorry, Tony." I started stuffing CDs back into the tower, out of order. Then I looked at him. "Wait a minute, you don't sound as mad as you could be."

Tony shrugged. "Well, that's because Larry Bryant turned into a minor account. When he was our only major client, I'd have cleaned dog poop off his shoes to keep him on. But we've got so many better accounts now, and Larry was always stingy. So, oh, well."

"Oh, well?" I put my hand on his forehead. "Who are you, and what have you done with Tony?"

"Very funny, Brenda. We don't need him any more, thanks to you."

"Don't thank me," I said. "Thank my brother and Clarissa. And Mexico."

"Huh?"

"Never mind."

Tony gave me a glare, looking more like his old self. "You lose any more accounts, though, Brenda, and it's curtains for you."

"I'm not dating any of our other accounts, so it'll be fine."

Tony got up, drifted toward the door. "It better be." He stopped. "Play some Steppenwolf, will you, Brenda?" He looked at me dreamily. I guess he wanted to reminisce about the good old days.

I played Tony's songs for him and endured the calls of people angry that we'd changed the format. Near the end of my show, John the hippie mechanic called.

"Hey, Brenda, cool. I love the new sound."

I told San Diego, "I have on the phone John Dishard, a member of the sixties band Bohemian Love Child. And I got ahold of their single, 'Black Mothers.' Here it is."

I played the song, which was kind of a folky dirge, all about kids dying in Vietnam. I'd found the song an hour before at the bottom of a box of reel-to-reels that Tony had brought in. I'd asked Marty to stick the reel on an ancient machine lying in a corner of the studio and then burn the song to CD.

John, still on the phone with me, got teary. "Oh, wow, man, that takes me back. Thanks, Brenda. Any time you need your car fixed, you just call me. Gratis."

At least we'd made one person in the city happy.

Another caller wasn't as happy. "Brenda?" came a breathy male voice.

It took me a minute to place it. "Tim?"

"Yeah." He paused a minute, breathing hard.

"You all right?" I asked. "I'm sorry you got fired. Do you want me to ask Nick if they're hiring at KBZ?"

"No," he said in a half whisper. "I'm glad Tony fired me. Now's my chance. I just wanted to warn you. Watch out for sharks." He started laughing, sounding a little crazy.

"Tim, are you sure you're OK?"

"Fine. Fine. Sharks are everywhere, Brenda. And do you know what sharks swim in?"

"Uh. Water?"

"Yes!" He sounded triumphant. The weird laughter came again. "Water. Sharks swim in water. Tell Tony Beale to watch out for sharks! Ha ha ha ha ha ha ha!"

"Tim?" I asked worriedly. "Why don't you take an aspirin and lie down for a while?"

"Beware, Brenda. Beware! Ah ha ha ha ha ha."

188

He hung up the phone, and his laughter cut off abruptly.

I stared at the phone, stared at Marty behind the glass. Marty said in my headphones, "Was that Tim going on about sharks?"

I nodded. Marty shrugged. "He's crazy. Always knew it."

I put down the phone. I jumped when it rang again, but it wasn't Tim, just another caller with a comment about the format change.

I finished my shift, took off, and went out to buy some more lingerie—tiny thongs, buy one, get one half price. I had to keep daring Brenda fed.

At seven fifty-five I was ready, in a black slinky dress with spaghetti straps over a sheer slip, vertically striped black stockings and one of the new thongs.

I paced the living room, waiting for Nick, as nervous as a fifteen-year-old girl on her first date. Not that my first date inspired confidence. I'd gone out with a basketball jock who'd taken me to one of our football games and tried to kiss me under the bleachers. That was fine, but his braces cut my lower lip, and my math teacher caught us and gave us both detention.

Now, a dozen years later, I was all dressed up, and my knees still shook.

David watched me moodily. "Going out to some fancy place, huh?"

I shrugged. "I guess." Nick had said that the food was good, but I didn't know how fancy the restaurant was. I was probably overdressed.

"Clarissa's taking me out for a burger again," David said. "She likes burgers. She lives on them."

"And candy bars," I put in.

Clarissa was in the shower. We heard the water running on the other side of the wall.

189

"Don't make fun of her," David said. "She's really cool."

I stopped. "You like her?"

"Yes. I do." He gave me a quiet look with his blue eyes.

"You're still married, David," I reminded him.

"Not for much longer."

I folded my arms, suddenly chilled. "I know, but they're going to make you fork out enough as it is. Be careful."

David didn't seem to be listening. "Clarissa has such a great attitude. I mean, she takes everything in stride. Anything that happens, even getting arrested, is just an experience to her. Nothing to worry about."

He smiled a little. I'd known Clarissa for a year, so I knew what he meant.

What I hadn't realized was how much David needed to be around someone with just such an attitude. His wife had driven him hard, from what I'd gathered, and had never been satisfied with anything he did, no matter how much money he made.

Clarissa, on the other hand, accepted David as he was. She did that with everybody, which was probably why her friends were so weird. She was friends with everyone from musicians who'd played with Nine Inch Nails to a girl who worked the cash register at the gas station on the corner.

Clarissa didn't care about what a person did or who they knew or how much money they made. She liked people for who they were. And she seemed to like David.

David, no matter how much he drove me crazy, was a good guy. He really did have a generous heart behind his crabbiness. I wasn't sure he and Clarissa would be a good match, but I was glad he'd found a friend.

I saw Nick's convertible pull up in front of the complex and started for the door. I opened it, then turned back. "David," I said, "do you know anyone who drives a white Toyota?"

He looked blank. "No. Why?"

"Just asking," I said. Toyota Man was back.

I left the house, went downstairs, and got into Nick's car. The man in the white Toyota took no notice of me or Nick. He stared up at the building, ignoring me completely. When Nick pulled out into traffic, the Toyota did not follow.

17

Carlos and His Amazing Organic Vegetables

Nick had dressed in nice slacks and a pullover shirt. No coat and tie, but dressy. I looked him over and decided that if he ever did wear a suit, he'd look lickably good.

He'd look good getting out of the suit, too. I pictured him with his coat hanging from his arms, his tie loosened, his shirt half off.

I shivered. *Yum.*

He looked over at me. "You OK?"

I must have been glassy-eyed. "What? Oh, yeah, just fine."

I wiped the drool from my mouth and kept feasting my eyes on him.

Larry had always been buttoned up, every hair in place. Nick wore his shirt with the top two buttons undone, revealing the damp hollow of his throat and the top of his fine masculine chest.

Nick's hair was never perfect, either. I'd seen him comb it and comb it, trying to make it flat on his head, but he never could. Strands would cross and stick out in the back and snake over his forehead. I always wanted to run my hands through it.

Nope, definitely never had this reaction with Larry. When Larry had first gone out with me, I'd been stunned that such a wealthy, perfect man had been interested in me, but after that, the excitement had faded.

I should have known that Larry had only been after my mother's property. No prominent businessman went for a girl with a pointed face and a mop of red hair. He went for a blond, long-legged woman with a cheerleader smile and a brain the size of a walnut.

Nick, on the other hand, wanted *me*. It was a heady feeling.

"I'm fine," I assured him again.

He gave me his half-smile. "Good."

I leaned back against the door and watched him drive. His eyelashes flickered as he kept track of the traffic around him. His hand rested loosely on the wheel, strong tanned fingers adjusting it as we went along. I thought about how those fingers touched me in all my intimate places, and I got all hot and melty.

Nick took us north, then drove off the freeway to La Jolla. As we crested the hill above the town, the twilight blue sea stretched before us to the horizon. Palm trees and pines rose together, black against the sky.

The village of La Jolla is trendy and upscale, a great place to bring a client or someone from out of town you want to impress. The restaurants are hip, the hotels posh, the atmosphere casual.

My mom and I sometimes came up here after our Saturday shopping and ate at a favorite restaurant that overlooked the cove. Only the filthy rich could actually afford to live here; the rest of us drove in from elsewhere, parked our cars, and wandered the streets.

Nick drove to a small restaurant on Girard called Le Grand Bistro, a place I'd walked by before but never been in. The facade was pseudo-Spanish with an arch of brick and artfully crumbling plaster. Inside it was ultramodern, with stark black walls and modern paintings, art deco chairs and tables, and a square fountain in the center.

The tables were full, but the maitre d' beamed as we came in. He gave Nick an enthusiastic handshake and clapped him on the shoulder. "Nicky, how are you? I have your table in the back. I'll tell Carlos you're here."

Nick smiled at the guy as though they were old friends. "This is Brenda," he introduced me.

The maitre d' flashed a smile at me and clasped my hand. "I'm Anthony. Pleased to meet you. If I can get you anything tonight, anything at all, you just let me know."

"Stop drooling, Anthony." Nick slid his arm around my waist. "She's with me."

Anthony gave me a wink, released my hand. "Well, whenever you dump this guy, you find me," he joked. "Your table is this way."

He led us into the darkened dining room. People lifted their heads or swiveled in their chairs to see who had come in. Nick guided me with his hand on the small of my back, his touch a comforting feeling of warmth.

We were halfway across when someone said, "Brenda?"

I knew the voice. My heart sank. Slowly I turned around.

There she was, my mother, all dressed up with her diamond earrings, sharing a table with a suited Jerry Murphy, who looked almost as good as Nick.

I stopped dead. "Mom."

Nick stopped, too. He looked at my mother, interested.

My mother stood up. Jerry stood up next to her. He touched her elbow and put on a polite smile.

Nick became Mr. Charming. "You're Brenda's mother?" he said, since I had gone mute. "It's nice to meet you. I'm Nick Jordan."

My mother took his hand, smiling warmly. "Oh, you're Nick. I've heard you two on the radio. I was hoping I'd get to meet you."

My mouth went dry. Nick's eyes crinkled with his smile. He swiveled his glance to Jerry, and a slight pucker creased his brow.

Jerry held out his hand. "Jerry Murphy." He grinned at Nick, knowing full well Nick was trying to determine the relationship between Jerry and my mom. "I'm Sarah's date," he said.

I wanted to crawl under the table. People around us were looking. They'd been wondering, too.

Nick smiled again. "Lucky man," he said.

My mother blushed. "Stop that. Why don't you two join us?"

I glared at Nick. He glanced at me. I tried to signal him with my eyes, tried to scream into his brain, "No! No!"

If Nick understood the signals, he ignored them. "That would be great. Anthony, would it be OK if we sat with our friends?"

I switched my needlelike gaze to Anthony and silently implored him to tell us that the restaurant would be swallowed into a pit of hell if we didn't sit in our assigned seats.

"Not at all." Anthony drew out a chair with a flourish. "Brenda, there you are. I'll get a bottle of wine for you. On the house."

"Thank you," Nick said.

"No menu for you tonight," Anthony carried on cheerfully. "Carlos is preparing something special for you and your lady. He brought the vegetables in from his farm himself."

"Great," Nick said, rubbing his hands. "I can't wait."

Anthony put napkins on our laps and glided off to greet new customers.

"Carlos was the chef when my father owned this restaurant," Nick explained. "He bought it from my father and made it into something really special. He's an amazing chef."

My mother turned an eager smile on him. "Oh, your family owned it? I love this restaurant. The food is wonderful."

I raised my brows. My mother had never mentioned coming to Le Grand Bistro before tonight. I glanced sideways at Jerry. He wasn't looking at me. He and my mom were both getting their fill of Nick.

The two of them must have sensed they had an ally in Nick. Nick was warm and friendly and charming. I sat there like a stone.

Mom and Jerry and Nick talked. They talked about Nick. They talked about Nick's job at KBZ. They talked about the fact that Nick and I both worked in radio. Jerry talked about his boat business, which had just opened its doors and was doing well.

"Sorry, Nick," Jerry said, putting his arm around my mother's shoulders. "If I advertise with any station but Brenda's, Sarah will kill me."

Nick laughed appropriately. "KCLP's gone classic rock," he replied. "It's smart to stay there. People with boats will be listening."

"The station changed again?" my mother asked me. "Why?"

I shrugged. "Who knows? Every time Tony gets bored, we get a new format."

"Brenda's doing well there," Nick said. He slid his hand under my hair and lightly stroked the base of my neck.

I started blushing. I don't know why. I'd had wild, hot monkey sex with Nick, and I was blushing like this was our first date.

Fortunately the food arrived, so my mom didn't have time to comment on my sudden embarrassment.

Carlos brought the food to us himself. Carlos was squat and sweaty and looked more like a short-order cook in a Mexican restaurant than a four-star chef.

But the man could cook. He served us a salad of greens and raspberries with a touch of vinegar and oil. Next we delighted in a shrimp bisque that was like velvet on the tongue, followed by an entree of a rib roast with lobster butter and shallots, accompanied by steamed organic vegetables, the ones that Carlos had driven in from his farm.

Because my mother and Jerry were with us, they got the special meal, too. And more wine. Nothing was too good for Nicky.

By the time we'd finished the entree, my mother and Jerry and Nick were talking like old friends. I watched them and chewed and tried to enjoy the food Carlos had exquisitely prepared just for us.

"How is David?" my mother asked me at one point.

"David?"

"Your brother," Nick explained to me. "The one who's living in your apartment."

"Oh, that David," I said, trying to be cute and failing. "He's fine. He's job-hunting."

My mother's expression turned worried. "He hasn't found anything yet?"

"No."

My mother continued to look worried. Jerry laid down his fork. "Any time he wants a job, you know, he

197

has one at my business. He did me a lot of favors in Chicago. I'm happy to repay him."

"David doesn't know anything about repairing boats," I pointed out. "He designs computer chips."

"It doesn't matter. I need people. And who knows? I might need some computer chips."

"It's a bad idea," I said in a hard voice.

Jerry shrugged. "Mention it to him. He can come and see me any time."

I could imagine David's face when I told him that Jerry Murphy wanted to offer him a job. David would turn three shades of purple and start shouting. My dad used to do that. David took after him.

When the ever-hovering bus boys took away our plates, my mother stood up. Jerry and Nick, the perfect gentlemen, hopped to their feet.

"I'm going to visit the ladies' room," Mom said. "Brenda, come with me."

I didn't want to. I wanted to hold onto the table and stay there. I did not want any one-on-one time with my mother, even in a restaurant restroom.

Jerry and Nick looked down at me, waiting for my answer. My mother picked up her purse, waiting, too.

I sighed, threw down my napkin, and stood up. Nick steadied me by my elbow as I slid out from behind the table. I threw him a dark look and followed my mother to the back of the restaurant and to the bathroom.

The ladies' room was as chic as the rest of the restaurant. A low, black-upholstered lounge sat along a wall across from a lighted vanity. The stalls were wallpapered in blue moiré, and the automatic sinks had folded washcloths with which patrons could dry their hands. No paper towel machines for Le Grand Bistro.

A few ladies lingered at the sinks, talking, brushing their hair, reapplying their makeup. I was happy to see them. While my mother went to the stalls, I sat down on the lounge and picked up one of the fashion magazines thoughtfully placed on the table next to it.

I flipped through it, ignoring the chatting ladies who were going on about a vacation in some sun-drenched village on the Italian coast.

My last vacation had been to a hole-in-the-wall hotel in Las Vegas, courtesy of Tony Beale, who'd finagled a trip from a discount travel agent in return for free ads. At the last minute, he couldn't go, so he gave the trip to me by process of elimination—meaning no one else at the station wanted to go. So I spent a weekend in a place with threadbare sheets, sandpaper toilet paper, and smoky air. It had taken me two weeks to wash the smell out of my clothes when I got home.

Lili Duoma had a full-page ad in the magazine opposite an article about a celebrity's beautiful house in Rancho Santa Fe. In the ad, a young woman clad in nothing but a see-through half-slip and four-inch-high heels hung upside down over a chair. Her long legs were draped artfully over the chair seat.

I suppose she was trying to be sexy. Maybe a man would think she was sexy. I thought she looked like a spider who'd landed on her back and couldn't get up.

I turned the page. My mother came out and washed her hands. The two chattering ladies departed, one saying, "Oh, you have *got* to go. We had breakfast every morning on the terrace—it was *so* beautiful."

My mother dried her hands on one of the towels and came out to the lounge. We were alone.

"Ready?" I said, springing to my feet.

"Brenda." My mother stopped in front of me, her arms folded. She didn't want to go anywhere.

I had to admit, my mother was looking better than she had in a long time. I'd always thought she was pretty, and she still was. She'd gotten her hair highlighted to put more of the red back in, and she wore makeup artfully applied so she didn't look made up at all. She looked nice. I wanted to tell her that, but I couldn't.

I tossed the magazine to the table. "Mom, I really don't want to talk about it right now."

"Well, I do."

I sighed.

"Don't act like a teenager, Brenda," she said. "We're both grown-ups. Jerry is very special to me. I want you to get used to that."

I swallowed. "I know you like him, but—" I'd been thinking about Mr. Perfect and his deceitful ways. "But how do you know Jerry isn't after you for your money? Your house is worth two million dollars. He might convince you to marry him so that he can get his hands on it."

My mother fixed me with a steely gaze. "Is it so hard to believe he's going out with me because he likes me? I know you and David think I'm a stupid old woman, so gullible and lonely that I'll let any smooth-talking man slide into my life."

"We don't think that," I said hotly. Well, maybe David did. He was acting like he thought that.

Mom ignored me. "Well, I'm not stupid. I'm flattered that Jerry likes me, but he likes me. And I'm not rushing into marriage, I'm just enjoying myself." She smiled a little. "Besides, I've always wanted a boy toy."

My face heated. *"Mom!"*

"Well, what about you?" my mother countered. "Don't tell me you're going out with Nick only for his personality. His nice butt has nothing to do with it, I suppose?"

"Mom, please don't talk about my boyfriend's butt."

"Oh, so you noticed it, did you? If you want to know, I'm glad you're seeing him and not Larry. Nick is a nice boy."

"The *boy* is only about five years younger than your boyfriend," I pointed out.

"At least you acknowledge he's my boyfriend."

I dug my fingers into my face. "This is all just so weird. Doesn't anyone get that but me?"

My mom and I are the same height. Her hair is red and curly like mine, her eyes just as blue.

"Of course it's weird," she said calmly. "It's the weirdest thing that ever happened to me—a sexy, good-looking man actually likes being with me. I married your father when I was very young, Brenda. I was twenty years old. He was the first man I ever had a serious relationship with. The only man."

Meaning he was the only one she'd ever slept with. She must have been sweet and virginal at twenty, ready to get married, because that's what nice girls did.

"I got pregnant almost immediately," she went on. "Your father didn't have time or patience for a pregnant girl who was always sick. Then when I had David, I didn't have time for your father. By the time you came along, I was happy just being with my babies. Now, for the first time, I'm alone. And for the first time, a man wants to be with me just because he likes me. I don't care if he does have ulterior motives, not right now. I'm enjoying myself. Understand me, Brenda."

"I do understand," I said. "You don't want to be alone. That's fine. But did you have to pick a guy old enough to be my brother?"

"Did you expect me to go to the retirement home to go boyfriend-shopping? Find someone who wanted to sit in a rocking chair and drink lemonade with me? Maybe play bingo at the church?"

I raked my hands through my hair. "I didn't mean that. But couldn't you have found someone your own age, at least?"

She laughed. "It's ironic, dear. Most single men my age are running after women your age. I guess the midlife crisis works both ways."

I was near to tears. "But—"

Mom stepped close to me. She had no sympathy on her face. "Let me explain, honey. I'm going to do this. Jerry makes me happy. Maybe one day I'll decide it's wrong or that I'm making a fool of myself. But for now, I'm enjoying it. All right?" She paused and drew breath. "I want this. Whether you like it or not."

"What I am supposed to do?" I asked. "Be friends with him? Call him my stepfather? He's only eight years older than I am."

"I really don't care," my mother answered. "You work out how you want to feel about him. For now, he's staying with me, and you'll have to get used to it."

"He's taking you away from me," I said in a small voice.

Guilt flashed in her eyes; then she got mad. Two red spots stood out on her cheeks. "Of course he isn't." She paused. "I've finally found someone who isn't too busy for me, and I like it."

A hard pain settled in my heart. We sized each other up for a few tense moments, then she turned around and marched out the door. I heard the soft sounds of clinking silverware and murmuring voices, then the door swung closed.

I started to cry. I stood in the middle of the chic bathroom and cried with my hand pressed to my face.

Then, sniffling, I went to the sink, washed the tears from my face and patted my skin dry with a washcloth. I studied myself as I tried to smooth my hair. My eyes were huge and blue in my stark white face.

When I could finally walk without shaking, I left the bathroom and made my way back to the table.

My mother, already there, was all smiles. "Miss us?" she asked our dates breezily.

Nick pulled out my chair for me. I sat down and tried not to look at Jerry as he nuzzled my mother's cheek.

I wanted to jump up and run out the door, but I was

here with Nick. He was my date, my ride. I couldn't leave until he was ready, unless I wanted to run down the street and catch a bus.

Carlos surprised the table with a dessert created especially for us. He brought out mountains of pastry cream surrounded by a shell of cake, topped with chocolate ganache. Fresh berries completed the picture.

We had to ohh and ahh and compliment the pastry chef and wash it all down with just the right dessert wine. The conversation dragged on. Everyone else was having a good time. I was jumpy as a dog wanting out of obedience school.

Carlos came out and sat with us, and he and Nick reminisced. Mom and Jerry didn't seem to mind. Jerry laughed and inserted appropriate comments and so did my mother.

I seethed. Nick didn't seem to notice my hints that we get out of there. Either that or he didn't care. And who was I to spoil his fun?

The only reason we left that night is that the restaurant closed. Carlos at last peeled himself off his chair and said he'd go help his staff clean up.

The waiters were clumped in the corner, talking and laughing like normal people. The busboys had finished removing the tablecloths and napkins and silverware from the unused tables and were trucking it all back into the linen closet.

Carlos walked us to the door, shook our hands, hugged Nick, told us to come back any time, please, we were old friends now.

We stood out on the sidewalk then, and talked. Or at least Jerry and Nick and my mother talked. I stood next to Nick praying that none of them would suggest we go to a bar or back to my mom's house to finish off the evening.

Finally, finally, Jerry and my mother walked off together toward my mom's car. Jerry put his arm around her waist. She turned and smiled up at him.

My heart broke.

Nick touched my arm. He knew something was wrong, I saw it in his face. He said nothing, though, just led me back to his car, and held the door while I crawled in.

18

Love, Salsa, and Kitchen Tables

"You OK?" Nick asked me.

We were drifting down La Jolla Boulevard in Nick's convertible, winding along the coast from the village back toward Mission Bay. I glimpsed the dark ocean from time to time, the view swallowed by houses, beach cottages, motels, and businesses.

"Sure. Fine," I said.

Nick didn't ask if I wanted to talk about it. He stared straight ahead, resting one elbow on the open window. Larry would have been all over me, blaming me for my mother's choice in men. Nick was being tactful.

The road got busier and narrower as we entered the beach towns. I wasn't sure why Nick hadn't zipped back to the freeway, which would have taken us south much faster. Back here, we had to stop for intersections, tourists weaving across streets, cyclists, and slow cars.

Nick seemed to be enjoying himself. The top was down, and the night air ruffled his hair. He drove along, humming a tune. I huddled in the passenger seat, arms folded.

"Why are you so happy?" I asked him.

He shot me a look of surprise. "Nice night, good food, I'm with a beautiful woman." He smiled. "What's not to like?"

I couldn't think of anything to say. I was smarting at my mother's last words to me in the bathroom, but I couldn't explain this to Nick. Not in a million years.

He looked at my face, and his smile faded.

He drove all the way to the end of Mission Boulevard, then pulled off into a park. I knew this park, having come out here a lot with my mom and David when we were kids. You could fish in Mission Bay or sit and watch the sailboats leaving the bay for the open water.

Nick parked the car, turned it off, turned off the lights. He turned to me, his seat creaking. "What's the matter, Brenda?"

His voice was so gentle that it melted me. I hugged myself and stared out at the water, afraid that if I spoke, I'd start crying and crying.

For a long time, I couldn't answer. He let me sit there, not pushing or prying. He was being nice after getting treated to more of my crazy family.

At last I asked, "What did you think of Jerry?"

He looked surprised by the question. "Jerry? He seemed OK."

I tried to laugh. "I'm sure you noticed that you and he are about the same age."

Nick absently traced the steering wheel. "Yes, I did notice that." He slanted me a look. "What are you trying to get me to say?"

I wiped my eyes with my thumb. "What I don't want

you to say is that you find it disgusting." Larry had said that. He'd said *creepy*, too.

"I wasn't going to. It's unusual, maybe, but not disgusting. Besides, it's none of my business."

"David won't speak to my mom anymore," I said glumly.

"That's too bad," Nick answered, his voice neutral. He studied the black water and the lights on the far shore. "Why are you worried about what I think of your mother's boyfriend?"

"Because I want you to like me," I said.

"I do like you. I think last night proved that a little."

He was trying to lighten the mood. I was too wound up.

I turned in the seat to face him. "How can you when my mother is dating a guy half her age, and my brother is bankrupt and gets thrown in jail in Mexico, and I'm a lingerie addict who slept with a man on New Year's without even knowing his name?" My eyes swam with tears.

He put a gentle hand on my shoulder. "You know my name now."

I sniffled. "You're probably thinking that we should have kept it a one-night stand."

"No." He smoothed a lock of hair from my face. "I wanted to see you again, and I do like you. I even like your family." He sounded sincere.

"Really?"

He grinned. "Yes, really. You and David should give your mom a break."

I wiped my nose. "What would you think—really and truly—if it was your mom that Jerry was dating?"

He considered. "Truthfully? I'd probably be surprised and upset at first."

"Only at first?"

"Yes," he said. "Until I got to know the guy. I'd be

worried about what he was after, and I'd probably check him out. I'd be protective. But if he was OK, and I didn't think he was a jerk or would hurt her or rob her blind, then I'd let it be."

"Would you?"

"Yes." He got quiet and looked out at the water again. "I really wouldn't mind if my mother was dating a man my age, because that would mean she was still alive for me to get mad at."

He rested his hands lightly on the steering wheel, but his arms and shoulders were tense. Remorse flooded me. "Oh, God, Nick, I'm sorry."

He was silent a long time. I touched his fingers and rested my forehead against his tight shoulder.

"I'm really, really sorry," I repeated.

"It's all right."

"No, it isn't. I'm stupid."

I felt his hand on my hair. "No, you're not. You're worried."

"You're way too nice to me. I'm selfish. What, I don't want my mom to have a real life?"

He stroked my hair again. "Were you close to your dad?"

"No." I sniffled. "That's the strange thing. My dad hardly paid any attention to me, or me to him. He liked David. I didn't care. They did all the male bonding things I wasn't interested in."

Nick was silent. I looked up at him. His gaze was remote, and I realized he could probably care less about me and my dad.

"What about you?" I asked softly. "Were you close to your parents?"

He nodded. "Very."

"What happened to them?" I whispered.

He fell silent again, and I hoped he wouldn't tell me to get out of the car and walk home.

"My dad had a stroke," he said, after a time. "He was a workaholic. He never sat down or slept if he could help it. My mother persuaded him to sell the restaurants and retire, but he hadn't been retired a year before he got sick. He died pretty quick. My mother—" He drew a breath, his mouth tight, as though he'd never said this out loud before. "My mother just gave up. He was her entire world, and when that was gone, she was gone, too. I guess she didn't want to live without him."

I stroked his fingers. "I'm sorry," I whispered.

His eyes glittered in the dark. "Thank you."

We didn't say anything more. What do you say after you've been whining about your mother and her boyfriend, and then a man tells you he wishes he still had a mother to whine about?

After a few minutes, Nick started the car again. He drove out of the park, across the bridge over Mission Bay, and south through Ocean Beach to Point Loma.

In silence he parked the car in the driveway behind his house, then opened the door for me. We walked across the grass to the courtyard and inside. If Mrs. Pankhurst had come out to watch, I didn't see her.

Our lovemaking that night was quiet and intense. I never saw a man who needed sex as much as Nick did that night. I don't know whether he was grieving or wanted comfort or simply didn't want me to talk any more.

He kissed me hard and rode out his climax while I held him; then he lay next to me for a long time without sleeping. He traced my breasts with his fingertips and nuzzled my hair as though he was enjoying simply being there with me.

After a time, he rolled back on top of me, kissed me gently, and started up again.

We fell asleep after round three and didn't wake up again until the sun was high. Nick made us breakfast (an egg casserole with salsa and cheese and tortillas), while I showered and dressed and brushed my teeth with the toothbrush I'd remembered to bring with me this time.

Downstairs, Nick smiled at me. Outside it had started raining, that gentle spring rain that mists out the mountains and the ocean. Inside, the kitchen was warm and filled with smells of Nick's cooking.

Because his dad had been a chef, the range was large and complicated, and he had two ovens in the wall. I looked at the large, shining chrome kitchen, ate my piquant breakfast casserole, and sighed happily.

"I like it here," I said.

Those were the first words I'd spoken since the night before, other than lovemaking babble.

Nick sat across the table from me, sopping up salsa with his last tortilla. "Move in," he suggested.

I stopped. "What?"

"Move in," Nick repeated. "This house is too big for me by myself. You can have your own toothbrush holder and everything."

I laid down my fork. My hand shook. "Nick."

His eyes went quiet. "You're going to say no, aren't you?"

"I'm going to say, maybe this isn't something we should rush into. We should think about it. We should talk about it."

He laid down his tortilla and wiped his hands on a napkin. "No, we shouldn't talk about it. I want you to move in. You don't. Nothing else to say."

"I didn't say I didn't want to. I said we should think about it."

He rested his arms on the table. "If it felt right to you, Brenda, you'd just say yes."

I looked down. "Maybe."

"So let's forget about it. We'll have our weekends, and

maybe later you'll change your mind." He got up and went to the refrigerator. "Want any juice?"

"Nick."

Nick's back quivered, but he stared into the refrigerator. I'd seen his face as he turned away. He was mad and hurt.

"Nick," I repeated. "Don't try to make me feel guilty so I'll stay."

He rummaged in the refrigerator like he'd forgotten what he was looking for. "You know, you have this annoying habit of deciding what other people are thinking and feeling. I'm not trying to guilt you into staying. I only asked if you wanted some juice."

"But you're mad."

"Yes." He let the refrigerator slam shut. "I am."

"Because I said no."

He faced me, resting the orange juice container against his hip. "Because I thought we liked being together. You don't want to move in, you don't have to. Can we talk about something else?"

I clutched the lip of the table. "Living with someone is different from going out with them."

"I know that," he said tersely.

"I love going out with you. I don't want that to stop."

He didn't look mollified. "You like the sex part. Not what comes after."

"Not right now," I said, getting desperate.

"And I've already said it's OK. Why are we still arguing about it?"

He set the juice container on the counter and turned to the stove as though he was going to start cleaning up.

I sprang to my feet. My chair went over backwards. I swung to pick it up and knocked my plate to the floor, where it smashed into white fragments covered with bits of tomato and pepper and onion.

Nick just stood there. I dropped to my knees and

started picking up the pieces. I cut myself and popped my finger into my mouth.

"Leave it," Nick said. "I'll clean it up later."

I stubbornly went on picking up pieces. "You have to understand. I just went through a bad breakup."

"I know." Nick sat down again and watched me scramble around gathering broken plate and bits of salsa.

"I'm just afraid—"

That it wouldn't work. That Nick would stop liking me once he knew the real me.

I'd moved in with Larry for two months and that had deteriorated the relationship gonzo-fast. Larry had realized he didn't like me. He didn't like the way I forgot to fold my clothes when I went to bed. He didn't like the way I'd leave dishes in the sink overnight. He didn't like the way I wasn't interested in making him coffee, buying him groceries, picking up his cleaning, taking his car to the shop, walking his dog, or saying the right things to his various friends, most of whom I didn't know.

Whenever I'd tried to stand up for myself, Larry took me down. He had a way of making me feel small, stupid, and incompetent. The harder I tried to be the perfect woman for him, the worse he'd make me feel.

Sex had become an obligation, not a joy. When sex is an obligation, cleaning out the garage is more fun. Ask me how I know.

Two months was all it took. Was all I could take. I'd moved back in with Clarissa, who'd said she figured I'd be back soon. She was smarter than I was.

I didn't want my relationship with Nick to break down until it become an endless argument about my shortcomings. That followed by bad sex. I liked what Nick and I had, good sex and good fun, and me watching Nick's gorgeous body every chance I got.

I didn't want it to change into Brenda trying to remember to hide her box of tampons because they disgusted her boyfriend, Brenda trying to pretend she knew how to cook and waiting for the tantrum when what she made turned out like crap.

Nick had never met the real me. I realized that like a slap in the face. He'd had glimpses, but he'd never gotten the real, neurotic Brenda full-force.

Nick knew the crazy, brazen Brenda, who was not afraid of being sexy. He'd never met the shy I'll-do-anything-you-say Brenda or even the in-between Brenda. By the time Nick had enticed me to bed on New Year's I'd been drunk and already stepping into the wild persona.

If I moved in, he'd quickly find out I wasn't that Brenda all the way through. When he got to know the real me, the girl somewhere between mousy, codependent Brenda and the new I'm-a-kick-ass-wild-woman Brenda, would he like her? Or run screaming for the hills?

Larry hadn't liked the real Brenda. Larry had tried to mold me into his perfect little woman and had railed at me when I couldn't be that for him.

Nick wanted exactly the opposite. Nick had told me that he liked being with me because I was unpredictable and lifted him out of his anal-retentiveness. (I had yet to see him be as anal as Larry, but maybe Nick thought he was anal because he'd lived with a father who was a chef. Chefs were creative and temperamental, I'd heard.)

Whatever the reason, Nick had told me I was liberating and sexy and fun.

Nick didn't want Boring Brenda. He wanted Lingerie Addict Brenda. He wanted the Brenda who bought him edible underwear and took him to roadhouses and unzipped her dress in the middle of restaurants.

If he finally met the real Brenda, he might recoil and run away just as he'd done New Year's morning.

Nick was offering me something I really, really wanted. And it terrified me.

"Brenda," Nick repeated, pulling me back to today. "I've already said it's OK."

I sat down on the floor. "It's not OK. You think I'm not in love with you."

He stared at me. "In love?"

"That's what I said."

He went quiet. Tears started to leak from my eyes. I said, "I'm messing everything up, aren't I?"

He rested his elbows on his knees, let his hands dangle over his spread legs. I let my gaze rest there while I tried to surreptitiously wipe away tears.

He asked, "You think I'd break up with you because you didn't want to move in with me?"

"Yes."

"You truly don't give me credit, Brenda."

"I've never been out with a man that I could."

He raised his brows. "You know, this Larry guy must have been a real loser."

I pulled my knees to my chest. "He's one of the richest men in southern California."

"That just means he's good at business. He's still a loser."

I'd never heard anyone call Mr. Perfect a loser before. He was the man all men aspired to be. I liked that Nick thought he was a loser.

Nick had a comfortable life and was doing what he wanted. He seemed to know everyone in town. So did Larry. But the difference was that people liked Nick. They beamed when they saw him coming. They called him "Nicky." They hugged him. They clung to his hand and wouldn't let him go until they'd heard every bit of news he had to tell them.

When people saw Larry coming, they got nervous. They tried to impress him. They looked relieved when he walked away. I'd always done the exact same thing.

With Nick, you wanted to lay your head in his lap and purr.

Especially the way his jeans stretched over his thighs. I thought about crawling over to him and laying my cheek against his knee. Running my hand down the faded seam of the jeans to where it wanted to go.

His look turned bemused. "You have salsa all over your face."

I reached up to the table, grabbed a napkin, and smeared my tears and the salsa with it.

He started laughing. "Come here."

Nick took my elbow and gently helped me to sit on his lap. He took a clean paper towel from the table and started wiping my face with it.

He had a strong jaw lined with golden bristles that he'd missed shaving. His lashes swept down to hide his eyes as he cleaned my face.

"I'm going to pretend you really meant that," he said.

"Meant what?"

"About being in love."

"Why wouldn't I?" I touched his cheek. "What's not to love?"

He looked at me for a long time. He wiped one last bit of salsa from my nose, then he tilted my head back and kissed me deeply.

He pressed the corners of my mouth with his thumbs, opening my lips. I snaked my hands under his shirt, burrowing for warmth against his hard chest. He pulled me to him with his hand on the back of my neck, and kissed me like he was desperate for me.

I slid my fingers to the button of his jeans and popped it open. His hardness under his zipper felt as if it would split the metal links any minute. I ran my hand along it, daring it to come out and play.

Nick growled. He lifted me and set my rump on the

edge of the table, then swept the plates and silverware to the floor.

I'd always wondered what having sex on a kitchen table would be like. Nick laid me back on the hard surface, and I cushioned my head with my arm. He unzipped his jeans, let them fall, and entered me right there. Thank God he had a condom in his pocket in preparation for our next montage. I hung onto the side of the table and enjoyed every minute of it.

It almost—almost—convinced me to stay. Who wouldn't want to move into a fine old house with a gorgeous guy who boffed you on the kitchen table after he'd cooked you a to-die-for breakfast?

No one.

I had to be seriously crazy. I was in love. No doubt about that.

But I wanted it to stay that way, all shining and happy and untouchable. I didn't want to break the fragile bubble that had begun between us. I needed to get over Mr. Perfect and the mess he'd made of my self-esteem before I walked in here with my suitcases. I wanted to enjoy what Nick and I had started, and not ruin it too soon.

When Nick finished, he dragged me onto his lap again and held me close. I shuddered with my pent-up feelings and physical joy, and sat in silence with him for a long time.

After that, we cleaned up the mess of the kitchen, and he drove me home.

He didn't ask me again to consider moving in with him. He didn't even ask to see me the rest of the day, or that night, or the next day. He didn't ask me anything.

I kissed him good-bye. His return kiss was quiet and coolly neutral. He'd told me he wouldn't break up because I'd turned him down, but he was not happy. I saw that in his eyes. The few steps we'd taken toward closeness last night had vanished with the light of day.

Getting out of his car and watching him drive away was one of the hardest things I'd ever done in my life.

I dragged myself upstairs, heart heavy. When I entered the apartment, I found David and Clarissa bent over a pot on the stove. Clarissa's long hair spilled forward, in danger of igniting. They both stared at me as I walked in and threw my bag on the sofa.

"What are you doing here?" David asked.

"I live here," I said. "Why are you cooking, David? You don't know how to cook."

Clarissa smiled her languid smile. "We're making fondue. Want some?"

19

Chocolate Fondue and the Hosing of Tony Beale

"What kind of fondue?" I asked. I followed my bag to the sofa. I felt tired and old.

"Chocolate." Clarissa lifted a spoon out of the pot. Chocolate dribbled from it in a swift stream. "I think it's a little thin."

Nick would know how to fix it. He'd know exactly what exotic chocolate or butter or whatever would make the fondue just right.

I thought about Nick licking chocolate from a spoon, put my hands to my face, and groaned.

"You don't have to have any if you don't want it," David said. "Anyway, I thought you'd be spending the weekend with whatshisname."

"Nick," Clarissa told him.

"Nick," David repeated.

I pressed my hands harder, groaned louder.

"What's wrong?" David asked. "You didn't break up, did you?"

"I don't know," I said.

"You don't know?" David prodded. Clarissa went back to peering at the chocolate and stirring it. "How can you not know?"

"I don't know, David."

He looked perplexed. "Brenda, you go through men like—like—well, I don't know, but you go through them fast."

I protested, "I've only had one serious relationship in my life." Maybe two. I wasn't sure what it was I had with Nick.

"Yeah, with Larry," he said. "You know, I was really proud when Mom told me you'd started going out with him. Brenda snagged herself a rich guy, I thought. Go, little sister. Too bad he turned out to be a two-faced jerk."

"Yes," I agreed. "Too bad."

"He likes himself too much," Clarissa said, staring into the pot.

I thought that a good way of putting it. Larry had such a high opinion of himself that he assumed everyone else did, too. I heaved a sigh, got myself up off the couch. "So what are you going to have with the fondue?"

David looked blank. "Have with it? What do you mean?"

"What are you going to dip into it? Cake? Strawberries?"

David's brow furrowed; then he and Clarissa exchanged a glance. "Oh."

At least something could still make me laugh. "What were you going to do? Lick it off the spoon?"

Clarissa shrugged. "I guess."

"I'll go get some fruit and pound cake. Don't eat it all without me."

They didn't argue. They went back to stirring their chocolate goop, heads together.

As I went down the stairs, I thought about what I'd do if I made fondue with Nick. I wouldn't bother with pound cake. I'd just dribble the chocolate all over Nick.

The thought made my heart pound and my face get hot. I needed to look at this relationship with a clear head, decide what I really wanted and how I was going to get there.

Instead, all I could think of was Nick in the shower, Nick covered with chocolate fondue, Nick with his jeans unzipped as he made love to me on the table.

Why did he have to be so pretty? Of course, looks aren't everything, are they? Larry was good looking. No, correction, Larry gave the impression of being good looking. He had the right hair, the right clothes, the right build, and the right car to set it all off.

If you took Larry and Nick, stripped them both naked, and threw them into the mud, Nick would come out of that mud still looking good. Larry would just look messy and annoyed.

Nick would have his hair plastered to his head and mud all over his body. He'd be grinning, and he'd try to hug the lucky woman waiting for him. Then the lucky woman would get to wash him off in the shower.

The vision was so strong that I had to sit down on the bottom stair. Our next door neighbor climbed past me with her hands full of plastic grocery bags. "Hi, Brenda."

I said, "Hi." She didn't ask why I'd suddenly sat down on the stairs. She already thought me and Clarissa and everyone who went into our apartment severely weird. I agreed with her.

I got up and went to my car, trying to focus on buying fruit. I wondered if Nick would taste good with mango.

The dirty white Toyota was in the parking lot, sans driver. On impulse, I walked over to the car and peered through its open window.

The car looked like any ordinary old car. A clipboard lay on the passenger seat with a sheet of paper attached to it covered with numbers and checkmarks, but they made no sense to me. On the back seat lay a khaki-colored raincoat, the trenchcoat kind. Other than that, the car looked perfectly innocent, if worn out. The car had California plates and had been bought at a dealership in La Mesa. Nothing sinister in that.

I figured it was my imagination that anything was wrong with that Toyota. I continued to my car, started it, and drove to a nearby grocery store.

Just because I was proved entirely wrong later really wasn't my fault.

When I returned, frozen pound cake in hand, Clarissa and David were bent over the stove, giggling, their faces smeared with chocolate.

My anal, social-climbing older brother was giggling over fondue. At least it was good to see him laugh again.

I thawed out the pound cake and cut up the fruit. I piled it all on a plate, and we stood around the stove, dipping strawberries and pineapple and cake into the chocolate.

The fondue wasn't very good. It was too grainy and didn't stick to the fruit. David kept adding butter to it, so we had a greasy, buttery chocolate-like substance with dried out cake. The fruit was good, anyway.

The phone rang. I jumped at it. Was it Nick, calling to beg me to come back to his house for another night with him? Please?

The caller ID said it was my mother. I eyed the number on the readout, debating whether to answer. I thought of what she'd said to me last night. In my guilt-ridden soul, part of me wanted to say she was right. The other part still cringed.

Should I answer it? Would she apologize for being abrupt, or continue with her lecture about how I was an ungrateful daughter?

I almost let it go. The only thing that stopped me was—well, she was my mother.

"Hello," I said, none too encouragingly.

"Brenda." She sounded relieved.

"Hi."

"I called to say—" Mom stopped, obviously debating about what she had called to say. "Please thank Nick for allowing us to share the meal last night. It was wonderful, and he was kind to let us."

"I'll tell him," I said.

"I like Nick," she went on. "He's a nice—"

"Yeah, you told me last night."

"That's not why I called," she said quickly.

"No?" I waited.

"I wanted to thank Nick for being gracious. And you, too."

"Me?" I was surprised. "What for?"

"For not being obvious, in public, how angry you are at me. You could have refused to speak to me or run off like you did the other day. But you stuck it out. You didn't have to."

I sat down on the couch. "I didn't want to embarrass Nick."

"I know. But it was nice of you."

Her tone held a note of apology. I knew, though, that she hadn't called to apologize. She was not about to back down. She was going to hang onto Jerry to prove a point, even if she couldn't stand the guy. Which she could. I'd not seen her so flirty and at ease and smiling in—OK, I'd never seen her so flirty and at ease and smiling as she'd been last night.

"Is that all you called about?" I asked.

"No." She cleared her throat. "Is David there with you?"

"Yes." I glanced into the kitchen where Clarissa was quietly eating all the pineapple. David stirred the sauce, but he was listening, a sour look on his face. He'd guessed who I was talking to.

"Can I talk to him?"

I lifted my brows. "I'll ask." I was not optimistic. I covered the receiver with my hand. "David, would you like to talk to Mom?"

"No," he said instantly.

"She wants to talk to you."

"Too bad." He thrust the spoon into the chocolate and gave it a hearty stir. "I'll talk to her when that so-called friend of mine moves out."

"That would be a 'no,' then."

David gave me a deprecating look. I lifted the phone to my ear. "He says he doesn't want to talk to you."

"Not until that so-called friend of mine moves out!" he shouted.

"He is not moving out," my mother said crisply. "David will just have to get used to it. The reason I wanted to talk to you two is to remind you that Easter is next Sunday."

Easter. My heart sank. Every year, we had traditional Easter dinner at my mother's house with ham and green beans and macaroni and cheese. We'd been having the same meal for decades.

Our family had always done a traditional Easter. When I was little, my mom had hidden Easter eggs for me and David to find, and then we'd gone to church, me in a new Easter dress, usually pink, although it clashed with my hair. Mom always let me have a pink dress, even when my dad argued that yellow or white would be much more sensible. Mom knew I wanted pink most of all and said it didn't matter that I had a mop of red hair to go with it.

After church, we'd have Easter dinner; then David and I would fight over the Easter candy, and then, once the battle was resolved, we'd eat chocolate until we were sick.

For the past seven years, David hadn't been home for our dinners, because his wife had wanted to stay in Chicago with her family. After my father had died, Mom and I had carried on alone.

Now, this Easter, David was finally home, and we could have a family dinner again. With Jerry.

"Yes," I said. "Easter. What about it?"

"I am going to make dinner. Like always. I want you to come."

"Oh," I said.

"Ask Nick along if you like. In return for last night."

I winced. Let's see, did I want to ask Nick to come and watch my family glare at each other over ham and green beans?

He might say a polite, cool no. He wasn't exactly happy with Brenda right now.

But Nick could cook. Maybe he could at least tell me why my potato salad always came out wrong. It was a yearly joke, Brenda's potato salad. Everyone kept insisting I make it so they could have a good laugh.

"OK," I mumbled.

Mom drew a hopeful breath. "You really will come?"

"Will Jerry be there?"

"Of course he'll be there," she said. "Why wouldn't he be?"

"He might have family in Chicago."

"We talked about it. He decided he wanted to spend Easter here, with us."

Us. Not her. Us.

I knew what she was doing. Mom wanted to drag Jerry firmly into the family tradition and thus establish that he had every right to be part of the family. I had to give her brownie points for trying.

"David won't come," I said.

"But you will?" she countered. "With Nick?"

I thought about it. If Nick was there, we probably wouldn't kill each other. "Yes," I said dully. I closed my eyes. I had a bad feeling about this. "I'll ask him."

"Please try to convince David to come along," she said. "He can bring a friend, too, if he'd like."

She wanted more buffers. More people to convince us that Jerry was acceptable.

I didn't want to argue with her. I was tired of arguing. "I'll tell him," I said.

"Please, Brenda."

"I can't promise," I said. "Don't ask me to."

She subsided. "All right. Thank you. I plan to have dinner around two o'clock. Come about one. You can make your potato salad."

Was that humor I heard in her voice? I didn't think it was funny. I said, "OK," again, and then I hung up the phone.

David was already glaring at me. "What? What does she want me to do?"

"Come to Easter dinner." I sat back and propped my feet on the coffee table. "And bring a friend."

His eyes narrowed. "Is Jerry going to be there?"

"Yes. He's here to stay, David."

David's mouth turned down, his face twisting into a nasty expression. "Screw that," he growled.

I knew that was the end of the discussion.

* * *

I wanted to call Nick, but I didn't. He didn't call me. I guess we were giving each other space. I didn't want space. I wanted Nick.

I moped around feeling sorry for myself. David and Clarissa decided to go out to dinner that night. Clarissa took one look at me and suggested I go along.

We went to a diner on the freeway, a trendy one, not a seedy one. I had to admit that going out with David and Clarissa helped my wayward emotions. Clarissa didn't talk much, but she was good at introducing off-the-wall topics. Without seeming to, she prompted David to talk and come out of his sulky shell.

My brother was smart. He knew things, and not in an arrogant, know-it-all way. He could be amusing and informative on a whole range of subjects. He was complaining less now about his wife and his failure in Chicago and conversing more about stuff that interested him.

I realized that Clarissa had succeeded in drawing David out of himself. She'd become his friend. David needed a friend right now, not someone to make relationship demands on him. Clarissa, for all her weirdness and black eyeliner, never demanded anything of anyone. David seemed relaxed around her, not threatened.

Watching them, I knew that she and David hadn't been together in the sexual sense, even though I'd left them alone plenty. That relieved me, because who knew what David's wife's divorce lawyers would do with that?

Clarissa was generous, too. She paid for the whole meal with her seemingly limitless supply of funds and shrugged when I said I'd pay her back.

When we returned to the apartment, I ran to check my messages, hoping Nick had decided he wanted another go on the kitchen table and called me. It would be good for him to think I didn't wait by the phone for him.

But he hadn't called.

I went to bed early so I could get in a good night's brooding. Clarissa and David stayed up most of the night. Whenever I woke up, I could hear them murmuring together in the living room.

I got through Sunday by running errands and shopping and doing those things you have to do to live, like buying toilet paper and paying the phone bill. None of the heroines in romance novels ever have to buy toilet paper. None of the books even mention the heroines having to relieve themselves at all. Those poor, constipated heroines.

Nick didn't call that day either. I wondered what he was doing.

Probably he was buying toilet paper, too. Living his life. If I'd agreed to live with him, we could be out shopping for toilet paper together.

I wondered if he was finished with me because I'd turned him down. Lying in the dark that night, I imagined Nick drawing a line through my name on his list of girlfriends, then picking up the phone and calling the next one. Maybe he was done with the Bs and had moved on to the Cs. Carol? Cathy? Carla?

I lay awake and hated them. Nick and his blue eyes and messy blond hair and firm butt was mine, all mine. Carol, Cathy, and Carla had better just take a number.

I didn't sleep much and went to work the next morning in a bad mood.

When I got out of my car and walked to the front door of the station, I suddenly got a strange crawly sensation of someone watching me. I swung around, but the parking lot, dark in the early morning, was empty. My car, Tony's car, and Marty's falling-apart pickup sat in their places, but no one else was there.

Still, I felt a prickle between my shoulder blades. I looked around for the white Toyota, but didn't see it. My incompetent stalker was nowhere in sight.

I tried to shrug it off. Maybe I just hadn't gotten enough sleep. It bugged me, though.

Inside the studio, Tony, wearing a very faded black Pink Floyd shirt, was singing along to Golden Earring.

"Reliving your childhood?" I asked as I scooted past him and into the booth.

"This is real music, Brenda. Back when being in a band meant something. Now it's all commercial trash and good musicians dumped after one album if it doesn't go instantly platinum."

"Yeah, it's a drag, Tony."

"It's a travesty!" He followed me in, leaned against the control boards. "Record companies run by guys in suits, DJs playing the playlist and nothing else. No creativity any more."

He sounded like my hippie friends.

"Could you whine about it not on my control board?" I asked, sitting down. I put on the headphones, but still couldn't shut him out.

"You're doing an interview this week," he said. "Some guy called John Dishard."

I moved the headphones. "John from Bohemian Love Child?"

"I guess that's him."

"One of those bands in the sixties that didn't go platinum," I told him.

Tony waved it away. "He apparently has a lot of fans in San Diego. His agent called me."

"He has an agent?" I thought about the little roadhouse and the crowd there. "He's moving up."

"Whatever, he'll be here Wednesday. So sweet-talk him, Brenda. Bat your eyelashes and make him say how wonderful KCLP is to all his fans."

"I don't bat my eyelashes, Tony."

"Show him your legs, then. You have good legs."

He walked away, whistling strains of ZZ Top. I rolled

my eyes, slammed my headphones back on, and started my show.

Could I resist turning on KBZ to listen in on Nick? No, of course not.

"Hey, good morning, this is Nick Jordan."

At the sound of his voice, all movement around me ceased. My eyes got glassy, and I let his warm, sweet voice flow over me.

I remembered salsa, the kitchen table, and how nice I'd imagined him looking covered in chocolate fondue.

He was talking about Le Grand Bistro in La Jolla. "I have a gift certificate here for the ninth caller for a dinner for two. It's romantic, guys. You take a lady there, I guarantee she'll fall for you. Brenda and I enjoyed it Friday night. Just tell them Nick Jordan sent you. The chef's a friend of mine."

He was right. He'd taken a lady there, and she'd fallen for him, hard.

I wondered if he was making a crack about me. No, Nick didn't make cracks. Nick was sweet. He opened car doors. He cooked breakfast. He looked stunned when I mentioned love.

He was the sweetest, most wonderful man I'd ever met. And when he'd asked me to move in with him, the first step in sharing his life, I'd balked. My own fear was punishing me.

"What's she doing?" I heard Tony Beale say from the control booth.

I couldn't see him, or the computer, or the buttons I was supposed to push, because tears were running down my face.

"Brenda," Tony said, right in front of me. "Brenda, Brenda, Brenda. Dead air, Brenda."

"What?" I looked up. I noticed that everything had gone silent. Except Nick's voice saying he'd gone to the movies Saturday night, and what did everyone think about *Aliens Ate My Homework*? Apparently, it had debuted at number one. He was giving away a pair of tickets for that, too.

So Nick had gone to the movies. With Carol or Carla or Cathy? My tears increased.

"Brenda!" Tony shouted. He shoved a CD in a slot and flooded the airwaves with the Rolling Stones. "What is the matter with you? Do you want me to fire you?"

"Shut up, Tony," I sniffled.

He snapped off the speaker. Nick's voice, along with that of an eager female caller, vanished.

"You are not allowed to listen to KBZ anymore," he said. "Every time you listen to Nick, you either get teary or gushy, but in all cases, you get plain stupid. What happened, you break up with him?"

I shook my head, tears raining down my face. "No, I'm in love with him."

"So what's the problem?" He sighed and sat down in the other chair. "Stop crying, Brenda. What happened? Tell Tony."

I wiped my face with the back of my hand. And then, God help me, I confessed all my troubles to Tony Beale. I told Marty, too, because he was listening in from the booth.

"So," Tony said when I'd finished. He leaned back on the chair and crossed his ankles. His paunch bulged out of the T-shirt and over the belt of his jeans. Not a pretty sight. "All you do is ask him to this Easter dinner. Show him you want him to get to know the family. Then after you're both stuffed with ham, you take him out to your backyard, show him the view, tell him you love him, and then give him the best blow job he ever had in his life. He'll forgive you."

230

I started laughing, tears drying on my face. "Thanks, Tony. Great advice."

"It'll work, Brenda," Marty said from the booth. He peeled open another Snickers bar. "Then move in with him. Why not? He can cook? Heck, I'll move in with him."

I sighed. "I don't know. I'm afraid to. What if it doesn't work out? What if we turn into nagging pains in the butt and hate each other?"

"What if you do?" Tony asked. "Then you feel stupid and go back home. But what if you hit it off, get married, and live happily ever after? You'll never know until you take the step. Don't let your fear keep you from something that just might make you happy. Give it a chance. I speak from experience."

I looked at him, interested. "Really?"

He gazed at the ceiling. "Oh, yes. Long time ago. Beautiful girl. Legs as good as yours, but her hair was blond and sleek and long, nothing like yours. Even now I could be bouncing our kids on my knees, but I got cold feet. She married a bridge designer and moved to Sweden. And I'm a swinging bachelor at a bar with a new lady every weekend."

I sat up, cut him off. "Tony, do *not* tell me about that."

Tony stood. He didn't look offended. "Hey, I still get dates, Brenda. It's the mystique of show business. Who knows, if it doesn't work between you and Nick, maybe I'll ask you out."

My eyes got big. I turned hurriedly to the microphone and snapped it on. "Hi, San Diego, Brenda here. Sorry about the silence; I was recovering from nausea."

Tony burst out laughing as soon as I dropped in a commercial. "Only kidding, Brenda. I just wanted to see your face."

It took until the end of my show for the nausea to go away.

* * *

At two that afternoon, I finished up taping the voice-overs Tony wanted me to do and left the studio. Tony headed out at the same time. I was on my way home, he on his way to wrap up a sales deal with someone who liked Pink Floyd.

"See you, Brenda," he said. "Don't forget what I said about Nick and Easter dinner. It'll work."

"Sure, Tony," I said.

We'd almost reached our cars, his right next to mine, when it happened.

A man sprang out of the bushes, a look of crazed triumph on his face. He gripped the nozzle of a long green garden hose in his trembling hands and hurtled toward Tony Beale.

"Tony, look out!" I yelled.

Tim, our former bungee-jumping, shark-baiting morning show host, screamed, "Sharks swim in water, ha ha. How do you like being all wet, Tony?" and turned the hose full blast on him.

I shrieked. A wave drenched my skirt before I could dive for cover. Tony got it full-force.

Tony threw up his hands, tried to turn away, hollered at Tim to stop. The stream pushed him back into his car; then Tim proceeded to soak him from head to foot. Tony's faded Pink Floyd shirt turned black with water, his jeans dripped, and what little hair he had left slid from his domed head and plastered itself to his neck.

I climbed to my hands and knees and then to my feet. My cotton skirt was ruined, my lace stockings shredded. Tony rocked back and forth against his car, swearing and screaming.

Tim kept the spray on him, laughing maniacally. I hurried to the spigot on the side of the building and turned off the water.

The hose deflated and the stream of water died off.

Tim held it on Tony until the water became a trickle. Then Tim stared at the nozzle as though he didn't know what had happened.

Tony peeled himself off the car. He wiped the water from his eyes. Tim looked at me, looked at the hose again, looked at Tony.

Tony started for him. Tim dropped the hose and took off. The last we saw of him was a flash of his back as he scrambled over a hedge and hightailed it for the street.

Tony stopped running, panting hard.

"Let him go," I said.

"I'm calling the police. He's crazy!"

"He only squirted you with water." I started laughing. Water rained down Tony's bald head and sloughed off his arms in wide rivulets. "Oh, God, I wish I had a camera."

Tony glared at me. He swiped his hand across his head, sending another wave of cold water over me. I backed away. "This is serious, Brenda."

"He hosed you down to get back at you for throwing him in a shark tank. You're lucky he didn't bring the shark." I shook out my skirt. "What else does he want to get back at you for?"

We both thought about New Year's Eve at the same time. About Tony gleefully wrapping the screaming, terrified Tim in a bungee cord and throwing him over the bridge. We looked at each other.

"He wouldn't," Tony said, paling. "I'm afraid of heights."

"It's your own fault, Tony." I opened the door and got my damp self in the car. I'd been sort of right about Tim, except he hadn't sued. He'd gone stark, raving loony.

"You're all heart, Brenda."

I backed out my car and glanced out the window at him. He'd pulled his sodden T-shirt from his paunch and was wringing it out.

"Stay away from Coronado Bridge," I advised, then I drove away, trying not to laugh at the panicked look on his face.

That night I gathered my courage and called Nick.

20

Aliens Ate My Homework

Nick wasn't home.

I left a message on his voice mail, trying not to sound too desperate to talk to him.

Clarissa and David had gone out somewhere. I stripped off my ruined skirt and stockings, changed my underwear, and lay back on my bed clad only in my bikinis. The fan above me turned lazily, stirring the cool air that came in through my open window.

I thought about things. I thought about the man in the white Toyota. I thought about Tim hosing down Tony. White Toyota Man hadn't been Tim. Tim drove a blue Honda, or at least he used to. I hadn't seen the Honda in the station parking lot either.

Poor Tony. He was an idiot, and yet at times he could be a good guy. But then again he hadn't stood up for Tim. I never knew what to make of Tony Beale.

Thinking about Tony and Tim was supposed to keep me from thinking about Nick. It didn't work.

I thought about the restaurant and Nick's hand on my back guiding me in, Nick introducing me proudly to the maitre d' as his girlfriend. Nick kissing me with wild abandon and laying me down on the kitchen table.

I still couldn't believe that a guy like Nick liked me. I wished for the hundredth time that I could remember what New Year's Eve with him had been like.

I only remembered downing martinis and sort of wobbling to a sofa and then things going blank. Nick must have found me and charmed me senseless. That wouldn't have been too hard for him to do, whether I'd been drunk or sober.

Thinking about Nick was supposed to prevent me thinking about my mother and how she wanted to make us one big happy family again. That didn't work, either.

I should feel sorry for my mother, I thought. She'd married young and lived her entire life everyone else's way. Wasn't she entitled to have some fun?

I could say that in my head, but my gut still churned. Having your mother dating at all was difficult to think about; watching her date a man eighteen years younger than herself was almost impossible.

It wasn't as though I didn't like Jerry. I had liked him, at least before he'd moved into my mother's bedroom. Nick liked him, too, the traitor. David had liked him before all this started. Heck, Jerry was the one friend who stood by David during his troubles. I should have warm feelings for Jerry just for that.

My life was all mixed up. Everything used to be simple. Go to work, go out with Mr. Perfect, visit my mom on the weekend.

Now my safe little world had dissolved, I was having sex on kitchen tables, and my family had broken apart.

The phone rang. Without looking at the caller ID, I picked it up. "Brenda's home for sad cases," I said.

Nick said. "Brenda?"

I sat up straight. "Nick." He'd called me back. He'd actually called me back.

"How are you?"

"Great." My mind blanked. I had no idea what to say. "How was the movie?"

"What movie? Oh, *Aliens Ate My Homework.* It wasn't bad." He hesitated. "How was your weekend?"

"My weekend? Oh, fine. Fine. My brother and Clarissa made chocolate fondue. It was terrible."

"The trick is to use high-quality cream," Nick said.

"I knew you'd know how to fix it."

"I grew up with a restaurateur. I didn't have a chance."

Just listening to his voice made me happy. And horny. I wished he were lying next to me, whispering in my ear how to make fondue.

I'd ask him over. I'd ask him to come here and lie down next to me and talk about chocolate fondue. Then we'd make some, and I'd pour it on him.

He said, "So why did you call?"

I jumped. "Oh." I'd completely forgotten why I'd called.

"Well?"

"Oh, I—uh," I racked my brain. What had I been thinking about? Oh, yes, Easter.

I gulped. "My mother wants me to invite you for Easter dinner. Ham and macaroni and cheese. And potato salad. I make the potato salad. Only I don't know how. Do you have a good recipe for potato salad?"

"Brenda—"

"I think I use too much mustard. Everyone puckers when they eat my potato salad. Is it too much mustard? Or maybe too much salt. What else do you put in potato salad?"

"Brenda—"

"They make me bring it every year, even though everyone hates it. I think my family just wants a good

237

laugh. But I want to show them this year. So if you help me, they can't laugh. I'm really tired of everyone telling me I can't cook. But if I invite someone who *can* cook—"

"Brenda," Nick almost shouted. "I can't come to Easter dinner."

I ground to a halt. "What? Oh."

"I'm going back to San Antonio this weekend."

"San Antonio?" I asked weakly.

"Yes. I've already bought the ticket."

"Are you spending Easter with your brother?"

"Partly."

I closed my eyes. San Antonio. Where he'd been engaged to a woman who was beautiful, poised, rich, and popular. I was a nerdy radio DJ with scouring pad hair, a dysfunctional family, and a taste for ultrasexy underwear.

"And the other part?" I asked.

"Tying up loose ends."

I gripped the phone. "Loose ends?"

"Things I should have done when I was there."

What things? I wanted to scream. Was his fiancée a loose end? One he forgot to sever? Or one he wanted to retie?

My own fault. I'd brushed him off. He'd asked me to move in with him, and I'd looked at him in horror.

"I guess it will be nice for you to see your brother," I said.

"It will." He seemed pleased I was so understanding.

I wiped my nose. "I'll probably go to Lili Duoma on Saturday. I've been thinking about getting a corset. You know, one of those black satin ones? I have the perfect dress to pair it with."

I couldn't resist. If he was going to run off to Texas to talk about loose ends with his beautiful fiancée, he could think about me in a black satin corset.

"Sounds, ah—nice," he said.

"They're a little expensive, but I think I deserve a treat. I've been working hard."

"You have been," he said warmly. "I'm sorry about dinner, Brenda, but I really need to do this."

"Oh, I understand." I made my voice light. "You were my first choice, but I guess I'll have to ask someone else."

He got quiet. I imagined him holding the phone tight, staring at the wall with his blue, blue eyes. "Someone else?" he said eventually.

"I haven't decided who yet. I have to think about it. Serves me right for assuming you'd be free."

He drew a breath. "I really have to go out there, Brenda."

"I know. You have a life. You can tell me about it when you get back." My heart was pounding. I couldn't help adding, "When are you coming back?"

I sounded like a little girl. I hoped he didn't notice.

"I don't know," he said. "I don't know how long it will take."

I wanted details. I wanted to shout at him to tell me exactly what these loose ends were and why they'd take so long, but I closed my mouth.

What man wanted a ranting, nagging woman demanding to know everything about his personal life? Nick would probably think San Antonio was peaceful. He'd never want to come back to California and his crazy redheaded girlfriend.

"Well," I said, forcing cheerfulness into my voice. "Have a good trip."

"I'll call you when I get back," he said.

I squeezed my eyes shut. "Sure. That'd be nice." Polite lies are probably the most painful lies of all.

"Enjoy your Easter dinner," he said. "Tell your mom and Jerry hi for me."

"Sure."

Another silence. If he was waiting for me to say something, I didn't know what it was. I'd accepted his excuse, told him to have fun. Nothing more to be said, except good-bye.

"Good-bye, then." I said it.

"See you, Brenda."

"Bye," I said again.

After a moment of silence, he hung up. I pushed the "off" button and rolled over to put the phone back on the hook.

I lay on my stomach, my hand still on the phone. I wanted to cry and cry until I couldn't cry any more. Instead I lay there silently, my eyes dry, the fan cool on my bare back.

I loved Nick. Nick was leaving. And it was all my fault.

Therefore, heartbreak for Brenda. Again.

I'd been thinking that Tony Beale's crazy idea for seducing Nick after Easter dinner wasn't such a bad idea after all. I could take him around the corner of the house, and in the quiet dusk where we wouldn't be seen, I could show him I was willing to get my knees wet in the grass for him.

He'd put his hands in my hair and look at me with blue, intense eyes, then he'd race back home with me and make frenzied love to me again.

Too bad I'd never have the chance to put the plan into action.

Because he'd get off his airplane in San Antonio, see the beautiful blond witch again, and decide to stay.

Good-bye weird girlfriend with her weird, weird family. Good-bye Brenda and her strange addiction to lingerie. Nick would be making love on a kitchen table with a girl with a sultry Texas accent and long sleek hair.

A few tears of self-pity leaked from my eyes. I wondered if I'd ever see Nick's lovely house again or eat his lovely food or look at his strong face and the way his eyes crinkled when he smiled.

I lay there for a long time, letting emotion after emotion wash over me. I could pretend to be brazen, wild, and a lingerie addict all I wanted, but I was still stupid Brenda eating her heart out over a man.

Some things never changed.

I laid there until the window went dark and the room got cooler and David and Clarissa came home. I threw on some clothes and went out to talk to them.

My heart heavy, I started trying to convince David to go to Easter dinner at Mom's house. He flat-out refused. When I told him we needed to grit our teeth and live with it, he slammed the door and left.

Clarissa just looked at me and said nothing.

Later that night, while I lay awake thinking about Nick, I heard them talking about it.

"So," Clarissa asked in her frank way. "Why don't you want to go to Easter dinner at your mom's?"

David snorted. "Don't *you* start. Brenda's bad enough."

"I just want to know." After a casual silence she said, "We never did Easter in my family. Christmas, we had presents and a tree, but that's all. My family was never religious."

"Yeah, well, we always did the whole thing," David said. "Very white-bread Protestant."

"So why don't you want to do it anymore?"

"I do," David said defensively. "I just don't want to share it with Jerry."

"You said he was your best friend."

David waited a few moments before he answered. "He was. That's why I can't believe he did what he did."

"I'd like to meet him," Clarissa said.

241

"You would? Why?"

"I don't know. You said he bought your plane ticket home."

"I know," David admitted. "He helped me. He took my side when no one else in the entire city of Chicago would. He said I could repay him someday." He snorted. "I didn't think he'd help himself to my mother in return. God, I can't even think about it."

"I want to meet him." Clarissa sounded stubborn, for her.

"Come to the damn dinner, then," David said. "Brenda's not going to let up on me until I give in and go. I don't know why she's Mom's best friend all the sudden."

I wasn't. But I needed some pretense of peace between us all.

"What did you think of *Aliens Ate My Homework*?" Clarissa asked, changing the subject with her usual abruptness.

David seemed relieved to follow her lead. "It was cool," he said. "I liked it."

Apparently, I was the only one in San Diego who still hadn't seen it.

On Wednesday, my friend John from Bohemian Love Child came to the studio. I interviewed him and played some of his favorite tunes from days gone by.

"This is so cool, Brenda," he kept saying.

"So tell us about the music scene in California in the sixties," I suggested. As I figured, that kept him talking for a while. He went on about the summer of love and Janis Joplin and how he and the band and some other friends had piled into one car and panhandled their way across America to Woodstock. He kept talking while I flipped through CDs and occasionally interjected a comment.

Halfway through, Tony came in and planted himself across the table from John. He slammed a manila folder down in front of him and helped himself to a mike and some earphones.

Tony looked white about the mouth. Ever since Tim's surprise on Monday, Tony had sidled in and out of rooms, glancing furtively behind him, and he wouldn't leave unless I walked him to his car.

He'd called the police on Tim, but when the police had checked out Tim's apartment, they found Tim gone, moved out.

So far, Tim hadn't returned to the station for more antics. He'd more or less disappeared. I imagined him lying in wait on Coronado Bridge, bungee cord in hand.

When John slowed down about his reminisces about Woodstock, Tony spoke up. "So John, did you do any marijuana in those days?"

I gaped. "Tony!"

John blinked. He opened his mouth to answer, looked at his mike, and turned red.

"Well, did you?" Tony insisted. "I mean everyone did, right? It was the scene."

21

Bohemian Love Child

I tensed, trying to decide what Tony was up to. John dithered. "Well, yeah, it was a big thing at the time."

"And LSD. That was a big thing too. And speed."

John shook his head. "Now, I never did any of that." He laughed. "We couldn't afford it. We slept in ditches, man."

"But you smoked pot."

I glared at Tony, willing him to shut up. John looked confused. "Well, yeah. Like you said, it was the scene."

Tony pursed up his mouth. "So you are sitting here telling my listeners, many of whom are kids, how cool it was to do drugs?"

John looked alarmed. "Oh, hey, I never said that."

"But you did it. You smoked marijuana when you were young, probably started when you were still in high school. I have a newspaper article here"—he tapped his folder—"of you getting busted for posses-

244

sion of marijuana in San Francisco when you were eighteen."

"So?" John said, defensive. "Lots of people got busted for pot. Didn't you?"

"No." Tony gave him a smug look. "I never did. Never once. I got high on music and my friends. Never needed drugs."

John looked at him askance. "Yeah? I bet you had a lot of friends with that stick up your butt."

"Well, now," I tried to break in. "How about playing us your favorite song you heard at Woodstock, John?"

"I was clean," Tony said, "and everyone knew it. They respected me."

"Sure, man," John said. "I bet they were really respectful."

Tony half stood. "Are you telling my listeners and their families that it's better to be admired by your friends than to say no to drugs?"

"And we're almost out of time," I shouted. "Everyone listen to this fabulous commercial."

I jabbed the button. A spot for Jerry's boat repair down on Shelter Island roared to life. I had done the voice over for it. Why everyone thought that men with boats would be attracted to a boat repair shop announced by a woman's voice, I didn't know. But Jerry had insisted. And since Brenda was the only female voice at the station, guess who got assigned?

I glared at Tony as my voice extolled the convenient location of Jerry's shop and his ten years of expertise. "What are you, Tony, a shock jock?"

"No, I just don't want people coming in here and telling kids that drugs are OK."

I ripped off my headphones. "We weren't even talking about it until you brought it up!"

Tony waved his folder in my face. "I found this article.

In fact, I found several. He was in and out of jail for weed, Brenda. If I came across these so easily, so will everyone else."

"They will now," I pointed out.

"So, Mr. Dishard," Tony said, "when we return to the air, please point out to the kiddies that you were wrong and that it's very uncool to do drugs."

John stared at him. "You want me to say what?"

"Tony," I said through my teeth. "If you refuse to interview any rock star past or present who has ever touched drugs, our interviews will be few and far between."

"Oh? So you think drugs are OK, then, Brenda?"

"No! Of course not. What is with you?"

John stood up. "I think I'm out of here."

"Wait," I begged. "Tony, why did you book him if you didn't like the marijuana?"

"I didn't know about it until this morning," Tony said. He turned to John. "All you have to say is that you were wrong about the pot and kids shouldn't do it any more."

I buried my face in my hands.

"Hey, man," John said, "whether I think so or not, I'm not going to pander to your agenda."

"Fine," Tony said. "Nice talking to you."

"You don't have to go, John," I said.

"Yes, I do." John turned to me, his face softening. "It's not your fault you have a jerk for a boss. See you around, Brenda."

He stalked out of the studio. I opened my mouth to remind Tony he was an idiot, but the commercials ended, and I dove back into my chair. The phones were lighting up.

"OK, we're back," I said brightly. "John Dishard of Bohemian Love Child was talking to us today about life in the sixties. John had to leave—"

"But he wanted to say," Tony interrupted, "that he

knows that doing drugs was very wrong of him, and he encourages kids, and their parents, to say no to drugs."

I thumped my head on the table.

"The phones are going crazy," Tony said in delight. "Who's our first caller, Brenda?"

I shut my mike off and hissed, "You're going to get us sued, Tony."

Tony grinned at me, a big, toothy, annoying Tony grin. He turned off his mike. "So what? I bet I just jumped our ratings to a weekly high." He chuckled. "The Brenda/Nick thing was gone. We needed something new." He clicked his mike back on again. "Now, Brenda, who's that first caller?"

On Friday, my mother called me at the station. She and Jerry had decided not to have dinner at the house, she said, but to move the celebration to the sailboat. "It's supposed to be a very nice day, and we can all use the fresh air. We'll sail up to the cove, and then have dinner."

"You want us to cook Easter dinner in the galley?" I asked, incredulous.

"Why not? It will be fun. We don't have to do anything fancy. Just the basics."

"What about my potato salad?"

She laughed. "You don't have to worry about making your potato salad. We'll keep it simple."

I felt stung, illogically. It was my potato salad, and one of these years, I was going to get it right.

"I'll make it at home and bring it along," I insisted.

"Whatever you like, dear. Now, what about David?"

"He's coming," I said.

She drew a relieved breath. "Oh, good. Thank you, sweetheart. I know you must have talked him into it."

"No. He decided on his own. We're bringing Clarissa."

"Clarissa?" She sounded puzzled. "Well, it will be nice to see her again."

Clarissa, in the year she'd lived with me, had never done anything with my family. If ever I invited her, she always claimed she had something else to do, or she just looked at me as though I was crazy. And now she'd not only talked David into going to the dinner but also into bringing her along. Things were weird all over.

"Is Nick coming?" my mother asked.

I bit down on my lip. "Ow. No. He's, uh, he's flying out to see his brother in Texas."

"Oh. Well, that's nice for him."

"Yes, Mom," I said.

"I know you'll miss him. But he'll be back before you know it."

"Yes, Mom."

"See you Sunday? Let's meet at the slip at noon."

"OK." I heaved a sigh of resignation. "We'll be there."

I thought Nick might call me Friday night or Saturday morning before he flew out. I thought he might call me on his cell when he reached San Antonio. I thought he might call me from his brother's house.

I thought wrong. My phone never rang.

I didn't tell anyone how that cut me to the heart. I went to the store Saturday afternoon and bought potatoes and eggs and mayonnaise and mustard and dill weed. David groaned when I brought the groceries home.

"Brenda, you're not making that potato salad again."

"Yes, I am." I dug a knife into the skin of the first potato. "You don't have to eat it."

David wrinkled his nose. "Thank God."

I gave him a freezing look and continued peeling. I wasn't very good at it. The potato ended up half the size of when I started.

I prayed for rain and crappy weather, but when Sunday dawned, it was a beautiful day. The blue sky arched softly overhead, and only a little mist hung over the mountains and out to sea. The mist would burn off before long, and the day would be fair and clear.

Just before we left, I shoveled my potato salad into a plastic container and snapped the lid shut. The potato salad didn't smell right, and I didn't know why. I'd lightened up on the mustard. Maybe it was too much dill.

Someone knocked on the door. "David, will you get that?" I shouted.

No response from my bedroom. None from Clarissa's either. I hoped the two of them would be ready to go on time. Clarissa thought the word "punctual" only applied to other people, and lately David had copied her attitude.

I thumped down the container of potato salad and ran to the door, wiping my hands. I flung the door open.

Nick stood on the doorstep. The breeze ruffled his never straight blond hair.

"Hey," he said. "Am I in time for dinner?"

"Nick!" I screamed. I threw my arms around his neck. It never occurred to me to be dignified.

"Brenda," he said, in a slightly strangled voice. "Why do you smell like potato salad?"

"Nick." David emerged from my bedroom wearing shorts, boat shoes, a T-shirt and windbreaker, and a baseball cap. "I thought you were in San Antonio."

"I was. I finished up early." He slanted me a smile. "I can take care of the rest of my loose ends on the phone."

David didn't know what he was talking about and didn't care. He thumped on Clarissa's door. "Clarissa, come on. We're going."

I slid my hand into Nick's. He gave it a squeeze.

I thought I'd slide to the floor, my legs felt so warm and loose. What was he doing back? Had he come back for me? Questions bubbled to my lips, but I couldn't ask them here in front of my brother.

Nick leaned down and said into my ear. "We'll talk later."

He'd better believe we would. We'd talk, and then I'd rip off all his clothes and jump his bones. I didn't care right now whether he'd come back because his old girlfriend refused to see him. I only cared that he'd come back.

"I hope the kitchen table is ready," I whispered.

He actually blushed, but he sent me a sparkling glance that told me it was more than ready.

Clarissa emerged. She was dressed almost identically to David, though her windbreaker was blue while his was red. They looked cute together.

In deference to the fact we were going to sail, I didn't wear any pricey, sexy stockings, but under my T-shirt and shorts I sported a matching bra and underwear. Black, silky, and sexy as all hell. Maybe sometime during the voyage, I could corner Nick alone and show him.

I was elected to drive to the marina. Nick sat in the front seat with me and held the potato salad. David and Clarissa climbed into the back.

I gunned the car down the street and pulled onto the freeway, which was blissfully light on traffic. I turned on KBZ and let it rip. I'd had enough of classic rock.

In the back seat, David said. "Brenda, what is this?" He leaned over and pulled up something that crackled.

I glanced over my shoulder and saw the shiny plastic packet with the bright pink and blue label. I tried to grab it. The car swerved. Nick's eyes went wide.

I righted the car. Clarissa started laughing. David said, "Edible underwear? Brenda, what is wrong with you?"

Nick grinned back at him. "It's mine. Brenda bought it for me."

David tossed the packet into the front seat. It landed on top of the potato salad. "Don't tell me. Just don't tell me."

"What flavor is it?" Clarissa sat forward, her black hair spilling in pretty contrast over her red jacket.

Nick studied it. "Strawberry."

"I like the mango," Clarissa said.

"You do?" David asked her in a worried voice.

"Yes. The raspberry is pretty good, too, but it turns your tongue blue."

David put his hands over his face. "Oh, God."

"What's wrong?" Clarissa asked. "Are you a prude?"

"No. I just don't want to talk about edible underwear with my sister."

Nick started laughing. I loved his laugh.

I turned up the radio. We sped along past Balboa Park and into San Diego, singing along with Barenaked Ladies. I felt happy and excited.

I had no way of knowing how that day would end up.

When we reached the marina, Mom and Jerry, who had come early to prep the boat, met us in the parking lot.

We weren't the only family to decide to have an Easter Sunday sail. Cars filled the parking lot, and the marina itself was teeming with boats. Whether the sailors were celebrating the resurrection of Christ or just good sailing weather, I couldn't tell.

Nick, sweet man, carried the smelly potato salad toward the gate to the slips.

A car pulled in behind us as we walked. David glanced back. "Hey, Brenda, weren't you asking me about a white Toyota?"

I swung around. Sure enough, the boxy two-door that severely needed a paint job was parking in a space far from other cars.

Nick noted the apprehension on my face. "What is it?"

251

I stared at the Toyota. "It's my incompetent stalker." Or maybe he wasn't so incompetent after all. He kept following me, didn't he?

Mom and Jerry joined us. "Brenda thinks she has a stalker," Nick said. His brows furrowed.

David looked concerned. "Why didn't you say anything, Brenda?"

I shrugged. "I thought it was my imagination. I've seen him around the apartments, but he never follows me anywhere or even looks interested in me. But here he is now."

In a strange way, I was relieved to see him. His arrival made the reunion of Mom and David much less awkward. They were united in concern for Brenda being stalked.

Nick handed my mother the potato salad. He looked at Jerry and David. "Let's go see what he wants."

Mom took the potato salad, holding it as though it were the Holy Grail. "He might be dangerous. Call the police instead."

"Brenda, you call," Nick said. "I don't want him running off before we can catch him."

The three men, one blond, one dark, one redheaded, all muscular, walked together toward the car. They presented a nice back view, even if one of them was my brother.

I followed them. So did Mom and the potato salad. So did Clarissa.

None of us called the police. I'd never bothered to get another cell phone after mine had been flattened on Torrey Pines Road. Clarissa didn't own a cell phone because she was a free spirit, like my friend Billy, and my mother said she'd never needed one in the first fifty years of her life, so why should she now?

The only cell phone between us was the one on Jerry's belt.

As we hurried to catch up to the guys, Jerry slowed and stopped. "Wait a minute."

"What?" Mom asked him. "What's wrong, honey?"

David gave her a white-lipped look.

"I know that guy," Jerry said.

"You do?" I blurted.

"Not personally. But I've seen him. In a Chicago business magazine. He's a private investigator."

David froze. "A private investigator?"

"Yeah, I read an article about him. He was going on about the investigation business and how easy it really is to get hold of private records, and how best to protect yourself from identity theft. It was a good article."

"So he isn't a stalker," Clarissa said.

"Yes, he is," David corrected her, a bitter twist to his mouth. "Except he's not stalking Brenda. He's stalking me."

22

Potato Salad and Other Disasters

"Your wife must have hired him," Jerry said. His face was dark with anger.

"No kidding," David answered. He gave a bitter laugh. "Poor guy must be bored out of his mind. I don't exactly live it up down here."

"Why don't we ask him?" Nick suggested.

David blinked. "What?"

"Why don't we ask him to join us? If he wants to investigate you, he might as well investigate you up close and personal. You can tell him exactly what's going on. He can even take pictures."

I snorted. David scowled at me. "It's not funny, Brenda. I can't believe this."

Clarissa put her hand on his shoulder. "Nick's right. It's a good idea. Better that he knows the exact truth than make something up about you."

David's look softened when he turned to her. "I don't want him dragging you into this. I don't want him making sleazy insinuations."

"So that's why we bring him with us," Clarissa said. "To show him we're just friends."

David looked at her a moment longer, then he nodded.

In that look, he betrayed himself. Nick and Jerry were studying the white Toyota, so they might not have seen, but I noticed what was in David's eyes. I think Mom did, too. David hated that he had to keep Clarissa at a distance, that he had to be just friends. In the weeks that he'd lived with us, he'd started to care for her.

He might not agree, but I think David had an advantage over me. Because he'd been forced to take the hands-off approach, he'd been able to get to know Clarissa before lust could render the relationship a confused mess.

Nick and I, on the other hand, had jumped into bed right off and were still trying to figure out what we were doing. I wondered who'd end up with the better relationship.

"Let's go, then," Nick said.

The six of us started for the car. The guy in the Toyota must have seen us coming, but he pretended to look past us out to the marina, as if he was a harmless Sunday sightseer out to watch the boats.

We surrounded the car. He slowly turned his head and saw me and my mop of red hair, Clarissa's dead-white face, my mother with her hands full of potato salad, and three muscular men—David, Nick, and Jerry—peering through his open windows at him.

As I said before, he was a young-looking guy with dark hair. He wore his trench coat. A camera, camera case, and clipboard sat on the seat beside him. He looked back at us and swallowed.

"Hi," Jerry said, giving him a big smile. "Aren't you Reginald Weiz, the private investigator?"

"Uh," the guy answered.

My mom chimed in sweetly, "Jerry recognized you. He's from Chicago, too."

"Oh. Uh—"

Reginald Weiz suddenly reached down and tried to start his car. Nick snaked his arm in and yanked the keys from the ignition. He dangled the keys from his fingers and said cheerfully, "We're just going out for a sail. Why don't you come with us?"

"We're making Easter dinner and everything," my mother said. "It will be much more fun than sitting in the car all afternoon."

Reginald gripped the steering wheel until his knuckles went white. "You want me to come with you out on your boat?"

"Yes." My mother beamed at him. "I made chocolate pie for dessert."

"Uh—" He started to splutter.

Nick opened the door. "Come on. We need to have a talk."

He and Jerry more or less hauled Reginald out of the car. "This is kidnapping," Reginald said plaintively.

"Not really," Jerry said. "We're not holding you for ransom or anything. Can you sail?"

"No."

"That's OK. You can help out in the kitchen."

"And if you complain about kidnapping," David put in, "I can complain about you stalking me."

Reginald looked at us warily. He probably thought we'd take him out to sea and throw him overboard. And maybe we would.

I grabbed his camera and case and followed as Reginald limped along between Jerry and Nick. The camera wasn't a digital one, but the 35mm kind, expensive, with a big lens. No doubt Reginald's film canisters were full of shots of David and Clarissa going in and out of the apartment together, driving off in his car together, sharing a burger and fries at the diner together. Creep.

No one else at the marina seemed to noticed that we'd abducted a guy out of his car and were dragging him onto our sloop. Clarissa and my mother carried the potato salad and bags of groceries. Jerry and Nick maneuvered Reginald on board, then turned to help the ladies.

"Hi Sarah, hi Brenda, hi David," our neighbor called. "Great day to go out, isn't it?"

It was indeed, a beautiful day. Made more beautiful by the presence of Nick, who steadied me as I stepped from dock to deck and down into the boat.

Nick had dressed for sailing in a sweatshirt over a polo shirt, shorts and boat shoes, not sneakers. Boat shoes have white soles, and you wear them so you don't get dark sneaker marks all over the pretty white deck. I'd learned that the hard way when I was about nine years old.

Jerry and David both reached to cast us off at the same time. David glared at Jerry, who made a surrendering gesture and stepped back so that David could unwind the lines. Jerry cranked up the engine, and we all took a place. Mom had already gone down to the galley.

Reginald looked longingly at the dock as we backed out. Jerry steered. David watched, his eyes pinched in fury.

"So, Nick," I said quickly. "Why don't you be skipper?"

One person has to be in charge of the boat—the driver, so to speak. They watch over the sails and monitor direction and speed; they tell the crew what to do, making sure everything goes smoothly and safely.

My father and David had always switched off on the job. They'd never let me do it, because, of course, I was handicapped by the fact that I was female. I'd obviously be too busy filing my nails or something to notice that the boat was sinking.

If Jerry skippered today, I'd never stop David from killing him. If David skippered, he'd relieve his anger by turning into Captain Bligh and running Jerry and the rest of us ragged. We'd only survive by mutinying.

But Nick was neutral. Neither David nor Jerry knew him well enough to like him or dislike him.

Nick looked at me, brows raised. "Never learned to sail," he said. "I was going to volunteer to swab the deck."

Great. That left me, and David was in a bad enough mood to take out his frustrations on Captain Brenda.

"I'll do it," Clarissa said. She shooed Jerry from the wheel and took hold of it. "I can sail a boat."

David glanced at her in surprise. "You can?"

Clarissa gave her typical shrug. "Sure. My dad taught me."

Without a word, she calmly took over.

The woman was astonishing. She could sail all right, with a competence that quickly put me and David to shame. Only Jerry could keep up with her, much to David's disgust. Nick said he felt redundant and went below to help my mom with the cooking.

Clarissa guided us out of the marina to the waters of Mission Bay. Lots of boats were out now, but she coolly steered and commanded us around them and through the narrow mouth of the Bay out to the ocean.

By the time we reached La Jolla, she had turned us into a well-oiled machine. David cranked windlasses, I wound lines, and Jerry moved the boom back and forth as we tacked and jibbed according to the wind. Once we'd reached the point where we wanted to stop, we brought in the sail, dropped the anchor, and Clarissa sat down on a bench, looking no more stressed than if she'd just come back from having her hair done.

The boat rocked gently, the sea calm, the wind fresh enough for sailing but not enough for a gale.

Jerry and David looked at each other. They'd just

worked together to haul sails without fighting. Jerry opened his mouth, probably to suggest that they could be friends again. David frowned, turned on his heel, and stalked away.

He couldn't go far. The boat was not that big. Jerry disappeared down into the galley, where I could hear my mom and Nick chatting and laughing together. The two of them were bonding over chopping carrots or something.

I abandoned David, Clarissa, and Reginald, who clung to a bench, looking slightly green, and climbed forward to the bow.

This was my favorite place on the boat. I sat cross-legged just behind the point of the bow and gazed out at the cliffs of La Jolla and the resorts lining the beaches. Kayaks and little boats scuttled about, and people in wet suits surfed or snorkeled. The occasional sea lion poked its head up from the water, sniffed the air, and dove back again. Sea birds swooped against waves as blue as Nick's eyes.

I always liked it up here, because I could be alone. The people talking in the stern or inside the cabin behind the tiny windows seemed remote, part of another world.

In my childhood, I'd come up here to shut out the voices of David and my father either bickering or talking about male things, my father complaining to my mother about whatever on those rare occasions that she joined us, and my mother exclaiming how beautiful everything was.

This was my special place away from it all, where I could feel the wind in my hair, the sun on my face, and the boat rocking beneath me like a cradle.

Sitting here, I began to think that Mom's idea had been pretty good. The sounds of my childhood were replaced by Clarissa and David murmuring together in the stern, punctuated by Clarissa's throaty laugh. Below me in the cabin, Mom spoke in her bright, bustling voice, and Jerry teased her. Nick's warm tones overlaid both of theirs.

"What's in the mystery container?" I heard Nick say. "Oh, potato salad."

"It's Brenda's specialty," my mother answered.

I jumped like a rabbit, scrambled back to the windows, and shoved my face against one. "Nick, no, don't eat it! It's terrible!"

Too late. He'd already scooped a hunk onto a spoon and put it into his mouth. He looked up at me while he chewed. His face became very, very still.

"It's—" He swallowed. "Interesting."

I thumped my forehead to the window frame. "It's awful."

"No, it's—" He gave up. "Hmm, hand me the olive oil. I have an idea."

I turned around and scooted back to the bow. I should have just dumped the container over the side. I didn't mind so much my family laughing at my potato salad— over the years, I'd gotten used to it. But I didn't want Nick to know the awful truth. I'd humiliated myself enough in front of him already.

More laughter from the galley. I cringed, trying to shut it out. My mother's voice floated up. "Reginald, do you like ham?"

"What? Oh, no, ma'am. I'm kosher."

"You can have potato salad," Nick said from inside the galley.

I buried my face in my hands.

After a while I heard someone climbing forward toward me.

I deduced that it was Nick, because Jerry or David or Clarissa wouldn't scramble as much. My mother wouldn't come to the bow at all, because she said sitting there made her sick.

Nick made it to the front after much climbing and holding onto ropes. He sat down beside me and swung his tanned legs to the rail. Wiry, golden-yellow curls traced his skin.

I wanted to touch him. I wanted to turn and put my arms around his neck and kiss him.

He leaned back, resting his hand just behind my butt. "Nice day," he said. He wore sunglasses against the glare. They were crooked, as though he'd knocked them when he climbed forward.

"How did you know," I asked, gazing at him, dressed and ready for sailing, "that we were going out on the boat today?"

"Hmm?" He straightened his sunglasses. "Oh, I called Jerry. He told me."

"Oh." I fell silent, watching the gentle waves and a kayaker heading for shore.

"Why are you here?" I asked after a while.

"I wanted to sit with you. Enjoy the water."

"No, I meant, here in San Diego? Why didn't you stay in Texas?"

"I finished what I needed to do," he answered. "And I was ready to come home. Besides, I couldn't think of a better way to spend Easter Sunday."

"You didn't want to spend it with your brother?"

He shook his head. "My brother's girlfriend is part of a huge extended family. They've more or less adopted him. He's covered."

I rested my cheek on my shoulder. "You're lonely without him, aren't you?"

"Yes." The terse word told me he didn't want to talk about it.

"You really didn't have to come out here and be with my insane family," I said. "I'd describe the situation as awkward."

He smiled a little. "Hey, I didn't want you putting on

lingerie for some other guy. I was surprised when I showed up at your apartment today that he wasn't there."

I blinked. "Who wasn't there?"

"The guy you were going to invite instead of me."

"What? Oh. No," I babbled, remembering what I'd said to him on the phone. "I decided not to ask anyone else." Well, it was the truth. Who else would I have invited? Tony Beale?

"Good." He studied me a minute, his sunglasses guarding his eyes. "I don't want to lie to you, Brenda. I went back to San Antonio to see my fiancée."

A lump rose in my throat. "I figured that's why you went."

"It was one reason."

He fell silent. The breeze flipped his hair; the sun burned it golden. The lines around his mouth, which were usually turned upward, had flattened.

"Don't keep me in suspense," I said, with a flippancy far removed from the dull ache I was feeling. "Are you going to marry her? Or did you push her off the Riverwalk?"

His mouth twitched. "I went back to see if I'd left Texas too soon, if I only imagined what I felt for you."

Imagined. Wasn't that nice?

He went on, "When I asked you to move in with me, the look on your face was—well, it floored me. You looked like that was the last thing you ever wanted me to ask you. I was surprised how much that hurt."

I touched his arm. "Nick, I never meant to hurt you. I just—"

"I know." He placed his warm hand over mind. "Let me finish. I realized that I'd rushed you. Then I wondered if I'd asked you so fast because I hadn't really finished with Cathy."

Ha—Cathy—I knew it!

"I wondered if I was substituting you for her in a long-term relationship," he said.

My heart burned. "Not really complimentary, Nick."

He smiled slightly. "I know. That's why I went. If I really was substituting you for her, it wasn't fair to you."

"Oh." *So he went to see his old girlfriend for my own good? Gee, that should make me feel so much better.* "And when you saw her—" I left it hanging.

"I didn't see her." He turned his head again, studying the shore and the cliffs. "I realized as soon as I got off the plane that I didn't need to see her."

"Why, was she on the runway?"

His teeth showed in his warm smile. "No. I realized that the face I most wanted to see was the one with your freckles and your blue eyes. I wasn't going after a long-term relationship because I was lonely. I was going after you."

I put my hand to my mouth. "Oh, God, Nick."

"I know that's not what you want right now. I know that Larry pushed you into things you didn't want to do. You're not really looking for commitment right now."

"I'm not?"

"You want wildness in your life. Unpredictability. I don't know if I can give that to you. I'm kind of stodgy."

I stared at him, the sexy man sunning his muscular, bare calves, letting the wind ruffle his sun-touched hair, the sexy man who'd taken me on his kitchen table in a frenzy of passion.

"You're not stodgy, Nick," I told him. "You're one of the most incredibly sexy men I've ever met in my life."

"Aw, you're just saying that," he joked.

I looked him up and down, taking my time. "Oh, yes, Nick. I was thinking the other day that if I stripped you naked and threw you in mud, you'd still come out gorgeous."

My heart started beating hard. Why did I have to think of that now? With my mother and David and Jerry and Clarissa and the private investigator from Chicago all cozy on the boat with us?

"If I did," he said, "that's because you made me that way."

I blushed. "You're trying to sweet-talk me because you didn't like my potato salad."

"Screw the potato salad." He put his hands on my neck, leaned down, and kissed me.

His lips were smooth and warm, his teeth playfully sharp. I ran my fingers through his wild hair, smoothing it with my palms. His tongue swirled and stroked in my mouth.

"Nice," he said when he stopped. "I missed doing that."

"Me too." I dropped my head back, ready to go on doing that.

His lips grazed mine. "Should we start all over again, Brenda?"

"We keep starting over again."

"I'm willing to do this over and over again until we get it right."

"OK."

I wasn't sure why he was talking about it, but with him holding me, I didn't care. He thought he'd messed up our relationship and wanted to make it right. I could have told him he was trying too hard. But right now I just wanted him.

"Right now, I just want you," I said.

He laughed quietly. "I share the sentiment. But that PI from Chicago is watching us. And he has a camera."

I turned my head. Sure enough, Reginald was standing up, gazing over the cabin at us. "Forget him. He's spying on David, not me."

"I don't want an audience." He scooped me up and settled me in front of him, my back against his chest. His legs hung on either side of mine. "I just want you," he said into my hair. "Come over tonight."

"OK."

I closed my eyes, happy. The sun was warm, the breeze cool, and Nick's body sheltered mine. He'd come back from San Antonio so he could kiss me again. He wanted me to come over so he could make love to me again.

I wriggled, settling back into his arms. I could feel his hardness underneath his shorts. I liked rubbing against it.

He liked it, too. He chuckled. "I won't ever trap you, Brenda," he said. "You can walk away from me whenever you like, free and clear." He held me a little tighter. "But not just now."

"Because if we stand up right now, everyone will see that you have a hard on."

"That's part of it." He pressed a kiss to my hair. "The other part is, I've never had a girl like you. You're wild, and you make me feel wild. I'm never quite sure what to do when I'm with you."

"That's fine," I said, enjoying him nuzzling my neck. "Just keep doing that."

"I don't want to bore you to death. So what did I do? Took you to my dad's old restaurant and made you have dinner with your mother."

I turned in his arms. "I liked the food."

And my mother and I had a much-needed argument. Nick had paved the way for some understanding, although we still had a long way to go. But at least I was here, wasn't I?

"Kiss me," I said.

He smiled down at me, and obliged.

I loved his lips. They were always smooth, like my French silk camisole. His face was cool from the wind, but his mouth was warm. Our tongues tangled, and his hand crept down to cup my breast, promising through the shirt what he'd do when it was bare.

I deepened the kiss, groaned into it. I looked forward to unbuttoning and unzipping his shorts, letting them fall down his thighs. His underwear would go next, baring the line of hair that pointed to his very long and very satisfying—

"Hey, you up there!" David suddenly shouted from the back of the boat. "Leonardo and Kate. Get back here so we can eat!"

Nick laughed. I cursed under my breath. David was good at ruining a moment. But at least David was teasing and not snarling.

Nick helped me to my feet. I went first, easily climbing over the deck that I'd climbed over hundreds of times. Nick came more slowly. He held onto the lines for dear life and waited a while before he would swing around the mast. I really needed to teach him to sail.

Clarissa still sat at the wheel, staring idly at the water. Reginald had gone below to the head, David told me. He was probably busy trying to figure out how to work it.

I ducked into the galley. Jerry and my mom stood in the middle of it, Jerry's brawny arms locked firmly around my mother's waist. He was leaning over her, kissing her like Rhett Butler kissing Scarlett.

"Ahem," I said loudly.

Mom jumped. Jerry let her go. She at least appeared embarrassed. "Brenda. I didn't hear you coming down."

"Obviously."

My mother gave me a severe look. Jerry folded his arms and tried a neutral expression. "Jerry, dear," Mom said to him. "Why don't you and Nick go up and Brenda and I will bring the food."

Jerry looked at Nick. Nick looked at Jerry. Both men nodded. "Sounds good," said Jerry. "All right," said Nick.

At that moment, Reginald stumbled out of the cabin in the bow, where the head was. "Damn door," he said. "Couldn't figure out how to open it."

Mom pushed past me. She crowded Reginald into the corner. "I've been meaning to talk to you. Why are you persecuting my son?"

Reginald looked suddenly panicked. "I'm not persecuting him. I'm doing my job."

"Taking pictures of him? Following him around like he's a criminal? He's done nothing wrong. That wife of his has already beggared him. Go back to Chicago and tell her you quit."

Reginald reddened. "Your son has been sleeping with that black-haired woman ever since he got here. If I can prove she was his girlfriend before the breakup, I will. I'm being paid much more than any of you can pay me to stop. Besides, I have my professional ethics."

"I wasn't about to offer you money," Mom said. "I am appealing to your sense of fairness. David is not sleeping with Clarissa. He's already in enough trouble. He knows better than to jeopardize himself."

"He went to Mexico with her. He got arrested. I bet he bought drugs."

I broke in, "I bet he bought a stupid souvenir vase with 'Mexico' written on it."

Reginald pointed at me. "He came back with you in a big Lexus. Probably got his drug-runner friends to bail him out."

"Oh, for God's sake, you are a moron," I said. "Larry brought him back as a favor to me. Larry's not a drug-runner. He's just a jerk."

"He certainly must like you to take a Lexus to Mexico and bail out your brother."

"I didn't have a choice."

On the boat, all had gone quiet. Nick and Jerry stood in front of the ladder. David had climbed down to listen, with Clarissa leaning in behind him.

My mother glared at Reginald like she really would haul him up onto deck and throw him over. She opened her mouth to berate him again, but Jerry broke in. "Why don't you go back to Chicago and tell your client that David is flat broke and barely surviving in San Diego?" he said. "That a man I admire has to sleep on his sister's sofa and scrounge through the want ads to see if he can become a fast-food cook? That he worked his ass off so his wife could spend all his money and complain when he didn't have any more? Tell her she bankrupted him and broke his spirit, but his family and friends are rallying around him and helping him the best they can."

Reginald was a pro. He simply looked at Jerry as though he was taking notes in his head. He wasn't about to break down crying and say he was ashamed.

David, on the other hand, had no such inhibitions. He swung a furious gaze on Jerry. "The last thing I need is you acting all sanctimonious and sticking up for me. I brought you here as a friend, and look what you did to me? Moved right into my house and my life like you owned it." He turned to Reginald. "If anyone needs investigating, it's him."

"David," my mother said wearily.

"And I don't even want to start on what *you* did."

"You sound just like your father," Mom said, her lips tight.

"Well, someone has to."

Jerry said sternly, "We need to talk about this."

"No." Nick said, breaking into the tension. "We need to eat dinner. That's why we came. Brenda, will you help me?"

Mom, Jerry, David, and Reginald fell silent. I expected David to explode and tell Nick to mind his own business, but everyone seemed to agree to let Nick take over.

Nick calmly took the ham, which had been precooked and warmed up and put it on a platter, and arranged cut fruit around it. He brought out the warmed up macaroni and cheese, the fresh green beans that he and Mom had fixed, and the loaf of bread Mom had bought at a bakery.

He thrust the ham platter at me. There wasn't enough room down here for all of us to eat at the table, so we were going to eat al fresco on deck. David actually moved aside so I could climb out, balancing the ham.

One by one, the silent members of our family gathering took whatever Nick handed them and brought it up to the deck. Reginald came out with a stack of plastic plates and silverware. Mom appeared with the bread. Clarissa carried the beans, Jerry the salad, and Nick brought up the rear with the infamous potato salad. I noticed he didn't give David anything to do.

We set it all on a folding table on the corner of the deck. I arranged the dishes to look pretty, because it seemed important for some reason.

Everyone crowded on the deck, and Nick took the plastic plates and passed them around. No one spoke.

"Why don't you start, Brenda?" Nick suggested.

His presence was magical. My brother and my mother acted as though they wouldn't put a foot out of line as long as he was directing. My heart was beating hard with anger and embarrassment, but I was grateful to Nick for basically telling us all to shut up and get on with it.

But he made one big mistake. He thought that Brenda Scott could be part of the peacemaking process. He hadn't figured on my famous ability to screw everything up.

I started for the table with all the food. Then I slipped on the wet deck.

My left foot went back; my right foot stuck. My arms went out. Nick reached for me, but it was too late.

I grabbed for the table. It overbalanced. I watched the table go over backwards as though it were a slow-motion scene in a horror movie.

Everyone gasped. The platter of ham, the bowl of green beans, the macaroni and cheese, and the bakery bread all slid through the spaces between the rails and flew out in a perfect arc down to the waiting sea.

Everyone stood there, mouths open as the Easter feast splashed into the ocean and sank swiftly beneath the surface.

I had managed to save one dish. I handed it to Nick, tears blinding me.

Nick took off the plastic lid. "Potato salad," he announced.

23

A Long, Cold Day in Hell, or Conversations with My Family

David clamped his hands to his head and shouted, "Brenda, you are the stupidest female on God's green earth!"

"It wasn't her fault," my mother defended me.

"Whose was it, then?" David snarled. "No one was near that table but my clumsy little sister. What were you thinking telling her to start, Nick? She makes a mess of everything."

I knew he was upset and lashing out at anyone he could, but I resented that the lashee was me.

"What about you?" I said in David's face. "You couldn't lift a finger to help. All you can do is stand around yelling at anyone who upsets you. Mom didn't have to invite you today. She could have blown you off, and that would have been fine with me."

"Since when have you taken her side? I thought you

were just as pissed off as me that she's sleeping with my best friend."

Reginald looked interested. I ignored him.

"So you're mad at her," I said angrily. "And Jerry. So am I. But that doesn't give you the right to be nasty to everyone in your path, including me, just because everything isn't going your way. I didn't do anything to you. I'm letting you crash at my apartment because I feel sorry for you. Because I'm your sister, and for some reason I want to help you."

Did David look ashamed of himself? Did he back down and apologize? Of course not. "Fine," he retorted. "If you feel that way, I'll move out. I'll sleep on the streets. Will you be happy?"

"Don't be so stupid!"

"You can always come home, David," my mother said. She stood by the cabin door, her arms folded, her lips tight. "Your bedroom is empty. But you won't, will you?"

"Hell, no. Do you think I could sleep knowing you and Jerry were humping on the other side of the house? I'm not about to listen to that all night, every night."

"I'll take that as a compliment to my sexual prowess," Jerry said mildly.

David glared at him. "Don't make me sick. Thinking about you and her makes me want to puke. Only I haven't had any food to throw up!" He pointed at my mother. "It was your stupid idea to have Easter dinner on the boat. At home, I'd be nauseous, but at least I'd have something to eat."

Out of the corner of my eye, I saw Clarissa take the potato salad from Nick. She daintily dipped a fork into it and chewed a mouthful.

She didn't pass out or make a face. She swallowed without fuss and handed the container to Reginald. "Want any, Reggie?"

Reginald, his face white, took it hastily and shoved his

own fork in. I have no idea if it was kosher, but Reginald didn't seem inclined to complain.

"Oh, great," David said. "All we have to eat is Brenda's disgusting potato salad."

"I didn't see you volunteering to help make anything else," I pointed out.

"This entire fiasco is because of you and her." David indicated my mother with his chin.

"I have a name," Mom said.

"Oh, that's right. Sarah. Should I call you Sarah, so we can all be friends together? Won't that be cozy?"

"Lay off her, David," Jerry said.

"Or what?" David swung on him. "You'll tan my hide? Am I supposed to get used to calling you Pa?"

"David, shut up!" I yelled.

Nick sat down next to Clarissa. He didn't eat the damn potato salad, he simply put his elbows on his knees and watched us.

David glared at me. "Why are you all gushy and happy with our mother? Or are you sleeping with Jerry, too?"

I rolled my eyes. Jerry didn't bother saying anything.

"That's enough, David," my mother said.

"Sorry, Mom. You gave up any right to make me obey you. And all rights to my respect. You've totally lost that."

"Oh, I have, have I?" my mother said, balled fists on her hips. "What would you have me do, David, put on black and lock myself away for the rest of my life so that you will respect me? Haven't I earned my own life? For thirty-three years I lived with a man who didn't like me, and now I'd like to live with one who does."

"What are you talking about?" David demanded. "Dad liked you fine. You and he never divorced or even talked about it."

My mother nodded. "No, of course we didn't, because

I became the woman he wanted me to be. I learned early on that I had to suppress my entire personality to keep the peace, to become the perfect wife and the perfect housekeeper and the perfect mother. Otherwise we fought every day. I was young and afraid of confrontation, so I kept the peace. I gave up everything I was and everything I wanted for a man who then didn't respect me because I had given up everything."

David shook his head. He didn't believe her. "You could have left him. You could have told him to screw himself and gone off to find your so-called life, sleeping with men half your age."

"No, I couldn't. I had you and Brenda. I loved you too much to leave you or to take you away from a house where I could take care of you. I never had a job; I didn't know how to work, and I never could have made enough money to survive on my own. I knew that. So I stayed."

David might not have believed her, but I did. I realized suddenly that she had done exactly what Larry had expected me to do—be everything he wanted me to be, never mind my own dreams and goals and needs. He'd wanted a woman who lived for him. If that woman wanted anything for herself, it simply didn't matter to him.

I'd been luckier than my mom. I'd had a choice, because I had my own career and my own life, as lame as it was. I could have told Larry and all his money to go fly a kite any time I wanted to. Mom hadn't had that choice.

"I didn't know that," I said.

"Oh, come on," David interrupted. "She's trying to make you feel guilty. 'I sacrificed so much for you, now I get to make a complete fool of myself.' That's what she's saying. It's the mother guilt-trip."

Mom heaved an exasperated sigh. "And you are giving me the son guilt-trip. You're throwing a temper tantrum because I'm not living my life to make you happy."

"I am not," David retorted. "This isn't about me. It's about you. You're only using Jerry for sex and to show the world you're not old. And he's using you for God knows what."

"This is getting a little personal," Jerry said quietly. "You can't possibly know what's between me and your mother. You haven't spoken to her in weeks."

"Because I don't want to speak to her," David growled. "Or you. And I didn't want to be here. This was a stupid idea."

He turned his back and stomped down into the cabin. My mother's blue eyes blazed with fury, and she went right after him. "Oh, no, you don't."

I hurried after them. The others stayed on the deck. I didn't blame them. I wondered if any of them would ever speak to us again. Even Reginald.

"I don't want to talk about it," David was yelling. It was his favorite cop-out line.

"You never want to talk about anything," Mom told him. "You stomp away, and we are supposed to believe that makes you strong and silent. But you're not strong. You're acting like a three-year-old."

"Who is the one acting childish here?" David demanded.

"You both are," I said. "I wouldn't be surprised if our friends left us and swam for shore. Or made us swim for shore."

"Why are you taking her side?" David shouted at me. "I thought you hated Jerry as much as I do."

"I don't hate him," I said. "But David has a point. Mom, are you seeing Jerry just to get back at Dad?"

Mom went quiet a moment. I don't think she'd thought of that before. "I like Jerry. I might even love him. And no, he's nothing like your father."

"See?" David said. "She's sleeping with him to prove

herself, because she was too afraid to have a life before. Did you hear that, Jerry? How does that makes you feel?"

"David, stop interfering in my life!" Mom shouted.

"You're my mother. What am I supposed to do?"

Mom opened her mouth to yell back at him, then all three of us heard a soft click as the door above us closed.

I climbed the ladder to the door and turned the handle. The door wouldn't open.

"Hey!" I yelled. I knocked on the glass.

Jerry squatted down to look at me. "You three need to talk about things," he said. "When you've come to some kind of agreement, we'll let you out again."

I stared at him. He stared back, no sympathy on his face. Nick leaned over his shoulder.

"Nick!" I cried. "Let us out."

Nick studied me for a moment. His expression was straight, and he, too, looked unsympathetic. He stared at me for a time; then he turned and walked away.

Abandoning me. The rat.

I climbed down the ladder and sank onto the aft berth. The galley was a mess, crowded with containers for heating up the dinner we could no longer eat. I hoped the pelicans and the fish were having a good time out there.

"This is your fault," David spat. I wasn't sure whether he was talking to me or my mother. Probably both of us. "You've ruined my whole weekend."

"You didn't even want to come," I said churlishly. "Geez, David, could you get past thinking everything is about you?"

"He can't help it," Mom said. "He was raised to believe that we all exist for him and that we don't have lives of our own."

"That's not fair," David said hotly. "And it's not true."

"He was the only son," Mom went on, looking at me, not David. "So of course he would take over ruling us when his father was gone."

"Stop it," David said. "I never thought that. I don't think like that."

"Well, you're behaving like that."

"Well, you're behaving like a slut."

"Don't call my mother a slut," I snapped.

"Oh," David sneered. "She has a great example in you. Look at you with your mountains of lingerie and spending your nights with Nick. Brenda didn't even know Nick when she first jumped in bed with him. Clarissa told me. She met him at Clarissa's New Year's party and had sex with him that night. What would you call that?"

Mom switched her gaze to me. "Is that true, Brenda?"

"Hey, why are we suddenly talking about me?" I complained.

"I'm the one being spied on," David said, "and I'm the only one not sleeping with anybody."

"So that justifies you being horrible to the rest of us?" Mom asked him. She turned to me again. "Did you really not know Nick when—on New Year's?"

"No," I answered.

She gave me a worried mother look. "Brenda, do you know how foolish that was? Nick turned out to be a nice young man, but what if he hadn't been? A one-night stand with a stranger is dangerous. What were you thinking?"

"I don't remember what I was thinking," I said. "Larry was there, and I had too many martinis."

"And you were drinking? Brenda, I want you to promise me you'll never do something like that again."

I buried my face in my hands. David said, "Look who's talking. How well did you know Jerry before you hit the sack with him?"

My mother swung on him. "I knew him quite well. We got to know each other while you were busy feeling sorry for yourself. And he was your friend, and I know your true friends are good people."

David snapped, "Don't you dare blame this on me."

"I am not blaming anyone," my mother said firmly. "Jerry and I talked, we became friends, we started seeing each other seriously. If you cannot accept that, then you can't. But stop railing at me because you don't like my choices."

David glared at her a moment, then stamped to the forward part of the cabin, arms folded. There was a berth in the bow, which was V-shaped, following the hull. David stood in the berth's doorway, gave us both a lofty look. "I can see you'll do what you want, no matter how we feel." He started to close the door. "This isn't over."

"I realize that," my mother said; then the door slammed shut.

Mom looked at me. I studied the floor, not wanting to talk any more. I was torn up inside, and nothing was helping.

Mom sank down on the berth on the other side of the galley, the same one Nick and I had almost made love on.

Everything went silent except for the slap of water on the hull, the murmur of voices above where the more rational part of our party waited for us to hash things out.

None of us seemed inclined to bang on the door and demand our release. I think we didn't want to face them. Mom sat on her berth and I sat on mine, and I imagined David sulking behind the door.

We remained quiet, buried in our own thoughts, hoping we'd stay there until a miracle occurred and all our problems went away—or the boat sank.

* * *

I don't know how many hours went by. I got hungry, but had no wish to rummage through the remnants of the Easter feast. My mother stayed dormant on her bunk, I on mine.

David had picked the fore cabin on purpose, I thought sourly. The head was in there. Anyone else on the boat who had to go to the bathroom was out of luck.

The sun began to slide west into the ocean. Still we sat there, not speaking, not moving. I heard the head flush, and then, a long time later, flush again.

The digital clock read five PM when Nick finally opened the door.

He took in the sullen faces of myself and my mother, and the closed door of the far cabin.

"We should go in," he said. "It's getting dark."

Without a word, my mother got off her bunk and started cleaning up the galley. I rose and stalked up the stairs past Nick in complete silence.

David stayed in his cabin, behind the closed door.

Clarissa took command again. She guided Jerry and me into winding ropes and moving sails, and we sailed gently and quietly back into Mission Bay.

At long last, we reached our slip. Reginald was the first off the boat. He looked back at us, hugging his camera and his camera case. "Thank you for an interesting afternoon," he said; then he turned and ran for the parking lot.

Nick helped us put the boat away for the night, following Jerry's instructions. David was still holed up in the cabin.

Nick stepped off the boat and helped my mother and then me onto the dock. We hadn't exchanged two words since I'd come up from below.

Jerry followed us. I shouted back at the cabin. "David, come on."

No response.

I lost my temper. "David, I'll just leave you here, I don't care."

Nothing.

"You can't do that, Brenda," my mother said. "You can't leave him behind."

"Yes, I can, if he's going to be stupid."

Clarissa said, "I'll stay with him."

"How are you going to get home, then?" I asked crossly.

She shrugged. Nothing perturbed the woman. "I'll call somebody."

I was too annoyed to argue. "Fine," I said, and started up the dock.

Reginald had already left us in the dust. I wondered if we'd ever see the white Toyota again.

Nick and I got into my car. In the rearview mirror, I saw Jerry and my mother stop at the top of the dock for a long kiss.

I started the car and drove out of the marina to the main streets.

Nick and I rode back to the apartment in complete silence. He held the empty potato salad container. He and Jerry and Clarissa and Reginald had eaten every bite of it.

I knew I should apologize for the fight and my family and the meal and the horrible day, but the words wouldn't come.

Nick didn't seem inclined to speak either. He didn't touch me or even look at me. He studied the passing scenery and the other cars on the freeway and never once turned in my direction.

I couldn't tell if he was giving me space, or if he'd decided never to see me again. My heart ached and burned.

I was glad Clarissa and David had stayed behind. The apartment would be blissfully empty. I parked my car in my designated slot and stopped the engine.

Nick still didn't look at me. I couldn't bring myself to ask him to come upstairs. I'd have to explain, have to apologize, and right then I had no words for either.

We sat for a long time in silence, neither of us moving, neither of us suggesting we get out of the car. Maybe we thought that if we spoke, somehow things would go wrong, somehow things would be over.

It got darker. The lights in the parking lot came on. The air grew colder. People walked past the car, glanced in, wondered what we were doing in there.

After a long time, Nick said, "Olive oil."

I turned my head. "What?"

"Olive oil. And crushed red pepper. That's what saved the potato salad. It was good."

"You don't have to say that," I said. "It was crap."

"No." Nick shifted the container in his lap. "You had a good base. I just added the finish."

"Do you mean that for the first time in my life, my potato salad turned out? And I didn't get any?"

He grinned. "It was great. I know you're starving, though. Let's go upstairs and I'll make you something to eat."

I snorted. "There isn't any food in my house."

"Then let's go somewhere. I'll take you out." He put his hand on mine. "OK?"

When a gorgeous guy asks you out like that, why argue? I started the car again and drove down the road to the diner.

Nick bought me dinner, a cheeseburger with all the works and a basket of greasy French fries. I ate them as though they were ambrosia.

We were quiet during the meal. Even strangers sharing a table have more to say.

I thought that when we returned to the apartment, he'd get out of the car, kiss me good-night, get back into his own car and drive home. Instead he silently led me up the stairs and inside.

As I said, the apartment was blissfully empty without Clarissa and David. I had no idea how long it would take Clarissa to talk David out of the cabin and get him home, so I decided to enjoy the peace while I had it.

I could no longer be silent, though.

"Nick," I began.

"Shhh." He took my hands in his and kissed me.

Our lips met, then met again. He kissed me for a while, then led me into my bedroom.

He stopped. He looked around at the pile of lingerie on the floor mixed with David's underwear and clothes. My bed was rumpled and also full of lingerie.

"Sorry," I said. "I wasn't expecting company."

I threw the panties and bustiers and camisoles and teddies off the bed and straightened the covers. Nick's bedroom was always neat. His whole house was neat. Not perfect, just neat. I was willing to bet Nick never broke plates or spilled salsa on the floor. I'm amazed he ever let me in to ruin the neatness.

He watched me, that little smile on his face. "Take off your shirt," he said.

Romance heroines were supposed to swoon or say, "Oh, no, sir, I could not." Brenda Scott grabbed her T-shirt and pulled it off over her head.

Nick looked at me in my bra, and smiled. "You didn't buy the corset?"

"What corset?"

"The one you said that you'd buy for today. Remember? When you called and asked me to Easter dinner?"

"Oh. That corset. No," I said hastily. "I didn't get it. I thought you weren't coming."

"Good," he said.

He kept looking me up and down. My nipples tightened behind the lace. "Why good?"

"Because that means you didn't buy it for someone else. Lie down."

Again, no resistance, no swooning, no protests. I plopped full-length on my bed.

He pulled my boat shoes off my feet, then my socks. He unbuttoned my shorts and slid them down my legs. He stood back and looked at me as though he'd unwrapped a package and liked what he found inside. Warmth swirled in my abdomen.

He said, "There's the Brenda I came back to find. It's all I thought about on the plane. Coming home to find lingerie-loving Brenda."

Now, now was the time for me to tell him, *You know, Nick, this is not the real Brenda. You like a pretend Brenda. I should be honest and show you the real me.*

Nick stripped off his clothes. His tanned chest and arms and thighs came into view. I lay there and enjoyed the view.

Oh, well, if he wanted lingerie-addict Brenda, I'd just have to accept it.

Nick's nose was a little sunburned from the day on the water, but the rest of him looked none the worse for wear. Gold hair curled across his chest and drew to that sexy line down his abdomen.

"How did I get so lucky?" I murmured.

He stood there in his bikini briefs, hands on hips. "Lucky?"

"To find a guy as gorgeous as you."

He laughed, showing white teeth. "That wasn't luck. I seduced you."

"You did?" I squeaked. "I mean, yes, you did. On New Year's."

"I saw you come in, so I asked the friend who'd dragged me there who you were."

"And he said, 'Oh, that's just Brenda'?"

Nick chuckled, warm and smooth. "No. He told me

he didn't know you. Someone else said your name was Brenda, and I spent the rest of the night trying to corner you." He ran a hand through his hair. "To tell you the truth, I don't remember exactly how I finally wore you down. But I guess I did. I woke up in the morning, and there you were."

I smiled at him. "Looking like something the cat coughed up."

He sat down on the edge of the bed. I enjoyed myself watching the muscles of his thighs. "No, you looked beautiful."

He stroked my hair. I rolled over and kissed his hip.

"You don't know," he went on, "what hell it was. I'd found the woman of my dreams and let her get away in one short night."

"The woman of your dreams?" I basked in the glow of his adoration.

"Yes. I didn't know anything about you, and yet, I just knew—"

I shook my head against the pillow. "You're sweet, Nick, but I'm not a dream woman."

"No, you're real. That's the best part."

I raised up on one elbow. "You'd just broken an engagement and come home to start over. I'd have looked good no matter who I was. You wanted something different, and I sure am different. Today should have proved that."

"Why are you questioning my taste? I told you today, it had nothing to do with breaking up with Cathy or wanting something different. When I saw you on New Year's, even when I was half-drunk, I knew you were the woman I truly wanted."

"Stop," I said.

"Let me get it out." He cupped my cheek, smoothed my temple with his thumb. "I want you and your red hair and your big blue eyes. I don't care who your

mother dates or how many private detectives are following your brother around. You're crazy and fun and
everything I'm not. You make me chase you into lingerie
stores and take you on the kitchen table. I never would
have done that before I met you. You made me wake up
inside. Since my parents' death, I'd pretty much been
asleep."

This was breaking my heart. I sat up. "Nick, you don't
know me, not really."

"I know enough."

"No, I'm not the person you think I am. Before New
Year's, I wasn't like this. I'm not what you want."

"You know, Brenda," he said gently, "you've gone
back to deciding what I feel. If you don't want this to go
any further than seeing each other on weekends, that's
fine. I'll go slow and take what I can get." He winked. "I
plan to take a lot."

"Nick," I began.

"You still don't sound happy."

"I am happy." I balled my fists, my hands sweating.
"You make me happy. But one day you'll wake up and
realize I'm not what you thought I was."

He went silent. He continued to touch my face,
smoothing my skin with his fingertips. I waited for him
to say, "You're right," to put on his clothes and walk out.

After a time, he said softly, "You know, I really hate
Larry Bryant."

"Oh good," I answered. "Why?"

"I don't know what he said to you or what he did to
you. But he must have made you feel like you weren't
sexy and attractive. He's wrong. You're all those things.
You're strong and you're smart, and you have me."

"I told you, I am over Larry Bryant."

"But you still think you have to be a different person
to get me to love you. You don't. You just have to be
Brenda."

"It isn't like that—" I broke off, looking at his smile. "Oh, wait. I'm stupid. You're sweet-talking me. You're saying all these things so you can get into my pants."

"Right now, I'm hoping you'll try to get into mine."

"Thought you'd never ask," I said.

I ended the too-serious discussion by making him stand up so I could yank down his briefs.

A little later, he lay stretched out beside me, stark naked, kissing my damp skin. I traced the hard muscle of his arm and shoulder, enjoying the cool air from the window that played over us.

Nick had come back for me. He wanted me. Correction, he wanted lingerie-addict Brenda, but right now lingerie-addict Brenda was just selfish enough to let him have her.

I pulled him to me and kissed him. He responded. He rolled me onto my back, parting my legs.

He made love to me slow and strong, lacing his fingers through mine against the pillow. Nick usually made love in silence, showing me his joy by his actions or by the little pucker between his brows that he got when he was puzzled or intense.

"Brenda," he whispered hoarsely when he was about to climax, and that raw sound sent me spiraling over the edge.

I'd drifted off to sleep, snug under the sheets with Nick, when someone knocked on the door.

I came awake all muzzy and saw that it was still dark. "My brother," I mumbled to Nick.

Not until I'd reached the door did I realize that I'd given David a key. That, and he was supposed to be with Clarissa, who also had a key.

Of course, knowing David and Clarissa, they'd probably both lost them or left them on the boat or let them fall overboard.

I opened the door. Tony Beale stood on the threshold. "Hi, Brenda," he said pushing past me. He barely noticed the silk negligee I'd thrown on over my bare skin. "Do you have any beer?"

24

Tony Beale Has Another Great Idea

"What are you doing here?" I blurted out.

"Shut the door," Tony said. He planted himself on my sofa. "Don't mind me."

I closed the door against the night and locked it again. "Tony, what are you doing here?"

Tony wore a Chargers sweatshirt and had a large, rather bulging fanny pack around his waist. "I can't stay at home," he said. "Tim might find me."

"Tim?"

"He's following me, Brenda. I can feel it. But when I turn around, no one's there."

I closed my eyes. "I don't believe this."

"Hey, he could be dangerous. Let me stay here, pleeeze?"

"Tony—"

Nick opened my bedroom door and walked out. He'd

288

put on his T-shirt and underwear. "What's going on?"

"Oh, hi, Nick." Tony's brows climbed. "Well, well, did I interrupt something?" He chuckled. "Hey, it's no problem. You two carry on. I'll just watch some TV. Oh, and I'll take that beer, Brenda."

Nick disappeared back into the bedroom. When he came out again, he was fully dressed. He sat down in a chair facing Tony, who had just popped open the beer I'd finally handed him.

"Now, what exactly do you want?" Nick asked him.

"I'm hiding out," Tony said. "From a crazed morning show host."

"The shark guy," Nick said, catching on fast.

"Yes, the shark guy. He hasn't gotten over being fired yet."

"Don't you have anywhere else to go?" I asked. "A hotel? He won't be able to get in to see you, if you tell them not to let him."

Tony looked surprised. "A hotel? That's too expensive. I knew you had a couch."

Nick darted a glance at me. "He's done this before?"

"No." I glared at Tony. "I can't imagine why he thinks he can crash here."

"Oh, come on, Brenda. After all I've done for you. I gave you the morning slot."

"And fired Tim, which is why you're trying to hide out here. Thanks a lot."

"Lighten up," Tony said. "I'm making you into a star. Speaking of that, I'm glad you're here, Nick. I've come up with a good cross-promotion scheme for both our stations. Plus we raise money for charity so everyone loves us. What do you think?"

Nick blinked a few times, still not quite sure what had just happened. "I'm not the station manager. And I don't know what you're talking about."

"Promotion. Ratings. It's what we live for." Tony hunkered on the sofa, elbows on knees, his eyes taking on that fanatic glow he got when he had one of his great ideas. "We have a big weekend party with competitive games, your station and KCLP. Pie eating, dart throwing, tug-of-war, wrestling, spoon races, anything you can come up with. The show hosts will compete against each other, and the whole thing is broadcast mutually on our two stations. The victors will win donations to charities from sponsors, and the station with the most donations at the end of the day will be the champion. They'll make the other station get weird haircuts or work in their underwear or something as the loser prize. What do you think?"

"I think it's two o'clock in the morning," Nick said. "But I'll tell my station manager."

"It'll be great. It would be even better if you and Brenda tied the knot there or something. Or got engaged. Are you two engaged?" He looked at us hopefully.

"Tony!" I shouted.

"Just asking. Don't get all bent out of shape. We can always ask that band Bohemian Love Child to do a set."

I gave him an incredulous look. "You insulted the band leader on the air. You accused him of being a pothead. Remember? I was sitting right there."

"Oh, he'll understand about that. It's show biz."

"It's not a bad idea, Brenda," Nick said gently. "It would be good publicity and good for charities."

"Nick, you can't take his side! He's the crazy man."

Nick grinned. "Maybe, but he knows his job. I'll suggest it when I go in tomorrow."

"Oh, God," I groaned.

A key scraped in the door lock. Tony turned pale and leapt behind the sofa. Before I could point out that Tim wouldn't likely have a key to my apartment, the door opened.

It was Clarissa and David, but they didn't see us. David had his arms around Clarissa's waist and was kissing her passionately. His hand groped for the door handle that had already swung away from him. Their mouths were locked, and Clarissa had her hands firmly planted on my brother's buttocks.

Tony popped up from behind the sofa. "Oh, wow. Is this an orgy?"

I sprang froward, dragged the startled couple inside, and closed the door. "Are you nuts?" I asked David. "I bet Reginald is out there right now snapping pictures."

"Pictures?" Tony beamed. "Someone's going to take pictures? Who's Reginald?"

"Tony, go away!" I pleaded.

David swept his gaze around the room. "What the hell is going on? Why is everyone here at two o'clock in the morning? And what's all this about an orgy?"

Clarissa clung to David's arm. She looked as languid as ever, but her eyes held a certain happiness. "Come on," she said to David, tugging him toward her bed-room door. "Let's get some sleep."

"Can I talk to David for a minute?" I asked.

David looked annoyed and exhausted. He gave Clarissa a brief kiss on the lips and told her he'd be right in.

I glanced at Nick. He nodded imperceptibly and sat back down. He started asking Tony questions about his charity idea, and I grabbed David by the arm and pulled him into my bedroom.

"David," I began.

He eyed me narrowly. "What?"

"You and Clarissa."

David threw a pile of underwear from a chair in the corner and sat down. "What about it? I like her."

Then, before my eyes, my defensive and prickly

brother softened. His eyes became the color of the sky just after sunset and held a glow of that hidden sun.

"No, you know what it is? She likes me. *Me*. She doesn't care what school I went to, or how much I made, or how many people I supervised, or whether I was asked to join an executive club. She doesn't give a damn. She only cares that I like snorkeling and eating those hot dogs with the cheese already inside."

"Are you sure, David?" I asked gently. "You've fallen in love before."

"Oh, I know. And I got burned. She knows I don't have any money or any prospects of money. She knows lawyers are trying their best to make me pay for the rest of my life. And she doesn't look at me like she's disgusted or feels sorry for me. She holds my hand when we go to the movies." He blew out his breath. "When she came to the cabin this evening and told me she'd decided to stay and wait for me, I just couldn't stop my feelings. I wanted to hold her. I felt like if I did that, everything would be all right."

He looked up, realized he'd been waxing poetic, and tightened his face again. "You have no call to lecture me, Brenda. I know you and Nick have been bouncing up and down on the bed."

"I'm not lecturing. I'm glad you and Clarissa hit it off. But you have to be careful until the divorce is settled. You know that."

David nodded. "I know. But no one can accuse me of getting money from Clarissa. She doesn't even have a job."

"No," I admitted. "But she always pays her rent, so she must get it from somewhere."

David shrugged. "I haven't asked her. None of my business. Maybe it's a disability claim or her grandmother left it to her."

I'd never noticed Clarissa having any kind of disability except maybe the tendency to sleep all the time.

She'd never mentioned any of her relatives, either, dead or alive.

"Anyway," I said. "You don't want Reginald running back to Chicago showing your wife that you're having an affair. They'll add it to the mix."

"I know." His chin jutted out. "Besides, we did not have sex. We just held each other."

He looked so indignant and virtuous that I suddenly wanted to laugh. "Reginald and your wife's lawyers will so not believe that."

"Why are you the only one who gets to fall in love?" he complained.

"You can fall in love," I said. "But wait until you're single."

"Love doesn't work that way, Brenda," David said, his voice softening. "It strikes when you least expect it. With the person you least expect. I think I'm grateful to Jerry for forcing me to move in here." He stopped, made a face. "OK, almost grateful."

"Let's not talk about it," I said quickly.

"Hey, no problem. I'd like to forget today ever happened. Except for the last part." He took on a contrite expression. "Sorry I yelled at you this afternoon. About the food. It could have happened to anyone."

I knew he was so forgiving because he and Clarissa had cuddled and cooed and then had probably gotten something to eat on the way home. Still, it was nice to see him in such a good mood, and who was I to turn away an apology?

"Well." David slapped his thighs and stood up. "Was that all you wanted to talk about?"

I nodded, rolling my lower lip with my teeth. I worried about David and wanted him to be careful, but I knew he'd only listen to so much from me.

"OK," he said. "Good night."

He left my room. I came slowly after him. He didn't

stop at the sofa (which Tony Beale was still hogging), but went on into Clarissa's room without knocking. He closed the door.

Tony watched him go, then gave me a cocky grin. "So is the orgy going to start now?"

I gave him a dirty look. Nick laughed and stood up. "No orgy for you, Mr. Beale. Brenda, get dressed and bring a change of clothes. We'll go to my house. Less crowded."

Tony started to look nervous. "What about me? You wouldn't throw me out to the mercy of Tim, would you?"

By this time, I surely would. I certainly didn't want Tony staying here without me to watch him. He might go into my bedroom and discover my mountains of lingerie. There are just some things you don't ever want your boss to see.

Nick saved the day, or at least the rest of the night. "If you can get yourself to my house, you're welcome to a guest bedroom. I have several. We'll figure out what to do about your rabid morning show host tomorrow."

Tony became happy again. "Great. You'll never know I'm there. As long as there's beer in the fridge." He wagged a finger at me. "But you get some rest, my girl. You have to be up bright and early in the morning and on the air."

"Yes, Tony," I said. I ducked back into my bedroom and slammed the door loudly behind me, hoping Tony Beale would get the idea that he was unwelcome.

He didn't, of course. He followed us to Nick's house, came inside, and helped himself to a beer from Nick's subzero refrigerator, chattering happily the whole time.

I left the two downstairs in the living room to become best friends, stretched myself across Nick's bed, and fell into deep slumber, comforted by the sheets and pillows that smelled enticingly of Nick.

* * *

Morning found Tony Beale sitting with his elbows on the table in Nick's kitchen with Nick busy at the stove making pancakes and bacon and eggs. Tony was talking nonstop and Nick was listening to him, for God's sake.

"We can make it a family day," Nick suggested as he shoved eggs around with his spatula. "Free admission, lots of food and drinks, and the sponsors can donate prizes."

I leaned on the doorframe in my robe and watched Nick's sinews working as he made breakfast for me. I'd been asleep when he'd come to bed, and when the alarm had gone off a half an hour ago, he'd kissed me on the forehead and slid away to fix breakfast.

"Nick," I said. "You're consorting with the enemy."

Nick turned around and flashed me a smile, but his eyes were guarded.

Tony took the opportunity to shovel his food into his mouth. "Aren't you dressed yet, Brenda?" he asked around a mouthful of eggs and cheese. "We need to go in early and get this stuff set up."

I rolled my eyes, turned away, and went back upstairs to take my shower.

Later that morning, Tony barged into the studio while I was greeting San Diego. He plunked himself down and turned on a mike. As soon as I paused for breath, he started talking about the big competition between us and KBZ.

He'd worked fast. The date had been set for two weeks from now at Mission Bay Park. "Take sides, join the fun, it's free, bring the kids, do something for charity," he bleated.

After I wrestled control of the show back from him and put on Jimi Hendrix ("This is for you, Katie and Billy"), I scowled at him.

"You put that together in a hurry."

"Me and Nick worked it out this morning. He's a great guy, that Nick." He peered at me. "Everything all right between you two kids?"

I started to answer, then stopped and bit my lip. "I guess."

Tony waved this away. "You two should get married. You'd be great together. You can live happily ever after and breed little DJs."

"Please stay out of my personal life, Tony. Or next time I'll let Tim have you."

"That's mean, Brenda."

The song ended. I turned on my mike and took a breath to continue, but Tony cut in. "This is Tony, we're back talking about our radio station festival at Mission Bay Park. Hey, we might be hearing a great announcement there about Brenda and Nick—are they going to tie the knot?"

"Tony!" I yelled.

Over my headphones, Marty snickered.

"Well, you'd better get married after what I saw yesterday," Tony chortled. "They spent Easter together—if you know what I mean about 'together.'" Marty played a suggestive sound effect.

I glared at Marty through the glass. He grinned and opened another candy bar.

I shut off my mike as I punched in a Heart tune. "I don't know why I don't just quit."

Tony grinned as Ann Wilson belted that she was crazy on someone—not Tony, because she'd have better taste. "Because you need a job," he told me. "Besides, you love me, Brenda."

I ground my teeth and prayed that Nick hadn't been listening to us during that little exchange.

Nick might not have heard, but the rest of San Diego had.

My mother called me at home that afternoon. "Brenda."

"Hello, Mom," I said, trying to sound neutral.

"I know you don't want to talk to me, Brenda," she began. "But is what I heard on the radio true? Are you and Nick that serious?"

"No, Mom," I said, holding onto my temper. "That was just Tony, going for ratings."

"I see." That was an "I see" that meant she didn't believe me, but she'd not press me.

"You'd tell me, wouldn't you?" she asked.

"Tell you what?"

"If you and Nick were that serious. If you were going to get engaged."

"We're not."

"But you'd tell me."

"Mom, Nick and I—" My voice broke.

My mom's voice softened. "What is it, honey?"

She sounded as gentle as she had when I'd been sixteen and my jock boyfriend finally made first string in the basketball team and dumped me because he reasoned he could get a better girl after that. The sad thing was, he'd been right.

"I don't know," I said. "I don't know what's going on with us."

She hesitated for a time, probably wondering how much advice I'd take from her. I didn't want answers right now; I wanted comfort. Would she understand that?

"Are you serious about him?" she asked.

"Yes."

"How serious?"

I swallowed tears. "I'm in love with him."

I imagined my mom nodding slowly. She'd known it all along, of course. "Have you told him this?"

"I tried." I remembered my panic when he asked me to move in with him and then him making love to me on the table. Talk about mixed signals. "But I'm just so afraid—"

"Honey, not every man is like Larry. Nick didn't strike me as being anything like him. Larry was always polite, but in a cold way. I could always tell he really didn't like me, no matter how polite he was. Nick is charming. He sincerely likes people, you can tell."

"I know," I mourned. "That's one thing I love about him."

She laughed. "Then what's the problem, Brenda?"

"I'm still afraid. What if he doesn't like me once he gets to know me? Or, even worse, what if Nick insists I be a certain person for him always, just like Larry did? I've just come out of being Larry's shadow. I don't want to lose me again."

Mom went silent for a moment. "I know, dear," she said. "I know what it is to be in someone else's shadow. But the right person can draw you out. They beam sunshine on you and chase all those shadows away."

I wiped a tear from my wet face. "Is that why you like Jerry?"

"Yes," she said, sounding surprised I understood. "That's one of the reasons I like him."

"Plus, he's got a great butt," I said.

"Are you talking about Jerry or Nick?"

"Both of them," I answered. "They both have great butts. We should take a picture of them walking away together."

We laughed, then I wiped away more tears.

"Well, I'm going to come to your little radio festival," she said, in the same way she'd told me she'd come to the school talent show when I was six, whether I liked it or not. "I'm bringing Jerry."

She waited for me to scream and tell her no way in hell was she bringing Jerry.

"OK," I said. "I'm surprised he's still speaking to any of us."

"He is a little annoyed at you two—and me. But he's still willing to give it a whirl."

"He must really like you." I admitted this grudgingly.

"He does. This is real, Brenda. I'm plenty old enough to know when it's real."

"I'm glad for you," I made myself say. I truly was glad for her. But I still felt awkward. Her relationship with Jerry was going to take some getting used to.

She hung up then, and I looked around at my underwear-infested bedroom. I thought of Nick's neat bedroom and his bed with hospital corners. I stood up and started picking up lingerie, sorting it from David's clothes, separating everything into piles—stockings, garter belts, teddies, camisoles, panties, bras.

I segued into a laundry frenzy. I threw everything I could into the washing machine and hand-soaped everything else. My sink overflowed with suds, and my shower blossomed stockings and bras and thin lace teddies.

I went out, bought a hamper, put a big sign on it that read "Dirty Clothes," and put all David's socks and underwear and T-shirts into it. I stripped the sheets off my bed, washed those, then made the bed again with hospital corners.

I worked into the night on my laundry project. Before I was done, Clarissa and David came home from wherever they'd been. They were holding hands.

"What's that smell?" David asked, sniffing.

"Soap," I said. "I was washing clothes."

"Oh, good." He smiled.

"Not yours," I said severely. "Yours are in a hamper."

His face fell. "Thanks a lot, Brenda."

"It won't hurt you to do your own laundry," I said. "Geez, David, you're thirty-two years old. Can't you work a washing machine yet?"

"Alicia's maids always did it," he said.

"That figures."

Clarissa slid out of her windbreaker and tossed it on the couch. "I'll show you, David. It's easy. The trick is not to put in your red shirts with your white underwear." She trailed into my bedroom. "Wow, it's clean in here. Is Nick coming over?"

I shrugged. "I don't know." I smiled weakly. "But just in case."

Clarissa went to the hamper and upended it all over the floor I'd just cleared. She sat down and started sorting things into dark and light piles. David watched her as though it was the most fascinating thing he'd ever seen.

Nick did not come over. At about eleven that night, I lost the battle with myself trying to be cool, and called him.

Tony Beale answered the phone. "Hi, Brenda! You want to talk to Nick?"

"Yes," I answered, unclenching my teeth. "That would be nice."

"He's not here," Tony said cheerfully. "He went to the store. We ran out of chips."

"You mean you ate them all."

"Well, yeah. You want me to take a message?"

I closed my eyes. I could imagine any message I left being relayed to Nick through Tony. He'd put on a falsetto voice and grin the whole time. Yuck.

"No," I said. "No message," and hung up the phone.

25

How to Be a Sex Object

The two weeks leading to our radio station competition went by fairly smoothly—at work. The sponsors liked the idea, and donations and ads poured in. Calls lit up the screens, and it looked as if KCLP might even have a chance at top five.

At home—well, different story.

Tony Beale had more or less moved in with Nick. Tony made sure he answered the phone every time I called. He told me one morning, "You should stay with Nick, too, so we can carpool."

"I don't want to carpool with you, Tony," I said.

"Is it because you think you can't have sex with Nick while I'm there?" He waved that away. "You kids can have all the sex you want. I'll just turn up the TV to drown out the noise."

I truly despised him.

"I'm trying to get Nick to work for KCLP," he went on. "Then all three of us can carpool."

"You have a home, Tony. Why don't you go live there?"

Tony looked hurt. "I'm being stalked, Brenda. Have a heart."

Nick did invite me out to lunch on Thursday. I was so glad to see him over my mound of French fries that I wanted to leap across the booth and make love to him then and there.

He wore a pullover shirt open at the neck so I could ogle his throat. Maybe I could smear a little ketchup there and lick it off—slowly.

I turned my thoughts to mundane matters so I wouldn't grab the ketchup bottle and go to town.

"So how's the house guest?" I asked.

Nick smiled wearily. "He's fine. He helps out cleaning up the kitchen. Mrs. Pankhurst doesn't like him, though."

I pictured Nick's across-the-street neighbor sweeping her walk and shaking her head at Tony Beale. "She doesn't like me either," I pointed out.

Nick looked surprised. "Yes, she does. She told me. She said you were cute."

"Really? Anyway, I don't think Mrs. Pankhurst's disapproval of Tony will make him leave."

"No." Nick took a bite of his burger, chewed it, swallowed. "If you're wondering why I don't kick Tony out, I feel sorry for the guy. He really is being stalked."

"By Tim? We haven't seen Tim at all near the station. That's the most logical place for Tim to stalk him. I think it was just one occurrence. Maybe Tim's figured out that the best thing to do is leave town and look for another job."

Nick was shaking his head. "I tried to drive Tony back to his house last night. Someone was waiting on his porch for him. It was too dark to see who. When I started to walk up the sidewalk, whoever it was ran away. But he'd made himself at home on the porch. I found fast-food containers and a blanket, like someone was camping out."

"A homeless person," I suggested.

Nick gave me a "you know better than that" look. "We called the police, and they took all the stuff, but they didn't find Tim."

I sighed. Poor, stupid Tony. "Why can't he stay in a hotel?"

"He doesn't like hotels, he says. He seems to feel safe at my house."

I snorted. "Sure, he does. You can cook. He likes to eat. I'm surprised he doesn't want to marry you."

"He asked me. I told him no," Nick said, straight-faced.

"At this point, Tony is having a better relationship than I am."

Nick set down his burger, wiped his fingers on his napkin. "You can always come over."

"Not with Tony there. I love you, Nick, but—" I held up my hands. "Not with Tony."

He watched me with a coolness in his eyes. "You like to throw that out so casually."

"What—about Tony?"

"No, that you love me."

My voice got quiet. "It isn't casual."

"It isn't to me, either."

We shared a long look that lasted until the waitress came to ask if we wanted anything else. Nick broke away to ask for the check, and I looked down at my plate.

When the waitress left, I reached for the slip of paper in Nick's hand. "I'll pick up mine."

"No, you won't," he answered. "You're my woman, and I'm buying."

I smiled. "Male chauvinist."

"Damn straight."

I poked my straw into my iced tea, mashing down the lemon wedge at the bottom. "I suppose you expect me to put out now."

He grinned, warmth replacing the strange coolness in his eyes. "Damn straight."

I smiled back, running my tongue across my lower lip. Our relationship had problems, but I might as well enjoy the sex while we were sorting things out.

Then I deflated. I thought of joyfully driving back to Nick's house—and Tony showing up. I thought of Nick in my apartment, but David and Clarissa would be snuggling on the sofa and making goo-goo eyes at each other.

My dad's boat again? No, the scene of former disasters was not a good place to make love, and besides, my mom and Jerry might waltz out there any time. The boat belonged to my mom, after all.

I sighed. "Maybe we should go to a sleazy motel room."

Nick looked interested. "That's an idea."

"I was kidding."

"I'm not." He drew out a twenty and a ten and laid it across the bill. "Tell you what, I'll pick you up at your apartment tomorrow evening at six. Pack something sexy." He smiled at me. "But then, you always do."

I smiled back and tried to keep my nipples from obviously pebbling. Whenever Larry had taken charge (and he did all the time), it had been annoying. Nick taking charge was sexy. Nick did it for fun. Larry expected obedience and appreciation.

I ran my tongue over my lip again. "OK," I said. "You take me to a sleazy motel room, I'll be a sleazy girl."

"Stop that, or I won't be able to stand up and walk out of here."

I shook my head in mock sympathy. "Poor Nick." I unfolded myself from the booth, stepped over to him, and whispered into his ear exactly what I wanted to do with that spontaneous hard-on he was having.

He shot me a hot look from under his lashes. "You are so going to pay for that," he whispered.

"Love you, too," I said. I kissed his cheek, waved good-bye, and sauntered away.

I ruined the exit by looking back at him. He was watching me with flattering scrutiny.

Our waitress told me to have a nice day. Then she said, "You know what, honey, that guy's a babe. I mean a *babe*. If you're ever done with him, you just come back here and let me know."

I smiled. I agreed: he was a babe. "I hope I'm not done with him until we're both in a nursing home," I said, and she grinned.

I thought about that as I walked to my car and then as I drove back to KCLP. Did I really want what I had with Nick to be forever and ever?

It dawned on me that maybe I did.

I had to sit in the parking lot for a solid five minutes waiting for my knees to stop shaking before I could walk back into work.

The sleazy motel Nick took me to the next evening turned out to be the ultraluxurious, superexpensive Majestic San Diego on the bay. It was the kind of over-the-top hotel where the ballroom-sized lobby is all marble and fountains and full of snooty bellhops and concierges.

Nick had managed to reserve us a large suite. We couldn't even get off the elevator to the floor it was on without a key. He'd gone all out.

I walked into a beautiful sun-filled bedroom, which

305

overlooked the blue Pacific, and shivered. I'd worn a two-piece dress with a light spaghetti-strap top and a narrow skirt. Underneath I wore a strapless lacy bustier with garters and black silk stockings. But it wasn't the temperature of the room that had given me goose bumps.

The bellhop followed us in and pointed out all the amenities of the suite until Nick shoved a large bill in his hand and persuaded him out the door.

I stood still in the middle of the room. Nick couldn't have known, and I didn't want to tell him. I closed my mouth and told myself to deal with it.

Larry had brought me here the past November to celebrate our first anniversary. The chic elegance of the room brought it all back: the champagne he'd ordered, the carted-in dinner complete with violinist, the hot tub for two, the horrible fight we'd had that ended in him walking out.

I shook myself. Larry was history. I was here with Nick. This wasn't the same room, or even the same style of room—Larry had booked a penthouse suite that had been bigger than my apartment.

I could use this opportunity to cleanse myself of bad memories. This hotel could see the beginning of fond memories of Nick and me.

With this positive attitude, I attempted a smile, which almost worked. My stiff lips moved upward, at least.

Nick locked the door behind the bellhop. "Alone at last," he said. "This is the part where you fall on your knees and tell me how wonderful I am."

I waggled my brows. "Unzip those pants and I will."

He laughed. He crossed the room and crushed me into his arms. "I missed you, Brenda," he said into my hair. "Brazen woman."

I tilted my head back. He leaned down and kissed

me. A good romantic-hero kiss. All thoughts of Larry dissolved.

He cupped my shoulders with burning hands and slid down the straps of my dress. "Brenda," he whispered into my lips. "I want you to be as wild tonight as you ever wanted to be. Don't hold back. I want it all."

I snaked my hands to the front of his pants and started unzipping. He was right; if this was all we could have, we should have it all the way.

We were interrupted by the soft chime of the doorbell. Yes, the suite had a doorbell. "Room service," an official sounding voice announced.

Nick unwound his arms from me and moved to the door, zipping his jeans back up as he went. I admired the view, tilting my head to observe the way the denim hugged the curve of his backside.

He opened the door. A man in a black suit waltzed in and presented a bucket of ice and champagne. Nick handed out another large bill, and the waiter, giving Nick an obvious wink, closed the door behind him.

"Champagne?" Nick offered.

I glanced at the flutes and the bottle. I was reminded of Larry simply popping the cork and thrusting the champagne glass at me. He never asked if I wanted anything.

I slid my arms around Nick's waist. "Later," I said.

He grinned down at me. "OK. Mind if I lick it off you when we get there?"

I sent him a coy smile. "Not at all."

I rested my head against his hard pectorals and inhaled his wonderful scent. He smelled like whatever soap he'd laundered his shirts with and his very own, oh-so-appealing aroma. I kissed his chest through the shirt, ran my hands down his abs. "I love your body," I whispered.

"Mmm. Yours is pretty good, too."

I'd never thought I had a great body. I guess lingerie can do nice things for you. He slid his hands under my shirt, cupping my waist through the bustier. He kissed me slowly, as if we had all night, his lashes sweeping down to hide his eyes.

"Are you going to undress me again?" he asked.

For answer, I popped the button on his pants and tugged down the zipper. He was hard and ready behind his briefs. I slid my hand up that hardness, and his kiss deepened.

I moved my mouth from his and yanked down his pants and underpants. He gasped a laugh, but before he could say anything, I dropped to my knees and did what I'd always wanted to do, took his long, beautiful shaft into my mouth.

He twined his fingers through my hair, just as I'd imagined. He politely did not press me onto him, but I felt his fingers shaking, as though he was holding back. That made me do even nicer things to him.

I didn't really know what to do; I had to let instinct take over. Larry had never wanted this kind of experience—I guess it was too messy for him and threatened his strict self-control. I had never considered it with the few guys I'd dated before; those relationships hadn't seen much in the way of intimacy. Inexperienced fumbling in the dark was as far as they ever progressed.

Nick seemed to like it, though. He made a soft groan, and his thigh muscles clenched. I swirled my tongue over him until he breathed faster and faster.

Finally he grabbed me under the arms, hauled me to my feet, and tossed me onto the bed. He didn't smile. With an almost stern expression on his face, he stripped himself, and then he stripped me.

He knew what to do with garters now. He unsnapped them and skimmed off my stockings, then my panties, then the bustier. The clothes landed on the bed, on the floor, in a complete mess. I opened my arms for him. He lay down on me without saying a word.

We both came very fast. I was screaming after a few thrusts, and it didn't take him much longer to get there. I arched my pelvis into his, and his hardness burned me all the way.

Then he was kissing my sweaty skin, his mouth hot. I smoothed his hair and enjoyed the deep, stretched feeling of having him inside me.

After a long time, he moved out of me, and we lay there touching and kissing, not talking. We drowsed, reveling in the softness of the bed. Nick dragged the pillows and sheets around us in a nice cocoon.

I got up sometime later and went to the bathroom. Nick lay tangled in the sheets, his eyes closed, his head pillowed on his outstretched arm. I smiled at the sight. He was so beautiful.

There was a telephone in the bathroom as well as a television. I guess you could make sure you didn't miss a minute of your game while you called housekeeping for more toilet paper.

Unbelievably, as I was washing my hands, the phone rang. I hurried to grab it, my hands dripping, not wanting it to wake up Nick. He needed plenty of sleep for what I had in mind for the rest of the night.

"Hello?" I said, expecting room service.

"Brenda?"

I should have known. "David. What do you want?"

"Why are you answering the phone?" he demanded. "You should have let voice mail get it."

"Why are you calling me? Is something wrong?" I pictured Clarissa or my mother being rushed to the hospital for some horrific illness or injury.

"Don't panic," he said. "Everything's OK. I called to warn you that Larry's been looking for you. He keeps calling, and he's showed up here twice since you left."

"What for?"

"He said he wanted to talk to you. He seems really mad."

I sighed. "Oh, great. Now *I* have a stalker."

"He yelled at Clarissa," David said, his tone turning angry. "He called her a liar when she said you were gone. I had to throw him out. I can't believe you ever went out with that jerk."

"I can't believe it either. You didn't tell him where I was, did you?"

"No," he said. "I just thought I'd warn you. I told him you were spending the weekend with Nick, and he said he'd scour the town for you."

"Crap." I dropped the towel and didn't bother picking it up.

"Don't worry," David said. "I think we put him off the scent."

"Good." I frowned. "Hey, wait a minute, how'd you know I was here? I didn't even know where we were going until Nick drove me here."

"Because I told Nick you liked the Majestic. He asked me for the name of a hotel you really loved. Didn't he say?"

"No. Why on earth did you tell him I liked it?" After the fiasco with Larry, I hadn't wanted to enter the lobby of this hotel, let alone stay in a room. Plus I had no memory of ever mentioning this place to David.

David said, "Last year, Mom told me you really raved about it. I figured you must like it, so I told Nick to take you there."

I groaned. My own fault. I hadn't wanted to reveal to my mom the downturn in my relationship with Larry, so I'd gone overboard praising the hotel. Let that be a lesson on how avoiding painful subjects can turn around and bite you.

"Well, anyway," David said. "I thought you'd want to know."

"Thanks, David."

"Have fun."

"Thanks, David."

"Don't kill Nick with sex."

"Shut up, David." I hung up on him.

I growled and raked my hands through my hair. Why the heck was Larry looking for me, and why right now? Had he finally gotten it through his skull that I didn't want him anymore, so he'd decided to ruin it for me and Nick?

Geez, why couldn't he get a life? Maybe I'd hire Reginald to follow him around and keep him from interfering with me and my dates with Nick.

I went back out, swallowing my annoyance. Nick was standing, stark naked, in front of the television, a remote on his hands. I stopped, all thoughts of David and Larry flying out of my head.

"They have adult DVDs," he said without turning around. "Want to watch one?"

His back muscles moved the smallest bit as he manipulated the remote. No adult movie could look as good as Nick did right now.

"Sure, why not?" I managed to say.

"Who was on the phone?"

I came to stand next to him so I could admire him close-up. "My brother."

Nick lifted his brows. "Checking up on little sister?"

I opened my mouth to tell him about Larry, then I closed it. I didn't want to ruin this night talking about—or fighting about—Larry. Larry wouldn't find us here, and I could tell Nick everything tomorrow. Not tonight. Larry was not intruding tonight.

I smiled. "Something like that."

311

"He knows why I brought you here." Nick's blue eyes crinkled with his grin. "I asked him for a swank hotel you liked so I could have my way with you."

"He just wanted to give me a hard time."

"I'll tell the front desk to hold our calls. I don't want any more interruptions."

I rested my fingers on the hard muscle of his arm. "I don't think he'll call back. I think he's happy being alone with Clarissa."

Nick absently pressed buttons on the remote. "They've really hit it off, haven't they?"

"Seems like it. I'm glad. She treats him nice. He needs that right now." God knows I'd been a real pain to live with, and David was still dealing with the fact that his best friend was sleeping with his mother. David needed someone to look at him adoringly and hold his hand, and Clarissa did that.

I let my fingers run down the smooth hardness of Nick's biceps; then I followed the same path with my tongue.

Nick grinned at me. "Let's try this one." He hit the "play" button.

We sat on the edge of the bed, two naked people, hip to warm hip, and watched the screen. The blank blue faded, and the movie came on.

It was the stupidest thing I'd ever seen in my life. Pretty soon Nick and I were laughing hard and holding onto each other. Laughing, we slid off the bed and onto the floor.

"I didn't know people could bend that way," Nick snickered into my ear.

"They can't," I said. "They're stunt dummies."

"You think so? That blond dummy's really built."

"Oh, yeah?" I countered. "That guy dummy has a great butt."

"Hey, stop looking at that dummy's butt."

"I'd rather look your butt," I said, nibbling his ear.

"You did when you came out of the bathroom. You stood there and looked at my butt for a good five minutes."

"I can't help it if I think you're gorgeous."

He pulled me on top of him and held me close. "Is that all I am to you? A sex object?"

I swiped his upper lip with my tongue. "You are right now. And anyway I'm supposed to be the sex object. I'm the woman."

He shot me a wicked look. "You *are* the sex object."

"Good," I said. I fumbled for the remote and hit the power button. The screen went black, and lovely silence fell.

We proved we could make love as well as any movie dummies. We rolled around on the floor, then on the bed, and finally, on the armchair next to the bed. I'd had no idea that being a sex object could be so much fun.

After much screaming and laughter, Nick lifted me in his strong arms and laid me back on the bed. He made sweet love to me again; then we both fell into a deep slumber.

I woke after an hour of comatose sleep, feeling relaxed and refreshed. The room was dark. I pushed the button beside the bed that opened the drapes. The bellhop had proudly demonstrated this button to us several times before Nick had paid him off.

Moonlight pooled on the bed, gleaming off Nick's skin, which was slick with sweat. I traced the muscles of his arms from biceps to wrist; then I softly kissed his forehead.

I could have this, I thought, always.

I was still scared, but the thought of not having Nick

in my life was worse. Maybe I should just take what I could get and be happy with that.

Look at my mom. She knew all the arguments for not seeing Jerry—the age difference would cause too many problems, he might only be using her for a free ride, her friends and family might shun her.

But she was going for it, clinging with both hands to something that made her happy. She knew that it might not last forever, but she was enjoying the heck out of it while she could.

I should take lessons from her.

And then there was David. He'd had riches and lost everything. Now he was discovering that eating cheeseburgers with a girl who was actually interested in what he had to say was better than millions in stocks and a perfect blond wife who disliked him.

My crazy family was smart, and I was stupid.

Nick is here. Enjoy him.

I leaned down and kissed his cheek.

Nick's eyes opened as though he hadn't been asleep. He smiled at me, and my heart turned over.

"Hey," he said. He gave me a long, deep kiss. "I think I'll take a shower. Join me?"

I nodded against the pillow. "Sure. I'll be right in."

Nick kissed my lips and got himself off the bed. I watched him walk away, then wiped the drool from my face and rolled over into the warm indentation he'd left. I heard the water start in the shower and heard Nick humming in a low baritone.

I was so in love with him that it hurt.

The doorbell chimed, followed by a soft knock. "Room service."

I smiled and got off the bed, wondering what further surprises Nick had asked them to bring. More champagne? Better adult movies? Paisley toilet paper?

I dug in my suitcase for the silk robe I'd brought and

slid it over my nakedness. I heard the slap of Nick's bare feet as he got into the shower, still humming. Rubbing my eyes, I opened the door.

Larry Bryant stood on the threshold. Before I could panic and slam the door in his face, he pushed past me into the room.

26

The Total Destruction of My Love Life

I yanked myself away from him, then I gaped. Larry's eyes were bloodshot, his dapper suit was rumpled, and his breath reeked of scotch. For the first time since I'd known him, I was seeing Mr. Perfect drunk.

My astonishment dissolved into anger. "What do you want, Larry? I'm on a date."

He glanced at the bathroom door, behind which the shower was still running. "Yes, I know. I figured you'd have picked this hotel for your love-in weekend. I called my old friend Frank downstairs, and he told me that, sure enough, my slut of a girlfriend was up here with her DJ lover."

"I'm not your girlfriend," I said. He grinned wolfishly at my tacit agreement that I was a slut. I plunged on. "I remember you telling me it was over. Wait a minute, why am I arguing with you? Get out!"

"Not until I give you this."

He pulled a piece of paper from his inside pocket and thrust it at me. It was a sheet of printer paper, folded in thirds. Mystified, I opened it.

Two typed columns of expenses filled the page. They said things like: "Flowers delivered on birthday, $300; Detailing car for date, $80; Diamond earrings, $2,000; Weekend at Majestic San Diego, $1,500; Private dinner prepared by caterer, $500; Consultation for nose job, $1,000."

At the bottom it said, in bold, capital letters: "Grand Total: $30,000."

"What the hell is this?" I demanded.

"It's a bill," Larry slurred, "for all the things I did for you and all the money I spent on you while we were going out. Including this hotel." He swayed a little, spittle raining on the page.

I remembered how thrilled I'd been by his expensive presents and romantic dinners, and then how he'd talked me into seeing a plastic surgeon—just for a consultation. He'd wanted to sculpt himself a girlfriend, I guess. I'd talked to the doctor and declined the surgery. My nose was fine the way it was, I'd decided. Larry had been livid.

I slammed the paper into his chest. "You're crazy."

Larry didn't take the sheet. It fluttered to the floor. "You owe me, Brenda."

"Ha! I should bill you for all the misery you've caused *me*. I guarantee it would wipe out that debt and then some."

Larry's look turned dark. He grabbed me by the shoulders. "I spent my hard-earned money and my precious time on you, and for what? For nothing, that's what."

His fingers bit into my shoulders, but I was so angry I barely felt the pressure. "No," I said. "You're just pissed

317

because you couldn't con my mother out of a million dollars."

"I should have had that money, Brenda. There was nothing wrong with what I wanted to do. But I didn't take you out to all those dinners and buy you all those damned presents and spend all my time with you so you could end up in the hotel I took you to with your boy toy. You were sleeping with him all the time you were going out with me, weren't you?"

"Of course not!" I yelled. "I only met him on New Year's."

He shook me. My teeth rattled. "Oh, yes, New Year's. That's when I finally caught you."

"Take your hands off me, Larry."

He shook me again. "You pretended to hate sex, but that's because you were screwing Nick all the time."

"You're insane, do you know that? Oh, no, wait, you're just drunk."

"S-L-U-T. Slut. Spell it with me, Brenda. S-L—"

A pair of brawny hands caught Larry on the shoulders and slammed him away from me and into the wall.

Nick, his hair dripping, his eyes sparkling fury, pushed his face at Larry's. "Don't you *ever* touch her again."

Nick had wrapped a towel around his hips, and water droplets slid down his back and arms. He must have either heard me yelling or come out to see what was taking me so long.

Larry looked at Nick with a twinge of fear. Nick was strong, and he was angry. His whole body radiated menace.

Then Larry's expression took on a note of cunning. That worried me.

"Nick, let him go," I said quickly.

Nick turned an outraged glare on me. Before he could

say anything, the door slammed open. David stumbled hastily into the room, followed by Clarissa.

David said, "Brenda, Larry's on his way. We followed him, but we lost him in the parking garage—"

He broke off when he saw Nick, naked in a towel, holding Larry against the wall.

"Thanks for the warning," Nick said, calm but angry. "But it wasn't in time to stop Larry manhandling your sister."

David reddened. "You bastard." He balled up his fists and started for Larry.

I wormed my way between the three of them and pushed Nick and David back. "Stop it. Don't hit him!"

"What are you protecting him for?" David demanded.

"I'm not protecting him. I'm protecting you. He knows the best lawyers in town. He'll sue you."

Larry swung away from them to the center of the room. He smiled a nasty smile. "Too late, Brenda. I can get Nick for assault just because he touched me. I'll have my friend start a case in the morning." His smiled widened. "You see, if I want revenge on my slutty girl-friend, there's nothing any of you can do."

He grabbed for me again, but just then Clarissa hit him in the back with a lamp.

Clarissa wasn't very big, and in her skinny black jeans and tight midriff-baring top, she looked even smaller. But Larry, drunk, stumbled under the assault. He spun around to see her hefting her weapon again.

He pointed at her, finger shaking. "I'll sue you, too."

"No, you won't," she said calmly.

Her tone was so ordinary and reasonable that Larry stopped, baffled. "Why not?"

"Because my last name is Sheridan."

Beside me, David frowned. "What is she talking about?"

Larry, too, looked puzzled. "What has your last name got to do with anything? I'll sue you until you pay me for the rest of your life and your children do, too."

Clarissa simply smiled.

"Wait a minute," Nick said. "Sheridan as in Sheridan Holdings?"

Clarissa nodded mutely.

I didn't know anything about Sheridan Holdings, except that I saw the name on the sides of buildings and in ads. Having no need for a holding company, I never really paid much attention. I had also never connected them with Clarissa Sheridan.

Larry's face drained of color.

"What's the matter, Larry?" I asked sweetly.

"Sheridan Holdings controls most of Larry's business interests," Clarissa said in her languid voice.

"And you're what, related to the owner?" David asked.

"He's my dad," Clarissa answered.

The four of us stared at her.

That explained how she could pay her rent and buy her candy bars and take David out all the time without having to work at a job like the rest of us. I was betting that Dad gave his baby daughter a hefty allowance.

"So how come you never told me this?" David asked in a strangled voice.

Clarissa shrugged. "What's the big?"

The big was that her father could have bought the apartment complex we lived in twice over. She could live in a palatial mansion. Instead she sat in our crappy apartment and ate candy bars and drank beer.

Larry stared at her in terror. "Shit."

Clarissa gave him a little smile. "So go away and leave Brenda alone. Or I'll tell Dad."

"Shit," Larry said again. He glanced at the rest of us

with his bloodshot eyes, as though he barely noticed us standing there. Then he ran for the door, tore it open, and dashed out.

The door clicked closed into silence. Nick stood against the wall, his arms folded, his towel enticingly low on his hips.

David stared at Clarissa in bewilderment. Clarissa lifted the champagne bottle from the melting ice, dribbling water all over the carpet. "Cool," she said. "Champagne."

She unwound the wire and popped the cork. Liquid frothed from the bottle's neck onto the carpet. She poured liquid into a flute with a steady hand and held it up. "Anybody want some?"

That broke the silence. David laughed and so did I, shakily. I got extra glasses from the bathroom. Clarissa handed around the champagne, and we all toasted getting rid of Larry.

Except Nick. He held his glass without drinking, a neutral expression on his face.

After Clarissa and David drained their flutes, Clarissa took him by the hand. "This is a nice room. Let's get one for ourselves."

David grinned. I hadn't seen him look so happy for a long time.

"What about Reginald?" I asked. "I bet he followed you here."

Clarissa considered. "We'll invite him up. We'll play video games or something and eat everything in the refrigerator."

She took David's hand and towed him from the room. He looked pleased to go.

I closed the door after them and shot home all the locks. The glowing "Do Not Disturb" sign was already lit up, for what good it had done us.

Nick was in the middle of the room, his champagne glass in his hand. Standing there all bronzed and muscular in a towel that could slip down his hips at any minute, he looked good enough to eat.

I went to him. He watched me, no expression on his face. I touched the fold of the towel. "Let's start by taking this off," I said.

He moved my hand and backed up a step. Something cold struck my heart.

"Why did you let him in?" Nick asked quietly.

"What? Oh, you mean Larry? I thought it was room service. He said he was room service."

"At two o'clock in the morning?"

I glanced at the clock next to the bed. "Is it that late already?"

"You let him in. Even when you saw he wasn't room service."

"I wouldn't say I *let* him in."

Nick clicked his glass down on a nearby table and sat on the edge of the bed. Worried, I stood in front of him. Maybe he'd see how sexy I looked in the form-fitting silk robe. "Nick, I didn't let him in. He barged in."

Nick looked up. "I know. He's pushy."

I exhaled in relief. "But he's gone now." I sat next to him, letting my hip roll into his. "And you came out to defend my honor. That's sweet."

The look in his eyes told me that "sweet" had been the wrong thing to say.

He sighed. "Look, I'm trying to be so cool here."

"You are. You're being—" I groped for words. "Really nice."

His bronzed fingers traced a pattern on the towel. "That's not what I mean. I mean that I don't think I can keep doing this, Brenda."

My dart of fear returned. "Doing what?"

"Having a pretend relationship with you."

I stared at him. "It isn't pretend. Sex tonight wasn't pretend. Me, on top of you, in the chair, wasn't pretend."

"I mean that I can't even have you to myself in a hotel room."

I shook my head. "Larry's a jerk. He was drunk. He came over to tell me he wanted to be paid back all the money he spent on me while we were going out. Look."

I sprang from the bed, snatched up the piece of paper that Larry had trampled during his hasty exit, and fluttered it in front of Nick's face. "He even made an invoice. Can you believe him?"

Nick glanced at the paper, then up at me. His eyes were cold. "I'm behind," he said. "I haven't even spent a tenth of that."

I ripped the invoice to shreds and threw the pieces up in the air. They wafted their way down, landing on the bed and the floor. One came to rest on the taut spread of Nick's towel.

"I am over Larry," I said desperately. "Totally. Completely."

"I know," Nick answered.

I sat down on the bed again. "Then what's wrong? I never thought Larry would find us here, no matter how hard he looked, but then I forgot he knows the managers of every hotel in town. He'd probably just called them all as soon as he knew we'd gone out for the weekend."

Nick lifted his head. "You knew he was searching for you?"

His expression made my mouth go dry. I faltered, "Yes. David told me when he called."

Nick folded his arms over his chest. He was closing himself to me, cutting me out. I put my hand on his arm. He flinched, but made no move to dislodge me.

"Oh, God, Nick, I'm sorry," I babbled. "I should have told you, but I didn't want to talk about Larry. Not right then. I wanted it to be just you and me."

"You mean you wanted to have sex," he said in a quiet voice.

"Well, yes." I balled my hand. "Wasn't it worth it? You can't tell me you didn't like that."

"Oh, I liked it."

Somehow him saying that made it worse. "Nick, I'm over Larry. I want to be with you. Only with you."

He looked at me again. He had no emotion in his eyes: not anger, not sadness. "You aren't understanding me. I'm not jealous of Larry, not in that sense. I know your relationship with him is over." He absently rubbed his arms. "How can I put this? I know you're over him. But you're also not into me."

I gaped, baffled. "What are you talking about? You and I have done things I've never done before. And you've seen all the slinky stuff I wear. I've never showed that to anyone. Ever."

A note of anger finally entered his voice. "Brenda, I'm not talking about sex."

"I know that. But I just—I don't understand what you mean?"

"I mean you practically lived with him, you more or less gave him your whole life. And yet you hate him. But when I asked you to do the same thing with me, you looked terrified and nearly ran away."

"But that's why," I persisted. "I didn't want what we had to turn into what I had with Larry."

"I'm not Larry," he said, his voice firm. "I decided I wouldn't try to push you where you didn't want to go, but it seems like you don't want to go anywhere. I thought that if I took it slow, didn't ask too much, then eventually you'd come to me. But you won't. You want to see me and want the sex, but that's all you want."

Tears filled my eyes. "I do want more. Nick, I love you."

He didn't believe me.

My tears overflowed. "I'll prove it," I sniffled. "Tell me how I can prove it."

He took my hand. His eyes were intense. "All right," he said. "Marry me."

"What?" I gasped.

"Let's go, right now. Let's get in the car and drive to Las Vegas. We'll make it in time for breakfast. We'll eat, and then we'll get married."

I gulped. "In the Elvis House of Love?"

He didn't smile. "We can pick a non-Elvis chapel. So, how about it?" He tugged at my hand. "Do you want to go?"

"Are you serious?"

"Yes." His mouth was hard. "I'm tired of being cool. I'm tired of being Mr. Understanding. I want you all the way, and I want you for keeps."

I wiped away a tear with the back of my hand. "And if I say no, you're crazy, does that mean I don't love you?"

"No. But it means you don't want me for keeps."

My heart tore inside of me, falling in little shreds like the torn bits of Larry's paper. "My mother was married to my father for thirty-three years. She was miserable all that time. David and Alicia were married for seven years. She married him for his career and hated him when he failed. When I got close with Larry—God, it was horrible." I rested my hand on top of my sleep-mussed hair. "It went from OK to horrible so fast. I don't want it to be horrible with you. Ever."

He looked at me for a long time. I saw him understand that he wasn't going to reach me, that I was too scared, too rabbit-in-the-headlights, to let myself be completely myself with him.

Something closed between us, and that hurt worse than anything ever had, much, much worse than Larry telling me that our relationship was over. Pain spun slowly inside my chest and trickled through the rest of my body.

"So I guess we're back to sex," he said softly.

My sense of humor pressed its way through the pain, trying to save me, I suppose. "Most guys would be happy to have great sex with no strings."

He smiled slightly, then switched his gaze to his toweled knees. "Yeah, well, I guess I'm not most guys."

Tears poured out of me. I wanted to be able to say, *Ok, let's go to Las Vegas,* but I couldn't do it. I wanted what I had, I wanted to bask in him, without worrying that the relationship was deteriorating, without worrying that something beautiful was turning to something ugly.

He knew I couldn't say it. He stood up. He gathered up his clothes, dropped his towel, and started dressing.

I had to watch him. The muscles in his legs and back moved as he pulled on his underwear, then his pants. Sinews played as he dragged on his shirt and tried to smooth his hair. Through it all, I sat still, hugging myself in my smooth silk robe.

"Are you going home?" I asked, sniffing.

He sat down on the wing chair where we'd had such a fabulous time to put on his socks and shoes. "Yes. I'll come back and pay for the room tomorrow." He stopped, a sock dangling. "You can stay. Unless you want me to drive you home."

"No, I'll, um, go home with Clarissa and David."

He nodded as though it was all settled and went back to pulling on his socks.

I really didn't want to stay here in this stupid hotel after it had ruined a second relationship for me. This place should be condemned.

But I also didn't want to ride home in Nick's convertible in painful silence. I'd live with it, find David and Clarissa, or if all else failed, take the damned bus.

I watched him tie his shoes; then he stood up and loaded his stuff into his suitcase. Across the room, the ice in the ice bucket finally melted all the way, and water started dripping over the sides.

Nick came to me and stood above me. I must have looked just great, my eyes all red from crying, my unsculptured nose puffy, my red hair sticking out every which way.

He leaned down and kissed me. It was a long kiss, a parting kiss, a kiss that meant he was savoring me for the last time.

He had tears in his eyes, too, when he stood up. But he didn't let them bother him. He turned around, picked up his bag, unlocked all the locks I'd so carefully locked, and walked out the door.

The click of it closing hit me harder than anything ever had in my life.

I curled into the fetal position on the bed and cried until I had nothing left. After my tears ran out, I lay for a long time in silence, like a stunned bird who's run headfirst into a window.

Eventually, I got up and took the shower I should have taken with Nick. I let the water cascade from my body, and I started crying again, tears mixing with the water on my face.

After a time, I made myself turn off the shower; then I stood staring at the faucet until the room cooled off, and I started shivering.

I dried myself and then drank a bottle of water from the refrigerator at the wet bar. I was dehydrated and needed to replenish for the next crying jag.

I lay down again facing the clock next to the bed. I

wanted to go home, but I didn't want to hunt for David and disturb him and Clarissa (and maybe Reginald). It was four in the morning. I didn't want to lie here, either, feeling as though my heart had been encased in lead.

The person I wanted to talk to was my mom. I knew it was the crack of dawn, and I would be incredibly selfish to wake her up with my problems, but I was hurting and I wanted my mother.

Before I could reason myself out of it, I picked up the phone and dialed her number.

"Hello?" Jerry croaked on the other end of the line.

I squeezed my eyes closed and hung up without saying a word.

27

Jerry to the Rescue

I lay for a while longer in the dark. The sky went gray, that depressing color it gets before the world floods with light. I was tired and my eyes were sandy, and still I couldn't sleep.

I rolled back over to the phone and dialed my mother again.

Jerry answered. "Hello," he said, sounding a little more alert.

"Hi, Jerry," I said, my voice ragged. "Can I talk to my mom?"

"Brenda?" I heard rustling as he sat up. "What's wrong?"

"Nothing. I just need to talk—" I started crying again, so I couldn't actually talk at all.

I heard him murmuring something in the background, and my mom answering him. Then my mom came on the line. "Brenda? Are you OK?"

"Nick broke up with me," I choked out.

329

"Oh, honey."

Then I was crying too hard to be coherent. My mother made soothing noises. She tried to get me to talk, but I couldn't. But I felt the tiniest bit better weeping onto the phone, knowing she was on the other end listening to me, wanting to comfort me.

She finally got me to agree to let her and Jerry pick me up. I had an attack of guilt then, telling her I'd be OK and not to get out of bed.

Jerry grabbed the phone back. "Brenda, you don't need to be alone right now. We'll come and get you and take you to breakfast, OK? Pack up your stuff and meet us in the lobby."

I love a man who can take charge. Well, I don't always, but right now I needed someone to tell me what to do.

I hung up, went into the bathroom to wash my face, and dressed in the jeans and plain shirt I'd brought to wear tomorrow on the beach with Nick. I shoved my lingerie and slinky dress into the bag without bothering to fold anything. Right now, I never wanted to see a piece of lingerie again.

Jerry and Mom arrived in Mom's new SUV, which she'd bought just after New Year's. The woman who'd spent her life driving neutral-colored Buick sedans had gone out and bought a bright red, two-door Cherokee. I guess I shouldn't have been so surprised when she started dating Jerry.

They took me to our favorite all-night pancake restaurant. Jerry ordered chocolate chip pancakes, though my mother stuck with something whole-grain.

When I was little, I'd always gotten the silver dollar pancakes, kid-sized just for me. I remembered sitting in the booth with my mom and dad and David and making little pools of syrup with my own kid-sized syrup container. I'd always felt just a little bit special.

This morning I ordered the lemon-zest and ricotta

cheese pancakes, then picked them apart with my fork without eating. If I poked them in the middle, the ricotta cheese oozed out the holes.

My mom oozed sympathy while my pancakes oozed cheese. "I know you love him, Brenda."

I nodded. I'd told them the whole terrible story, starting with waking up with Nick on New Year's morning, and letting Zoe (or Chloe) persuade me to buy lingerie, and turning myself into a lingerie addict. Then meeting Nick again and him thinking I really was the lingerie addict—a wild, brazen, sexy woman—and me fearing that he wouldn't like me when we got too close.

My mother held my hand across the booth, and Jerry handed me napkins so I could wipe away the tears.

It was Jerry who surprised me with his common-sense advice. "Why did he go?" he asked me.

I shrugged and swiped my nose with the paper napkin. "He's tired of me."

"No, he isn't," Jerry said. "Don't try so hard to make him like Larry. He's a different person."

"How do you know?" I asked, feeling sour. "You didn't know Larry."

"I told him," my mom broke in. "I told him how glad I was when you two split up. I don't mean I was glad you were hurt, but Larry wasn't good for you."

"That's for sure," I agreed.

Jerry said, "Nick left tonight because you keep trying to stuff him into the mold of Larry."

"I know he's not like Larry," I argued. "That's why I love him."

"But you don't trust him. You don't believe he's smart enough to see the whole Brenda and love you. Nick went through a bad relationship in Texas—he knows what they're like. But he seems willing to try for a great one with you."

"You mean, I'm not willing."

331

"I get it, you know," Jerry said. "Relationships are scary. Especially when you think it might be the right one." He closed his hand over my mother's. She looked happy.

"But asking me to run off to Las Vegas right then and there," I protested. "That's more than scary."

"Yes," Jerry agreed. "He was trying to push you too hard, but I can understand. He wanted you to trust him. And you didn't."

A tear leaked down my cheek. I was tired of crying, but I couldn't stop. "I love him."

"That's not the same thing as trust. You can get hurt bad, Brenda, there's no guarantee you won't. But you seem like you want to rush into the hurt before it's even there. Maybe you're trying to get it over with?"

"Maybe," I said. I was hurting so badly, though, that I doubted the wisdom of this approach.

Jerry leaned across the table. "You love this guy. You think he might be the right one, don't you?"

I nodded. "But it's too late now."

He smiled. He had a nice smile, Jerry did. "It's never too late. If he's the one for you, don't let him get away."

Deep inside I felt a sudden prickle of hope. "Don't let him get away?"

"No," Jerry said. "Get out there while there's still time and get him back. Show him you love him. And most of all, show him you trust him."

"How?" I was a pathetic baby.

"Use whatever it takes, Brenda. Whatever it takes."

I sat silently, the occasional sniffle jerking my body. I thought about what Jerry had said, I thought about how much I loved Nick, and I thought about the prickle of hope. I thought about how Nick's blue eyes had moistened when he'd kissed me good-bye. I thought about how those same blue eyes went dark when he made love to me.

Jerry started eating his pancakes again. My mother sipped her orange juice, watching me.

I asked them, "Are you two going to get married?"

Jerry shot my mother a look. My mother smiled sweetly. "Why do you say that, dear?"

"Because I think you should." I gave Jerry a shaky smile. "Jerry would make a great dad."

Jerry reddened, but my mother looked pleased. She snaked her fingers through Jerry's, and he returned the caress with a look that broke my heart.

The rest of that day, I cried and thought about Nick, cried and thought about what Jerry had said, cried and thought about Nick some more. I fell asleep early that night after my near-sleepless stay at the Majestic San Diego and woke up Sunday morning determined to begin the Get Nick Back campaign.

I went shopping and ordered stuff on-line, then made plans and phone calls. I made my bed again and did more laundry. I cleaned out the refrigerator, bought real food to put in it, and then I cooked spaghetti and meatballs. Even David liked it. He and Clarissa offered to do the dishes. We were so domestic.

Monday morning, I marched into the studio, all flags flying. I was wearing lingerie, yes, a slinky teddy with a low-cut red blouse and a leather skirt. Marty stared at me in mid–candy bar bite.

No, I wasn't frumpy Brenda any longer, or wimpy Brenda worried that Mr. Perfect would be mad at her, but I wasn't completely lingerie-addict Brenda, either. I was me—all phases of me.

Showing Nick who I was would be scary. I'd be exposing everything with no guarantee that he'd like it. But I had to know. Love is like that, you know? It's scary, and it hurts, and it's worth everything you throw at it.

"Good morning, San Diego," I said brightly. "This is Brenda Scott. I have a message for Nick at KBZ." I dropped The Calling into the CD player to wail "Wherever You Will Go." "Thanks for a great night."

I turned off my mike. Marty started swaying to the music in the booth while chewing his candy bar.

As predicted, hurricane Tony hit the studio in five seconds flat. "Brenda, you're doing it again! What happened to classic rock?"

"I want to get a point across."

"What, that you have the hots for Nick? We all know that. And anyway, he broke up with you."

My heart twisted, and my will faltered. "He told you?"

"Yeah, I had to ask him why he'd breezed home from a sex date with you at three in the morning. So stop with Nick and Brenda already."

I almost put my head down and started crying again. Then I clenched my fists. No. I would not let Tony Beale weaken my resolve. I would get Nick back.

I turned on KBZ in the background. Nick was playing his usual songs, following his clock, playing his spots. When I heard his voice, I almost slid off my chair in a puddle. But he only announced the song and cued a commercial. He made no indication that he had heard me over here at KCLP.

When my song ended, I turned on my mike again. "So Nick asked me an important question this weekend, and this is my answer." I punched up the ZZ Top version of "Viva Las Vegas" and let it rip. That should give him a clue, I thought.

It didn't. Nick wouldn't come out and play. At KBZ, he went on with his show and his bits and his commercials. I played all kinds of off-the-wall music, answered phones, teased callers about what Nick had asked me.

Nick never responded. Whether he didn't like Brenda any more, or his program manager wouldn't let him respond, or he just didn't hear me, I didn't know.

But Jerry had said, "Whatever it takes." So I did whatever it took.

The next day I sent Nick flowers, a big bouquet of roses and other bright red fluted flowers whose name I didn't know, plus balloons and a big cookie.

The card said, "From your edible-panty stalker. I love you." I'd had to tell the wording to the florist twice before she believed me. Then she couldn't write it down because she was laughing so hard.

Nick still said nothing on the air. But I knew he got the bouquet, because the DJ after Nick teased him about it and offered to eat the cookie if Nick didn't want it.

I called Carlos up in La Jolla and asked him if he'd make a special dinner for Nick and then take it to him. I offered to pay for it, but Carlos chuckled and said no, he'd be happy to. I guess chefs get bored cooking the same thing over and over, and like to experiment once in a while. Or maybe he just liked the idea of helping young love.

The next day I left the station as soon as my shift was over and drove to Nick's house. I parked across the street and spent time making friends with Mrs. Pankhurst. I explained that I'd ordered a special surprise for Nick and wanted to watch it arrive, although I didn't want Nick to see me.

Mrs. Pankhurst was delighted that I wanted to do something nice for Nicky, so she agreed to let me watch him from her living room window. She even provided the binoculars.

I moved my car to the alley behind her house, then went back inside to play cribbage with Mrs. Pankhurst until Nick came home.

Nick arrived at about four in the afternoon. Tony, who was still hiding out in Nick's house, arrived with him. I bit my lip as I watched Nick get out of his car and walk up to the courtyard. The sight of his tall, strong body reminded me how much I missed having his arms around me. I wanted nothing more than to dash across the street and tackle him and kiss him all over once I got him on the ground.

The presence of Mrs. Pankhurst and Tony kept me from doing anything so stupid.

Nick and Tony went inside. Right on cue, Carlos's minions arrived in a van and started carrying covered dishes up the walk. It was a nice day, so they set up a table in the courtyard. Nick came out, of course, to see who was setting up a dinner next to his fountain. Carlos himself came forward to explain.

Through the binoculars I saw Nick listening to Carlos, his head bent, the sunshine catching in his blond hair. Damn, he was so incredibly sexy. Nick, not Carlos.

Tony came out, looked around, and rubbed his hands in delight. He plunked down on a folding chair and tucked a napkin into his collar.

Nick left the courtyard for the front walk. He scanned the street, searching for me, I'm sure. Mrs. Pankhurst and I ducked behind her living room curtains, giggling.

Bemused, Nick returned to his dinner. He sat down, and Carlos, with a flourish, uncovered the first course.

Nick ate the food—and remembering Carlos's cooking, I didn't see how he could have passed it up. Carlos remained to watch his creations be consumed. He carried on an animated conversation with Tony. Nick didn't say much; he just drank his wine and ate his salmon in papaya salsa in silence.

The three sat at the table until they finished dessert; then Carlos and his gang packed everything up again and put it back into his van. Carlos shook Nick's hand, clapped him on the back, and drove away.

Tony went inside, patting his paunch happily. Nick remained behind. He came out into the street and looked up and down in a determined way.

I froze behind the curtain. He knew I was out there, somewhere, and he was waiting for me to emerge. The look on his face made me think he wouldn't greet me with warm fuzzies.

Mrs. Pankhurst, still smiling, beckoned for me to follow her. She took me through her kitchen, down some steps to a laundry room, and out through a back door.

"Nicky needs some good surprises in his life," she said. "It was nice of you to do this for him."

She regarded me with thoughtful eyes, as though not quite sure of my sanity but willing to forgive me for Nicky's sake. "He went through a bad time when his mother and father died. I was glad to see him come home from Texas and settle down again. Being out there wasn't good for him."

Mrs. Pankhurst sure knew how to twist the knife. She was reminding me that Nick had gone through grief, then an engagement that nearly broke his spirit, and then came home to meet a crazy woman who stalked him with eclectic French food.

"I want to make him happy," I said. "I really do."

"We all want to see Nicky happy," she answered. "Oops, that's him ringing the doorbell. Go on, hurry."

She slammed the back door behind me. I scooted down the grassy hill in my heels and dove into my car.

As I inched the car out of the narrow alley, I saw Nick talking to Mrs. Pankhurst on her porch.

I nonchalantly pulled the car into the street. Nick turned and saw me. He did not look happy.

I waved to him out the window. "Hope it was good for

you!" I shouted; then I gunned the car and squealed around the corner out of sight.

For the next couple of days, I left Nick alone. Let him relax a while, maybe even think he was safe. I listened to his show every day, but he never mentioned the meal or the flowers or seeing me pull out of Mrs. Pankhurst's alley. I wondered how he felt about Carlos and Mrs. Pankhurst assisting me.

I wondered how he'd feel about the one last thing I would put into motion at the festival. It was kind of an all or nothing deal, and my insides got cold whenever I thought of it.

But I was determined. I recruited John and Katie and Billy to help me, and I practiced all night.

Saturday dawned with promising weather for the radio festival, which made everyone happy. I arrived in my big KCLP T-shirt and shorts and baseball cap. David and Clarissa came with me. I remembered how Mom had vowed she'd come today, too, and I hoped, I really hoped, that she—and Jerry—would show up.

The fest proved to be quite popular, which made Tony and KBZ's manager happy. Tents went up for food and beer and soft drinks, games were available for the kids, and a DJs' booth was erected on a stage under an awning. People started pouring in about ten o'clock, attracted by live music, food, prizes, and the opportunity to watch radio personalities make fools of themselves.

Nick arrived, looked extremely edible as usual. I didn't follow him, but when we happened to pass each other on the DJ stage, I said, "Hi, Nick. How was your week?"

Nick wore a black T-shirt with his station's logo on it. His tanned arms showed taut muscle, as though he'd been working out more than usual lately. His blue gaze raked me up and down, as though he was surprised to find me in something so mundane as shorts and a T-shirt.

He didn't know how mundane I'd actually dressed.

"I think you know how my week was," he said.

I slanted him a smile, pretending I wasn't aching inside. "Carlos is a good cook."

"Yes," Nick agreed. "He's also a good friend."

I wondered what the heck that was supposed to mean. Was it good or bad?

I didn't have the chance to ask, because his program manager grabbed his attention, and we all went back to work.

The softball tournament started. I am so not a jock, but every able-bodied person at KCLP got recruited, along with friends and family to fill in the gaps. So there I was playing left field, with my brother David at first base and Jerry playing shortstop. Incredibly, Tony Beale was our pitcher.

He proved to be not bad at it. He put the ball over the plate in a nice steady underhand throw. He wasn't perfect, but he kept the other team jumping.

The innings went on. Neither team was brilliant, but neither was too terrible either. KCLP racked up a steady stream of points, and even I got a base hit—although I couldn't run home, because the next guy popped up and we were out.

I was fine, even enjoying myself, until Nick stepped up to bat.

Because I was out in left field, I could only see Nick's tall, lithe form at a distance as he brushed off the plate with his foot and hefted the bat. My knees went weak. Nick swung a few times, looking Tony straight down the pitch.

Tony tried to get him to swing at bad balls, but Nick was too canny for that. He waited until Tony gave him one he liked, and Nick hit it hard. Out to left field.

It was a grounder. I scrambled to get it as Nick ran easily to first base. While I chased the damn ball and

David screamed, "Come on, Brenda, get it!" Nick took himself to second.

I grabbed the ball. I dropped it again. Nick ran on to third.

I grabbed the ball again, and this time it stayed in my glove. I dashed for the infield. No way could I throw that ball far enough in time to get it to the third baseman, Marty. Nick saw my dilemma and used it to his advantage. He started to sprint for home.

I ran across the field right for him. Nick realized he'd not make it home before I got to him, so he turned and backtracked to third. I hurtled straight into him.

We both went down into spring-scented grass. I held the ball against his chest and glared at him in triumph. "Out!" I yelled.

"Safe," he said.

His foot rested firmly on third base. "I touched you before you touched it," I said. "You're out."

"Safe," he insisted.

Our teammates converged on us. "He's out of there," David declared.

"Safe!" the KBZ people screamed.

Nick tried to get up, but I was still on top of him. He watched me through his lashes, and I saw it.

The spark was there, the one I thought had died. He'd gotten that little sparkle in his eyes when he'd seen me at Swesto's coffeehouse, when I'd asked if he'd like to start over. He'd had it during every date since then, even the ridiculous ones. It was the sparkle that meant he was happy that he and I were within arm's reach of each other.

Nick didn't hate me. My heart beat hard, rejoicing. I leaned down and kissed his lips.

Nick responded to the pressure with a push of his own lips, but he didn't reach for me.

"Hey," Tony said, leaning over us. "No kissing the other team."

"I'm trying to convince him he's out," I said in a choked voice.

Nick looked up at me. "Safe."

Our gazes met. The sparkle was still there.

But he made no other sign, no touch or caress or attempt to return my kiss.

The umpire declared him safe, and, grumbling, I finally climbed off of him. Jerry helped Nick to stand, and I strolled away, muttering that the umpire was blind.

KBZ won the game by one point. "Nick was out," I said to Tony. "We'd have won if the umpire had agreed that Nick was out."

"Give it a rest, Brenda," Tony said. "It's all in fun. Time for DJs on pogo sticks."

I tried very hard to talk him out of making me jump on a pogo stick. Tony insisted that guys liked to watch girls on pogo sticks. I told him he was a creep, but I walked over and grabbed my stick.

I had the advantage, though. All the other competitors were guys. They were so busy trying to beat one another that they failed to notice me happily pass them all. In triumph, I won.

The day wore on. Bohemian Love Child arrived and played. John Dishard showed incredible restraint toward Tony. "It's for charity, Brenda," he said, flipping his gray braid over his shoulder. "I'm cool with that."

Billy and Katie came with him. They greeted me enthusiastically, then trooped over to say hi to Nick.

My heart beat faster as I watched the three of them start a conversation—my ultimate Get Nick Back feat was about to begin.

"Psst!"

I glanced around, made sure that no one was looking,

341

then plunged behind the stage where the hissing had come from.

John stood waiting for me. "Ready?"

I drew a breath. "Yeah. I guess."

He gave me a sharp look. "Come on, Brenda. We went over this all night. Don't back out on me now."

"OK, OK." I peered around the jumble of speakers and junk on the stage. Katie and Billy had taken Nick aside, like I'd asked them to. They'd been easy to recruit, brightening like kids at their first Bob Dylan concert.

"Of course we'll help, honey," Katie had said. "It'll be fun."

John picked up his guitar and gave me a nod. "It's cool, don't worry."

I clenched my fists, wondering if I really, really wanted to do this. But, what was the worst that could happen? Well, Nick could turn his back and walk away, leaving Brenda awkward and rejected in front of hundreds of people including her boss and family and friends. That's all.

Great idea, Brenda.

But I had to try.

Taking a deep breath, I plunged out from behind the stage. A branch of the oleanders that grew close to the stage caught on my hair. I tugged it out, leaves flying.

When I straightened up, I saw Nick looking straight at me. I realized that the bush had also pulled my T-shirt half-way down my arm. At that wonderful moment, John walked out right behind me.

Nick's face was white. Geez, did he think I'd been back there alone with John? OK so I had been, but not for the reason he was thinking. His assumption hurt. I'd told him how I felt.

"Show him," Jerry had said.

Well, here goes nothing.

The plan went off so well that even I couldn't screw it up. Billy and Katie got Nick to walk toward the stage with them. They'd spent a lot of time last night coming up with ideas for getting him to come over there, each of them more ludicrous than the last. Finally John just told them to haul him over there and not worry about it.

I guess they came up with something, because Nick strolled with them toward the band shell. I could see Katie giggling.

Marty grinned at me when I climbed onto the stage with John. He'd set up to broadcast, and was ready, sitting behind his board with his headphones. Behind me, John put on his acoustic guitar and strummed a little tune to warm up.

Seeing that something was about to start, other people started drifting toward the stage. The sight of all of them made my heart thump hard, and my legs turn watery. Katie and Billy closed in on either side of Nick. More people came up behind him.

Little by little, they gradually maneuvered him right in front of the stage.

I stepped up to the microphone in front, shaking all over. From up here I could see the entire festival. The sun shone hard and hot on children dragging their parents toward the cotton candy machines. The beer tent overflowed with drinkers and noise. My mother and Jerry had moved to the back of the crowd and were smiling at me. David and Clarissa were over by the dart and balloon booth talking to—Reginald? The not-nervous-as-hell part of me registered that as interesting. Tony Beale was nowhere in sight. Thank God.

I looked down. Nick stood right in front of me. He folded his arms, looking resigned. I searched for the spark I'd seen when we were on the softball field.

Nope. No spark.

343

Us colliding on the softball field had been more or less serendipity. I could see the words whirling through Nick's brain. *What's she going to do this time?*

My throat was dry as the desert east of the mountains. That's pretty dry. And I was hot all over, like I was out in that desert under the August sun. Nick looked so great with his hair mussed from the wind and wearing shorts and a T-shirt that I wanted to haul him back behind the stage and show him what I was missing.

Well, the next few minutes would tell me whether I'd won him or lost him.

"Are we on, Marty?" I asked, my voice shaking.

"Hang on," he said. He talked to the guy waiting at KCLP, then showed me three fingers, two fingers, one finger, and pointed at me to start.

"Hey, San Diego," I said.

Tony was going to fire me for sure. But let him. I'd become a popular morning DJ. A newspaper story the other day said I was funny, smart, and entertaining, and called me San Diego radio's freshest voice. "Where has Brenda Scott been all my life?" the writer said. "I love this lady." I might just have a future. Maybe.

"This is Brenda Scott," I croaked. "I'm here at the radio festival to do a special tribute to the guy I love. Nick and I—"

I broke off. I didn't want to explain that he'd told me we'd be better off apart. It hurt too much to say it out loud. "Nick is very special to me. Even though I drive him crazy and have ever since New Year's, when he didn't mean to—" I took a breath. "Ever since New Year's I've been making him crazy, but it's only because I'm not good at expressing how I feel. Just saying 'I love you,' doesn't really work, so I'm going to say it a different way."

I nodded at John. Nick stood frozen, eyes on me. I

don't think he would have moved even if Katie and Billy hadn't been hemming him in.

John started playing. I'd sat up with him all night choosing a song and then learning how to sing it. We finally settled on The Beach Boys, "God Only Knows," because, although John wasn't a big Beach Boys fan, it was something I could sing and said what I wanted to say.

My voice was shaking and warbled. I'd practiced and practiced with John all night, and had the song mostly down, but now I could barely breathe.

Nick watched me, his face devoid of expression. Kind of like he was just waiting for me to finish, so he could walk away. The hurt inside me grew like a bubble.

John played, really getting into it, and putting in fancy licks where there weren't any in the original song. I sang my heart out.

The crowd sang along, laughing, having a great time. But from my perspective, it might as well have been just me and Nick. Me wailing and Nick standing there in complete silence.

And then it was over. John played a crashing chord, and Katie and Billy and the audience clapped and cheered.

"Thank you," I said. "That was for you, Nick. He's standing right here in front of the stage, and that's great, because I have something to give him."

I unhooked the microphone from the stand and pulled a folded piece of paper out of my pocket.

It was an airline ticket to Las Vegas. I'd bought two. In the movies, when someone hands someone else a plane ticket, it's a thick thing with lots of pages in a folder. It looks dramatic. In the age of the Internet, I'd bought it online and printed it out on a sheet of paper. Not dramatic. But still a ticket.

I leaned down, microphone still in hand. "Nick asked me a question a week ago. This is my answer."

I handed him the paper. He stared at it in suspicion, and for a long moment, I thought he wasn't going to take it.

Then he reached out a stiff hand and plucked it from my grip. He opened it, looked at it, then folded it again with a neutral expression.

I started to relax. He hadn't torn it to shreds or stomped it into the mud. Good sign, right?

"Does that mean yes?" I asked, hope evident in my tone. I took a deep breath, put my whole heart into my words, and looked him straight in the eye. "Will you marry me, Nick?" The words echoed to the ends of the park.

The silence that followed was stunned. Nick's eyes got bleaker still, and I realized the enormity of what I'd done. I'd probably just lost my job and lost Nick, and I'd humiliated myself in front of countless people. The story would be splashed across the newspapers and on the local news—I spotted a guy from one of the channels with a camera.

I'd have to move to Tahiti, change my name, and become a nun in some strange religious cult.

Then people in the crowd began to applaud, and to cheer, and to shout. "Marry her! Go on, Nick, say yes!"

Whistles split the air. They started a chant: "Yes, yes, yes, yes."

The only quiet one was Nick. He stared at me for a long time, his blue eyes telling me nothing.

Then he folded the ticket and slid it into his back pocket. I noticed then that Katie wasn't smiling any more. She looked worried.

Nick reached up and took the microphone from my numb hand. "Excuse us, San Diego," he said into it. "Brenda and I need a little privacy."

He clicked the microphone off and laid it on the stage. Then he took my hand and helped me down.

346

His movements were quiet, his touch gentle. He guided me through the crowd and away from them with his hand on the small of my back.

"Nick," I started.

"Don't say anything, yet."

We broke out of the crowd, them still chanting and cheering. As far as they were concerned, me and Nick getting married was a done deal. When was the wedding?

Nick smiled at people and waved at the cameraman. All the while, he guided me determinedly away; finally we moved through people who had no interest in the stage show, and then to the part of the park that was relatively empty. Back on stage, John had started up "Summer in the City," getting the audience to sing along with him.

Nick didn't stop until we reached a maintenance shed that stood open on the edge of the parking lot. I ducked inside the shed and Nick followed. He pulled the door half-way shut, but left it open enough to allow the warm daylight in.

The shed smelled like cut grass and moist, rich earth, the smells of spring. Rakes stood against the wall, and sacks of fertilizer and potting soil were stacked neatly on the floor. A coil of hose lay in front of a worn lawn-mower tractor. The air inside the shed was cool, and I could feel the heat of Nick's body so close to me.

My heart was thumping. "So," I said, trying to sound bright. "Did you bring me in here to talk, or should we close the door all the way?"

He only looked at me. The shadow made his eyes dark. The little hope I had when I was keyed up on the stage was dying.

It bit the dust all the way when Nick pulled out the ticket and handed it back to me.

28

The Healing Power of Pecan Pie

I didn't touch it. "You didn't like the song. I knew I should have picked something else, but I can't sing Evanescence or Fiona Apple."

He said nothing.

"OK, I can't sing the Beach Boys, either," I babbled. "I can't sing at all. Everyone in San Diego is laughing and I'll probably have to pay fifty FCC fines for putting something that horrible over the air waves."

Was it my imagination, or did his lips twitch? His eyes didn't soften, though.

"The song was fine," he said.

"If you don't want the ticket, why did you take it?"

"I didn't want to embarrass you."

I laughed shakily. "I wasn't already embarrassed? It was lame, I know that. But I really meant what the song said. I won't be anything without you."

"That's not true. You'll be Brenda."

My laughter faded. "What does that matter if you don't like Brenda?"

He slid the piece of paper inside the opening of my shirt. "Brenda, I can't—"

I put my hand against his lips. *Oops, big mistake.* I immediately wanted to run my fingers over his lips to feel their satin smoothness.

Talking, I scolded myself. Stick to talking.

"Don't say no, yet," I begged. "Take the ticket. Think about it. Be on the plane if you still want to go."

"Brenda—"

"No, don't. Please. Let me hope. Give me that, at least."

Nick's eyes softened, but his voice did not. "The flowers and the dinner were one thing. By the way, you impressed Carlos. He told me not to let you get away."

"Oh, good. I like Carlos."

"But—"

"Please don't say 'but.' If you come with me to Las Vegas, I'll show you the real Brenda. I promise. You've never met her, and I don't know if you'll like her, but I'm willing to risk it."

His breath warmed my fingers. I was starting to like this.

He gently moved my hand away. "Don't take me to Las Vegas to prove something."

"But I *do* want to prove something. I want to prove that I can be with you—the real me with the real you—without me being afraid. I want to prove that you are the one for me, that I'm willing to do what it takes to make it work."

Nick looked away. "No, you were right at the hotel. I was mad at you, and I wanted to push you into doing things you weren't ready to do."

"I *am* ready. I'm ready to say anything, Nick. I'm ready to *do* anything. I just got on the air and asked you to marry me in front of southern California, and I *sang*, for Pete's sake. Look—I don't even have on any lingerie." I pulled the collar of my T-shirt down to expose my shoulder and part of my breast.

Nick's brow creased. "What are you wearing under there, then?"

"Nothing."

He choked. He put his hand to his mouth to catch his coughing. "Nothing?"

"Au naturel." I grimaced. "These shorts are really chafing me."

"You were wearing a bra out on the softball field."

Oh, so he'd noticed that, had he? "Well, running and catching. And pogo-stick jumping. Kind of necessary. I took it off after."

He nodded once, still looking dazed.

"I packed my bag for Las Vegas," I went on. "There's no lingerie in it. Not a stitch."

"I don't have a problem with your lingerie, Brenda."

"I know. But it's not the real me. I only started wearing sexy lingerie after you and I made love on New Year's. I figured if I slept with a guy I didn't know, I might as well dress the part. Underneath my clothes anyway. And then you came back, and the lingerie addict just took over."

"We never slept together on New Year's," Nick said softly.

"And so I thought that—" I broke off, dumbfounded. "Huh?"

"We never slept together on New Year's," he repeated.

I stared at him. "What are you talking about? I woke up, and there you were. Right next to me, buck naked. You look great naked, Nick."

He stood there calmly, still looking really good, despite the fact that he was dressed. "I ran into the friend who took me to the New Year's party," he said. "I hadn't seen him since then. He told me that it was all a joke."

A pit opened up in front of me. "Joke?"

"I'd had way too many margaritas. When I started looking at you and saying how gorgeous you were, Mark and his friends decided to play a joke. They over-spiked my drinks, and when I passed out, they stripped off my clothes and put me in your bed. With you." He gave me an unreadable look. "We never touched each other. We were unconscious. When I woke up, I couldn't remember anything, and I just assumed—"

I'd just assumed, too. What else do you assume when you wake up next to a beautiful blue-eyed man, and neither of you has a stitch of clothing on? I should have realized that Clarissa's weird friends would have found that funny.

Some of the color started to drain out of my world, leaving behind shades of gray. Nick was telling me that I wasn't really a wild woman, but only Brenda Scott, the boring, good girl. I hadn't really done anything impulsive and crazy.

"Oh, God." A chill formed in the pit of my stomach.

"Does it matter?" Nick asked gently. "I'm glad they did it. It made me want to find you again."

"But what you found was a lie."

His eyes warmed. "No, what I found was you."

"You don't understand." I looked at him in anguish. "I've been basing my entire life since New Year's on something that never happened. The things I've done— I never, ever would have if I hadn't thought—"

"Stop," he said, putting his hand on my arm.

I whirled away and paced restlessly in the tiny space. "I started buying lingerie because I thought I was sexy Brenda, and I wanted to be her. You wanted to find me again because I was sexy Brenda. But I'm not. I'm just mousy Brenda with scouring-pad hair, pretending to be something else. I bought all those slinky things and flashed you at a restaurant because I thought that's who I was—"

351

"It is who you are," Nick said.

I kept pacing, desperately blinking back tears. "No. The real Brenda would never dream of doing all that stuff. Or of buying you edible underwear or having sex with you on your kitchen table—"

He smiled a little. "That part I liked."

I stopped. "I did too."

"I thought you did that because you liked me."

"I did. I really like Nick, that's what was going through my head the whole time."

"Not just because you were trying to prove to yourself that you were sexy?"

"No—" I broke off. "Or, maybe." I put my head in my hands. "I don't know any more."

He leaned against the doorframe, looking almost relaxed, while I was watching my life fall in shards at my feet.

"But you did it," he said. "Do you regret that?"

"Regret having sex with you? Not hardly."

"So what's the problem?"

I waved my arms. "The problem is, I'm not what you thought I was. I'm a lie."

"But you did all those things, Brenda. You took me to your dad's boat, you bought lingerie, you made love on my table, you flashed me at Tonio's. That was you." He caught my hand as I tried to resume my pacing. "You did all of that."

I stilled, mesmerized, as always, by his touch.

He kept talking. "You never could have done the humorous radio stuff and gotten all those listeners, if you weren't funny and sexy and brave for real."

Something inside me was telling me he was right, but I was too agitated and hurt and scared to listen, or to believe.

"Maybe I shouldn't have sung that song," I said

faintly. "You must be dazed from the terrible sound waves."

"I'm serious. I've spent the last couple weeks getting to know you, Brenda. Even if things don't work out with us, some other guy is going to be damn lucky to get you."

That's when I knew we were broken up for real. When the guy starts saying that your next boyfriend will be a lucky man, then he's finished with you.

Except—

"You said if things don't work out," I said. "Does that mean maybe they will?"

He shrugged. "I don't know. I think we should just take things as they come for now, and not push it."

Another bad sign. Asking for no pushing.

"We should get back to the festival," he said.

I clung to his hand as he tried to release me. "Could we—um—kiss? For luck?"

"No." He gently let go. "I know you're not wearing any underwear, and I might try to ravish you on that tractor over there."

I glanced at the lawn-mowing tractor with its wide, worn seat. "That might be fun," I said.

Nick shook his head. "No. Let's go." He turned around and pushed the door open. Sunshine flooded me, stinging my eyes that were salty with tears.

"By the way," Nick said, as he held the door for me. "You wouldn't have thought that sounded fun if you weren't really sexy Brenda."

"You're just trying to make me feel better," I muttered, and ducked outside.

Thank God no one was waiting for us. No Katie and Billy looking hopeful, no Mom and Jerry looking hopeful, no fans looking hopeful.

I did see Tony Beale, but he wasn't looking at us. The shed was on the edge of the grounds by the parking lot, and as we emerged, he was threading his way through cars in the lot.

I ducked behind a tree. "Ugh, there's Tony. I do not want him to see me right now."

"Neither do I," Nick said. "You would not believe how much that man eats."

"I believe it. He's—" I stopped.

As Tony passed a car, Tim the ex–morning DJ suddenly rose from inside it. Before Nick or I could start to Tony's rescue, Tim grabbed the startled Tony by the arm, smacked him on the back of the neck, and pushed him into the car.

As we watched, startled, Tim jumped into the driver's seat and roared away.

Both of us unfroze at the same time. Nick sprinted for the parking lot, and I ran beside him. We saw John just closing the door of his pick-up. Back at the stage, his band was playing on without him. When he saw us chasing Tim and Tony, he brightened. "Come on, get in!"

He jumped into the cab as I flung myself up and into the passenger seat, with Nick right behind me. I was fully aware of Nick's body jostling mine as we tried to settle on the seat. Over it was worry about what Tim was going to do to Tony. The man was unhinged.

John's engine roared to life, and he zoomed off in the direction Tim had taken. Driving wasn't easy. Other people were heading out, and we got stuck in a line exiting the parking lot. Tim managed to swerve around the line, earning himself honks and waving fists and raised middle fingers. By the time John made it to the street, Tim had disappeared.

Nick lifted himself halfway out of the window. "He turned that way," he pointed.

John obeyed the direction and stomped on the gas.

Pretty soon I saw Tim in his blue Honda shooting onto a ramp to the freeway, heading south.

John headed south, too. Again I noted that John's old truck zoomed along faster than any new Porsche, a testimony to his mechanic talent. I sensibly buckled myself in and hung on as he wove through Saturday traffic.

Tim stayed in sight, though we couldn't catch up to him. We almost immediately ran into people pouring onto the I-5 from Sea World and the I-8. Tim faded into a sea of cars and trucks and SUVs.

John plunged through the traffic, and Nick and I held on for dear life. We were jammed together in the cab, and the part of me below the panic enjoyed being thrown hard against him on every turn. His skin was warm, his arm and shoulder and hip strong against mine.

We lost Tim for a time as we hurtled past Balboa Park and through downtown, then I saw his car rise on an exit ramp.

"He's taking Coronado Bridge," I screamed.

"Crap." John swerved over two lanes, earning some waving fists, and zipped up the exit to the bridge.

Coronado Bridge curves out in a pretty arc from the I-5 over San Diego Bay to Coronado, an almost-island connected to the mainland by a slender finger of land that encircles the bay. A nice drive on a Sunday afternoon.

Tourists were out in full today, driving leisurely from downtown San Diego to hotels and shops and beaches on Coronado. I ground my teeth and cursed them for not parking and taking the ferry.

Tim in his blue Honda was easy to spot, because he was pulling over. When we'd done the bungee-jumping stunt on New Year's, the police had cleared the area and shunted traffic away. Today, cars whizzed on past, honking as Tim tried to park.

By the time John maneuvered his way behind him,

Tim had dragged Tony from the car and to the side of the bridge.

Other passing motorists stopped, creating a jam. Nick and I ran across the road, dodging cars, Nick running ahead of me.

Tim was wrapping Tony in a bungee cord, laughing like a crazy man the whole time. People who'd stopped to help hesitated, unsure of what was going on.

"Publicity stunt," Tim called, smiling up at them. Tony struggled, but weakly.

"Call the police!" I shouted at the crowd forming. I still didn't have a cell phone.

A couple people pulled out their phones. Traffic piled up, horns honking, drivers shouting, asking what the hell was going on.

"It's OK, Brenda," Tim called to me. "He has a bungee cord. I just want him to know how it feels."

Tim hauled Tony onto the lip of the bridge. Tony was wrapped in the bungee cord like a fly in a spider's web. He teetered on the edge.

Nick tackled Tim and pushed him to the ground. I grabbed for Tony. I missed, and he started to topple over the side. He screamed. In panic, I grabbed his legs and held on tight, my feet skidding against the pavement.

John grabbed me around the waist. He pulled me backward. I hauled on Tony's legs. Finally, Tony's weight shifted to the safe side of the ledge, and we both toppled to the pavement. Tony landed on top of me.

"Brenda," he whimpered.

Nick had Tim. Tim looked confused. "He has a bungee cord," he said.

"Fine," Nick said, panting. "But you need to anchor it to a rig. What were you going to do, hold it in your hand?"

"Oh," Tim said.

Tony groaned. His eyes rolled back in his head, and he sagged heavily against me.

His face came to rest right between my braless breasts.

The police and a nice man in a white coat took Tim away. An ambulance came for Tony, and I rode with him while Nick and John followed in the truck.

Tony held my hand and looked at me with adoring eyes. "You saved my life."

"It was your own fault," I said. "You shouldn't have made Tim do all those publicity stunts. You scared him crazy."

His eyes bugged. "I scared *him?* He almost killed me."

I patted his hand. "You're OK now, Tony."

"I'm never driving on that bridge again," he vowed. "If there's anything I can do for you, Brenda, anything at all, you just ask me."

"Hmm," I said, thinking.

"Nick really loves you," he said.

"What?" I glanced at the tech who was checking Tony's readouts and avidly listening to our conversation.

Tony didn't seem to care. "He said he knows he should walk away from you, but he loves you so much that he can't."

Right, he gave me back the plane ticket, the one still rustling around in my shirt, and turned down my proposal because he loved me.

"He—told you this," I said, my throat tight.

"Oh, yeah, he's been all broken up since your big fight. And then when you started sending him presents and that great dinner the other night, he almost broke down. By the way, thanks. That fish thing sure tasted good."

"Carlos's specialty," I said faintly.

"It was Nick's favorite. He said that Carlos used to fix

it for him ten years ago, whenever Nick helped out in his kitchen. Nick was totally bowled over."

Nick hadn't seemed bowled over. If he'd been bowled over, he'd have said, in his sexy voice, "Yes, I'll marry you, Brenda," and swept me into his arms.

"I told Nick all about you," Tony babbled, probably helped along by painkillers. "How scared you were when you first came to work for me, how you caught the eye of the rich Larry Bryant, how you blossomed under my guidance."

"Oh, right, Tony," I said. "I'd be nothing without you."

Tony ignored my sarcasm. "I told him that you two kids were made for each other. That underneath all your weirdness, you're a real sweetheart. A girl who'd do anything for anyone. I told him that Larry really screwed you over and that you'd gone a little nuts because of it."

I made a squeak of frustration. "Thanks a lot, Tony. I think you scared him away."

"I tried to offer him a job at KCLP, but he wouldn't take it. Not even when I offered him an obscenely high salary. But it isn't the money, he said. Nick doesn't need money—his father got filthy rich on his restaurants, did you know that? So he doesn't need money. But he loves the team at KBZ, so he stays."

And likely he didn't want to ruin his career by working for Tony Beale.

Tony went on, "So you need to marry him. He can support you. You can't live forever on a DJ's salary, you know, even on morning drive time."

"You could give me a raise," I pointed out. "I did just save your life."

He squeezed my hand again. "And I'm really grateful. I was thinking more along the lines of giving you and

Nick a weekend at a beach house. I can get a promotion swap."

I studied at the swaying ceiling of the ambulance. Oh, sure, Tony would offer Nick the moon to lure him from KBZ, but would the cheapskate pay to keep me there? Tony never changed. Even being nearly killed didn't do the trick.

"This Nick guy sounds great," the tech said. "Are you going to marry him?"

I opened my mouth to tell them to both mind their own business, but I subsided. Tony would never shut up because I told him to, and the tech was too cute and buff to yell at. I closed my mouth and let them get away with it.

Nick and I and John stayed with Tony in the emergency room while a doctor, a cool-faced woman with a dark blond bun, looked Tony over. She announced that there didn't appear to be much damage, but she told him to check in overnight for observation.

Nick helped Tony to the front desk and filled out his insurance paperwork for him. John kept up a running commentary that emergency care should be given free to all citizens without having to hassle with insurance. The nurse behind the counter looked harassed. John told her it was because of all the oppression. I decided to rush off to the cafeteria to get coffee for us all.

I met Clarissa coming out with two coffees in her hand.

Before I could blurt, "What are you doing here?" she said in her languid voice, "Oh, hi, Brenda. He's on the third floor."

I blinked. "Who is?"

"David," she answered calmly. "He's going to be OK. Your mom's with him. He got the injection in time."

359

She started to move past me, but I blocked her way. "Clarissa! What injection? *What happened?*"

"David had a reaction to the pecans."

I wanted to grab her and shake her. "What pecans?"

"In the pies. He entered the pie-eating contest. He was doing good, then he got the reaction. He puffed up and couldn't breathe."

"He's allergic to pecans, the idiot."

Clarissa shrugged. But despite the blandness of her dead-white face, she looked worried. "I guess he forgot."

"He forgot his tenth birthday party?" I asked, incredulous.

I'd never forgotten. Someone's mother had brought a pecan pie and David and his friends and his tagalong little sister, Brenda, had dug in. What had happened afterward wasn't pretty. Pecan pie everywhere, David gagging on the floor, his friends screaming in panic, freaking out like the ten-year-olds they were. Mom, so calm, had rushed David to the hospital, and I'd cried because I thought he was dead.

The tenth birthday party vanished. "Where is he?"

For answer, Clarissa jerked her head toward the elevators and started walking. Abandoning Nick and Tony, I followed.

In a room on the third floor, David lay in bed in a hospital gown. He was awake and scowling. His face was bright red and swollen, as were his neck and hands and elbows.

My mother and Jerry were there, my mother sitting weakly on a chair at David's bedside. To my surprise, Reginald was there, too.

Mom jumped up when she saw me. "Brenda, I was looking for you. Thank God you got here."

"I'm OK, Mom," David said in his crabby I'm-embarrassed voice.

"He almost died," Clarissa informed me. She handed my mom one of the cups of coffee and settled down to drink the other one.

"But I'm OK," David said firmly, giving me a severe look. "Don't you go off on me, too."

I was shaking, but I forced myself to stay calm. "You forgot your tenth birthday?" I asked, trying to sound humorous.

"I remembered as soon as I started spitting out pecan pie. Vividly, believe me."

My mother's eyes filled. "Reginald was with him. He got David into his car and to the hospital."

Reginald looked modest. "I knew he was allergic to pecans." When we looked surprised, he said, "I've been investigating him. It's in his dossier."

Jerry put his strong, brown hands on my mother's shoulders. "It'll be OK. David won't eat any more pecans."

"Cross my heart," David said. "I never want to see a pecan again."

Mom wiped her eyes. "Jerry, Clarissa, can I talk to David and Brenda alone?"

"Sure." Jerry leaned down and kissed her cheek. "I'll go see what passes for cheese Danishes in the cafeteria. Clarissa? Reg?" He gave my mom another kiss, winked at me, then led Clarissa and Reginald out of the room and closed the door.

Mom turned to David. He looked panicked. She was going to bring up The Subject, the one we hadn't fought about since Easter. Except now he couldn't run away and hide in a cabin to sulk.

I was in no mood to fight, either. I'd just done a chase through the streets of San Diego and saved Tony Beale from toppling off Coronado Bridge and falling way, way down to San Diego Bay. Plus I was in the middle of trying to persuade Nick to run away to Las Vegas with me. I thought of him downstairs. I chafed, and not just because of my lack of underwear.

"Mom," I began, "maybe this isn't the best time—"

David nodded fervently.

"No," my mother said. "I want to say what I need to say. I'm going to tell Jerry to leave."

Silence fell. David and I stared at her.

"Why?" I blurted out.

I thought of the way Jerry had kissed her before he'd left the room. I remembered the look he'd given her when he'd held her hand at the pancake house. That man loved my mother, no question about it.

"Because I realized today that my family is more important," my mom said. Tears trembled on her eyelashes. "You two are the most precious things in my life. If me having a relationship, or a fling, or whatever you want to call it, will keep you away from me, then I don't want it. I'd rather have you."

"Mom." I teared up, too. "Jerry loves you."

David growled. "Oh, now, don't both of you start crying. This is why I like Clarissa. She's not weepy."

Mom ignored him. "I don't want to hurt Jerry. But if I have to choose, I can't not choose you." She took my hand, squeezed it. "I told you on the boat that my life with your father had been unhappy. But it wasn't, not really, because I always had you. And even now that you're all grown up, you're still the best things in my life. I don't ever want anything to take that away."

Waves of guilt and love and sorrow struck me one after another. "Oh, Mom," I said, and then I was hugging her, and we were both crying.

"There they go," David said to the room.

"Shut up, David," I said from my mother's shoulder.

"I'm the one who's sick here," he complained. "Why aren't I getting any hugs?"

My mother and I converged on him and smothered him in icky mom and sister hugs until he told us to back off. But he liked it, I could tell.

We straightened up and wiped the tears from our faces. "Mom, you can't break up with Jerry," I said.

"She can if she wants to," David interrupted.

I glared him to silence. "I will not be selfish and make you break up with him so that I'll feel better. You love him, don't you?"

My mother nodded. "I'm afraid I do. But—"

I held up my hand. "No buts. I see the way he treats you. He cares about you and he's kind to you, and he's helpful to me and David." I shot a stern look at David again. "Or at least, he tries to be helpful to me and David. We don't always let him."

"Since when has he tried to be helpful to me?" David asked plaintively.

I put my hands on my hips. "Oh, let's see, he bought your plane ticket home when you had no money and nowhere to go. And he says you can work at his business any time you want."

"He repairs boats," David protested. "I can't repair boats."

"I'm sure you can do something. And isn't it better than sitting on your butt living off me and Clarissa?"

David frowned as though trying to figure out why working would be better than living for free in my apartment. "Maybe," he growled.

I turned back to my mother. "We're not going to stand in the way of you being happy. Are we, David?"

"We're not?"

I gave him the eye. He sighed and said, "No, I guess we're not."

"We're going to let you have a good life, and if that life includes Jerry, then it does. Right, David?"

"Right," David said grudgingly.

"Jerry's a good guy. Right, David?"

"Right." The word came out between his teeth.

"You will stay with Jerry," I said to my mother. "Marry him if you want to, and be in love. OK?"

Mom smiled, her tears still flowing. "OK."

"And if he turns out to be a greedy bloodsucker, we'll dump him in Mission Bay," I offered.

"That sounds good," David said.

Mom nodded. "Yes, all right. But he isn't a greedy bloodsucker. He's very sweet."

"Yuck," David said.

"And anyway," I finished, smiling, "he's to-die-for gorgeous."

My mother and I exchanged the woman's secret grin. "Yes," she said, "he really is."

"Oh God," David said. "I think I'm going to be sick again."

29

The 9:05 to Las Vegas

When I left David's room, I found Jerry waiting in the hall. Clarissa sat a little way down the corridor with her feet up while she read a magazine and chewed on a cheese Danish. Reginald sat next to her reading a dog-eared *People* magazine.

"Everything OK?" Jerry asked. He looked a little uneasy, as though he'd known what Mom was going to do. He was smart enough to understand that if Mom had to make a choice, she wouldn't choose him. She loved her children, and he was the dispensable party.

"Everything's fine," I said. I went to him and hugged him hard.

Surprised, he returned the embrace.

"Thank you, Jerry," I said.

"For what?"

"For everything." I released him then kissed him quickly on the cheek. "Thanks for making my mom fall in love."

"I was glad to do it."

I shook a finger at him mockingly. "Now, you make her happy. Or, I'll beat you up, OK?"

He grinned. "I swear, I'll treat her nice."

"Good, then that's settled." I pulled my shirt down straight. On to my next problem. "Now I have to find Nick."

"I saw him," Jerry said. "Downstairs. I told him about your brother."

I started for the elevators. "Is he waiting?"

"No."

Jerry's somber tone brought me up short. I turned. Jerry's grin had deserted him, and he looked unhappy.

I swallowed the lump in my throat. "Break it to me gently," I said.

"He's gone," Jerry replied softly. "He said that Tony was settled into a room and that he was heading back to the festival with your friend to get his car. He figured you'd want to go home with your mom."

I blinked away a tear that threatened to leak from my eyes. "Does he want me to call?"

Jerry looked at me sorrowfully. "No. I'm sorry, Brenda."

I folded my arms over my chest, trying to hug away the pain in my heart. "It's not your fault." I studied the ugly multicolored hospital carpet a moment, trying to keep the tears inside. "Thanks."

"I'll tell you what. Let's you and me and your mom go grab some dinner. I'm sure David will welcome the chance to get rid of me and be alone with Clarissa."

"No. You're nice but—" I looked at him, blinking until my eyes unblurred. "I'm going out of town tonight. To Las Vegas. I might as well go and enjoy myself, even if Nick turned me down."

"Are you sure?"

"I'm sure. I need to be alone for a while."

"In Las Vegas?" He raised his brows, his brown eyes concerned.

I smiled ruefully. "Why not? Maybe I'll hit a jackpot. Or meet a hunk."

"Just be careful, Brenda."

"Oh, I'm staying at one of the cushy hotels. No dives this time. I think I'll make Tony Beale pay for it." I smiled, cheered up a tiny measure.

We said good-bye again, and he hugged me and patted me on the shoulder. I was glad that I could now view him as a friend. He really was a nice guy.

With a good butt. I gave it a surreptitious look as he walked back to my brother's room.

Clarissa put aside her magazine, threw away her half-eaten Danish, said a weary good-bye to me, and strolled back to see David.

Reginald stood up. "Need a ride?" he asked.

I eyed him narrowly. "Aren't you going to stay here and spy on my brother?"

"Nah. I'm done with this case. Your brother's not doing anything his wife can get him for. I kind of like him, actually. So, I'm going back to Chicago with my report." He shrugged. "Besides, how much action can he get, stuck in the hospital with an allergic reaction?"

The airport was hectic when I arrived, but once I'd checked in, gone through security, and made my way to my gate, most of the evening flights had gone. Only the late travelers were drifting in, quiet and tired.

It was dark now, so the windows reflected the interior of the terminal instead of giving us a nice view of the hills. Most of the people around me were waiting for the Las Vegas flight, excited about going to the glittering city.

Three women obviously on a girls' night out drank martinis and laughed loudly over jokes only they understood. A couple with T-shirts reading "Just Married" canoodled in a corner. A gray haired man with a hard face explained to another hard-faced man exactly which games had the best chance of success. "Pai-Gow poker, that's the one to play," he said. "Even the dealers say that."

They all had an itinerary, a plan, something to anticipate. I sat among them and tried not to give in to the dull feeling in my stomach.

Hey, maybe I *would* hit a jackpot. I could buy a ticket to one of those all-male strip shows and scream like a fool over some gyrating male dancer. And I could try to pick up one and take him back to my hotel room—

No, wait, I couldn't. I wasn't really a wild, sexy woman, remember?

Or was I? I thought about what Nick said, that I really had done all those crazy things and that there must have been something in me that wanted to do them.

No, it was Nick. I knew in a flash that I would not have done all that stuff and encouraged wild lovemaking with just some guy I'd met at a party, or a male stripper.

I'd done it for Nick. Crazy, lingerie-addict Brenda was inside me, and Nick had brought her out of me. Mr. Perfect hadn't been able to do that in all the time he'd gone out with me. Nick had released her in one night.

I'd become the wild woman because Nick had touched me and made me crazy for him.

And I wanted to keep being that Brenda. I didn't want to shut her away because Nick was gone, and we really hadn't done anything on New Year's. We'd done plenty later, and I really had woken up with him, both of us naked, and oh, he'd looked good.

I would not let lingerie Brenda crawl away and hide. I wouldn't let radio Brenda go either. I had created a funny, on-air persona that I never knew I had inside me, and people liked her. Even I liked her.

I started regretting that I'd not packed any lingerie. But Las Vegas had some high-class lingerie stores. I should know; I had all their catalogs.

I could still be sexy Brenda. I could still be lingerie-addict Brenda. I could still be on-air Brenda (and I'd remind Tony Beale of how many listeners I'd gotten for him every chance I could). Even if Nick had dumped me, even if he'd refused my peace offering and proposal, I could still be zany, fun, lingerie Brenda.

Any maybe some day, I'd get over Nick and meet someone else.

Could happen.

Right.

The plane arrived. People filed off, looking happy to be headed home or to a hotel. Once the trickle of people petered out, the hostesses called for the rest of us to board.

I was among the first to get on. I swung my carry-on bag into the overhead compartment and plunked down into a window seat. Someone else sat down in the aisle seat, a thin man in a windbreaker, who chatted across the aisle to a thinner woman, likely his wife.

The seat between us, Nick's seat, remained stubbornly empty.

The next boarding party came on, then the last. I pulled up the plastic window shade, pressed my face to the cool glass, and peered out into the darkness.

The lights on the wings rotated in a flashing orange glow. I saw people working below, loading bags, refueling the plane, driving carts. They might all have broken hearts, too, I couldn't tell.

The flight attendant came on the loudspeaker and welcomed us in her chirpy voice to the flight from San

Diego to fabulous Las Vegas. Because this was the Las Vegas flight and we were all ready to party, we'd get started with free daiquiris. People cheered.

I stared determinedly out the window. I'd drink the daiquiri when they brought it to me, but I saw no reason to get excited about it.

The plane remained at the gate for a long time, and the passengers started to get restless. At long last, we taxied out and rumbled at the end of the runway for a time. Then the gentle electronic chime sounded, signaling we were clear for take-off. The pilot floored it, slamming me back against my seat. I guess he was in a hurry to get to Las Vegas, too.

As we climbed bumpily into the sky, out over the Pacific—I knew that, even though it was too dark to see it—I closed my eyes. Nick and I were over, and I was going to Las Vegas alone.

The loudspeaker clicked, and the attendant came on again announcing she would be coming around with the drinks. I heard someone stop by the end of my row, probably someone with dried-out peanuts.

"Excuse me," someone said in Nick's warm, velvety voice. "May I slide in?"

The thin guy on the aisle said, "Sure." I heard the click of the seat belt as the man climbed out of his chair.

Warmth filled the seat next to me, then Nick's strong hip touched mine. "Sorry I'm late," he murmured. "I delayed them so long, they made me take a seat up front. I almost didn't make it. But I had to stop and get you a gift." He thrust a flat box about a foot square into my hands.

The box had the Lili Duoma logo printed on it. Without looking at him, I pulled the top off with shaking fingers. Nestled in tissue paper that had the Lili Duoma logo all over it lay a midnight blue silk camisole identical to the one that Nick had ripped weeks ago on the boat during our interrupted intimate moment.

Tears flooded my eyes. I looked up at Nick, who watched me with blue, blue eyes. I tried to say something. Nothing came out of my throat.

Then I decided to hell with dignity.

I threw my arms around him, nearly smacking the guy on the aisle seat. Nick crushed me to him. I lifted my face, and he kissed me. He kissed me long, he kissed me deep. He ran his hand down my back and slid his fingers under the waistband of my jeans.

I kissed him back furiously. He pulled me closer to him, his arms hard around me. His thigh pressed mine, and the arm of the chair nearly cut my stomach in two.

"Ahem," the flight attendant said from the aisle. "You need to fasten your seat belt, sir."

Nick broke the kiss. He glanced up and gave the flight attendant his warmest smile. I saw her start to melt.

I hung onto Nick and put my head on his shoulder while he snapped his seat belt.

"Sorry," he said, and I saw her melt further at the sound of his voice. "Brenda and I are getting married."

"You are?" she asked, intrigued. "Then why did you almost miss the flight?"

"I was buying the wedding gift."

"Awww," the thin man's wife said across the aisle. "That's so sweet."

The attendant asked Nick his name, then she marched back to the intercom. "OK, not only do we have a couple on their honeymoon, but we have one that's going to Vegas to tie the knot: Nick and Brenda in aisle twelve!"

"Woo hoo!" someone shouted, then cheering erupted again.

"Hey," the aisle-seat guy said. "Are you Nick and Brenda from the radio?"

"That's us," Nick said. "I finally wore her down."

"Oh, wow, I heard you today at the festival. I guess you said yes, huh?"

Nick looked at me with warm eyes. "I did," he said.

"Hey, Julie," aisle-guy said to his wife. "It's Nick and Brenda from the radio."

A lot of people had listened to us, it seemed. We got many congratulations, and the people in front of us and behind us reached over the tops of their seats to shake our hands.

In the midst of the babble, Nick leaned over and whispered into my ear, "I love you, Brenda."

"Sexy Brenda?" I whispered back.

He kissed me again, warm and deep. I heard a few "awww's".

"All the Brendas. Wild Brenda, and sweet Brenda, and funny Brenda, and sexy Brenda."

"That's a lot of Brendas."

"I know."

He smiled at me, warm and promising. I squirmed, wishing the fifty-minute flight would hurry up and finish so I could drag him to the hotel room and jump his gorgeous bones.

"I like them all," he said.

I swallowed. "What made you change your mind?"

"The song." He chuckled. "I went home, to my empty house, and I kept hearing that Beach Boys tune in my head. And it hit me that really, God only knows what I'd be without you. I didn't want to be without you. Never, ever. If you're willing to go for it, I'm going to grab onto you and not let you go."

I was hanging onto his hands with every ounce of strength I had. I wasn't going to let him go either.

"I love you, Nick," I said.

"I love you, Brenda," He kissed me, then he whispered into my ear, "You're exactly the Brenda I want."

THE PIRATE HUNTER
JENNIFER ASHLEY

Widowed by an officer in the English navy, Diana Worthing is tired of self-important men. Then the legendary James Ardmore has the gall to abduct her, to demand information. A champion to some and a villain to others, the rogue sails the high seas, ruthlessly hunting down pirates. And he claims Diana's father was the key to justice.

When she refuses to tell him what she knows, James retaliates with passionate kisses and seductive caresses. The most potent weapons of all, though, are his honorable intentions, for they make Diana forget reason. They make her long to believe she's finally found a man she can trust, a man worth loving—a true hero who could rescue her marooned heart.
